HE HAD A DANGEROUS LOOK IN HIS EYE

"Come here," he murmured in a husky voice as he fixed his heated gaze on her.

She took a backward step, her lip still clenched between her teeth. "What for?"

"I want to kiss you. Come here."

She stood rigid, unsure of what to say or do. He was spoiled, she knew, and used to having his way with women. She wanted to run, but her feet wouldn't move.

Sensing her hesitation, Luke advanced on her. When he reached her, he took her into his arms and stared into her eyes. Then he whispered a final warning.

"Brace yourself, sweet darlin'. This time I mean to kiss you all the way to hell and back."

*　　*　　*

"In *Wildcat* Sharon Ihle succeeds in bringing the vibrant color and unbridled passion of the west to full-blooded life. . . . A love story that rings with exuberance, reality, and triumph."

—*Romantic Times*

"A tender love story . . . passionate and strong-willed."

—*Rendezvous*

Also by Sharon Ihle

Wild Rose

Available from
HarperPaperbacks

Wildcat

⚞ SHARON IHLE ⚟

HarperPaperbacks
A Division of HarperCollinsPublishers

HarperPaperbacks   *A Division of* HarperCollins*Publishers*
10 East 53rd Street, New York, N.Y. 10022

Cover illustration by Jean Monti

First printing: October 1993

Printed in the United States of America

HarperPaperbacks, HarperMonogram, and colophon are trademarks of HarperCollins*Publishers*

❖ 10 9 8 7 6 5 4 3 2 1

With love to my very own "sisty ugler"
Donna MacIver Sanfilippo
I don't know, kid—what do you think?
For my money, those Cannary sisters ain't got
a thing on Marilyn and Jane!

And

With special thanks to:
Judi Lind, a sister of another kind.

1

Dakota Territory
July 1876

  The minute the brass heel on Annie's new square-toed shoe touched down on muck-splattered Main Street, she was gripped with the urge to reclaim her seat on the oxcart and go back to Cheyenne—maybe even beyond to Denver, where she'd lived for the past eight years.

It wasn't just the scruffy little town itself, although even in the mercifully faint light of dawn the hastily erected settlement of log cabins and store fronts clearly was no place for a lady. Nor was it the suffocatingly narrow Y-shaped gulch that contained those crowded buildings, a canyon of high dark mountains against every horizon.

More likely it was the emotional letdown of knowing that her search had finally come to an end, the bursting of a bubble she'd kept inflated in her chest these past few years. Or maybe it was fear. At any rate, at least a part of the waiting was over now. It was time for her first glimpse at what had become of her oldest sibling.

Annie stepped onto a small crudely built board-walk as wagon masters jostled for position on the narrow street. The four rigs ahead of hers were blocking the entire avenue, and the six drivers behind were shouting endless streams of obscenities at the other rigs and their own oxen.

Her driver, a bullwhacker called No-Teeth Ed for obvious reasons, spewed a few blue curses of his own, circled around to where she stood, and said, "I'll get someone from the grocery store to help you with your things." He eyed the supplies in the back of his wagon, frowned as he picked out her double-strapped trunk, and grumbled, "Gonna take at least six strong men and four fat boys, but I'll see what I can do."

"Thank you," she replied, ignoring No-Teeth Ed's reference to her cumbersome luggage.

After he ducked inside the building, Annie glanced down at the boardwalk attached to the front of Smiling Will's Grocery, noticing that his wooden "porch" did not extend to the meat shop flanking the store to the north or bathhouse to the south. Looking up the street farther, she realized that all the boardwalks seemed to be laid out in a haphazard design with no clear pattern. *Odd little town,* she thought. What in God's name was Martha doing in a crude, uncivilized place such as this?

Were a few of the things she'd heard about her sister actually true? For the hundredth time since she'd set out on her mission, Annie had second thoughts. Her excitement about a reunion with Martha hadn't dimmed—her heart tripped every time she imagined that joyous moment—but what if Martha *had* changed dramatically? What if she really had become the hellion they made her out to be, a woman who behaved like a man and eschewed all of society's conventions? Would she even acknowledge that she had a sister, much less be happy to see her again?

Somewhere in the back of her mind, Annie knew that all of those things were not just possible but probable—especially after her less than friendly welcome in Cheyenne, Wyoming. When she'd arrived there and set out to find Martha some three weeks earlier, she'd begun her search by referring to her sister under the sobriquet so commonly used by the newspapers—Calamity Jane.

That had gotten Annie what she wanted—information about Martha's whereabouts—but it also earned her a fair amount of verbal abuse from the ruffled townsfolk who had not only had enough of Calamity Jane but had run her out of town. The last time she'd been seen, they'd said, Calamity was driving an oxcart into the Dakotas, hurling foul language at the beasts with the best of them. And good riddance.

This, of course, assumed that Cheyenne had hosted the *real* Calamity Jane. Annie had ferreted out several impostors during her search for her sister, women whose loose behavior most probably contributed to Martha's horrid reputation. But this time, her instincts told her, she was finally on the right trail. As for dealing with hostile townsfolk and their opinion of the infamous Calamity Jane, Annie had learned a valuable lesson: Not *everyone* was pleased to know that she was related to such a wild woman.

With this in mind, she hadn't mentioned her sister to No-Teeth, who treated her with barely concealed contempt as it was. And since they'd ridden into the gulch so early this morning, she had yet to set eyes on any of the townsfolk, much less mention the name, Calamity Jane. Wondering just how to conduct her search here and still retain some semblance of decorum, Annie straightened the polonaise of her lavender-and-white calico dress, tucked a loose strand of strawberry-blond hair up inside her faded prune-colored sunbonnet, then squared her shoulders.

Moments later, No-Teeth burst back out the door with a tall, gangly boy hot on his heels. "This here's Miss Cannary, Justin. Introduce yourself, take her where she wants to go, then get on back here and help me unload these supplies."

Justin screeched to a halt at Annie's side. His sputtered promises were meant for the bullwhacker, but the exuberance with which he delivered them was a direct tribute to the fine sample of womanhood standing before him. "Y-yessir! F-fast as I can!"

Annie smiled at the young man, noting the crimson boils on his neck and the clusters of pimples on his nose and chin. Setting his age at somewhere between fifteen and eighteen—some four or more years younger than herself—she extended her hand. "I'm Ann Marie Cannary. Maybe you can help me find my sister."

Justin glanced down at that offered hand, his fingers trembling with anticipation at the idea of touching such a goddess. Here stood the kind of woman he'd dreamed about since the day his voice had begun to deepen! Tall enough to reach the cupboards, sturdily built, though tiny of waist, this lovely vision looked vibrant and healthy, capable of bearing many fine babies. And, as an extra plus, she wore no makeup, not even a faint smudge of rouge on her heart-shaped lips. Plain, yet attractive; dressed like a queen, but humble as a serving girl. Perfect. A new woman in town, and she wasn't even a whore!

Determined to be the first to catch the attention of her sparkling gray eyes, Justin wiped his hand on his stained trousers, inched it toward hers, then lost his courage and quickly shoved it into his pocket. "Glad to make your acquaintance, Miss Cannary. My name's Justin Hawkes, and if you don't mind my saying so, you're a sight for sore eyes!"

Annie stifled a chuckle as she murmured, "Ah, thank you."

"You're welcome!" he said. "We don't get too many fine ladies out this way. Don't get none, now that I think about it." He laughed in a high squeaky voice, reddened, and glanced down at the boardwalk where he fixed his gaze on an unusually large knothole.

Trying to put the young man at ease, Annie brushed his arm with her fingertips as she said, "Again I thank you for the warm welcome, Justin. I don't know if the driver mentioned it, but we broke a wheel skidding down Splittail Gulch just outside of town, and after the repairs were made the wagon train decided to push on. I'm exhausted and would like nothing better right now than to find my sister and get some rest. Can you help me do that?"

Justin's eyebrows, the slant of his eyes, even the curve of his mouth, naturally swept upward, making him look as if he'd been dragged around by the hair as a young child and his features had just frozen that way. He flashed Annie a huge grin, making his face seem even more windblown, and his green eyes sparkled as he said, "I kin help you do anything you want. Just ask, and it's yours."

Humbled under such adoration, Annie returned his smile. "I'm looking for my sister, Miss Martha Jane Cannary. Do you know her?"

Justin scratched his head. "*Miss* you say?" At her nod, he scratched some more. "I don't know any women ain't hitched in this town—unless, a course, you count the ones up in the badlands."

Annie wrinkled her nose. "The badlands? Where are they?"

Again Justin reddened. "'S'cuse me, ma'am—I forgot myself there for a minute. The badlands is . . . ah, well, it's where no decent woman would even walk, much less—"

"I see." She realized that he must be referring to the whoring district, and brought the discussion back around to her sister. "And you're absolutely sure you never heard of Martha Cannary?"

Wishing to hell he *had* heard of her, and still hoping to stumble across a way to make this vision in lavender indebted to him, Justin slowly shook his head. "Sorry ma'am, I ain't never come across a woman by that name. And," he added, suddenly concerned she might seek help elsewhere, "if I don't know who she is, no one does."

Although she couldn't say she was surprised he hadn't heard Martha's real name, Annie let out the breath she'd been holding in an exasperated sigh. Now she would have to resort to her sister's more famous name—the one that might just turn this young man's adoration to disgust.

"I understand Martha sometimes uses another name." She leaned in close to whisper the rest. "Is there a—a Calamity Jane living in this town?"

Justin's green eyes bugged out. "Calamity . . . Calam's your *sister?*"

Annie put her finger to her lips as she glanced around at the workers. "Yes, I believe she is, but why don't we keep that information as our little secret for the time being. Is she here? Do you know her?"

Justin's Adam's apple bobbed in double time, as much to help swallow the shock of discovering anything so genteel as Annie in Calamity's past, as to trap the urge to burst out laughing. "Hell yes, ma'am! Everybody—oh! Pardon my bad manners and terrible language, I—"

"It's all right," she assured him. She had heard much worse remarks since she'd been old enough to walk. "I just want to find my sister as quickly as possible. Are you saying that she does live here, and if so, do you know where?"

Still reeling with the shock, but feeling less nervous, somehow less respectful of the well-dressed woman, Justin nodded. "Yes, ma'am, on both accounts.

Calamity stays in a log cabin up the street a ways."

At the idea of being so very close to Martha after all these years, Annie's pulse ran a foot race with her suddenly rapid breathing. "Take me there please. I can't wait to see her."

Justin snaked his finger under his hat and scratched at his scalp. "You sure that's what you want to do, ma'am?"

"Of course I'm sure!"

He shook off his disappointment and turned to the wagon where No-Teeth and another skinner were unloading supplies. Hollering up at the bullwhacker, he said, "Toss Miss Cannary's trunk on down to me, will you?"

"*Toss* it?" The veins on No-Teeth's ruddy neck bulged. "Try hefting a corner a that mother, then tell me to toss it. Humph." He turned back to the other bullwhacker, muttering blue oaths under his breath as he picked up a sack of ten-penny nails.

Justin reached for the trunk, intending to pull it off the wagon himself, and gave it a tug. It wouldn't budge. "What you got in here, ma'am? Rocks?"

"Supplies," she answered quickly, wondering if those supplies could possibly be put to good use in a ramshackle town such as this. Annie stepped up beside Justin and waved at her belongings. "Can't we worry about the trunk later? I want to see my sister now."

He shrugged, then called up to No-teeth. "Kin you and Dusty get that trunk down off the wagon?"

"We'll see what we can do. Anything breakable in there, ma'am?"

Annie considered the marble slab for a moment.

"Nothing as delicate as china, but please be careful."

"Yes, ma'am. We'll handle it like it was the last egg in the Dakota Territories." Then, again under his breath, he addressed Dusty. "Don't know what in tarnation a gal like that expects to find out here but trouble. And plenty of it."

Dusty tossed in his two cents, and a couple of ribald remarks as well, but Annie and Justin were already out of earshot. Ducking between rigs and oxen, the latter sprawled wearily beneath their harnesses, the pair crossed Main Street. Justin sidestepped a slippery, consistently muddy section of low-lying road kept that way by animal urine and droppings. "Best keep your skirts up high, ma'am, elsewise you'll likely get your hems in a mess. Best keep an eye on where you're going."

The caution was unnecessary. Holding her nose with one hand, Annie used the other to keep her skirts off the filthy, uneven road, not even relinquishing her grip when Justin called her to a halt outside of the Custer Saloon.

"Wait here a minute, ma'am. Might's well see if she's still in here 'fore we go any further." He pushed his way inside the establishment and took only a brief glance into a corner of the room before wheeling around and returning to the boardwalk with the back swing of the door. "She's in there all right. Sure you want to see her now? I'd say she's, ah, well . . . swizzled clean up to her eyeballs."

More disappointed than shocked, Annie nodded. "It won't be the first time I've seen her in her cups." She held out her hand. "Shall we?"

"B-but—" Justin glanced inside the Custer as if to make certain he knew what he was talking about. "This here's a *saloon*, ma'am. You sure you want to go in there?"

Again, it wasn't the first time for Annie. As young children, both Annie and Martha had made countless trips to neighboring saloons in order to coax their parents back to home and hearth. Although she was none too thrilled with the idea of repeating such an ordeal, she said, "I'm quite sure, Justin." Then, still hoping for his escort, she parted the swinging wooden doors and stepped inside.

Annie waited a minute for her eyes to adjust to the darkness of a room whose lamps were so low they barely flickered. Cheap whiskey, stale cigar and cigarette smoke, and every manner of body odor imaginable collided in her nostrils. Taking the smallest breaths possible, she made a cursory glance around the saloon.

Three gamblers apparently not yet aware the sun had risen, and definitely oblivious to the newly arrived female, were huddled around a poker table. A bartender slept in his high chair at the end of the counter, and two patrons were snoring, one draped across a tabletop, the other rolled up like a wood louse at the foot of his chair.

Annie frowned and glanced over her shoulder. "Justin?" she whispered. "I don't see my sister in here. Where did she go?"

He leaned forward and pointed to the table against the south wall, the one where the snoring man in buckskins sat.

Annie looked at the man, studied him from several angles, and looked again. Then she turned back to Justin in astonishment. "That . . . that *man* over there is Calamity Jane?"

Justin nodded solemnly. "I tried to warn you."

Too stunned for further comment, unable to believe that such a wreck of humanity could really be her sister, Annie motioned for Justin to follow along behind her as she approached the table. She stopped three feet from the slumbering sot, searching for the right words, and when she finally found her voice it was weak as she inquired, "Martha Jane Cannary? Is it . . . *you?*"

The "man" in buckskins sputtered against the scarred tabletop and drew in a long breath through a snore loud enough to rattle the empty whisky bottle lying belly up next to his head.

Justin pounded the table with his fist. "Calam! Wake up! Ya got a visitor."

Calamity's head, half-covered with a dirty felt hat, raised up a notch, then another, and hovered there for a moment like a hummingbird agonizing over the best petunia. Then she dropped back to the table, landing face first.

"My Lord!" Annie hunkered down beside her. "Martha? Is it really you? Are you all right?"

Calamity groaned, then turned her face to the side and let her breath out in a noisy wheeze.

Hardly able to tolerate the stench of days'-old whisky breath, Annie grimaced as she reached for the stained hat. Careful to remove it by using just the tips of two fingers, which she immediately wiped on her calico skirt, she tossed the hat aside, grabbed the knot of dull, matted hair at the back of the woman's head, and lifted her up off the table. Was it Martha or another imposter?

Annie had no trouble recognizing the raw-boned features of her older sister, Martha Jane. She looked just like their father, Robert Cannary, with a no-nonsense kind of face that brooked no arguments and told no lies.

Annie slid her fingers past the bun and up to Martha's temples, and she cradled her sister's wobbly head between her hands. "So it is you," she whispered more to herself, tears running down her cheeks. *Martha Jane Cannary*—the first link in Annie's missing family. Dear God! What could have driven her sister to such extremes? How could she have let herself become so . . . so very disgusting?

Instantly ashamed of herself for judging Martha in the very same moment she'd found her, Annie shook off those feelings of disappointment. She and Martha were finally together again. At the idea of the sisters Cannary rising anew as one, a dream she'd carried inside for eight long years, those bottled-up emotions finally flooded up to the surface.

"Thank the Lord," she whispered. "Praise God we're together again."

At the sound, Calamity's eyelids fluttered open, closed, then opened once again, fixing on Annie with an unfocused gaze.

Thinking that her sister was actually looking at her, Annie smiled into those grim brown eyes and said, "Hi, sis. Remember me?"

Calamity opened her mouth wide—and burped. Then she collapsed against the table again.

Annie gripped the table edge, swooning from the latest assault by her sister's odoriferous breath, and shook her head to try to clear it.

"Come on, Miss Cannary," Justin said, taking her by the elbow. "You ain't gonna get nowheres with Calam just yet. She's been sitting here with a whisky bottle since we got the news about Custer's defeat some two days ago. Gonna take about that long to bring her around to her senses, I 'spect."

Annie jumped to her feet. "*Two* days? Why hasn't someone helped her or seen to her? Has she eaten?"

The men at the poker table across the room stirred. "Hey! You want to keep it down over there?"

"Who is that, kid? A new saloon gal?" called another.

"Nuthin' to mind yourselves about," Justin hollered back. "We're just a leavin.'" Then he whispered under his breath. "Come on now, Miss Cannary. You got to leave 'fore trouble starts."

Indignant, and wondering why in heaven no one had helped Martha before now, Annie planted her hands on her hips. "I am not going anywhere without my sister. Do you think you can carry her?"

Justin groaned. "I'd ruther not, if you don't mind, ma'am. Calam, well, she gets a mite cantankerous if you pester her when she don't want to be pestered."

Singular in her purpose, Annie circled around behind her sister's chair. "I'll take full responsibility for whatever happens." She slipped her hands into the damp cradles of Martha's armpits, glanced up at

Justin, and said, "Well? Aren't you going to give me a hand?"

Bedazzled by the 'real' lady once again, Justin hopped to. He spun around and said, "Just slide her up past my butt and give me her hands. I'll take her out of here piggyback."

Annie managed to wrestle her sister to her feet, but before she could get her over Justin's backside, Martha raised her arms up high, opened her eyes to rheumy slits, and bellowed, "I'm Calamity Jane and I sleep where and when I want to! Get your gawddamn hands off'n me and leave me the hell alone!"

Then she passed out again, collapsing in an almost perfect line against Justin's skinny spine, which was where they wanted her in the first place. Annie looped her sister's hands around Justin's shoulders. When the unconscious woman was secured, hanging off Justin's shoulder like a freshly killed deer, Annie led the way through the swinging doors and out into the street.

"Straight northeast, ma'am," Justin directed as they started up Main Street. "And don't forget to mind your skirts."

Annie took brief notice of the rows of buildings crammed cheek by jowl against one another, their jerry-built frames decorated with false fronts. Up the street, several businesses were still housed in tents. Most of these structures, whether made of canvas or wood, contained a saloon or gambling hall, each a regular den of iniquity, Annie thought, again wondering how her sister could have chosen this sinner's haven as her home.

"Turn right here, ma'am," Justin said through a strained groan. "Just duck into that little alley, then kick open the door of the log cabin what got the elk rack hanging above the entry."

Even more careful of her steps than before, Annie followed Justin's directions down the offal-splattered avenue, turned into what was little more than a space between buildings, and stopped as she came to what appeared to be the correct cabin. It sat facing another log structure, the distance separating the two hardly more than a small aisle. The cabin with the elk horns was a lopsided, mud-sealed cartoon of what a house should be, the droopy roof patched and looking as if it might collapse at any minute.

Her brow puckered, Annie glanced back at Justin. "*This* is where my sister lives?"

"Yes, ma'am." He groaned as Calamity slipped another couple of inches down his back. Adjusting his burden, his face flushed and he said, "Would you mind opening the door so's I can put her down? If I don't get shuck of her soon, I'm afraid I'll be humped over for life."

"Oh, of course!" She turned and quickly pushed the door open, standing aside for Justin to pass. Once he and Martha were safely inside, Annie followed and closed the door behind her.

Her attention was drawn to two things at once. The *whomp!* her sister's body made when Justin dumped her onto a low-lying rope bed—and the curious stares of a pair of men playing cards at a table near the far window.

"What's up, kid?" asked the man with the stallion-tail mustache as he downed a shot of whiskey and then rose to his feet.

"Bring us a little treat, did you?" said the other as he too finished his drink and stood up.

Justin colored as he shuffled backward toward the door. "Gosh, no, fellahs. This here is—is Miss Cannary. I'll let her make the introductions." He turned to her. "Want me to fetch your trunk now, ma'am?"

Keeping one eye on the well-dressed but unkempt men, she said, "Ah, yes, if you please—and one more thing, Justin." She poked her finger up inside the tight sleeve of her blouse to extract her money pouch. "Let me pay you for your services."

"Oh, no, ma'am," he said, backing out the door. "I *want* to do anything I can to help you out. Anything a'tall. Be right back!" Then he disappeared down the alley.

When Annie turned around, both men had moved to the center of the small cabin. The one with the mustache extended his hand. "Name's James Hickok, but most folks call me Bill."

She reached for his hand, pausing in midstride. "*Wild* Bill Hickok?"

He nodded, then turned to his companion. "And this is—"

"Just Luke," he cut in, seeing the naked adoration for Wild Bill in the young woman's eyes, and respectful enough of his friend to allow him his moment of celebrity.

She tore her eyes off the legend long enough to acknowledge the presence of the other gambler, a man, it appeared, who hadn't bothered to shave for several days. "And, ah . . . nice to meet you, too."

Even though the second man had the blackest, most mirthful pair of eyes she'd ever seen, Annie turned back to Hickok, hardly able to believe she was standing in the same room with such a famous man. "It's a real pleasure to meet you, Mr. Hickok. I've heard so very much about you! My name is Ann Marie Cannary. I'm Martha's sister."

Hickok's normally impassive features lit up. "You're *Calamity's* sister?"

Proud finally to be able to say it out loud, she said, "Yes, sir, I am a full sister to Martha Jane Cannary, otherwise known as Calamity Jane."

He whistled. "I didn't know she had anyone besides Lena and Lije."

Annie gasped and rushed up closer to him. "You know about Lena and Elijah? Have you seen them? God in heaven!" She slapped her forehead. "Are they here, *too?*"

Hickok shot Luke a warning glance. "No, ma'am, ah . . . they're not." His gaze shifted to the unconscious woman on the bed, lingering as if weighing his options, and then he turned back to Annie and said, "Sorry, but no. Calam just mentioned her kin in passing."

Her spirits falling just a bit, Annie shrugged and stepped away from him. "That's all right. I'm sure she'll tell me all about them the minute she wakes up."

Annie glanced at Martha, hoping that moment would be soon, but she was snoring again, her mouth open in a most unladylike manner. When Annie turned back around, she realized the man with the black eyes had moved—was still moving. In a circle. Around her.

"So you're Calamity's sister, huh?" he asked, taking in her feminine demeanor, the round curve of her cheeks and jawline in contrast to her sibling's boxy, almost masculine bone structure. For a moment, Luke entertained the notion that this Annie might actually be a real, live lady. But a sister of Calamity Jane, a lady? How could that be? Over his shoulder, he addressed his friend. "One for you and one for me, you think?"

Hickok raised his eyebrows as straight as a carpenter's level. "Could be." He laughed, then caught the fierce gleam in Annie's eye. "Then again, maybe not."

Chuckling along with Wild Bill, Luke returned his attention to the woman, settling his gaze on her eyes, more on their brilliant color, a soft dove gray shot through with tiny shards of silver—brazenly innocent eyes. His laughter faded. Then he noticed her manner of dress. Her gown was a plain little affair without frills or trim to accentuate her finer points. This was accompanied by an ugly oversized bonnet that nearly hid her lovely features, a face as mysterious as it was attractive.

Surely that ladylike exterior hid the heart of a wildcat. How could a sister of Calamity Jane's be anything *but* a hell-raiser? At the thought of unwrapping that plain package and finding such a woman beneath, Luke's heart stumbled across the next beat like his boots did over the threshold last Saturday night. And a little bead of sweat trickled down from his temple.

Gathering his breath, and his wits too, Luke boldly

brought his fingertips to Annie's cheek and caressed the smattering of freckles there as he whispered, "It is *Miss* Cannary, isn't it, sweet darlin'? What's say you and I get to know one another a little better?"

Annie swatted his hand away, too intent on Hickok to put up with any silliness from his companion. "What's say you keep your hands to yourself."

Luke chuckled, at ease with this sister of the rudest, crudest woman he'd ever met. "You're Calamity's kin all right."

Ignoring both the man and his remark, she brushed by Luke and addressed Hickok. "I'm afraid I'll have to ask you and your friend to leave now. As you can see, my sister is feeling poorly, and I just got into town after a very long journey. We both need some rest. If you don't mind?" She pointed directly at the front door.

Hickok took a step toward her, staggered, then reached for the chair back to steady himself. Luke, who'd kept his consumption to a minimum, marched toward the table and stood between his friend and their sassy visitor. Then he gave her his most sarcastic grin. "I'm afraid you've made a little mistake, sweet darlin'. You can't throw us out of our own cabin."

"What? B-but, I thought—Justin told me Martha lives here."

Luke nodded, his grin sideways now, almost but not quite a smirk. "She does, cozy as it might get at times, but that she does."

Annie's fingers fluttered to her breast and she took several steps backward. "The *three* of you? Why that's . . . that's just plain vulgar!"

Luke turned to Bill and laughed. "*Vulgar?* This from the sister of the—"

"Now, be nice," Hickok said as he pushed his way around Luke to explain to Annie. "I realize this might sound a little sordid to you, ma'am, but I assure you—your shister has nothing but our utmost respect."

Luke's head fell back, and he howled with laughter over Bill's mispronunciation.

Hickok chuckled, hiccupped, and nearly fell onto his chair.

Annie's gaze darted from man to man, then froze as Hickok approached her, his arms outstretched as if preparing to apologize. He lurched backward, teetered for a moment, then leaned forward and regained his balance by draping his arms across her shoulders. "You'll have to excuse our manners, Miss Cannary," he murmured, using her as a support. "We've been up all night long."

Roused by the commotion, Calamity lifted her head and managed to focus well enough to see Hickok holding another woman. Instantly enraged, she sobered long enough to tumble off the bed onto the floor. Then she lunged at the couple, bellowing at Hickok, "You dirty bastard! Think I'm so moon-eyed I can't see you got a gal with you? Take your gawd-damn hands off'n her!"

She crashed into the pair, and Annie would have been knocked to the floor if not for Luke, who managed to snag her elbow at the last moment. He pulled her out of harm's way and swung her into his arms. In the process, Annie's bonnet was torn off by

Calamity's flailing fingers, and her hairpins flew in every direction.

Luke glanced down the length of his arm, stunned to find sheets of reddish-blond hair spilling over his black shirt in luscious contrast. For a moment he couldn't draw a breath. More than merely fascinated, but captured by the sight of those silken locks and the complement of her sparkling gray eyes, Luke held Annie fast. She was even more entrancing than he'd supposed. He dropped his gaze to her surprised mouth. Annie's lips were slightly parted, as if she were preparing to deliver a speech—or a kiss.

Encouraged by the recent shot of whisky, and far more inclined to believe that her expression suggested the latter, Luke bent his head low over that mouth, arching Annie's back in the same motion, and whispered, "As I was saying earlier, sweet darlin'— why don't we get a little better acquainted?"

Before Annie could react to the gambler's rude assault, the door burst open and Justin stood on the threshold, his mouth agape. "Miss *Cannary!*"

Realizing how unseemly the embrace must look to the young man, and shocked to realize that she hadn't tried to break away before now, Annie began to pound on Luke's chest. "Turn me loose, you animal!"

Those were fighting words to Justin. He bristled and flexed his muscles. Buoyed by the trumpets of his fallen hero's army—Custer's Seventh—blaring in his mind, he launched a charge on the lecherous gambler.

As Luke struggled to capture Annie's flailing fists, he caught a glimpse of the youth bearing down on him. He spun around on one boot heel and managed to duck the blow at the last second.

Justin launched his fist just before the target moved. He swung on by Luke, missing him completely, but connected with Annie's jaw instead. Although the blow itself was glancing, the young man stumbled against them, sending both Luke and Annie to the floor in a heap.

Unable to stop his forward momentum, Justin crashed into the cupboard door, his skull colliding with the corner of the cabinet. He stood rigid, unblinking for a long moment, then spiraled down to the floor.

Annie, who was dazed but not unconscious, lay on her back, her arms and legs spread as if making angels in the snow. Luke was sprawled across her bodice, one leg draped between her thighs, the other tangled in her skirts.

He raised himself up on his elbows, shook his head several times, and then glanced down at the disheveled woman beneath him. Her eyes were drifting from quicksilver bright to foggy morning gray as she struggled to clear her head. Her luscious mouth was still parted, beckoning him it seemed, and damn near as pleasurable a sight as turning up the last card in a royal flush. A woman, he decided then and there, he should definitely get to know better. A *lot* better.

The devil dancing a jig in his ebony eyes, Luke grinned and said, "Welcome to Deadwood, sweet darlin'."

Then he lowered his head.

2

When the dust had settled—and there was a considerable amount, given the fact that none of the cabin's occupants was inclined toward house-keeping—Calamity and Wild Bill had disappeared. Justin lay groaning on the floor, his hands clamped to his head like a blacksmith's vise. And Luke, the self-appointed welcoming committee of one, had just settled his mouth against Annie's parted lips.

She groaned, feeling her way through the purgatory of consciousness, a condition of being neither here nor there. As her circumstances slowly became clearer, she realized that a man was lying on top of her, his scratchy whiskers poking her delicate skin, his mouth flush against her own. Something wet—his tongue?—slipped between her teeth just then and he began probing her, exploring her innermost crevices as if laying the boundaries to a claim. Taking liberties she'd never allowed any man—and was not about to allow now.

Fully conscious at last, and angry too, Annie slid her fingers up beneath his unruly mop of sable hair, pinched his earlobe between her thumb and forefinger, and then gave the little nub of flesh a vicious twist. "Get *off* of me!" she demanded, her voice so deep and guttural it surprised even her. "*Now!*"

"Owww . . ." She twisted harder. "Jesus—*ow!*"

Pleased that she'd gotten the gambler's attention along with some measure of control, Annie released the pressure just enough for Luke to break free. When he did, she quickly rolled out from beneath him and climbed to her feet. Breathing heavily, she turned to face him. And found an enraged bull.

"I ought to kick your butt all the way to hell and back!" he said. Rubbing his ear as he staggered to his feet, Luke noticed the arrogant tilt of her chin. He shook a finger at her. "Don't think I don't mean what I say! The next time you make a grab for my ear, that's exactly what I'll do!"

Annie hardened her gaze. "And the next time you even *think* about putting a hand on me, I'll twist that ear into a taffy rope!"

Realizing that if she were anything like her rowdy sister, she meant what she said, Luke backed away. "Yeah, well . . . I was only trying to welcome you to Deadwood. I'd think you'd be a little more grateful."

"*Grateful?*" Annie pointed to the torn sleeve of her dress and dragged her fingers through her tangled hair. "I haven't been in this town for ten minutes, and already I look as if—as if . . ." She paused, trying to find a delicate way to explain what she meant.

"As if you'd just thoroughly welcomed your man after a long day of working the mines?"

Shocked by such audacity, Annie's mouth fell open. An insufferable man, this gambler was, as cocky and insensitive as any she'd ever met. Annie took a breath, intending to berate him, but she heard boots scraping the floor behind her, followed by Justin's weak, trembling voice.

"Miss Annie? Are you all right? I hope I didn't hurt you too much."

She twisted around to him, vaguely recalling the sight of his fist as it struck her chin. The young man was down on one knee struggling to regain his footing, and a little scarlet creek zigzagged down the side of his face. "Goodness sakes, Justin! Where did that blood come from?"

"I banged into the cupboard, but I'm all right now." He blinked his eyes several times in succession, then squinted over by the table to where Luke had retreated. Inclining his chin toward the gambler, he asked, "You need some help with him, ma'am?"

Annie glanced at Luke. He poured a shot of whiskey, held it high as if toasting her, then downed it in one gulp.

"Ma'am?" Justin repeated, his voice a bare whisper as he realized that he'd offered to take on Luke McCanles, who handled a gun as expertly as he did cards. "Y-you only got to say the word, and I—"

"No, thanks, Justin," she said, ushering him out the door. "I can manage now."

He shot another, more nervous look at the gambler, and said under his breath as he stepped across the threshold, "You just holler if you need me for anything else. Like I said, I want to hep you any way I can."

"Thank you again, Justin. I'll remember that." As she glanced outside, Annie saw that her trunk was pushed up against the cabin. "And thanks for bringing my things up so quickly. Are you sure I can't pay you?"

"No, no. Like I said—I'm yours anytime, ma'am. Anytime a'tall." He was suddenly in a hurry to take his leave, not from Annie, but from the gunmen, especially the one he'd been foolish enough to attack. "I'm sure the fellahs will bring your trunk in later after they find a place to put it." Then he gripped the handles of the cart he'd used to deliver her luggage and started up the alley.

Annie reached for the door to close it, then considered the rude gambler and left it ajar. She turned and surveyed the cabin. There wasn't much to examine. Besides the small rough-hewn pine table where he was dealing cards to himself and an imaginary challenger, the only other furniture was the rope bed to the left of the entry and the two unoccupied chairs at the table. No rug or even an oil cloth covered the floor, and the one small window near the front door wore a scrap of soiled muslin by way of a curtain. The window aft was covered by only a thin film of grease and ash.

At the foot of the bed stood a carving table, and beside that the stove. Above them, jutting out past the tabletop just enough to catch a shoulder—or as was the case earlier, Justin's temple—was a bank of two cupboards, holding everything from canned goods to dishes.

A narrow door just behind the gambler's chair led

to a back alley, Annie supposed. Or the privy. Above her head at the entry, a long, deep ledge stretched the width of the cabin. From a corner of this loft dangled a pair of men's long underwear the color of a rusted milk pail.

Sensing that she'd missed something, Annie glanced around the cabin one more time. "What happened to my sister?" When Luke didn't answer right away, she said louder, "Where is Martha?"

He cast a lazy eye in her direction, then picked the cards up off the table. Taking his time, he arched the deck in the palm of one hand, shuffling them, then repeated the performance before he finally spoke to her. "You're mighty cheeky for a woman fresh off a skinner's wagon."

She rolled her eyes and tried again. "Please excuse my impudence . . . *sir,* but I am concerned about my sister. Do you have any idea what could have happened to her?"

Luke canted his head over his left shoulder. "Might be in the bedroom, but I can't say I noticed where she went for sure."

Annie glanced at the narrow door. "Oh, I didn't realize this was another room." She picked up her skirts and started for it, but before she could reach up to knock, Luke issued a sharp warning.

"I wouldn't do that if I were you. If Calamity did go in there, she didn't go alone. Bill's with her."

The implication in the man's tone was all too clear. Annie spun around, her eyes wide as she said, "You don't mean to say that they're . . . well, they couldn't have—"

"It happens." Luke swung his legs around to the side of his chair and faced her. "It's nature's way, you know? Birds do it. Bees do it . . ." He winked.

"B-but—"

Luke spun back to the table and poured another two fingers of whisky. "Why don't you just let them be? They'll be out soon enough, I expect."

As embarrassed as she was indignant, Annie swept by the man, her brass heels clattering angrily against the plank floor. When she reached the bed she sat down on the edge of it. Grateful for the soft straw mattress after the rugged ride on the oxcart, she sighed and began rubbing the small of her back.

"I could do that for you if you like," Luke said. "I'm told I have 'magic' fingers."

Annie looked across the room, too weary to be shocked, and said, "How very nice of you to offer, but no thanks. The only thing I want from you is your silence. Do you think you can manage that?"

Luke chuckled. "How can I answer a question like that and stay quiet at the same time?"

This time Annie's sigh was heavy with exhaustion. "Look. I'm tired. I'd appreciate it if you'd just—just go. Please leave so I can get some rest."

Annie buried her face in her hands and waited for the gambler to vacate the premises. And waited a little longer. When five minutes had passed and she still had heard no movement, she took a peek between her fingers. Luke was sitting at the table grinning at her, his black eyes practically glowing with mirth.

She dropped her hands into her lap. "Well? Do I have to go for the sheriff in order to get a little privacy?"

Luke's grin widened. "There isn't much for sher-iffing around here yet. In fact, Bill and I have even helped out in the name of the law on occasion. Hell, for all I know, today I *am* the sheriff."

Annie groaned. "Please," she whispered, hating to beg, "if you have any gentlemanly tendencies inside you at all—will you go and let me get some rest?"

"I live here, remember? And I'm kind of tired myself." Luke stood up, straightened his holsters, and then hooked his thumbs in the waistband of his pinstriped trousers. "You're either going to have to find yourself some other quarters, or scoot over a little. You're sitting on my bed."

Annie leapt off the mattress, dusting her bottom vigorously, looking as if she'd just been told she was warming a nest of rattlesnakes.

Luke advanced on her, his expression somber.

Sensing that she could no longer try to reason with him, Annie backed toward the door, tripped over an irregularity in the floor, and fell back onto the bed. A scream rose up in her throat, then died there as he reached the edge of the mattress and leaned over. He hovered above her like a vulture patiently waiting for his opening.

"W-what are you going to do?" she asked weakly.

Luke grinned. "What would you like for me to do?"

A thin ray of sunlight drifted in through the muslin curtain, highlighting the gambler's features, and for Annie it was her first really good look at him. He needed a bath and a shave, fresh clothing and a hair-cut, yet oddly enough, he was easily the most hand-

some man she had ever seen. Handsome, overtly masculine—and familiar somehow. Had they met before?

She took a better look. Luke was definitely shaggy,
yet polished too, skillfully using his boyish charm to
his advantage through those playful ebony eyes and
grinning apple cheeks. And he was strong, from what
she could gather. His shirt was open at the throat and
rolled up at the sleeves, offering glimpses of his thick
muscular neck, curly black chest hairs, and massive
forearms—the body of a man capable of far more
strenuous work than dealing cards.

Exactly what did he do to earn his keep, she wondered, and why did she feel as if she already knew him?

"Having trouble making up your mind what it is
you *do* want from me, sweet darlin'?" he asked, the
twinkle in his eyes matching the hint of laughter in
his voice.

"N-no! I want you to leave. Just leave me alone."

"You absolutely *sure* about that?" He ran his hands
down the front of his thighs, then slid them up to his
matched holsters where he adjusted the leather sheaths.

Annie's gaze obediently followed those hands,
snagging for one stubborn moment at his crotch.
Even though she had no idea what was driving her to
such brazen behavior, her cheeks burned as she recognized the indiscretion. Her hand instinctively flew
to her mouth, and then to her raw cheeks where
Luke's stubble had scratched her skin. She tried to
look away, but as if driven by forces she couldn't see
or understand, Annie continued to stare up at him,
her fingers lingering there on her upper lip, sliding
back and forth, soothing those whisker burns.

Luke chuckled softly, pleased by what he saw in her expression—awareness of him, not as a famous pistoleer even, but him as a man. "Well, sweet darlin'? I've got to tell you that I'm not used to this waiting. Women generally know exactly what they want from Luke McCanles. In fact—"

"Luke McCanles!" Annie said, jackknifing to a sitting position. "Are you *Lucky* Luke McCanles from DeWitt's Ten Cent Romances?"

No longer simply grinning, but beaming, he said, "you're looking at him, sweet darlin'." Deciding to tease her a little after what she'd put him through earlier—his ear in particular—he plucked his hat off the bedpost and slowly fit it to his head. "Are you planning to stay in Deadwood more than a day or two?"

Annie's mouth was suddenly dry, too dry to speak, and her mind was in complete chaos. Lucky Luke McCanles was standing not a foot away from her! The best she could manage by way of an answer was an enthusiastic nod.

Luke cocked the brim of his hat to the side and said, "Then I expect we'll probably run into each other again. Who knows? I might even give you another chance to get better acquainted with me. Maybe next time," he added with a wink, "you'll be a little quicker on the draw." Then he ambled out the door.

As tired as she was, Annie took a long time to fall asleep. Thoughts of the real reunion between herself and Martha had her mind churning with excitement, while memories of Luke and his stolen kiss kept her pulse racing at top speed. She'd actually been *kissed* by the famous Lucky Luke McCanles!

Annie could hardly believe that a man of his stature would even *look* at a plain, disheveled mess like her. He'd been spoiled by much prettier women, and badly—of that much she was certain by the way Luke carried himself along with the quick, easy grin he flashed as if he were constantly on stage. Spoiled, yes, but Lord, what a man to spoil.

Why had he wasted even a moment of his time on her? Visions of that kiss, of those black eyes boring into hers, finally drifted to the back of Annie's consciousness, floating just out of reach as she fell asleep.

When she finally awakened several hours later, it was with a great deal of trepidation, a sense that she was in some kind of danger. Had Luke returned? She inched her eyelids open, half expecting to find a pair of sardonic raven eyes twinkling down at her. Instead, she found herself staring up into a single black orb—the barrel of a pistol.

"Get your scrawny ass up off'n that bed!" Calamity snarled.

Annie couldn't move or speak, so stunned was she to find her long lost sister standing before her.

"I told you to get off'n the gawddamn bed!" Calamity cocked the hammer and waved her gun even though it wavered in her trembling fingers. "Now *move!*"

Annie rolled to the edge of the mattress and scrambled to her feet, but before she could explain who she was or why she'd come to Deadwood, her sister grabbed her by the neck and shoved her up against the door.

"Do you know whose man you're a messing with or what the consequences are?" Calamity bellowed. "I'm Calamity Jane and I do what I damn well please. Right now, it'd please me a hell of a lot to blow you right back to where you come from!"

"Don't shoot, Martha!" Annie choked out, her breath nearly cut off by her sister's strong fingers. "It's me—Ann Marie. Don't you remember?"

Calamity eased her grip as she tried to clear her vision and focus her mind on the past. *Ann Marie— her sister?* Calamity cocked her head. The young woman did bear an uncanny resemblance to her mother, Charlotte Cannary, and her hair, although streaked with more vermillion strands than before, was very nearly the same crop of cornsilk she remembered from the last time she'd seen her younger sister. But how could Annie be here? And why?

Calamity released her grip on both the gun and the woman. The pistol clattered to the floor. This "sister" stood motionless—wide-eyed with fear, yet curiously familiar somehow. Calamity brought her fists to her eyes and rubbed hard. When she opened them again, the stranger was still there. Then this "Annie" smiled, looking even more like their mother.

"It truly is me," Annie whispered, feeling as if her heart were not merely in her throat but lodged there. "Muffin."

At the sound of the pet name that Calamity—and only Calamity—had called Annie as a child, she choked out, "Oh, Gawd! Oh my Gawd, it really is you."

"Yes—*yes!*" Annie gathered Martha in her embrace even though Martha's buckskin clothing positively reeked of perspiration, cheap tobacco, and a few other equally pungent odors she couldn't identify. In spite of the discomfort, she held her sister close, spilling tears as well as emitting cries of joy and muttered endearments.

When Calamity had taken all the hugging and tears she could tolerate, she set her sister apart from her and examined her from head to foot. Even though Annie's hair was a rat's nest of tangles, and her dress wrinkled and torn, she said, "Gawd, just look at how pretty you got!"

"And, and . . . look at you!" Annie replied, unable to manage the same compliment. Martha wore stained buckskin trousers, a man's dark blue work shirt beneath, a tattered, fringed buckskin vest, and a gun belt with matching holster. The only feminine thing about her was her long cinnamon-brown hair, but even that, loose and hanging down her back, was dirty and matted. Again, Annie had to wonder, What could have driven her sister to such extremes?

Calamity's expression turned indignant at Annie's intense perusal, but her skin, well-baked by the sun, didn't betray the depth of her embarrassment. "I ain't much to look at I 'speck," she said, "but then I guess I never was."

"Oh, of course you were—*are,*" she said, ashamed at her thoughts. "It's just been so long since I've seen you, I wanted to take a really good long look."

Calamity flashed a good-humored grin, one that also contained a message—she hadn't become the woman she was today by believing every little bit of flumdiddle that came her way. "Oh, hell—that's 'nuff of that stuff. Let's catch up with each other." She grabbed Annie's hand and dragged her across the room to the tiny table.

"Sit a spell and tell me what you been doing for the last—what's it been—five, six years?"

Annie slid onto one of the spindle-back chairs, shaking her head as she tugged herself up close to the table. "Eight years last May to be exact."

"Gawd." Calamity propped her cheeks between her hands, and then reached for the bottle of whisky Luke had left behind. She dumped three fingers into his glass, grabbed another off the windowsill, and poured a like amount into it. With a broad grin, she shoved it across the table to her sister. Lifting her own drink, she said, "To you and whatever miracle brought you back to me."

Annie glanced at the glass of whisky but didn't pick it up.

Calamity waited, her trembling fingers unable to steady her tumbler. Finally she set the drink down and cocked one auburn eyebrow. "What's the matter, Muffin? You too good to drink with me?"

"Oh, no," Annie said, reaching across the table for her sister's hand, but Calamity jerked her fingers away. "Don't be angry with me. I just don't happen to like the taste of whisky, so I don't drink."

Calamity narrowed her gaze and raised one corner of her mouth. "If I recall—and when I do remember something, I usually recall right—you not only enjoyed an occasional hooker of Ma's raw pioneer whisky, you taught yourself to down it in one gulp without shuddering."

"Not *me*," Annie objected. "*Mom*. She's the one who taught us all the 'delights' of whiskey. I figured out a long time ago it was just her way of keeping us quiet—didn't you?"

Calamity bristled and tossed back her drink. "Ma never wanted me quiet—she talked to me all the time, all night long sometimes!"

Watching her sister pour another glass of booze, Annie dropped that topic and drifted back to the past. "Of course Mom kept you up all night—you were her favorite."

"I was that all right," Calamity quickly agreed, "but only cause I was oldest and she could talk to me about anything—and did." She said it with conviction, as if parental favoritism was a simple fact of life. Then she jumped to another subject. "We both know all the old stuff . . . tell me something new. How did you fare with the Parkers?"

Annie shrugged, a good part of her attention still caught in the ruins of the last subject. Frowning, she thought back to the family who'd taken her in after the Cannary children had been orphaned. "I did all right I suppose . . . for a slave. But as a daughter? Abominably."

Calamity reached across the table. "Did they beat you or something? I thought they was right fine folks."

"Oh, they were all right, I suppose, and no, they didn't beat me much. They were pretty decent folks for adding a thirteen-year-old girl to their brood without knowing how much use she'd be." The Parkers, she recalled, were generally emotionless even where their own children were concerned, exacting and hard-driving folks, and yet they had been generous enough to take her in. "It wasn't so bad, really, but once they found out how well I could cook, sew, and keep house, they pretty much worked me to the bone. I figure we broke even. I got a home, they got a maid."

Calamity grieved to learn the fate of yet another Cannary child, one of six siblings she'd promised her father she'd look out for as he lay on his dying bed. Her sudden wave of guilt coaxed her into taking another drink before she could comment on Annie's trials. "If I'd known how unhappy you were, I'd a come running for you. I swear I would have."

Annie glanced up at her sister sharply, then dropped her gaze to the table. Would Martha *really* have come if she'd known? Promises of long ago came trickling into Annie's thoughts. First Martha's vow to keep the family together no matter what after Pa died. Then, as the brood drifted apart bit by bit anyway, the hollow guarantee that she would collect Annie and the others as soon as she got settled. Empty promises all.

Bitter tears stung Annie's eyes, drawing to the surface an anger that she hadn't realized she still carried deep inside herself. Without thinking, but trying only to find some way to shove those horrid feelings back down into their dark grave, she reached for her glass and took a large swallow of the liquor.

Calamity watched her sister with interest, unaware of her thoughts, knowing only that she wasn't as certain as she had been that Annie would make a good drinking companion. Sure of one thing, however—that her sister's sudden mood had something to do with the fact that the family had disintegrated—Calamity spoke more softly than she had in years. "I ain't gonna make excuses for the things I did or didn't do. My life ain't been real easy since Pa died either, you know. If I coulda come for you I would have. Just leave it at that. Now how'd you find me?"

Still shuddering from the effects of her first drink in years, Annie sniffed back her tears and took another sip of whisky—to calm her nerves, she told herself. This time it went down smoother and she felt ready to offer a brief version of the past eight years. "The Parkers moved to a farm just outside of Denver City, and I stayed with them there until I turned eighteen." She wiped her nose. "By then the youngest boys had grown up enough to have some less-than-sisterly ideas about me, and I can't say I was too happy about the way Mr. Parker looked at me every now and then, either."

Calamity swore under her breath. "The old goat. I thought he was a pretty good man or I never woulda—"

Annie waved her off. "It doesn't matter. Mrs. Parker wasn't too crazy about the way her men were looking at me either, so when I said I wanted to move to town on my own, she helped me pack and gave me enough money for my first week's room and board at Mrs. Peabody's."

"So you went off by yourself?" Calamity's dull brown eyes lit up. "Just like I done?"

"Yes, just like you." Finding a common ground with the sister she'd once worshiped, Annie finally lifted her glass and touched it to Calamity's. "Maybe we're more alike than I thought. Here's to the sisters Cannary!"

Since Calamity would drink to anything, she toasted Annie back, then finished the contents of her glass. "Eeee—ya—haaa!" she bellowed in her best bull-whacking voice. "That's some mighty fine whisky, wouldn't you say?"

Annie grimaced, trying to hide another, more violent shudder. She nodded but kept her lips pressed firmly together.

Calamity laughed, then leaned across the table. "Tell me about Denver."

"Not much to tell," Annie said through a hiccup. She took a deep breath, relaxing, feeling warm, *good* all over. "I worked at several different stores, but really liked the bakery best. If it hadn't been for Mr. Bradfield, I'd probably still be there rolling pie dough and making chocolates."

"Mr. Bradfield? What'd he do?"

Feeling much looser, lighter of heart somehow, Annie didn't want to spoil the mood by discussing a foul specimen such as Cornelius Bradfield. "Nothing really. He was just a man, and you know men, don't you? Most of the ones I've met have been, oh, I don't know exactly how to put it, but more often than not, they seem to be—"

"Assholes," Calamity supplied for her.

Annie cringed. "I—I wouldn't put it that way. Let me just say I've never met a man worth marrying, and certainly never one as famous or exciting as Mr. McCanles or Mr. Hickok."

Those innocent words stumbled over a festering sore spot in Calamity's mind. No longer the adoring sister, but a woman—and a jealous woman at that— her eyebrows drew together in a very sharp, unflattering line as she demanded, "Speaking of men, I want to know what in hell you were doing with mine this morning!"

"Yours?" Annie giggled as she said, "Mr. Hickok and Mr. McCanles?"

"Luke don't belong to no one." Seeing the sudden sparkle in her sister's eyes, she added, "And don't go thinking about corralling him for yourself. He don't much like women of your sort. You know, ladies and such. He likes 'em kind of rough around the edges."

"Oh," Annie murmured, disappointed somehow.

"I want to know what in the hell you were a doing with Bill."

Annie giggled again. "I still can't believe that you share a cabin with two men as famous as Wild Bill Hickok and that handsome Luke McCanles. Why, if not for the shameful way it looks, I swear the idea would give me the swoons."

Calamity didn't see anything humorous in the conversation, and she definitely hadn't lost track of her earlier question. "I'll give *you* the swoons!" She doubled up her fist and shook it. "And I'll give em to you right now if you don't answer me. What were you trying to do with Bill?"

Annie straightened up, unaware until then of just how serious Martha was. "I wasn't trying to do anything with him. I was talking to him one minute, and the next thing I knew—"

"I fell against her," the man in question finished as he strolled out from the bedroom. "She kept me from falling. Now shut up with that kind of talk, Calam. You're sounding like an old crazy woman again."

Annie could hardly believe the change in her sister at Hickok's words. Martha smiled, softening her features until she looked almost coy and genteel.

"Sorry, Bill. I'm a trying to do better."

"I know you are," he answered wearily. "Try a little harder, would you?"

" 'Course. Anything you say."

Annie glanced up at the man responsible for this sudden transformation and noticed that he'd brushed his long flowing hair and groomed his mustache. His clothes—riding breeches and a dark blue flannel shirt complete with scarlet set in front—were rumpled, but he looked cleaner, somehow.

Nodding toward the women as he started for the door, Hickok said, "I'm heading over to Rosa's for a little breakfast. You gals care to join me?"

Breakfast? Had she slept for twenty-four hours? Annie snuck a peek out the dirty window, but in the dark little gulch, it was impossible for her to tell the time of day. "Is it morning or night?"

"Dusk," Calamity answered as she eyed Annie's torn dress and general appearance. She looked at Bill and shook her head. "Thanks for the invite, but me and my sis still got some catching up to do. See you later."

Hickok turned to Annie. "It was a real pleasure to

meet you, ma'am." He took his white brimmed hat off the bedpost, donned it, and said, "Calam and I would like to buy you a nice meal before you head on out of town—that is, of course, if it's all right with her."

" 'Course it is!" Calamity agreed quickly. "How long are you figuring on stayin, kid?"

"How long?" Understanding their mistaken impression, Annie smiled first at Wild Bill, then at her sister. "Long enough for you to get packed and come with me to find the little ones."

"To *what?* I ain't leaving Deadwood!"

Prepared for just that reaction, Annie shrugged and said, "In that case then, I've come to stay."

Hickok and Calamity exchanged horrified glances. Then she turned an incredulous gaze on her sister. "'Stay' as in *live* here?"

Annie smiled. "For the time being, those are my intentions. I guess if I have to, I might even open my own sweet shop until we're ready to move on."

Calamity sat there agog, unable to find her tongue.

Hickok shook his head, chuckling to himself as he walked out of the cabin. Just before he pulled the door shut, he called into the room, "Best set her straight, Calam. Best do it *now* before she gets any other crazy ideas."

3

Late that afternoon in Colorado Charlie Utter's Camp—a small collection of wagons and shelters set up at Whitewood Creek—Luke stumbled out of the tent he and Bill had shared before moving to the cabin in town. He yawned, stretched his arms high overhead, then scooped a double handful of cold water out of a bucket hanging on a nearby tree and splashed it over his face. With another scoop he doused his tousled hair then ran his fingers through it in lieu of a comb.

More awake now, and cooler too, he peered into a mirror nailed to that same pine tree and took careful stock of himself. His eyes webbed with crimson veins, there were dark circles below them complete with lines of exhaustion puckering the corners, and his complexion had faded from a nice rich tan to parchment yellow—at least, that's how he saw himself. Too many late hours, he ruminated, too much drinking, and way too much commiserating with Bill over the recent death of their friend, George Custer, at the battle of the Little Bighorn.

"A damn waste of time," he muttered as he dragged his fingers across his rapidly growing beard. Time better spent in making his fortune while there was still a fortune to be made in these hills. Hell, he'd never even much *liked* old Iron Butt Custer, who had been more Bill's friend and, to a lesser extent, Calamity's. As far as Luke was concerned, the general wasn't much more than an overblown loudmouth who took too many chances with too many lives. And where did all that bravado get him? Dead—just like the poor fools who'd ridden with him.

"Oh, Joe!" called a miner making his way to camp after a long day of placer mining.

Luke swiveled toward him. "Oh, Joe!" he echoed in the universal greeting of miners. Then he turned back to his reflection. It was time to get a shave, he decided, thinking of the rising temperatures in the gulch and the itch already growing unbearable beneath those coarse stubbles. A shave and maybe a bath, even though not three days past he'd spent more than two hours in a bathhouse up to his neck in bubbles. He turned his head to the side. A haircut wouldn't be a bad idea either.

This sudden urge to groom himself—and on a Monday, no less—startled Luke. What did it matter whether he bathed, shaved, or cut his hair? Hell, he could go another two weeks like this and still be the best-groomed man in the Black Hills, if you didn't count the shopkeepers lining the gulch. So why bother?

As if in answer, a pair of silver eyes flashed in Luke's mind. These were followed by the luscious memory of hair the color of daybreak flowing down over his sleeve like a river of silk. He closed his eyes and began rocking on his heels, with a silly boyish grin on his face. He thought of Annie's prim, almost spinsterish appearance before the bonnet had been torn from her head to reveal her true beauty. What a perfect disguise, he thought with a chuckle. And it almost worked—she almost *did* look like a real lady. But looks, as he'd discovered early in life, were deceiving.

Not that he'd know an honest-to-God lady if he actually came across one. He'd learned young that even if a woman looked and acted like a lady, it didn't necessarily mean that she *was* one. Between that and his days of drifting around the countryside with Wild Bill, Luke had learned two major truths about women: The bad ones always had a little good in them, and the self-proclaimed "good" ones generally had more than just a little bad inside.

On which side of the fence did Annie belong? If on the good side, how often did she fall off her lofty perch? Luke thought back to her soft, sweet mouth and the tentative, almost innocent way she'd moved beneath him when he kissed her. That had to have been an act, he decided, especially as he recalled her incredibly strong, pincerlike fingers.

Luke absently rubbed his ear. Ah, yes—Miss Ann Marie Cannary. *No lady, that one, and thank God for that,* he thought as he remembered her fascinating eyes. She was costumed as a lady perhaps, showing a calm, even-tempered woman on the surface, but beneath that layer of gentility roiled a tempest. Not so unlike the eye of a storm.

Ann Cannary was a woman in the same mold as her sister, the kind of woman Luke could understand. She was a regular hurricane who'd practically torn off his ear, and then fallen onto his own soft bed. He thought of the look in her eye when she'd recognized him, the way her lips seemed to part in invitation—a look he'd seen with satisfying regularity during his years as a showman. His grin widened.

Maybe, he thought as he grabbed his hat off a low-lying tree branch, he'd rushed away from the cabin a little too hastily that morning. Then again, he mused as he adjusted the brim to just the right tilt, now that he and little "Stormy" Ann had taken the opportunity to rest up, they would both be fresh and full of vinegar. A real match.

As Luke took a final glance at himself in the mirror, he curled his upper lip and ran his tongue across his teeth. "Yep," he said to himself, satisfied that his smile was bright and free of tobacco bits. "I believe I'll just go give that little girl a reason to stay around Deadwood for a while."

Calamity was still trying to set Annie straight some fifteen minutes later when Luke made his way back to the cabin. He pushed open the door, strolled into the room, and said, "Jesus! What in hell is going on in here? I could hear you two caterwauling all the way down to the creek."

Calamity turned to him, fists curled against her hips. "Li'l sis here thinks she's a staying in Deadwood!"

"And I am!" Annie pushed away from the table and rose, steadying herself against the chair back as the whisky she'd downed sloshed around in her empty stomach. She hiccuped, then set her chin defiantly. "There's no use trying to talk me out of it . . . either of you."

Luke took in her wildly tangled hair, torn dress, and cheeks that glowed as if lit from within. She hiccuped again, then raised her chin to an even haughtier level.

With a shake of his head, he grinned and said, "Oh yeah, you're Calamity's sister all right. And a regular little sweet spot in the eye of the storm at that."

Annie wrinkled her nose at Luke and turned to her sister. "What's that supposed to mean?"

Calamity cut loose with one of her horse laughs. "Most folks around these parts get a nickname sooner or later. I think you're about to get one on the sooner side."

Luke nodded. "Damned if she isn't. Stormy fits her pretty good, wouldn't you say, Calam?"

Annie blinked, surprised to find her vision blurred. "Stormy? What kind of name is that? Is it good or bad?"

"I think it's a right fine name," Calamity said. "A little bit good *and* a little bit bad, just like most folks' is. Why, you even look like you've been caught in a storm, don't she, Luke?"

"That she does."

Annie's cheeks reddened at the mention of her dishevelment. She quickly gathered her hair into her hands, twisted it into a lopsided knot, and donned her prune-colored bonnet.

Luke grimaced at the sight. Never, *ever*, had he seen an uglier hat on a woman—or a man.

Calamity began to chuckle at Luke's expression as she made her way to the door. "My 'Stormy' li'l sis here has a damn fool idea about staying in Deadwood to start up her own shop. I've been trying to talk sense into her all morning. I'd appreciate it if you'd give it a try for a while." She reached for the bullwhip she kept propped against the jamb. "I got to go do a piss."

"*Martha!* Mind your language!"

Calamity shouted over her shoulder as she walked through the doorway, "Gawddamn it, stop calling me Marthy! My name's Calamity Jane and I say or do whatever I want to!" She cracked the whip once for emphasis, and disappeared.

Luke pulled the door shut and then turned to regard the newly christened Stormy. She took a couple of steps backward, straightened her shoulders, and stood her ground. The ugly bonnet rested crookedly on her head, and the sleeve of her "proper" dress was torn and hanging off her shoulder like the tongue of an exhausted mule. And her skirt! It looked like the sheets at the Hot Town brothel—wrinkled, used . . . and used some more.

Between her ruffled appearance and the tilt of her nose, which he assumed went with her I'm-a-lady act,

Luke couldn't help but laugh as he removed his hat and sent it spinning toward the bedpost he always hung it on. It caught on the large wooden knob, spiraled around like a roulette wheel for a moment, and then settled into its usual tilt.

"So is it true?" he asked as he slowly and deliberately crossed the room to where she stood. "You're actually thinking about staying in Deadwood for more than a day or two?"

Unsure as to how to behave around such a celebrity, Annie sidestepped him and moved closer to the table. "Y-yes. I'm going to open a sweet shop."

"Sweets?" Luke reached for the coffee pot sitting on the stove. He shook it, judged it to be about half-full of day-old coffee, and set it back down. As he lit a match to a crumpled copy of the *Black Hills Pioneer* and stuffed it beneath some half-burned kindling, he winked at her and asked, "Just what kind of sweets do you plan to peddle around here, Stormy? We've already got about all the sugar we can handle up in the badlands."

Annie suddenly realized what he was implying—especially after her encounter with Cornelius Bradfield—and she swallowed a gasp. But how did one proceed with someone like Luke McCanles? Was he merely testing her, teasing a little in the bargain? If not, would a display of anger be overreacting?

Too much in awe of him as yet to unleash her temper, Annie just smiled and said, "Chocolate dainties and taffy, *not* sugar, are my specialties."

Understanding now that her extraordinary strength probably came from long hours of taffy-pulling, he rubbed his ear as he said, "I'll keep your skills in mind the next time I think about crossing you." With his back still to her, Luke chuckled softly and added, "But that's not likely to happen often. Another saloon might even make it in Deadwood, but I'm not so sure a sweetshop is even worth opening."

Undaunted, Annie grinned broadly. "There must be lots of folks in this town who'd rather have a sweet than a shot of rotgut whisky."

Satisfied that the fire had taken hold beneath the pot, Luke turned to her, leaned back against the stove, and grinned. "It appears that you're not one of those folks. Hell, I can smell your whisky breath clean over here."

Annie instinctively brought her palm to her mouth, blew against it, and inhaled. Then she saw the mirth in those onyx eyes. "Oh, you—I only had a little toast with my sister. I have a few rules about drinking, and my biggest one is that I don't indulge."

"But you *did* indulge—of *my* whisky—and without my permission. Staples like booze come mighty dear in the hills. I ought to charge you." Again he winked. "Or maybe you'd rather take it out in trade?"

He could have done just about anything but remind Annie of Mr. Bradfield and his lecherous, bartering ways. Forgetting Luke's celebrity for a moment, remembering only herself and the vows she'd made when she left Denver, Annie all but spat fire as she said, "I don't have to listen to that kind of talk, and I'm not going to." She started across the room, but Luke lurched forward and caught her by the elbow, ensnaring her.

Less sure now that Annie was as ribald and hardened as her sister, he decided to give her at least the
benefit of a doubt. "Sorry if I offended you, Stormy. I
guess I was a little out of line."

"A *little?*" She glanced down at her arm, at the
strong fingers circling it, and said, "Please let me go."

Luke released her immediately and found himself
face-to-face with that ugly bonnet again. It had
slipped even farther askew during her struggles with
him and now hung at the side of her head like a feed
bag with a broken strap. He didn't know whether to
laugh or give in to a sudden urge to tear the damn
thing off of her head and fill his palms with silken
strands of her strawberry-blond hair.

Feeling off balance and uncharacteristically indecisive, he did neither. Instead, Luke turned back to the
stove and muttered, "Sorry if I was a little rough, but
maybe that's why your sister's trying to warn you off
this town. I don't know what kind of life you're planning to live here, but Deadwood is definitely no place
for a single 'lady.'"

"But it's just a town, isn't it?" she asked, only
mildly curious about the peculiar way he'd said *lady.*
"It needs a lot of work and careful planning to grow,
but I don't see why I can't be a part of that growth
for a little while. What's your *real* objection to my
staying here?"

Luke didn't miss the challenge in her words or the
mulish twang in her tone—both traits that were very
much like Calamity's. To make her wait for his
answer, he slowly turned back to Stormy and made a
slow, precise perusal of her. Starting with her

entrancing silver eyes, Luke ran his gaze down the length of her body, pausing at her breasts as if measuring them. Then he flashed a knowing, wicked grin.

When she flinched, giving him the embarrassed reaction he sought, he said, "I don't much care whether you stay or go, Stormy. I just thought I ought to warn you about the way folks are in these parts. For what it's worth, I'm the closest thing to a gentleman you'll find in this town."

Annie half expected some kind of ribald remark following Luke's admission, but no mirth, no wink, not even a little twinkle appeared in those obsidian eyes. He seemed to be weary with the conversation and worn out with her. And probably sick of the sight of her to boot, she decided, taking stock of her disheveled clothing.

Angry at herself for stirring up the locals and presenting herself so shabbily on her very first day in Deadwood—and with such a famous citizen at that—Annie heaved a sigh as she said, "I thank you for the warning, Mr. McCanles, and I promise to think about what you said. For now I'd just like a little privacy so I can freshen up and change clothes." She waved toward the door. "If you don't mind?"

"You can have all the privacy you want." He jerked a thumb toward the bedroom. "In there."

Annie gasped. "Oh, but I can't go in there. That's where Mr. Hickok, ah, well it wouldn't be right for me to invade a private bedchamber."

Smelling burning coffee, Luke returned to the stove. As he poured the boiling liquid into a cup, he explained, "That room belongs to your sister, but since you can find Bill in there on occasion, I would say that it isn't so private."

Sure there had to be a good explanation for Martha's behavior, Annie said, "If you're suggesting what I think you are, then I assume that Mr. Hickok and my sister are at the least engaged."

"*Engaged?*" This time when he turned to face her, Luke's features were pinched and somber. He took a tentative sip of coffee, choked it down, then slammed his cup down on the table. "Hell, Bill couldn't marry your sister even if he wanted to. He and Agnes Lake tied the knot in Cheyenne about four months ago."

Annie swept around to where he stood. "Are you *sure* about that?"

"Damn right I'm sure," Luke replied, pausing long enough to take another sip of his coffee, and then shuddering at the bitter taste. "I was Bill's best man."

"B-but—" Annie glanced around the cabin as if to reassure herself that they were quite alone. "I don't understand. Where is this—this *wife?*"

"Back in Cincinnati waiting for Bill to strike it rich and join her." He tried to say it as casually as possible, as if such things were ordinary events, but deep inside, Luke had some definite reservations about the way his old friend was conducting himself these days. Even the marriage to Agnes, a woman some eleven years older than Bill, was more a business transaction than anything else, and that hadn't set right with Luke either.

Annie gripped the edge of the table, reeling from shock.

Thinking that the whisky had caught up with her,

Luke reached out and took her by the arm. "Why don't you go lie down awhile?"

Annie was embarrassed by her tendency to swoon at any discussion of personal matters—courtship, the marital embrace, *adultery* as was the case here—and with a man no less! How would she ever conduct herself among these people if a topic such as this was considered part of the normal conversation?

"Come on, Stormy," Luke said, trying once again to lead her to the bed. "You've obviously never had anything quite so potent as our moonshine. Just a thimbleful can take the kick out of a mule and grow hair on its teeth."

She pushed away from him. "It's not the whisky, honest. I'm just a little . . . well, surprised, I guess, to find out that Bill is married."

"So is he, I suspect from the look of it." More than ready for a change of subject, Luke peered at her bonnet. "And you know something else? I really hate that hat! Why don't you do us all a kindness and put it out of its misery. Hell, I'll even shoot the damn thing for you if you like."

Annie considered telling Luke why she wore such plain clothes and unattractive bonnets—to keep men like Cornelius Bradfield from staring at her or worse, harassing her—but before she could make up her mind, Luke went on with his offer.

"Hell, we could even carry it on up to Boot Hill and give it a proper burial. 'Here lies the ugliest bonnet ever made. May it and the pattern for the hideous thing rest in peace forever. A-*men!*'"

Stormy burst out laughing, and Luke was drawn

first to the chimelike sound, and then to her sweet mouth. Even as she laughed, her full lips retained their natural heart shape, and her grin, deeper than usual, prompted the appearance of the cutest set of dimples he'd ever seen. *Dimples!* Where had she been hiding them?

Luke moved in close, unable to stop staring at her mouth. He thought of the little currents of electricity he'd felt between them last night, of the sweet taste of her, and sensed in an instant that the kiss he was about to bestow would mean more to him than his usual "gift" to an adoring female. He continued to study her, marveling at the sensation, this feeling that *he* would be the one receiving the souvenir, not she, and slowly lowered his head in spite of it.

Annie watched the changes in Luke—the darkening of his already impossibly black eyes, the softening of his expression, and the sensual curve of his lips— and guessed his next move. She knew she ought to be backing away from him. He *looked* as if he planned to kiss her again. He didn't just look it, he *was* going to kiss her again, and this time, somehow she knew it would be gentler and kinder, the kind of kiss a young man gives to a woman he adores. She didn't know *why* she knew it. She just did.

Annie felt herself flush from head to toe. What should she do? Allow the kiss, or break out of his embrace? If she did the latter, should she become indignant, blushing and coquettish, or completely outraged? Oh, God, where was *Dr. Tuttle's Guide for Unmarried Ladies* when she really needed it? Why had she only bothered to read the section pertaining to the marital embrace, the secret little do's and don't's allowed in the bridal chamber?

Luke drew to within a whisper of her lips.

Annie closed her eyes in uncertain surrender.

And Calamity's shrill voice ripped through the cabin walls like a rusted whipsaw. "Eeee—ya—haaa!"

At the outburst, Luke released Stormy and stepped away from her. She blushed and averted her gaze. A second later, Calamity exploded through the doorway.

"Did ya hear?" she hollered, her usually grim eyes fired with excitement. "Injun Joe hit it big down to Number Seven below Discovery! He's over at Number Ten Saloon now buying drinks for the town!" She whirled around in a cloud of her own dust and started for the door again. "There'll be a hot time in the old town tonight or my name ain't Calamity Jane!" She cracked her bullwhip. "Eeee—ya—haaa!"

"Martha!" Annie called, rushing toward the door. "Wait! What about me?"

Calamity turned back, then frowned. "Oh, sorry, kid. I almost forgot about you in all the excitement." She glanced behind her sister at Luke, who'd also come to the door, then motioned to him. "Help me get this trunk inside, would you? I suppose she's gonna want to unpack a few things tonight."

Luke nudged Stormy aside, sure that he could handle the luggage himself, but when he reached for one of the straps and began to drag the heavy trunk toward the cabin door it barely moved. "Jesus," he said, moving it along an inch at a time, even with Calamity pushing the other end. "What do you have in here? A piano?"

Waiting until after her belongings were safely stowed in the cabin, Annie explained. "The bottom of the trunk is full of my cooking supplies. You know . . . copper pots, oversized spoons, a marble slab—"

"A *marble*—" Almost pleased to have an excuse to leave, as Luke was still unsettled by his reactions to Calamity's sister, he gripped his lower back. "That's it for my help tonight. I'm going on over to Number Ten for a little of Injun Joe's hospitality."

Calamity wiped the sweat from her brow as she watched him disappear through the door. Turning back to her sister, she said, "And I'm gonna join him. Anything else you need doing 'fore I set out for the night?"

"Set out? B-but I thought—you mean you're just going to leave me here alone?"

Calamity shrugged. "You'll be safe enough if you lock up. This will give you a chance to unpack a few things, too."

Annie's heart sank. "Of course, but I also thought we could finish our talk over a meal or something. I haven't eaten since—"

"Lord almighty, I forgot about that! Course you must be purty near to starvin'." Calamity stalked across the room to the open cupboard and began removing several items. "We got beans, some molasses if you like them a little sweeter, and—" She paused long enough to open a sack of week-old biscuits, take one out, and bang it against the stove. Turning toward Annie, she smiled. "And biscuits that still got some life in 'em. Will that do you?"

"I-I suppose," she murmured, trying not to appear

too disappointed or ungrateful. "But what about you? You have to eat, too. Why don't you at least stay long enough to have supper with me?"

"Not tonight, Stormy, kid. I ain't hungry, and 'sides"—she narrowed her gaze, still unable to reveal the source of the ceaseless ache inside her—"I can't tell you what just yet, but a lot of bad has happened around here the last couple of days. Something good like this strike comes along, I just got to join in the celebration. Understand?"

Annie shrugged. "Not really, but I don't have to. Why don't I just come with you?"

Calamity chuckled and turned back toward the door. "Number Ten's a saloon, honey. It looks to me like you've gone and raised yourself up to be a lady. If you want to stay one, you got to think of your reputation. Saloons and ladies mix about as well as water and bacon grease." She glanced back at her sister and smiled. "We'll finish our catchin' up tomorry. Then we'll work on making arrangements to get you settled somewhere's besides Deadwood."

"As long as you're here, I'm staying in this town, and that's that," Annie insisted.

As if she didn't hear those last words, Calamity reached for the horseshoe nailed to the crossbars on the log door and pulled it shut behind her. "Use the pole near the jamb to lock yourself in," she hollered through the cracks in the wall, "and don't let no one come in till mornin'!"

After Calamity left Annie inched open the door. Her sister was nowhere in sight, but music and gaiety filtered down through the murky gulch—the sounds of people in the company of other people, a celebration of life in a harsh and sometimes brutal land. Annie pulled the door shut after her and dropped the pole across it.

This wasn't at all the way she'd envisioned her reunion with Martha, not even close. Nor would she let it end here. Too many years of loneliness and too many disappointments to count had led her to this town and her sister. She just couldn't let herself be left behind, abandoned all over again by the only person she'd ever trusted. Not here, and not tonight.

Armed with the kind of determination that had kept her going after she'd been orphaned, Annie marched over to the stove, withdrew a stale biscuit, and began chewing on it as she tried to think of what to do next.

Deadwood, rough and unfinished as it may be, was the town in which Martha lived. Therefore, it was the town Annie intended to claim as her own, too, a town in which she would have to adapt. After that, she would set out to help her sister reclaim at least a little of her femininity. Maybe by then Martha would see things *her* way and join the search for the rest of the family.

But what could she do tonight? Ladies did not walk the streets of Deadwood after dark. Would she have to become a little less of a lady, or was there another way?

She glanced at the bedroom door, hesitating for only a moment, and then peeked inside the room. Another rope bed and a freestanding closet nearly filled every inch of space.

Annie went straight to the closet and riffled through the clothing until she found a relatively small pair of trousers, a man's shirt, a miner's hat, and a pair of worn boots. Although she wasn't exactly sure what she intended to do with them, she marched back into the main room and donned the ill-gotten goods.

The stained trousers were at least a size too big, the shirt was in need of laundering, and the boots were so big and full of holes that she had to stuff each of them with a pair of dirty socks. Finally Annie stood before the cracked looking glass tacked to the bedroom door and scrutinized her image.

Even though she'd never thought of herself as anything more than plain, save for her blessedly beautiful hair, she did recognize that her feminine curves were much too apparent in the tightly belted miner's garb.

If she was going to go after her sister—and she knew now that this was exactly what she intended to do—she would not only have to dress like a man in Calamity's tradition but *look* like one as well. Maybe, she thought with sudden inspiration, if Martha were to see her ladylike sister dressed in her mirror image, she would realize how truly coarse and vulgar she'd become, and want to improve herself all the more!

What she needed in order to achieve that end, and at the same time preserve her modesty, was some kind of coat or jacket. Since she hadn't noticed anything of that order in the bedroom closet, she glanced around the room, and her eyes rested on the long johns hanging from the ledge near the front door. Thinking that she might find more clothing up there,

Annie crossed the room, took a small ladder down from its peg on the wall, and climbed up to the loft. The area contained a mattress on one half and, as she suspected, piles of clothing on the other.

Wasting no time, Annie rummaged through the fancy shirts and trousers, wondering which showman owned the colorful silk neckties and soft felt hats with silver conchos sparkling in the darkness. When she finally spotted a fancy leather vest made of black-and-white cowhide trimmed with fringe all around, she shrugged off a moment's guilt about "borrowing" such a fine piece of clothing and scrambled back down the ladder.

The vest covered her from breasts to hips, and the fringe hung well below, almost to her knees. She decided that she looked like a well-heeled miner, or maybe even a misplaced Texan—but, in any event, definitely a man. The question was, Could she go through with it? What if her disguise didn't work? What if she was accosted—or worse, what if Martha became so angry she banished her from her life? What if . . .

No. No more what ifs. She was here in Deadwood with one of her four long-lost sisters, and, God willing, she'd soon be reunited with the rest. If she had to compromise her reputation, her safety, or even her life to make sure Martha knew how determined she was to engineer that reunion, then so be it.

Feeling stronger and more hopeful, Annie tugged the opening of the fancy vest closed and said, "Well, Stormy . . . *Stormy?*" How easily the sobriquet flowed off her tongue, she thought, liking the sound and the strength of her new name. "Stormy," she repeated, this time in a whisper.

Grinning to herself, she tugged the ragged miner's hat down over her glorious hair, pulling it low on her brow, then turned in a slow circle, making a final assessment of her reflection. With her dimples receding, she nodded her final approval and wondered: Was even a town as rude and crude as Deadwood ready for another Cannary sister?

4

Stormy made her way along Main Street relatively unnoticed except for a couple of miners who waved and called her Joe. Keeping her head low, she waved back at the men, pleased by what she assumed was mistaken identity, and continued on her way.

The street was crowded, alive with chatter between excited miners and men hot on the scent of prosperity. The workday was over for most, and twilight had cast dark shadows over the gulch, yet above the men's voices Stormy could still hear the rasping of saws and steady drumming of hammers. More saloons under construction, she figured, even though she'd already passed at least a dozen such establishments.

When at last she came to a log building with a sign reading Nuttall & Mann's No. 10 Saloon nailed to its false front, Stormy took a tentative peek inside. The room rippled with jubilant miners, some gathered around tables, others belly-up to the bar, and still others milling around with drinks in hand.

A raucous piano tune she couldn't identify provided background music for a mélange of conversations sprinkled with a few feminine giggles. It was an interesting, if somewhat barbarous, gathering. But how would she ever find Martha in that crowd without bringing unwanted attention to herself? Perhaps going there had been a mistake after all.

A stranger bumped her from behind and then said in a voice rife with impatience, "Coming or going? Get the hell out of the way."

With the decision made for her, Stormy pushed her way into the saloon and then flattened herself against the wall near the door. Keeping an eye out for Martha, she inched her way along the rough-hewn panels of pine until she finally saw her sister sitting at a table with two scruffy-looking men.

Strangely enough, Annie was more afraid of her than of the men. She'd heard tales of Calamity Jane punching not just men but women right in the face! Would the fact that they were sisters protect her from Martha's hot temper? She thought back to her childhood and the already volatile older sister who had lit after her on more occasions than she could remember, and decided to proceed with caution.

Although her throat was as dry as the smoke-leaden air, Stormy squared her shoulders and strode up to the table. "Evening," she muttered in a deep voice.

Calamity glanced up at the stranger, nodded, and returned her gaze to her whisky glass. Then she whipped her head back up and narrowed her eyes. *"Muffin?"*

"The name's Stormy," Annie said in her roughest, meanest voice, "and I'll thank you to remember it— Martha."

Calamity's mouth dropped open. *This* was her little sister—*the lady?* "Ah, yeah—that's right. Stormy it is. What kin I do for ya?"

Annie hung her thumbs in the side pockets of the vest. "I thought I'd join you."

"Join—you mean *sit* in here?"

Struggling to keep her expression rigid and determined, Stormy gave a sharp nod.

Calamity stared long and hard at her sister, teetering between tossing her out of the saloon and indulging her curious behavior a while longer. Settling on the latter, she looked around at the men. "Well? What are you waiting for? One of you sapheads get up off your ass and give a gal a seat!"

Old Frenchy Cachlin the Bottle Fiend never argued with anyone, much less Calamity Jane. He leapt to his feet, swept the empty beer bottles off the table and into his carpetbag, and then padded away in search of more "collectibles."

Stormy slid onto his chair. The man to her left, who was dressed in a faded frock coat that reached his knees and a battered derby, leaned in close and peered at her as if he couldn't quite bring her into focus.

"This here's Swill Barrel Jimmy," Calamity said by way of introduction.

Swill Barrel continued to stare at her. "Damned if it *ain't* a gal . . . and a right pretty gal, at that."

"Shut up about that!" Calamity leaned across the

table and thumped him across the top of his head with the handle of her bullwhip. "You just forget you ever saw her, you lead-skulled polecat! This here's my sister, and I'm here to tell you that the first time one of you yahoos so much as looks cross-eyed at her—" she paused long enough to thump him on the head again, "will be the last time." She dropped the whip, pulled her pistol out of its holster, and drew a bead between his eyes. "Understand?"

"Whoa, Martha! Ya don't have to tell me twice!" Swill Barrel's chair screeched a loud protest as he pushed away from the table and hopped to his feet. "I ain't got no interest in you or a sister of yours." He touched the brim of his ragged derby, nodded toward Stormy, and staggered toward the bar.

Stormy chuckled as she whispered, "Swill Barrel? What kind of name is that?"

"I already told you that purty near everyone in Deadwood's got a nickname," she snapped, very unhappy at her sister's surprise visit. "Swill Barrel's an ex-Confederate soldier who ain't never got over the war. He got his name cause he pretty much lives out of the garbage from restaurants and bawdy houses. Understand?" She hooked the leg of the chair he'd just vacated with the toe of her boot, dragged it up tight against the table, and propped both of her feet across the seat. Then she picked up her whisky, tossed it down, and slammed the empty glass against the tabletop. "Now that we got that settled, tell me what in bloody blue hell you think you're doing in here!"

An icy shiver wriggled down Stormy's spine at the

look in Martha's eyes, but she managed to maintain her tough exterior as she said, "Same thing you are, I guess."

Calamity raised an auburn eyebrow. "Is that so?" She lifted Swill Barrel's glass off the table, wiped the rim with the sleeve of her shirt, then filled it with whisky and shoved it across the table. "Then you'd best get to drinking up. I'm way the hell ahead of you."

Stormy shook her head. "No, thanks. The drink I had with you earlier feels like it's still bouncing off the inside of my skull."

Calamity chuckled in spite of her foul mood. "It's the high altitude. Kinda doubles the jolt for a while, and definitely takes getting used to, but it does cut down on the rotgut bill some." She poured herself another glass of whisky but didn't pick it up. Speaking in a far softer voice, she quietly asked, "Why are you here, kid? Tell me the truth."

"I couldn't stand being left alone tonight, and I thought it was time you—"

"Not here in the saloon, kid, here in Deadwood. This is no kinda town for someone like you."

At Martha's soft, caring tone, Stormy's heart swelled and her throat grew tight. "I want my family again," she whispered, blinking back a tear. "I want us to be real sisters again. If I have to live in the saloons of Deadwood to be with you, then I guess I will."

More moved than she would ever let on, Calamity looked away from her sister and took a sip of whisky.

"I mean to find everyone," Stormy continued.

"Lena, Lije, and the little ones, and if I have to go back to Salt Lake City where I last saw them, I'll do that too. In fact, that's where I was headed when I heard you might be up here. Wouldn't that be something if they're still there, Martha?"

"I'm *not* Marthy anymore."

"Sorry, Calamity, but wouldn't it be wonderful— all of us together again? I was hoping you'd want to go with me to help find everyone."

Calamity looked up for a moment, then quickly dropped her gaze. "I kin help you with Lena. You passed within ten miles of her place on your way to Deadwood."

"I *did?* Where is she? How is she?"

Calamity chuckled. "She's just fine. Her and her husband, Johnnie Borner, got a farm just outside of Fort Laramie."

"Her *husband?* But Lena's just a kid!"

This time Calamity cut loose with one of her horse laughs. "Been a while since you seen Lena, I guess. She's right close to twenty. Gonna have a babe any day now, too."

"A baby?" Stormy sighed. *Imagine that,* she thought to herself. Her younger sister not only married, but about to become a mother. Until then, Stormy hadn't realized how very much she'd lost of her family through the years. What other surprises were in store?

"What about Elijah?" she asked Calamity. "Have you seen him lately?"

Calamity's expression grew rigid. She raised her glass but not her gaze, then brought the whisky to her lips and drank it down.

Stormy repeated the question even though she felt a terrible sense of foreboding. "What happened to Lije?"

Avoiding her sister's gaze, Calamity twirled her empty glass around in the same spot on the table for several moments before she finally muttered, "He was with Custer."

Stormy's fingers and stomach seemed to knot at once as if connected somehow. She glanced down at the table, and for one reckless moment, she considered taking the drink her sister had poured for her. Instead, she leaned back in her chair and folded her hands in her lap. "You're saying that he's . . . gone, then?"

"Dead and buried right near the Little Bighorn River where them damned Sioux kilt him. My fault, I guess, since I got him the job as one of Custer's scouts right along with me." She sighed. "Shoulda died with him at the Little Bighorn, too, but I was sick that day and couldn't ride."

Stormy closed her eyes against the tears of sorrow that fought for release. She swallowed, pushing a mournful sob back down in her throat. But nothing, she knew, would rid her of the sudden feeling that a great dark fog had enveloped her, drenching her with a sense of quiet pain and terrible loss. From within the aching core of that fog, Stormy heard her sister calling to her.

"Take it easy, kid," Calamity encouraged, patting the back of her hand. "He's with Ma and Pa now, so it might not be as bad as all that. I been sitting around the last two days hardly able to think of anything but poor Lije, until I thought of him with them. I'll bet he's feeling a damn sight better now than you are. Have your drink. It'll perk you right up."

Stormy shook her head. "Drinking doesn't make anything better. Good news does. Tell me what you know about the little ones. I sent a wire to Brigham Young while I still lived in Colorado, but so far, he hasn't answered it. Do you know if the same family took all three of them in?"

Taking her time with the answer, Calamity slowly refilled her glass. How could she explain about her failure to keep watch over her little brother and sisters? Or admit that they were in some ways as lost to Calamity as Lije, wandering for all she knew in the vast desert beyond the Great Salt Lake? How could she explain that she'd never tried to find them, when she wasn't even sure of the reason herself?

Sighing wearily, Calamity raised her bloodshot eyes. "I don't know where they are, and that's the God's honest truth."

"What do you mean, you don't know? You surely must have some information about their whereabouts."

Calamity stuck her finger into her glass of whisky, twirled it, then pulled it out and sucked it dry. Keeping that callused finger near her mouth, she said, "After you moved in with the Parkers, I went up to Helena to find work—remember?"

"Of course I remember. That was the last time I saw you." She thought back to the day. "I was thirteen and you were going on fifteen and still wearing dresses." *And you will be again,* she amended silently. "It seems to me that someone promised you a job at a hotel in Montana."

"That 'hotel' turned out to be a whorehouse, and the bastard what give me the job beat me bloody, and then he . . ." She paused, shutting out the horror of the memory. "Let's just say he was a true asshole through and through."

Stormy sucked in her breath. "Oh, my God! He didn't force you to do . . . anything, did he?"

Calamity narrowed her gaze. "I wasn't what you'd call willing, I can tell you that! Say, that ain't what that Cornelius fella done to you, is it?"

"No, not that he didn't try a time or two." Mere mention of the man's attempts to seduce her made Stormy shudder. How did her sister live with the memory of the man who'd completed such a brutal attack? "I'm sorry that it did happen to you, that a man made you do . . . I—I don't know what to say."

"Ain't nuthin' you can say. 'Sides, it was a long time ago." She made a tight fist then banged it against the table. "I made the bastard sorry if it makes you feel any better, and on down the road, I made a few other sons a bitches even sorrier they belonged in the same species as him." She smiled, then her mouth fell into its usual grim line. "Anyways, after I hitched a ride back to Salt Lake, I found out the Parkers had hauled you off to Colorado, and the little ones had been adopted by three separate families that were headed west." Her volume increased to its usual roar. "Nobody knew the names of the people what took 'em or exactly where they were heading, and that's why I don't know where the hell the little ones are. Ain't no way to track 'em I kin think of!"

Hickok strode up to the table and rapped his

knuckles against the scarred finish. "Dammit all, woman, I can hardly hear the piano player over your big mouth." He turned to Stormy. "You . . . up. Sit over here." He jerked the chair out from under Calamity's boots and they fell to the floor with a thud.

Hickok pointed to the now empty chair and Stormy, who obeyed him instantly, quickly slid over to the new seat. Then she looked to her sister and rolled her eyes.

Calamity chuckled. "He ain't picking on you. Bill don't never sit with his back to the door," she explained. "And he don't do nothing with his right hand so's he can keep it free in case he has to grab his gun. He don't drink, play cards, or fondle the girls with that hand. Ain't that right, Bill?"

Using the same even monotone he nearly always spoke in, he said, "Shut up, Calam." Then Hickok shoved Stormy's untouched drink over to her, sat in her chair, and poured himself a glass of whisky. He took a mouthful, swirled it around like fine wine for a few moments, then swallowed.

Calamity tore her adoring gaze off him long enough to turn to her sister and say, "There's talk of making Bill sheriff of Deadwood. Wouldn't that be something? They want him to clean this town up like he done in Hays City and Abilene." She swung back around toward Hickok. "I think you'd make a right fine sheriff. Just what this town needs."

"Shut up, Calam." Hickok glanced to his right. "New in town, are you mister?"

Stormy suppressed a grin, then answered him in her natural voice. "Sort of. I got in early yesterday morning."

Hickok frowned as he leaned in for a closer look. "Ann? Is that you under all that?"

"It's Stormy," she said correcting him. "That's my new nickname. Mr. McCanles gave it to me."

Catching the sparkle in her sister's eyes, Calamity rustled her way into the conversation. "Didn't I warn you not to get all gooney-eyed over that sorry excuse for a gambler? You stay away from Luke McCanles—he ain't nothing but trouble fore a gal like you. 'Sides, like I told you, he don't much like 'ladies,' goes in more for the soiled-dove type."

Hickok raised his brow. "She's got a point about Luke, Stormy, but what I'm wondering is why you're in here. Even if you're not quite the lady you seem to be, you struck me as being a cut above"—he glanced at Calamity—"the kind of folks you usually find in a saloon."

Used to Hickok's ways, Calamity took no offense. "I tried to talk her into leaving, Bill, I swear I did, but she just won't go."

Stormy confirmed the story. "I came to this town to get to know my sister again." She thought of mentioning how she and Calamity had been responsible for convincing their drunken parents to return home and that being inside a saloon wasn't nearly as traumatic to her as he might assume, but she thought better of it. Wild Bill Hickok didn't seem like a man who put up with much idle chatter. Stormy offered a brief summary. "I couldn't very well do that with Calamity sitting here and me back at the cabin, so I decided to join her."

"Is that a fact? Maybe you haven't noticed, but the

air and language in here is pretty near the same shade of blue as the morning sky. If I was your kin, I'd be a little concerned about you getting corrupted. You're better off back at the cabin."

"That's what I been trying to tell her myself!" Calamity bellowed, working to get his attention back on her—where it belonged. "She just ain't interested in listening to nobody."

Hickok turned to Calamity and heaved a weary sigh.

"You don't got to tell me again," Calamity said, picking up her drink. "I know. Shut up. Just shut up."

In the far corner of the room, with his back against the wall, Luke stared at his cards as if the fierce gaze might change the nine into a queen. It didn't. He tossed in his hand, then absently dragged his fingers across stubbles that were rapidly growing into a thick beard. This was not his night at all.

He rose. "That's it for me, pards."

A miner who'd lost big to Luke the week before grumbled, "Ya haven't given me a chance to get even."

"I will," he promised, moving away from the table, "and the way my luck's been running lately, you'll be getting caught up sooner than you think."

Bored with the game, with saloon life in general, Luke started for the door. As he made his retreat, he saw Bill sitting at a table across the room. Wondering if his friend wouldn't just as soon play a little one-on-one like they'd done last evening, and wondering too—

he had to admit—how Stormy was managing all by herself back at the cabin, he threaded his way through the drunken revelers and approached the table.

"I'm not worth a damn at poker tonight, Bill. Want to head on back to the cabin?" He glanced at the miner sitting next to Hickok, trying to identify him. The stranger smiled, flashing the cutest set of dimples Luke had ever seen. He froze for a moment, then bent down and peered up under the edge of the floppy-brimmed hat.

"What in the hell . . . *Stormy?*" He glanced at the drink sitting directly in front of her, took in her scruffy, weather-beaten appearance, then turned to Calamity and said, "God help us all, there really are two of you."

"Not quite," Calamity said. "I ain't taught her how to shoot straight yet!" Chuckling, she reached behind her, yanked the chair out from underneath an unsuspecting miner, and muttered a quick "thanks" to the man who was now sitting on the floor. Then she dragged the extra chair around to the front of her table and gestured toward Luke. "Why don't you sit a spell and have a drink with us."

Although the last thing he wanted was a drink, Luke was far too curious about Stormy to leave. Smiling at her as he sat down, he remarked, "Calamity has usually managed to cut up a couple of miners with her whip, or at least to coax one into dancing to the tune of her pistol by now. What about you, sweet darlin'? Maimed anyone yet?"

Stormy, who still wasn't sure how to conduct herself around such celebrities as Hickok and McCanles, glanced at Luke out of the corner of her eye. His normally mirthful expression was the same as always, but he also had the look of a hawk—an all-knowing, all-seeing raptor. What was he looking for? Or was it simply her new apparel?

He'd changed clothes, too, and now wore a crisp white shirt, rolled up at the sleeves and left open from the throat to the third button. Over this he'd draped a shiny vest of gunmetal gray satin, and his hair, neatly brushed, but still long and shaggy, was topped by his black-and-silver hat. He was dressed to the teeth, but he still hadn't shaved.

An inward blush blossomed in the pit of Stormy's belly at the memory of those whiskers flush against her skin, his mouth so intimately crushed against her own. She closed her eyes against the unsettling sensations and gripped the edge of the table.

Observing her all the while and guessing she'd had too much to drink, Luke settled back against his chair. "So much for conversation. Anyone else at this table still capable of coherent thought?"

Hickok chuckled. "Ease up on her, Luke. She's new at this."

"And she's not going to get any better!" Calamity thumped the handle of her bullwhip against the table. "I'm a-takin' her back to the cabin now."

Stormy shook a finger in the air, determined to set them all straight, but before she could form the first word of protest, a drunken miner stumbled over his own feet and fell heavily against her, spilling his drink down her back.

Stormy leapt out of her chair. "Oh my God!"

The miner, clutching his aching belly, muttered an apology laced with curses, and staggered away.

Intending to help dry Stormy off, Luke jumped up beside her. As he reached for his handkerchief, he recognized the fancy cowhide costume he once wore while a part of Buffalo Bill's Dramatic Company. "Hey! Where in the hell did you get that vest?"

Shaking the liquor off her fingers and arms, Stormy absently explained. "I borrowed it. Do you have a scarf or a hanky I can use?"

"A handkerchief isn't going to clean up that mess." He was incensed to see his favorite show vest dripping with rotgut. "Take it off!"

Alarmed by the idea of exposing herself as a female in a room full of drunken men, Stormy leaned forward and whispered, "I can't."

"What do you mean, you can't? That's my property and I want it back now."

Stormy parted the vest just enough for Luke to catch a glimpse of how well defined her breasts and waist were in the miner's garb. "Surely you can see why I can't take it off in here."

"Oh . . . hell," he grumbled, glancing around at the bounty of love-starved men. "Then I guess we'll just have to go back to the cabin. Come on. I'll walk you."

Calamity, who wasn't at all pleased by the circumstances, struggled to her feet. "Wait a damn minute," she bellowed. "You're not taking my li'l sis anywhere. I'll go to the cabin with her."

Hickok tapped his gun barrel against the tabletop.

"Sit down, Calam," he said quietly.

"B-but—"

"*Sit,* woman."

She grumbled under her breath but plopped back down in her chair.

"See you later, I guess," Stormy called to her sister over her shoulder as Luke gently pushed her through the crowd.

"Keep an eye on him!" Calamity hollered back, even though the pair was already out of earshot.

Hickok chuckled softly. "What are you so worried about, Calam?"

Her lower lip drooped as she muttered, "That there's my li'l sis. She ain't . . . like me, exactly."

"Aw, hell, woman—Luke's not going to hurt her any. He just wants to make sure she knows how to do a proper laundry job."

"Laundry job," she repeated with a sneer. "You'd best hope that's all he's figuring on doing, Bill, 'cause if that son of a bitch puts so much as one finger—"

"Shut up, Calam."

She sighed. "Do you have to keep a sayin' that to me? I'll bet that ain't the way you talk to your precious Agnes!"

He grinned and stroked his silken mustache. "Agnes knows when to keep her mouth shut."

"Agnes her bagness," she grumbled. "Why'd you go marry her, anyways? Hell, if I'd a known you was looking for a wife, I might a married you myself."

Hickok raised one eyebrow. "Would you now?"

Calamity shrugged, then downed her drink. "Maybe not. It doesn't matter one way or the other anyways," she muttered, no longer talking to Bill, but herself. "Nuthin' matters to me. Not losing the little ones, not Lije getting himself kilt, and not my sister coming to look down her nose at me. Don't none of it matter a'tall."

Calamity reached up to her cheeks and wiped a sudden profusion of moisture away, oblivious to the fact that it sprang from her own tears. "I don't care about nuthin!" She hiccuped, then raised her chin and gazed toward the bar. "Sylvester!" she hollered. "Bring us another bottle! They'll be a hot time in this old town tonight! Eeee—ya—haaa!"

Back in the cabin, Luke closed the door, held out his hand, and snapped his fingers. "The vest please."

Stormy peeled the garment off and handed it to him. "I hope it's not damaged. I just needed something to cover myself with, and it seemed to be the perfect size."

So was she, Luke decided as her lithe form came into view. Even in tattered doeskin clothing, Stormy exuded softness and femininity, a complete contrast to her more androgynous sister. The exception was the raggedy, lop-eared miner's hat she wore, which was, he decided, second only in sheer ugliness to her prune-colored bonnet.

"While you're at it," he added, "why don't you take off that disgusting hat? Your taste in headgear is positively appalling."

"This was the only one I could find," she said as she pulled it off along with the pins she'd used to secure her locks to the top of her head. Her thick hair tumbled down over her shoulders and back as

Stormy dropped the hat and shook her head. When she raised up again, preparing to reknot her hair at the back of her neck, she caught Luke's gaze. What she saw in his eyes both thrilled and frightened her.

He had a dangerous look about him, something basic, an almost animalistic gleam coupled with a subtle glimmer of amusement. The look sent a chill down her spine even as it warmed her. Unsure of his next move—or her own—Stormy bit her bottom lip.

The innocent gesture caught Luke like a blow to the gut. Sudden desire spread through him, warming him like a hot towel. Eager for a taste of her, and sure that Stormy was every bit as anxious as he, Luke dropped the vest to the floor. He tore off his hat and sent it flying in the general direction of the bedpost, for once uninterested in where it landed. Then he fixed a heated gaze on her.

"Come here," he whispered, his voice dark and husky.

"I—" She took a backward step, her lip still clenched between her teeth. "What for?"

"I want to kiss you. Come here."

Stormy stood rigid, unsure of what to say or do. *He's spoiled,* her conscience warned her, *used to having his way with women.* She knew she should run, but her feet wouldn't move, and her mind seemed to shut down completely.

Luke advanced on her. When he reached her, he took her in his arms and stared into her eyes. Then he whispered a final warning.

"Brace yourself, sweet darlin'. This time I mean to kiss you all the way to hell and back."

5

Luke was upon Stormy before she could blink, as his strong arms wound around her, tugging her up close to his body. His breathing was rapid, knotted, and his dark eyes shone with determination. God, he was handsome, so masculine and exciting, but how could she just allow him this indulgence? To be embraced so intimately, ravaged by a man she hardly even knew, went against everything Stormy believed in—even if that man did happen to be Lucky Luke McCanles. She wanted him to notice her, yes, perhaps even to court her, but this . . . this was too much.

She would have to dissuade him somehow, yet still manage to retain the demeanor of Stormy Ann Cannary. And to do that, she would have to appear to be the kind of woman he liked, yet manage to avoid his advances at the same time—no matter how good they made her feel.

At the last moment, as his whiskers skimmed across her mouth, Stormy flattened her palms against his chest, leaned back, and said, "Wait!"

Luke's head remained suspended in place for a moment. "Wait? What in hell for?"

"I—I have rules about things like this."

Luke relaxed his grip. "Rules? What in hell are you talking about?"

"I—I can't stand . . . beards. That's my number one rule. I never kiss a man with a beard." She rubbed her cheek. "It hurts too much."

Unable to argue against such forthright honesty, Luke released her. "No beards, huh?"

"Never." With a shake of her head, Stormy ducked out of his embrace and made her way to the stove. "Sorry, but that's the way it is."

"Sorry?" Wasn't *she* the one missing out here? he wondered. Shouldn't he be making the rules, not this silver-eyed sister of the most immoral woman he'd ever met? He turned toward her. "Well, sweet darlin', I hope you won't be holding your breath waiting for me to rush out and get shaved. You'll have to take me up on my offer now the way I am, or I'm afraid I'll just have to be on my way."

Although half of her was dying to find out exactly what it meant to be "kissed all the way to hell and back" by Luke McCanles, the other half, the part of Stormy with the common sense, turned to Luke and flashed him a smile. "Then I guess I'll be saying good night, Mr. McCanles. Thanks for walking me home."

If he'd been dealt a royal flush, Luke couldn't have been more surprised. This wasn't the way most

"Skeeters" behaved—women he and Bill had to fight off, and sometimes didn't, during their years on the show circuit. Skeeters—bloodsucking mosquito women, as they called them—would do anything at any time just for the mere chance of being the girl of the week, or even the night, of a famous man like Wild Bill Hickok or Lucky Luke McCanles.

He knew Stormy had been impressed by his celebrity. He'd seen it in her eyes when she figured out who he was. Why wasn't she as accessible as the others? Was she just teasing him a little?

He watched her light the stove and set a pot of water over the flames. She moved with graceful confidence, the man's shirt she wore showing off the strength in her softly rounded shoulders. Luke's gaze followed the river of golden-blond hair down to the center of her back, then lower still to the curve of her bottom clearly outlined in those tattered trousers. Shaken by a sudden surge of heat radiating from deep in his loins, he took a long, steadying breath. Then he swaggered over to where Stormy stood and began caressing her shoulders from behind.

"Last call, darlin'," he whispered against her hair. "Or I've got to be on my way."

A ripple of desire rolled down Stormy's back then pooled low in her abdomen. She gripped the edge of the stove and willed herself to remain calm and collected. When she felt in control—as much as she could muster with Luke's hands on her—she slowly turned and flashed him another grin, this one complete with batting eyelashes.

"Good luck at the tables—oh, and don't worry

about your vest. I'm sure I can clean it up with a little warm water and a good scrub brush. Good night."

Luke narrowed his gaze, waiting, watching for some crack in her little act, but she kept the same innocent expression, the kind of look that made him want to throttle her as much as he wanted to kiss her. With a sharp nod, he turned on his heel, marched over to the bed, and collected his hat. Just before leaving he glanced back inside at her and said, "Good night, sweet darlin'! If you change your mind, I'll be at the Progressive Hall Saloon."

Stormy didn't change her mind, but she did spend the next few hours wondering what she'd missed as she unpacked her things and piled them on the unused section of the loft. Luke was unlike any man she'd ever known—cocky and arrogant, yes, but beneath that flashy exterior beat a heart much like her own, she suspected. She'd seen it in his dark eyes. Mirth and wit were always apparent there, but something more, a sense of loss or loneliness lay just behind the sparkle. She had the definite feeling that Luke wasn't nearly as happy as he appeared to be. Whatever it was that drew her to him, Stormy identified with him in an instant, felt a bond with him somehow.

How should she proceed with this man who was so spoiled and obviously used to having his own way? She wouldn't find the answer in Dr. Tuttle's guidebook, that much she knew without thumbing through the worn pages again. It also wouldn't tell her what to do with the feelings Luke had stirred in her, feelings that lingered even now as she thought of him.

Dr. Tuttle only warned that having such carnal desires was a sure path to hell, and acting on them, a sin of utmost depravity. Gentlemen, he'd written, always fled from women who showed the slightest sexual desire, even after marriage. Did that include gentlemen like Luke? Men who didn't quite measure up to all that the word implied?

Stormy didn't know. She only knew that Luke hadn't fled because of her responses. Without a doubt, he still wanted to take her all the way to hell and back. Maybe he hadn't noticed how quickly she'd reacted to his touch. She wasn't sure whether to curse herself for missing what might be her only chance with him or pat herself on the back for remaining true to herself and the code of a real lady.

Only when she set about arranging the kitchen to suit her needs was she able to forget about Luke and concentrate on what had to be her biggest area of concern: fitting into Deadwood society and making enough money to earn a living. She dragged the heavy marble slab out of the trunk and managed to hoist it up on the carving table. Then, using the supplies she'd brought along, she made a batch each of anise-flavored and lemon taffy and cooked up a small sampling of her special twisted chocolate drops.

When she finally collapsed on her bed—Luke's bed, actually—Stormy slept till dawn.

She awakened to the sound of fists pounding against the cabin door. "Just a minute," she called. Not bothering to search for her robe, she wrapped herself in Luke's blanket and stumbled to the door. "Who's there?"

"It's me, Calamity Jane—and I can out-shoot any man in this town!" This declaration was followed by the sounds of gunfire.

Stormy quickly unlatched the door, grabbed the sleeve of her sister's rawhide jacket, and pulled her inside. The pistol Calamity was holding clattered to the floor as she tripped and nearly fell over the threshold.

Stormy kicked the gun into the room, then glanced up and down the alley before closing and latching the door. She followed Calamity into the tiny bedroom and watched her drunken sister struggle to get out of her clothes. Knowing better than to try to help her in such an inebriated condition, she quietly asked, "Where are Luke and Mr. Hickok?"

Calamity shrugged, then fell onto the bed as she tried to fight her way out of her jacket. "Hell, damned if I know. They decided you and me ought to have some privacy! I don't need no privacy! This cabin belongs to Johnny the Oyster. He never said who I could or couldn't keep in here with me!"

She hiccuped, still fighting the confines of her jacket, then tried to outsmart it by jerking her left arm upward and her right downward. The garment clung to her even more tightly, binding her like a strait jacket. She shrugged again and let her head fall against the mattress.

Stormy moved to the edge of the bed. At the revolting sight of the sister she'd once revered, anger raged throughout her. Again she wondered how Martha could have let herself slide so low. Why hadn't she fought harder to become less like their mother, and at least make a stab at being respectable? "Are you going to be all right?" she asked.

Calamity opened her mouth, burped, and finally said, "Uh-huh."

"If you're sure you don't need me, I thought I'd go out to look for work. Calamity?" she said sharply, knowing her temper had taken over her tongue. "Are you listening?" The only answer she got was a muffled grunt.

Used to family members who went to town and got so drunk they forgot to come home for days at a time, Stormy recognized that she would get no more answers from Calamity until she'd slept awhile. She whispered, hoping somehow that her sister's subconscious would hear. "I'll see you later—maybe not till supper if I can find someone to hire me today." Then, studying the awkward position her sister was in, she took pity and pushed a small flat pillow beneath her head.

As Stormy tiptoed through the room and headed toward the cupboard to collect her samples and fix a little breakfast, she suddenly wondered if finding employment in a town like Deadwood would mean the new beginning she was looking for, or the complete end to her sanity.

When Stormy's new shoes touched down on the boardwalk in front of Smiling Will's Grocery Store two hours later, the brass heels were covered with mud and slime from every kind of animal waste imaginable. There was nothing she could do about her shoes, but she did make sure her plain white blouse was properly tucked into the waist of her brown calico skirt. Then she adjusted her prune-colored bonnet until it showed a little more of her face but still kept her from appearing too flashy.

Space was at a premium in all the establishments along the narrow gulch, and Will's grocery was no exception, she realized when she stepped inside. Boxes and crates were stacked floor to ceiling from the front of the store to the rear, where a long counter supported the cash register and other items for sale. Stormy headed for the counter, where a heavyset woman labored over a set of books.

"Excuse me," she said. "I'd like to speak with the man who owns this store if I might."

The woman snapped her head up and adjusted her glasses. "What do you want? I'm Mrs. Will Hawkes and just as much the owner as he is."

Stormy didn't doubt it as she took in the beady eyes, the drooping mouth of a person who didn't laugh often, and the wealth of wrinkles at her brow. Sensing that she had to be *very* careful with this woman, Stormy quietly said, "I'm looking for work."

"Humph." Mrs. Hawkes leaned across the counter and looked her up and down. "Don't have enough meat on your bones to give an honest day's work. 'Sides, I ain't looking for no help."

"Actually, I have goods to offer, not just my labor." She held up the bag. "I'm a candymaker by trade, and I can also bake a pretty decent pie."

Mrs. Hawkes's frown reached new depths. "Candy? Lemme see what you got."

Stormy laid the bag on the counter and removed several pieces of taffy and chocolate, each piece wrapped in the waxed paper she'd brought with her from Denver. "The taffy is lemon or licorice flavored and the drops are pure milk chocolate."

Mrs. Hawkes pushed her glasses up farther on her nose then carefully unwrapped a chocolate drop. "You made these yourself?"

"Yes, ma'am, early this morning."

"Humph." She popped the candy into her mouth, then closed her eyes and began to suck it.

Justin popped through the curtain at the rear of the store just then, his arms stacked with boxes clear up past his eyebrows. "Where am I supposed to put the peaches, Ma?"

"Just put them up front on the floor near the other canned fruits. We'll shelve them as soon as we got room." She turned back to Stormy, slurping before she said, "Ox train come through yesterday. We've got more supplies than places to put them for a while."

"I understand what you mean," Stormy said. "I came in on that ox train. In fact, your son helped me with my things."

"Miss Cannary? Is that you?" Justin weaved his way to the front of the store, dropped his burden, and hurried back to the counter. "Morning, ma'am." Remembering his hat belatedly, he ripped it off his head and stuck it under his armpit. "Everything turn out all right for you at the cabin?"

Mrs. Hawkes's eyebrows met at the bridge of her nose. "You were at her cabin?"

Stormy shot Justin a nervous glance and said, "Justin was kind enough to deliver my trunk after I arrived."

Although she listened to what Stormy had to say, Mrs. Hawkes's full attention was on her son, especially on his moon-eyed expression. She whipped her graying head around. "What's your name and where're you from?"

"Stormy," she automatically said, still surprised at how easily her new name slid off her tongue. "I'm Stormy Ann Cannary, ma'am, from Denver City, Colorado."

"You got a husband with you looking for gold, that it?"

"No, ma'am. I'm not married."

"She come to stay with her sister," Justin said, his blue eyes sparkling with excitement.

"That's right," Stormy went on for him, afraid he might explain exactly who her kin was. "Martha Cannary is my sister and I live with her in a log cabin a few blocks up the street."

"That's the pure truth, Ma." Justin offered Stormy a wink since his mother wasn't looking at him any longer. "Martha Cannary. Know her well, I do."

Mrs. Hawkes rubbed her index finger back and forth against the mole near the point of her chin. "Martha Cannary?" she echoed. "Can't say I know her. She been here long?"

Stormy shook her head. "Only a month or so. What about the candy? Do you like it?"

She shrugged. "I've had better, but it'll do."

"Then you mean I can have the job and sell my candy out of your store, too?"

"The job? You're gonna work for us, Miss Cannary? Really?"

"Down, boy," Justin's mother grumbled under her breath. "We can't afford to hire on any extra help right now."

"But I'm not asking for much, Mrs. Hawkes. I just want to sell my candy out of your store until I can afford a store of my own. I'll split the profits with you fifty-fifty, and help with your other sales in the bargain. You really don't have a thing to lose."

Mrs. Hawkes narrowed one eye. "And you don't expect any wages?"

"No, ma'am. Just half of what my sweets bring in."

As she slowly unwrapped a piece of taffy and popped it into her mouth, Mrs. Hawkes glanced from her son to Stormy, then back to her son again. When she spoke, her voice came out muffled. "What are you standing around for? Don't you have work to do?"

"Yes, Ma," he said, backing away. "Kin she stay on? Kin she?"

She answered as she chewed, her jaw laboring to keep the candy from sticking to her dentures. "You make mighty good taffy. Don't think I've ever had lemon flavor before. How'd you get lemons up here?"

Stormy whispered, "It's a secret recipe, but I'll tell you this much. It's an extract of lemon flavoring, not lemon juice. Do you think the miners will like it?"

Mrs. Hawkes nodded, then unwrapped another

piece—licorice, this time. She sucked on it for a moment, moaned softly, then slurped as she said, "I think it just might be worth giving it a shot. We'll try this fifty-fifty business for a week and see how it works out."

"Ya-hoo!" Justin hollered.

Mrs. Hawkes pointed a chubby finger at her son. "Go on now! Get on back to work or I'll hire Miss Cannary to do your job and fire you!"

"Yes, ma'am!" He donned his hat, scrambled around the counter to give his mother a big hug, then disappeared behind the curtain that led to the back room.

After he'd gone, Mrs. Hawkes leaned across the counter and asked, "How old are you?"

"Twenty-two. Why?"

"My boy is mighty taken with you, but he's still more whelp than bulldog. I don't want you getting his hormonals all worked up, if you get my drift."

Stormy's cheeks blossomed at the very thought. "Don't worry, Mrs. Hawkes. I'm not interested in finding a husband right now, and even if I were, I'd choose someone a little closer to my age."

"Just so we understand each other. And by the way—my name's Eudell. I don't mind if you use it."

"Thank you, Eudell. Don't mind if I do."

Stormy spent the rest of the morning and a good part of the afternoon handing out free samples of her candy and waiting on customers. As she talked with the miners, she took an informal poll about their likes and dislikes where flavors were concerned. Chocolate taffy seemed to interest them the most, followed by licorice, peppermint, and lemon in that order.

Her arrangement with Eudell for baking pies also turned out to be especially pleasing. The grocery would furnish the supplies, and Stormy would bake the pies while retaining 50 percent of the profit. If her goods went over as well as she hoped they would, she figured she'd have more than enough money to pay both Calamity's and her own way out of Deadwood before the leaves began to turn.

As the day wore on, more and more miners came into the store, and it soon became apparent they were there not simply to shop but to gawk at the new woman in town. Word traveled fast in a small settlement like Deadwood, where women were scarce as plastered walls and lace curtains, and apparently there wasn't a man in town too shy to approach her and introduce himself.

This didn't set too well with Justin. He risked his mother's wrath time and time again trying to remain as the number one man in the eyes of Miss Stormy Ann Cannary, up to nearly tossing one miner out the door when he deemed him a little too friendly with the new employee.

Despite all that, the candy was receiving rave reviews, along with requests for more, so the day was far from a disappointment. Stormy was down to her last five pieces of taffy when an especially scruffy-looking miner approached her, hat in hand.

"Afternoon, missy," he began, not bold enough to raise his gaze to hers just yet. "Heard yur new in town, and that yur giving out free candy." He finally looked into her eyes. "I'd be right grateful—say! Ain't you the gal I seen over at the Number Ten last night?"

Stormy recognized Swill Barrel Jimmy in an instant—even worse, saw the potential impact of her impulsive foray. She quickly glanced at the counter where Eudell Hawkes was counting out a customer's change, and was relieved to see that her "new partner" apparently hadn't overheard the remark. Turning back to Swill Barrel, she kept her voice low as she said, "I'm afraid you're mistaken. I'm sure we've never met. Have a piece of candy."

As if he couldn't bear to look at her beauty any longer, his gaze fell to the floor. " 'Course it weren't a lady I seen. I guess that gal with Calamity just looked a little like you."

"Calamity?" Eudell Hawkes called out as she made her way over to where they stood. "Did I hear you mention Calamity Jane's name, Jimmy?"

He nodded, his jaw too busy pummeling a piece of taffy for speech.

"Well, you can tell her for me—she'd better not show her face in *this* establishment again. She is *not* welcome in my grocery store. Now or ever!" She turned to Stormy. "A very disgusting young woman, someone I hope you never have the displeasure to run into." She clucked her tongue in disapproval, slurped on her piece of taffy, and added, "I have to go into the back room for a moment. Please mind the store."

Biting back an angry retort, and forcing herself not to defend her sister—a woman who was largely indefensible—Stormy muttered, "Yes, ma'am. I'll be happy to."

After Swill Barrel left, Stormy set the tray containing the few remaining pieces of candy next to a jar filled with pickled quail eggs, then began dusting the shelves, anything to give vent to her frustrations. Twice in the last twenty-four hours she'd pretended to be someone she was not, and this time she'd gone so far as to allow a near stranger to denigrate a member of her family—even if the member in question did happen to be the infamous Calamity Jane.

Years ago, ladylike or not, she would have let fly at the woman, or at the least defended Martha in no uncertain terms. But not today, and not with someone as obviously rigid in her thinking as Eudell Hawkes. Had she let Martha—or even herself—down by remaining quiet?

From the corner of her eye, Stormy noticed another customer filling the doorway. Then she heard the sound of boots thumping against the plank floor and spurs jingling like a pocketful of loose change. Stormy glanced in his direction, then glanced again, her feather duster hanging from her hand at half-mast.

It was Luke. Not the man who'd left her breathless last evening. And not the one who'd stolen a kiss during her first few hours in town. This was a Luke she'd only seen sketched on the cover of a dime novel: Lucky Luke McCanles, showman and pistoleer.

He wore the same fancy black-and-silver hat she'd seen before but had added a fresh white shirt, a crimson bow tie, and a vest and trousers of fine broadcloth pin stripes in charcoal and black. Over this, he'd donned a matching waistcoat with satin lapels, and around his waist he wore an ornate belt of black leather with silver conchos all around. Hanging from this belt at each hip were two long-barreled pistols, silver with mother-of-pearl inlays as far as she could tell. He looked so fresh, so clean . . . and so exciting, it was all she could do to suppress a little cry of joy.

Luke strode to the back of the store, leaned an elbow against the countertop, and smiled. "Afternoon, sweet darlin'. I understand you're giving away free samples—of candy, that is. I thought I'd stop by and . . . indulge myself."

Stormy gripped the edge of the counter and pressed her knees against the shelves below to steady them. She blinked her eyes, sure that what she'd seen was imaginary, quite unable to believe that she was actually standing here watching the pages of a novel come to life. Here stood Lucky Luke McCanles— trailblazer, Indian fighter, lawman—looking as if he'd just stepped off the cover of one of his novels. And he was smiling at her—*her,* Miss Ann Marie Cannary from Denver City, and no one else.

Stormy tried to swallow but found her throat dry. She thought of brushing a few wayward strands of hair off her brow but discovered that her arms didn't work. In fact, the only functioning organ in her entire body seemed to be her heart, and it was beating so rapidly, Stormy feared she might collapse from sheer exhaustion at any moment.

Luke grinned and said, "You don't mind, do you?"

Mind? She blinked again, trying to understand what he was talking about. When she looked into his eyes she saw a kind of euphoric delight, an expression that went beyond mirth and sent her mind further into chaos.

Worse yet, Luke's grin seemed to deepen as she stared at him. Then he began to slide his fingers across his chin, rubbing the back of his hand up and down along his right cheek, grinning that bad-boy grin as he continued to stroke his baby-smooth, intoxicatingly scented cheek.

"Y-you shaved!"

"I guess I can't get anything past you, now, can I."

Stormy laughed, sounding almost girlish. "I didn't mean to holler like that, but I—well, I thought you said that I would, you know, have to accept you the way you were or not at all."

Luke shrugged. "I changed my mind." He stifled a chuckle as high color crawled up along her neck and fanned out on her cheeks. What was this? A blush from Stormy Ann Cannary? "Don't you want to know why I'm here?"

Suddenly mute, she nodded.

"It's simple," he whispered huskily, glancing from side to side to ensure their privacy. "I've come to collect." He took her hand and pressed it against his cheek. "Smooth enough for you?"

As if burned, she jerked her hand away the minute she made contact with him. "Y-yes, it's . . . fine."

"Then let's go."

She glanced up into his eyes again, those deadly

serious ebony eyes, and then quickly looked away. "I—I'm not through giving out my candy samples. I promised I'd stay until they were all gone."

Luke took only a moment to decide. Then he reached for the four remaining pieces of taffy—three lemon and one licorice—unwrapped them, and stuffed them all in his mouth at the same time. He held his hands up and mumbled through the gob of candy, "All gone."

Stormy was laughing into her handkerchief when Eudell Hawkes breezed through the curtain from the back room. "Oh, Mr. McCanles. Good afternoon. It's been awhile since I've seen you around. We could have used you and those big guns of yours Saturday night. Lawd, I thought the roof was going to come down the way those ruffians were carrying on—and till all hours of the morning, too!"

He tipped his hat and gave her a smile, one he hoped was tight enough to keep the taffy juice from running down his chin. She didn't seem to notice his discomfort.

She turned to Stormy, saw the empty tray on the counter, and said, "My, my! That candy of yours went over better than I expected." She whirled back around toward Luke. "Did you get a sample of Miss Cannary's fine taffy?"

Luke nodded, pointing to his bloated cheeks.

Speaking for him, Stormy said, "Yes. In fact, Mr. McCanles has just offered to walk me home so I can get started on tomorrow's supply."

"Humm, I suppose you should. We might as well find out if these folks are willing to pay for what they got free today. That'll be the real test. Then we can try your pies."

"That sounds fair enough." Stormy collected the used squares of paper—wrappings she intended to reuse until the "starch" went out of them—then circled around to where Luke stood waiting. "Good afternoon, Eudell. And thanks again for giving me a chance."

Luke nodded toward the older woman, touched the brim of his hat, then offered his elbow to Stormy.

By the time they reached the cabin, Luke was finally capable of coherent conversation again. The first words out of his mouth as he showed Stormy into the room were, "What in hell kind of flavoring did you put in that taffy?"

She chuckled, the sound a little twittery, clearly echoing a sudden attack of nerves at least to her own ears. As she set the bag and wrappings on her marble slab, she said, "It's licorice and lemon, but I made those flavors in two separate batches of candy. It's not my fault you decided to combine them."

He laughed to himself as he stalked over to the bedroom door, opened it, and peeked inside. It was empty. Turning back to Stormy, Luke smiled and said, "There's only two things I'm interested in combining, sweet darlin', and there isn't another soul in the cabin to keep us from doing just that." He paused, waiting for her to move. "Well? Are you going to make me come after you again?"

Her heart in her throat, Stormy's conscience told her to turn and flee, but instinct held her back, coaxing her to stay, to allow herself the thrill of this intimacy. How could she not? This was something she'd secretly dreamed of since she'd begun reading those novels. This was, in fact, a dream come true.

"All right," he conceded when she didn't respond. "But I think you should know that I have a few rules when it comes to this sort of thing myself."

"Rules? For *me?*"

"Yes—you." He stood not two feet from her now. "My biggest rule is that I never, *ever* kiss a woman who's wearing an ugly bonnet. Take it off."

Without question, she obeyed him. With trembling fingers Stormy reached for the ties of her bow and tugged them loose. Then she carefully removed the hat and tossed it over to one of the chairs.

"Better?" she said evenly, trying to seem less nervous than she felt.

"Definitely." He caught the tip of her chin between his thumb and forefinger. "There is one more thing . . ."

"Oh?"

"See if you can't relax a little. I also have a rule against kissing wooden statues."

Stormy could feel the blush rising inside of her. She willed with all her might for it to stay beneath her clothing, hidden in her breast. *Relax,* he'd said. *Relax.* But how could she? This was the most exciting, the most thrilling moment of her life. She took a deep breath, dangled her arms at her sides, squeezed her eyes shut, and let her head fall back.

Then slowly, tormenting her a little with his careful precision, Luke settled his mouth over hers.

6

This was nothing like Luke's uninvited assault the day she'd arrived in Deadwood. No, this was a gentler Luke, a man so fluid and smooth, he'd maneuvered the hard planes of his body against the soft curves of hers until there wasn't an inch of her that wasn't touching him. And he managed to do it before Stormy had a chance to figure out what he was doing.

She should have been scandalized by the liberties she'd allowed him thus far, or at least offended. But Lord, had she ever felt so good, so completely, so utterly, alive? She was tingling with sensations as Luke worked his tongue between her teeth, probing her mouth as before—this time caressing more than invading. This time, making her want the intimacy with a shamelessness that shocked her.

A kiss like this, her conscience whispered, most surely would start her down the path to hell. Would Luke be able to bring her back from those fiery gates as promised?

She didn't care. It no longer mattered. All that mattered was Luke. Luke and his hands. Luke and his magical mouth. Stormy melted against him, wanting more, needing something to ease the terrible tension building inside her. Then, as slowly and precisely as he'd begun the kiss, he ended it. He lifted his head, hovering above her mouth for one agonizing moment. His raven eyes glittered with savagery, and his boyish apple cheeks were no longer round, but hardened, more rigid and defined.

Before Stormy could understand what it all meant, he swooped back down on her, capturing her lips one more time in a hard, searing kiss. This too Stormy allowed him. What if she never felt this way again, not *ever* in her entire life? How could she not indulge herself these few stolen moments?

When Luke's mouth left hers again, sliding down along her throat this time to follow the path of his wandering fingers, she allowed him those caresses as well. His touch hypnotized her, it seemed, for Stormy could no longer control her own body.

Through it all, she became aware that Luke's fingers were no longer merely stroking her throat but busying themselves lower still. Incredible as it seemed, he was . . . opening the buttons . . . of her blouse. She stood rigid for a moment, then shuddered with both pleasure and horror as he reached inside her chemise and began to caress her breast.

That final intimacy was the act that brought Stormy back to her senses. She locked her elbows and pushed out of his embrace. "W-what do you think you're doing?"

His voice husky with desire and frustration, Luke reached out to reclaim her. "Nothing you didn't want me to do."

Stormy spun out of his arms and turned her back to him as she buttoned her blouse. "I—I don't know what you mean. I never said you could do anything but kiss me."

Luke slid his hands across her shoulders, gently kneading the knots out of her suddenly tensed muscles. "Your body gave me all the permission I need to do more than kiss you, sweet—"

But he found he couldn't add the word *darlin'*, as the endearment he'd casually bestowed on dozens of women simply didn't fit her any longer—if it ever really had. He suddenly felt humbled for reasons he didn't understand, and instinctively softened his tone. "What's the point of teasing ourselves this way? We both know what we want."

But he was wrong, so terribly wrong. Stormy had no idea exactly *what* it was she wanted. She only knew that she'd let herself get carried away. And that she'd allowed Luke far more than just the simple kiss she'd agreed to.

Stormy did the only thing she could think of. She apologized. "I'm sorry if I gave you the wrong impression. It wasn't my intention to lead you on."

"But you *did* lead me on, and now I think we should finish what we started."

Finish? As in . . . ? The question never completely formed in Stormy's mind, as there was no need. The answer practically shouted at her from Luke's glistening eyes and the determination in his expression.

She backed away from him until her bustles met the edge of the stove. Then she gave him a weak smile, and said, "Again, I'm sorry if you misunderstood. Can't we just let it go at that?"

"No." Luke's long stride ate up half the distance she'd put between them.

Holding her hands up, she warned, "You'd better stop right there."

He kept on coming.

"I mean business, Mr. McCanles."

"So do I."

There was no grin on his face, no flash of humor in his dark eyes. He was just a man. A man who wanted a woman in the worst way. Stormy broke to her right and headed for the door.

Luke lunged forward, snagging her before she'd taken a full step. Then he hauled her back into his arms. "I don't want to play cat and mouse games with you anymore. I just want you."

Stormy's eyes rolled to a close. She swooned, or something close to it, and leaned against Luke's broad chest. Never had she imagined the impact such words could have on her, or the sheer thrill of hearing them from a man like Luke McCanles. This had to be a dream. A wonderful, delicious dream from which she never wanted to awaken.

Luke brushed his mouth across hers, then whispered against her lips, "I took a room at the Grand Central Hotel last night. It's a lot more private than this falling-down excuse for a cabin. Why don't we head on over there?"

Afraid of what she might see, of what she might

do, and afraid to end the dream, Stormy squeezed her eyelids even tighter.

"Well?" Luke's voice was sharp, more impatient than ever. "Shall we?"

The abrupt change in his tone brought Stormy out of her reverie. She blinked, shook her head, then stared up at him. "I—no," she managed to say. "I have . . . rules about such things."

"More rules?" Luke groaned, then plunged his fingers into the thick bank of hair at his forehead. "Jesus, lady—now what do you want from me? I've bathed and shaved. What's left?" He lifted his fingers, letting a few strands of his sable hair fall across his left eyebrow. "Do you expect me to shave my head?"

In spite of her chagrin, Stormy chuckled. "No, of course not."

"Then what?"

Unable to think of an excuse other than the truth, she laid her cards on the table. "I've decided not to indulge in more than a kiss or two until the day . . . I'm wed."

"Wed?" The veins in Luke's neck bulged. "As in *married?*"

"That's correct."

"What the hell kind of a rule is that?" Luke's expression turned as dark as his eyes. "Can't you come up with something a fellow can at least *think* about?"

Stormy's gaze flickered toward the door, and she bit her bottom lip.

"Aw, hell," he said. "When did you come up with

that rule? Riding up the gulch with the ox train?"

Maybe the truth hadn't been the wisest choice after all. How could she tell Luke that she'd made up her mind years ago not to bed her first man until the night she wed, or even suggest to him that she was a virgin and still expect to see him again? If what her sister had said was true—that Luke was attracted only to bawdy, experienced women—he'd walk out the door and head for the badlands the minute the words were out of her mouth.

So how should she answer him? An out-and-out lie wouldn't do—she'd already compromised her principles enough by her unexpected response to his kisses—yet she couldn't exactly tell the truth either. Maybe the best answer was silence. Calculating, coquettish silence.

With her heart pounding and her palms damp, Stormy glanced at Luke, offered him a secretive smile and a fluttering of lashes, then slowly looked away.

"Aw . . . *hell.*" He drove the toe of his boot against the iron leg of the stove. "Isn't that just the way my luck's been running lately!"

Stormy emitted a little sigh of relief. "Maybe it doesn't have a thing to do with luck. Maybe you're just spoiled."

"Spoiled?" He nearly choked on the word. *"Me?"*

"Yes, you. Maybe you're just mad because you're used to having everything your own way."

He shrugged. "So? Even if you're right—and I'm not saying that you are—what's wrong with that?"

"Nothing much, I suppose, if you want to live your life unchallenged."

"I've been challenged, lady, plenty of times, and I don't consider myself spoiled or lucky because of it."

"I guess what I meant to say was that maybe you've never truly *appreciated* what you've been given, since everything comes to you so easily. In that way, don't you think you're a little spoiled?"

She had him there. Especially if she happened to be referring to his luck with women. There had been only one woman in his entire life he'd ever looked up to or who'd ever offered him any kind of challenge—and she'd committed adultery with his very own father. Luke didn't need more challenges like that any more than he needed another dose of Stormy's brilliant observations about him. In fact, if he had any brains at all, he'd simply turn tail and head on up the road.

But he couldn't. Not yet, and not this way, even though she'd left him frustrated, a little bit angry, and a lot confused. Hell, how could he? He couldn't blame her for wanting to turn her life around, in fact, he admired her all the more for it. If Stormy had lived a life even half as troubled as her sister, she'd been through a lot. Even to try to become respectable showed a lot of determination. And guts. Why, just hopping on an ox train and going in search of her sister in this godforsaken country—a sister like Calamity Jane, no less—took more guts and determination than most men had.

A lot more, Luke had to admit, than even he'd had at times. He'd never so much as written a letter to ease the estrangement from his own family. That sudden realization made up Luke's mind about his next move.

"Come on." He took Stormy's hand and started for the door. "Let's go on over to the hotel and—"

"I guess you haven't been listening to me." Stormy planted the heels of her shoes against the rough flooring and tried to jerk out of his grasp.

"Yes, I have." Luke flashed his showman's grin. "You didn't let me finish what I had to say. I was trying to ask you to join me for supper at my hotel—in the dining room with everyone else."

"That's all? Just supper?"

"That's it. The ox train brought in a fresh supply of beef, and as scarce as cattle are in these parts, it won't last long. Now are you going to come have a steak with me before they're all sold out, or would you rather scratch through Calamity's cupboards again?"

Just the thought of the cold beans and stale biscuits she'd eaten last night and again this morning would have been enough reason for Stormy to accept. She could almost smell the heavenly aroma of sizzling beefsteak and see mounds of potatoes smothered in onions.

But a far greater inducement—the fact that Luke was acting like a suitor, a gentleman courting a lady—prompted her to say, "Thank you for the invitation, Mr. McCanles. I'd love to join you for supper." She glanced back toward the chair to where she'd tossed her hat. "It won't take me a minute to get ready."

"It won't even take a second, sweetheart. You're coming with me now—just the way you are." Luke gave her a gentle tug and started for the door again.

"I'm looking forward to supper tonight. I won't have my appetite ruined by that damned hat of yours."

The Grand Central Hotel, which was just across the street from the row of cabins Calamity called home, had been open for six short weeks. The food ranged from good to excellent, thanks to the culinary talents of Lucretia Marchbanks, a former slave who'd picked up the nickname "Mahogany" because of her coloring.

Intent on her steak, Boston-baked brown potatoes, fresh peas, and a double helping of Mahogany's huge fluffy biscuits, Stormy had fallen silent. Luke, who'd never been one to waste a lot of time sitting at the supper table, wiped his mouth with his napkin, dropped it in the center of his empty plate, and then eyed his dining companion as she worked on her meal.

Those dimples of hers were popping in and out as she chewed, drawing his attention again and again to her pert little mouth. Did she realize the effect she had on him? Just watching her eat was almost too much to bear.

Of course she did, he decided. That's why she made up that last little rule. She was teasing him, making him wait until he'd do almost anything to be with her. But she hadn't completely fooled him. He'd been with enough women to know that Stormy wanted him as much as he wanted her. Even if she was trying to change her life, she would be his soon enough. He didn't mind waiting a little if it made her feel better about herself. He would give her time to come to him on her own . . . a little time anyway.

But Lord, how he wanted her, Luke realized as he continued to stare across the table. *Now.* She'd almost finished her meal and was tiptoeing through her few remaining vittles like a kitten in wet grass, taking her fill but making a grand show of delicacy, of gentility even. Eating, he supposed, like a lady. Behaving exactly the way a proper, well-mannered woman should. A woman like . . . Sarah Shull.

Jesus, how long had it been since he'd thought of her? Sarah, the gentle-voiced woman of exotic beauty who'd always led the parade in Luke's adolescent dreams, the woman who owned his twelve-year-old heart from the moment he first set eyes on her, even though she was at least twice his age. To him, she'd been the epitome of what a lady should be, a delicate, proper woman of grace who knew exactly how to behave under even the most trying of circumstances. The kind of woman he'd hoped to find for himself one day.

Most men would have agreed with him until the day Sarah and Luke's father, Sheriff David McCanles of Watauga County, North Carolina, made off with county funds and left Luke, his brother, and his mother to face the shame alone. Right up until that day, Sarah Shull had been thought of by all who knew her as a real fine lady. But she turned out to be merely an *imitation* of a lady—one who'd fooled an entire town, Luke worst of all.

Just thinking of her name brought a bitter tide of memories to Luke's throat. His voice sharp and far more impatient than he'd intended, he asked Stormy, "Are you about done?"

Stormy, who'd swallowed at least three more pieces of steak than her stomach had room for, leaned back in her chair and issued a miserable groan. "I haven't eaten that much at one sitting since . . . I don't think I've *ever* been quite this gluttonous! What the chef in this hotel does with a few eggs and a sack of flour is a sin."

"Mahogany is a great cook all right." Luke wanted out of the room, and out *now* before Stormy did or said something else to remind him of the past—of Sarah Shull. He pushed his chair away from the table. "Maybe next time we'll save enough room for a taste of her pie."

"She makes pie, too?" Again Stormy groaned, this time in defeat. "My baked goods won't stand a chance against hers."

"You'll do all right." He rose and circled around to Stormy's chair. "Besides," he added as he helped her up, "Mahogany won't sell her wares outside this hotel. I think she has some kind of 'rule' against it."

As Stormy chuckled over what she assumed was his reference to her endless list of rules, Luke took her by the elbow and escorted her from the narrow dining room. They went into the gaily decorated lobby, which the restaurant shared with the hotel, just as four gunmen strolled in through the front door. One of them, a man whose nose had obviously been broken several times over, bumped against Stormy, nearly tearing her out of Luke's grip.

"Hey!" Luke hollered, glancing at Stormy to make

certain she was all right. "One of you fellows owes the lady an apology."

The man with the misshapen nose hesitated, snickering along with his companions before he slowly turned back to them. He grinned at Stormy, touched his hat, and then settled his cross-eyed gaze on Luke. "The lady don't look any worse for the wear. You're McCanles, aren't you?"

Although he was none too impressed with the stranger's idea of an apology, Luke offered a grudging nod of his head. "That's right."

"McCall here," the man said, even though Luke hadn't asked. "Jack McCall. You be sure and tell your 'bodyguard' that I'm in town, and that I plan to stay awhile, too." Snickering again, he turned back to his friends and continued on into the restaurant.

Luke hadn't heard Hickok referred to as his bodyguard in years, and he wasn't in much of a mood to hear it again. But he swallowed his sudden rage along with the urge to reach out, grab the man by his shirt collar, and beat him bloody. Who was this McCall? he wondered. Why did he seem intent on stirring up trouble?

Alarmed by the intensity in Luke's dark eyes, Stormy tugged the sleeve of his shirt. "Is something wrong? You look as if, as if . . ."

Forcing a smile he didn't feel inside, Luke took Stormy by the arm and resumed their stroll through the front door. "Everything's fine. I was just trying to remember where I'd seen that man before, that's all." Then, eager to put as much distance between himself and McCall, Luke guided her across the street and up the alley without another word.

Once inside the cabin, he lit the lamp on the table and turned the wick up high. "You know, there are no guarantees that Calamity will show up to stay with you tonight. Are you sure you'll be all right here alone?"

Stormy pointed to the pole on the wall. "I know how to bar the door, and in spite of what my sister said, I can handle a gun almost as well as she can. My mother taught us all to shoot from the time we were big enough to hold a gun. I can pick a Juneberry out of a crow's beak at fifty yards." She nodded toward the gun propped against the wall near the door. "I'll be just fine."

Luke followed her gaze, then burst out laughing. "If you're planning to use that, you'll be picking pieces of that crow out of a pine tree at a hundred yards! That's old Martha, Bill's ten-gauge shotgun."

Stormy squinted and stared into the darkened corner. "In that case, you have even less reason to worry about me. There's no way I'll miss my target if I use that."

"You'd better hope not. You get one shot with old Martha, then—*boom!* You'll be sitting on your butt like Calam was the first time she shot it!" He laughed at the memory.

Hearing something in his tone other than amusement, Stormy quietly said, "You like my sister a lot, don't you."

"Calam?" Luke paused to consider the woman who'd gradually become one of his closest friends. "Yes, I do, but more than that, I admire her. Your sister is a rare breed, in case you don't know it."

"I know she's special. She's also the most capable woman I've ever known."

"Humm, she's all of that," Luke agreed. "But more. She knows exactly what she wants, and she's not afraid to go right out and get it. I don't know any women, and not too many men who can lay claim to that kind of bravery."

Go right out and get it. Stormy smiled, wondering if he would feel the same way if she were to tell him she planned to do just that—with him.

Encouraged by the softness in her eyes, Luke impulsively took her into his arms. "I'd better be going. Is a good-night kiss allowed, or do you have rules against that sort of thing too?"

She hesitated, instinctively holding back for a moment, but Stormy had no intention of denying Luke or herself—even if he threatened to kiss her all the way to hell and back again. She wanted him. On her terms, yes, but badly enough to allow a few of his own. She closed her eyes and parted her lips.

Ignoring the conflicting messages Stormy's behavior suggested, Luke took her face between his hands and nestled his mouth against hers. Then he gave her a kiss so gentle and caring, the depth of his own tenderness surprised him. Had he ever kissed a woman in quite this way, he wondered, or with so much . . . emotion?

Calamity chose that moment to burst through the doorway. When she saw her sister in Luke's embrace, she promptly drew her pistol and fired two rounds into the loft above her head.

At the sound of gunfire Luke dropped to the floor and in the same motion flung Stormy toward the safety of the bed, heaving himself in the opposite direction. Drawing his pistol as he rolled, he came up on one knee, hands clasped around the gun's grip, and pulled back the hammer.

"Aw, dammit it all, Calam!" Luke jammed his pistol back into the holster when he saw who the intruder was, then climbed to his feet. "Can't you knock when you enter a room, like a normal person?"

Calamity kicked the door shut behind her and started for him. "Soon as you figure out just what a normal person is in these parts, you let me know and we'll talk about it. In the meantime," she waved her still-drawn gun in his face, "you got a little explaining to do. What in hell do you think you're a-doing with my little sis?"

Stormy, who'd landed against the edge of the mattress, then tumbled to the floor in an ungraceful heap, scrambled to her feet. "He didn't do anything wrong, Martha, he was just—"

Calamity whirled around to her sister, her face coloring rapidly. "For the last time, see if you can't remember that I *ain't* Marthy no more!"

"Sorry, Calamity, but as I was saying—"

"Where in bloody blue hell have you been? I've turned this town upside down looking for you!"

Luke tried to calm the enraged woman as he adjusted his belt and holster. "Now don't go working yourself into a lather, Calam. Stormy and I have been over at the Grand Central Hotel for the past hour or so, and before that—"

"You went to the hotel?" Calamity asked her sister. "With *him?*"

"Well, yes, but—"

"I took her to the hotel *restaurant* for a steak." Luke stomped past Calamity and headed for the door. "I didn't realize I had to get your permission to have an innocent meal with your sister." He grabbed his hat off the bedpost and slammed it down on his head. "Believe me, it *won't* happen again." Then he yanked open the door, stepped outside, and banged it shut.

Bits of mud fell from the loft above Calamity's head, sprinkling her filthy hat with a new layer of Dakota dirt. Unaware of the dusting, she wheeled around to where her sister stood and sheathed her gun. "So Luke took you out for a steak, huh?" Stormy didn't answer. She just stood there glowering, her arms folded across her breasts, her feet spread. "Well, hell!" Calamity went on. "How was I supposed to know that? I went looking for you in every bar in Deadwood—and I expect by now you know there's a considerable number of them in this here town. Anyways, I guess I got a little worried when no one had seen hide nor hair of you."

"That's because you were looking in the wrong places. You won't find me in one of Deadwood's saloons again. I only went to the Number Ten last night to make a point with you."

"A point, huh? I guess I musta missed it."

"I wanted you to understand that I'd do anything to become your sister again—your sister, by the way, *not* your daughter."

Calamity scratched her head through her hat. "Now what in tarnation is that supposed to mean?"

"Just that I resent you coming in here and acting

like a mother or something. You had no right to run Luke off like that. He was my guest, not yours, and if I thought he needed cooling off, I'd have done it myself." With that, she spun on her heel and marched over to the stove.

Calamity stood rock-still for a long moment. Then she strolled over to the table, pulled out a chair, turned it around, and straddled it. "Well la tee dah," she said in a mocking voice. "Excuse me for trying to take care of you a little."

Satisfied that the flame had taken hold beneath the kettle of water, Stormy blew out the match and joined her sister at the table. As she sat down, she softly sighed. "I didn't come looking for you so you could take care of me. I just wanted us to be sisters again. Is that so difficult for you to understand?"

Calamity's gaze flickered away from Stormy. She slowly took off her hat, dropped it to the floor near her feet, and began removing the pins from her hair. As she pulled her fingers through her tangles, she quietly said, "Did it ever cross your mind that maybe I don't want to be anyone's sister again—ever?"

It *had* occurred to Stormy that Martha might not have been as excited as she was by the reunion, but she'd never seriously entertained the idea for long, and certainly not to the extent that Martha was suggesting now. Could that be the reason Calamity Jane always got so mad when Stormy referred to her as Martha? Was it too much of a reminder of who she was and where she had come from—or, even worse, of what and *whom* she'd left behind?

Calamity leaned toward the window and grabbed

the bottle of whisky off the sill. "Well? I thought you wanted to talk."

"I do, but can't we do it without that?" She canted her head toward the bottle.

Calamity ignored her sister's suggestion and helped herself to a glass instead. "I ain't exactly looking for another mother either, kid. Why don't we start by getting that straight."

"Fine, then if you have to have a drink to talk to me, go right ahead. Before you have too many, would you please have the decency to explain what you meant by not wanting to be anyone's sister again? Is that the reason you didn't come after us—any of us? You just didn't want us anymore?"

Calamity slid her fingers around the whisky bottle. She stared at it, her eyes vacant, as glassy as the bottle, but said nothing.

"Is it because of Mom?" Stormy persisted. "Were you afraid that you couldn't take care of us the way she would have if she'd lived?"

"Jesus, kid!" Calamity burst out laughing. "Listen to you! When did Charlotte suddenly become a saint? Have you forgotten what she was before Pa married her, or what the townsfolk thought of her no matter where we went?"

Stormy's mouth drew into a tight line. Of course she hadn't forgotten that their father had married their mother straight out of a house of ill-repute, neither could she forget whispers about how miserably Bob Cannary had failed in his efforts to reform her. Even after marriage, Charlotte Cannary had turned her bold brown eyes on anybody's man, used bawdy language in the presence of man, woman, or child, and seen no reason to curtail her constant smoking, drinking, and carousing.

"I haven't forgotten a minute of our childhood," Stormy said. "I just thought you might have felt a little inadequate or unable to care for us all."

"Damn ya all anyway! Don't you go telling me what I think! I didn't come for you or the little ones because . . . *gawd!*" She rolled her eyes. "Take a look at me—what in tarnation would someone like me have done with a passel of kids, huh? I figured you was all better off adopted out to real families."

"Not all of us were adopted," Stormy gently reminded her. "And it's possible that some of us who were didn't wind up with people who loved them. Did you ever think of that?"

Calamity could feel hot tears sliding up her throat to burn the inside of her eyelids. She grabbed the bottle of whisky and poured three fingers neat into the glass. "Wasn't nothing I could do about that," she finally said in a hoarse whisper. "Nothing a'tall. I guess that's why I don't want to be nobody's sister again. I ain't too good at it."

"Oh, Marth—Calamity," Stormy said, leaning across the table to pat her sister's hand. "I never meant to suggest anything like that. It's just that you're all I thought of growing up. Do you know how often I dreamed that you'd ride up in a big carriage with a husband of your own, and that the two of you would take me away to live with you? That thought—that dream—kept me going all this time. I guess I was expecting too much of you then, and maybe now, too."

Calamity withdrew her hand and picked up her glass. She held it near the flame from the lamp so she could study the amber-colored liquid, but did not take a sip. After several moments of observation, she set the glass back down on the table, chuckled lightly, and said, "So you figured one day me and my husband would come and save you, did you?"

A mist shone in Stormy's eyes and her throat felt clogged, too tight to speak. She nodded.

"And now that you've seen me, what do you say? Still think I coulda found one a them knightly husbands, then talked him into rounding up a bunch of snotty-nosed kids that weren't his?"

"It doesn't sound so impossible. I'm sure there are a lot of men who'd have been willing to do just that if you'd given them a chance."

"Hey, kid," Calamity said, "take another look at me. I ain't flashy like Charlotte with her flaming red hair and big brown eyes, and I ain't delicate and pretty like you. I'm just plain ol' me, plain being the word you ought to pay the most attention to. I never had a chance in hell of lassoing that kind a husband, and you know it."

"But that's not true! If you'd just wash up and put on some decent dresses—" Calamity's scowl cut off Stormy's attempts to remind her about how to become a lady. "Anyway, I met a lot of women in Denver City that weren't nearly as pretty as you, and they all had their pick of husbands."

Calamity chuckled, her gaze drawn again and again to her still untouched drink. "Their pick, you say. Tell me this, li'l sis, would you have taken any one of them?"

Stormy shrugged. "None that I can remember right now, but—"

"You wouldn't have, and neither would I." She absently pushed the drink aside and leaned across the table. "I *could* have rounded up a man for myself, I suppose, but hell, any woman who wanders west of the Mississippi can get a husband!" She laughed one of her boisterous, bullwhacking whoops. "In fact, it's so easy to get a man out West, I figure by the time you get to California, you could put a dress on a cow, teach it to walk upright, and by sundown, she'd have a husband, too."

Stormy joined in Calamity's laughter, giggling until her stomach hurt. "All right," she said. "I think I'm beginning to understand."

"Good. Now you know why I couldn't come for you, and why I don't want no husband."

A sudden profusion of tears welled up in the corners of Stormy's eyes, yet she wasn't the least bit sad. She felt happy, almost euphoric. She and Calamity were talking to each other like a pair of good friends, like the sisters she wanted them to be again—even if Calamity wasn't quite coming around to her way of thinking. Stormy lifted the corner of her skirt, dabbed at her eyes, and then smiled and said, "Yes, I think I finally do understand why you didn't come back for us." She winked. "But I still think you ought to try to find yourself a husband."

"What in hell for?" Calamity said, fighting her tears. "Damned if I can't do just about anything a man can do, and besides—I ain't exactly no young little thing out dangling a line for the man of my dreams. Hell, I'm purty near twenty-five already!"

Stormy brushed her off. "Oh, that shouldn't stop someone like you. You could get married tomorrow if you wanted to."

Calamity shook her head. "Don't think I'll *ever* want to. Don't think I could be happy having a fellow try to lead me around by the nose. I get along pretty good just by borrowing a man when I need one."

"*Borrowing* a man?" Stormy wrinkled her nose. "Whatever for?"

This time, Calamity's laughter came out in more of a howl. "For pleasure, kid," she said through her chuckles. "Life out here can be tough enough without denying myself a few little pleasures."

Her attempts to turn her sister into a lady completely forgotten, Stormy centered her thoughts on Calamity's final sentence. Pretty sure that a lady wouldn't even think of such a question, she found herself asking for an explanation anyway. "*Pleasures?* From a man? J-just exactly what do you mean by that?"

7

Stormy expected some kind of reaction from her sister, but she hadn't figured on the thundering laughter that came rumbling up from Calamity's throat.

Her cheeks burning, Stormy got up from the table and went to the stove to remove the bubbling water from the heat. Although she didn't mind allowing her sister a small amount of amusement at her expense, she couldn't keep the irritation and embarrassment out of her voice as she said, "I'm making hot cocoa. Would you like some?"

"Cocoa?" Calamity shot a longing glance toward her glass of whisky, and then shrugged. "Oh, sure, kid. Why not?"

Stormy added a little of the chocolate flavoring she generally saved for her candymaking into two cups of boiling water, and sweetened them with a dash of sugar. As she carried the steaming mugs back to the table, she said, "I asked what I thought was a perfectly reasonable question. If you're done laughing at me, I'd still like to know exactly what you meant by getting pleasure from a man."

As she warmed her hands over the vapors spiraling up from the cup, Calamity apologized. "I didn't mean to laugh at you, kid. I guess with you missing half the day and all—say! Exactly where have you been all this time?"

"I went out looking for work early this morning. I tried to tell you when you came in, but you . . . fell asleep."

"Yeah, yeah, maybe you did. I must'a forgot what you said."

Despite the reason for her sister's memory loss, Stormy smiled. "In case you're wondering, Eudell Hawkes agreed to let me sell my candy out of the grocery store until I get a place of my own." She refrained from adding, or until we leave town.

"You're working for Hawk-faced Hawkes?" At Stormy's nod, Calamity's jaw fell open, then slammed shut. "I'll be go to hell! That beady-eyed bitch won't even let me set foot inside her precious store, but she goes and hires my sister! If that don't just beat all."

Not wanting to admit that she hadn't told her new employer exactly who her sister was, Stormy brought the conversation back around to a subject of far more interest. "I needed work and they hired me. Now, please—tell me what you meant."

Calamity picked at the fringe on her jacket. "I ain't sure how to go about it, kid. I mean, I figured you hadn't done much for playing grab-ass under the sheets yet, but it seems to me that someone must a told you a little about those goings on by now."

"Well, no one did." She took a sip of cocoa, almost scalding her tongue before impatiently adding, "Will you?"

"Damned if it ain't a sight easier to just plain do it than it is to talk about it! What exactly do you want to know?"

"Pleasure." She said the word so softly, so carefully, that it was more a gentle breeze than a whisper. Keeping her gaze on her cup of cocoa, she went on. "I want to know how you can get pleasure from a man, and if it's really and truly . . . allowed."

"*Allowed?* Gawd! You don't know a blasted thing." Calamity turned her chair around, leaned back in it, and propped her boots against the table-top. "The first part's the hardest. By that I mean, finding a man who knows what to do, then talking him into doing it. For me, that was the easy part. I had to dress up like a man to join Custer's army as a scout—wouldn't a-taken me if they'd knowd I was a gal. Had my pick of fellahs."

"Dressed as a *man?*"

"Gawd, kid, not every waking minute! I had one hell of a hot time that first night me and the fellahs took a skinny dip in the lake. Like I said before, had my pick of the litter, so to speak." She closed her eyes, grinning at the memory, and then opened them to add, "By the way, that's how I got the name, Calamity. This nice young captain gave it to me 'cause I stirred up such a commotion."

But Stormy never even heard the explanation of

her sister's sobriquet. Her thoughts were still fixated on the first statement. "Y-you actually bathed with a—a group of men in your . . . without—"

"Bare-assed naked as the day I was born."

Unable to comprehend how anyone could function with such a complete lack of modesty, Stormy sank against the back of her chair with a low groan.

"Ain't nuthin' wrong with what I done," Calamity insisted. "That's the kind of gal I am. It ain't that I'm suggesting you go join the army or anything like that, kid. I was only explaining pleasure best as I can."

Still in shock, Stormy slowly shook her head. "I don't see how you could possibly have gotten anything but ashamed swimming around in a lake with all those men."

Her chin up, Calamity said, "Who said anything about swimming? I got exactly what I wanted, and then some. Now you answer me a question or two. Why are you suddenly so interested in all of this? Does it have something to do with Luke?"

Caught off guard, Stormy bit her bottom lip. "I guess maybe it does."

"Has he tried something with you?" Calamity leaned forward and pounded her fist against the table, ignoring the chocolate drink that she caused to splash over the rims of both mugs. "If that man has put his hands on you and you didn't want him to, I'll bust his—"

"It's nothing like that. It's . . ." She blushed. "It's me I'm wondering about, not him."

"You?" Calamity scratched her head. "How do you mean?"

Stormy gave a tiny shrug but couldn't look her sister in the eye. "I really like Luke, more than anyone I've ever met before. I realize that I've only known him for two days, but I can't help feeling the way I do." At the thought of just owning up to those feelings, Stormy gave in to a fit of giggles.

Calamity rolled her eyes. "Gawd."

"Sorry. I'm a little embarrassed to be acting so silly. But I can't help it when I think of Luke. He's so terribly exciting and handsome, not to mention famous! Why, I've just never known anybody like Luke McCanles." Stormy thought of the kisses they'd shared, the way he'd molded her body to his, and had to take several calming breaths before she could go on. "Besides all that, I, ah . . . think Luke might want to get to know me a little better, too."

Calamity, who'd seen women fall all over themselves to get near the infamous Luke McCanles, slowly shook her head. "You and every other gal who licks his boots."

"I—I don't know what you mean by that, Calamity. I just know that he's the one I'd like to—" she paused, searching for the right words, then borrowed her sister's expression, "I'd like to dangle my line in front of him and see what happens."

Calamity blew out a long, low whistle. "I can tell you exactly what'll happen if you try a thing like that with Luke McCanles. He'll jump on you like flies on Swill Barrel Jimmy. Is that the way you want to get to know him?"

Stormy's blush deepened, warning her that this conversation had gone completely beyond the boundaries of good taste, but she forced herself to proceed. "No, of course not. I want Luke to court me, not jump on me. How can I get him to do that?"

"Court you?" Calamity threw her head back and laughed. "I hope you ain't talking about getting Luke to marry up with you. He definitely *ain't* that kind a fellah."

At this Stormy felt a surprising stab of disappointment, confusing her further. "Oh, Martha, don't you see what I'm trying to say? My whole problem is that I *don't* know exactly what it is that I want from Luke. I only know that I want him, not why . . . or even how."

Calamity offered a sympathetic shake of her head. "Sorry if this little bit of news upsets you, kid, but I think the only way you'll catch Luke's attention is by crawling under the sheets with him. I don't believe he has much use for women anywhere else."

She hadn't thought it possible, but Stormy's cheeks burned even hotter. "Are you suggesting that I offer myself in the, ah . . . marital embrace?"

"The mar—the what?"

"You know, the thing a woman does in the dark with her husband."

Her lips wobbled under the strain, but Calamity managed to keep her chuckles to herself this time. "If you got to call it that, then yes, that's what I'm talking about."

"I'm not even sure I can bear the idea of letting a man do that to me after I'm married. I'm certainly not going to—"

"Listen up, kid," Calamity interrupted. "That's the

part I been trying to tell you about—this marriage embrace business is where all the pleasure happens."

"Pleasure? From the *marital embrace?* I don't understand. I thought. . . . Wait here. I want to show you something." She pushed out of her chair and headed for her trunk to retrieve her copy of *Dr. Tuttle's Guide for Unmarried Ladies.*

The slender volume in hand, Stormy hurried back to the table and began flipping through the worn pages. Pointing to the section she'd been looking for, she spun the book around for her sister to read. "See what it says here? You must be wrong about getting pleasure in that way. This lady wrote in to Dr. Tuttle saying that she is ashamed—*ashamed,* mind you—to occasionally find a modicum of enjoyment in the marital embrace. If that's the pleasure you're talking about, it's wrong!"

"Wrong? How can feeling good be wrong?"

Stormy pushed the book across the table. "Here. Read for yourself what the doctor has to say about such things."

Calamity squinted, then dragged her finger across the page one word at a time. "You . . . must . . . *stop* . . . it . . . at . . . once. The consa-sa—"

"Consequences."

"Excuse my ignorance, but I ain't had much call to keep up with my reading of late." She stared at the word, then tested it. "The con-see-quences . . . of . . . this . . . vile . . . habit . . . will . . . cause . . . insan-*insanity?*" Calamity's gaze shot over to Stormy, then dropped back to the book. "Decay . . . and . . . softening . . . of . . . the . . . brain." She slammed the volume closed. "You actually read this crap and believe it, too?"

"It's all I have to go by."

"*Gawd!* Where in tarnation did you get this stupid book?"

Stormy's back stiffened, but she answered truthfully. "From Mrs. Peabody. She was the respectable lady who owned the boarding house I lived in while I was in Denver City."

Calamity snickered. "Would I be wrong if I guessed there was no *Mr.* Peabody?"

"No, in fact there wasn't. Oda Peabody was a widow."

"I think I know what killed her husband."

After waiting until her sister stopped laughing, Stormy pleaded with her. "Please don't make fun of me, Calamity. I'm only trying to learn what every other woman seems to know but me. I thought there was something wrong with me for liking the way Luke kisses me, for having feelings that . . . I don't know how to put it, but I feel kind of *funny* all over when he looks at me—or touches me."

"Ain't nothing wrong with that kid, and I ain't been making fun of you. In fact, now that I know how you feel about Luke, I'm thinking maybe you ought to let your hair down with him. I ain't gonna take exception to nothing I see or hear between you two no more." Calamity drew her pistol and announced, "What I take exception to is the load of crap printed on these pages, but don't you worry another minute about it. I think I got a way—a *cure,* that is—to keep old Dr. Tuttle from filling your head with any more lies."

Before Stormy could do a thing to stop her, Calamity tossed the book into the air, took aim, and blew it clear across the room. Not finished with *Dr. Tuttle* yet, she fired into the volume several more times as it lay in tatters on the plank floor. The guide bounced around like a beetle in a frying pan, bits and pieces of paper flying in every direction, then at last what little of it was left lay deathly still.

Stormy opened her mouth to protest, but burst out laughing instead.

Chuckling along with her, Calamity began to reload her gun.

Outside the cabin a man bellowed in anger. Then someone kicked the door open.

"Calamity!" called a voice. "Are you in there and is everything all right?"

"Is that you, Bill?"

In reply, the acrimonious form of Wild Bill Hickok appeared. Behind him, was a pale-looking Colorado Charlie Utter.

"*Christ*, woman!" Hickok yelled. "You could have shot my legs out from under me!"

Calamity inched her chair closer to the window and spoke in a much smaller voice than normal. "Sorry about that, Bill. If I'd a-know'd you was out there, I wouldn't a-done it."

"Like hell you wouldn't have." His features still contorted with rage, Hickok took a quick survey of the inside of the cabin. "What in hell got you so riled up? A bobcat or something?"

Her expression as sheepish as it ever got, Calamity shook her head. "I shot up that there book over yonder."

Hickok glanced behind him, saw the tiny pile of shredded pulp, then looked back at Calamity in astonishment. "You unloaded your gun into a *book?*"

She shrugged and shot an uneasy glance in her sister's direction.

Hickok reached for the full glass of whisky sitting on the table. "Might be a good time for you to lay off this stuff for a while, Calam." He downed the whisky in one gulp, then slammed the empty glass against the tabletop. "Might be clouding your judgment."

Calamity's gaze flickered over to her cocoa, and then settled on Stormy. Chuckling a little, she said, "Whatever you say, Bill. Is there something else I kin do for you?"

"There sure as hell is." He pointed to a spot beside the empty glass. "Just lay your gun down right there, and sit on your hands until I've left. I came by to pick up the rest of my clothes, but I'll be damned if I'll get my butt shot off over a few pieces of broadcloth." He turned toward the door. "Charlie? Get on over here and see she doesn't move while I'm in the bedroom."

Looking reluctant to come into the room any farther than necessary, Utter took a few grudging steps and planted himself three feet from the threshold. The door behind him remained open.

Calamity gave him a grudging nod of acknowledgment, and made a fast introduction. "This here's my sister, Stormy Ann. She come up from Denver for a visit." She glanced at Stormy. "That there's Colorado Charlie. Bill, Luke, and him set up a camp out by Whitewood Creek."

Smiling at the stranger, Stormy said, "It's a pleasure to meet you, sir."

Utter whipped off his hat, revealing his rapidly

receding hairline, and offered a slight bow. "Plea-sure's all mine, ma'am."

"That'll do, Charlie." Calamity raised one auburn eyebrow and shot him her best mean-eyed polecat look. He got the message immediately. Utter turned on his heel and headed for the doorway.

After he'd stepped back into the alley, Calamity chuckled and whispered low so he couldn't hear, "I never liked ol' Charlie much. Too damn skinny, and that ax blade he's got for a nose! Gawd, can you imagine trying to kiss a man like that? He'd split a gal's face in half without even trying!"

Stormy laughed along with her sister and then said, "It's Mr. Hickok I'm more worried about. I feel as if I've thrown him out of his own place. Maybe I ought to take a room at the hotel so you two can, well, have your privacy again."

"Privacy?" She hooted. "We ain't never had none a'that. 'Sides, Bill'd rather sleep in a tent out by the creek than in a bed. We'll catch up with each other now and then if'n we want to. You're a staying right here with me."

At Martha's words, and the sisterly bond they implied, Stormy could feel her eyes growing moist again. She glanced away as Hickok came out of the bedroom, his arms laden with clothing.

"That about does it," he said to Calamity. "I left most of my show gear stowed up in the loft. See if you can't keep from burning the cabin down and ruining it all, will you?"

She beamed up at him. "Sure, Bill. I'll take right good care of 'em."

He nodded absently. "You seen Luke?"

At the sound of that name, Stormy leapt into the conversation. "Yes. I just had supper with him over at his hotel."

"Did he mention where he was heading after that?"

"No, but I think he might have gone back there to check on some men we ran into as we left. I don't think he liked them very much."

Hickok shifted his load, leaving his right hand completely free. "Friends or strangers?"

Stormy shook her head. "Strangers to Luke, I think, but they seemed to know him. One of them—I can't remember his name right now—asked Luke about his bodyguard. That made him a little angry."

"What did this stranger look like?"

With a shrug, she said, "Kind of average, I guess. He was about Luke's age, but shorter, with brown hair, a small mustache—oh, and a kind of squashed nose. It was all bumpy and flat, as if it had been badly broken."

Calamity offered a guess. "That sounds like Crooked Nose Jack McCall."

"That's it!" Stormy slapped the table. "His name was McCall."

Hickok frowned. He glanced into the alley and said something to Utter. "I think we'd best be on our way. A steak suddenly sounds mighty good to me. See you later, Calam. Evening, Stormy."

"Good evening, Mr. Hickok."

"*Mr.* Hickok, she says," he muttered under his breath, then joined his friend in the alley.

After the men had gone, Calamity climbed to her feet. "I got to be going too, kid. Don't know if I mentioned before that I drive an oxcart for No-Teeth Ed now and again. I was supposed to run a load of supplies up to Lead and Spearfish this morning, but I felt a little too sick to make it."

"*Sick*, Calamity?"

Acting as if she hadn't seen her sister's knowing expression or heard the mocking tone in her voice, Calamity rubbed her belly. "Yeah, sick. I think I had a touch of the torpid liver, but I'm much better now. Anyways, I'll be gone the best part of a week, maybe longer." She rolled her long hair back into a ball, jabbed a hairpin through it at the base of her neck, then tugged her hat down low over her forehead. "I'd be lying if I didn't say that I'm a mite worried about what to do with you while I'm gone."

"Me?" Stormy got up from her chair. "You don't have to give me another thought. Between candy-making and clerking in the grocery, I'll be plenty busy. In fact, it's time I got started on tomorrow's taffy."

"What about later tonight, and all the other nights? You going to be all right here alone?" She winked. "Maybe I can talk Luke into coming over and staying with you."

"No!" Stormy turned back to the stove, hiding a sudden blush. "I'll put the pole over the door when I get home from the grocery each day, and stay in at night. If anyone tries to come in, I'll just grab old Martha there in the corner and blow them right out of their boots."

Laughing to herself, Calamity made her way to the stove and wrapped her arm around Stormy's shoulders. "If you need any help a'tall, just look up Bill or Luke. They'll come a-running in a minute. Promise?"

With a smile and a quick kiss to her sister's cheek, Stormy whispered, "Promise."

Then, before all the new, disturbing emotions swirling inside of her could surface, Calamity turned on her heel and walked out of the cabin.

After climbing up to the third floor of the Grand Central Hotel, Calamity made her way to room 302 and rapped sharply on the door.

Luke, who'd been on his way out, tore the door open in midknock. "Hey, Calam, what are you doing here?" he asked, stepping across the threshold. "I was just heading over to Number Ten."

Calamity flattened her palms against Luke's chest to halt his progress, and then pushed him back inside the room. "That card game can wait on you a minute."

Luke had no idea what to make of this newest burst of bizarre behavior from a woman who never ceased to surprise him. He allowed himself to be driven backward but complained loudly, "What in hell do you think you're doing?"

Inside the room now, Calamity kicked the door closed behind her. "What I got to say is private—and *real* special to me. You got to listen and do what I ask. You owe me, Luke, you owe me good, and you know it."

Damned if he didn't. Luke would never forget how she'd tended him back in Cheyenne when he was so bad with the fever. Calamity had nursed him day and night, never once considering or lamenting the risk to her own health. Without her, he probably would have died. He owed her, and big.

With a heavy sigh, he pulled the chair out from beneath the desk in his room, swept a layer of imaginary dust from it with the brim of his hat, and then bade her to sit down.

Calamity ignored the courtesy and got down to business. "I ain't got time for nonsense. Here's the problem. It's my sister."

Concerned about his health again, this time for entirely different reasons, Luke began to slide toward the door. Keeping his gaze on Calamity's hands, their proximity to her whip and guns in particular, he said, "You don't have any reason to come running after me. I already told you once, I haven't—"

"Shut up and listen. I got to go on a supply run for a few days, and while I'm gone, I want you to do something for me. Before we get to that, there's a few things I got to mention about Stormy . . . things, I reckon, you ought to know."

With a shake of his head, Luke continued on his way to the door. "I don't know what for, Calam. If you don't want me to see her, I—"

"Shut up and listen, will you?"

Luke pulled up short of the door and faced her. "Go on, but make it quick. I'm paying a hotel bill these days. I'd like to get in a game while there's still some money to be made."

Calamity nodded, then paused, giving herself a moment to plan her strategy. Although she had absolutely no compunctions about stretching the truth for her own benefit, the last thing she wanted to do was tarnish her sister's good name by out and out lying. Careful with her wording, she finally began. "Stormy's life ain't been as easy as you might think. She's had kind of a rough time, with men in particular—scarred, she is." Calamity sighed dramatically. "'Course, it's them little ones bothers her the most of all. She still goes on and on about the loss of them babes, blames herself," she tossed in, adding a page from her own diary.

"*Babes?*" Luke said out, strangling with both surprise and disappointment. "You mean to tell me she's got—"

"Two still in diapers last time she saw them." Abruptly changing the subject before Luke could question her too closely, Calamity went on. "Anyways, it's not something she likes to talk about. I just wanted you to know how things has been with her, and maybe understand her skittishness a little better. She likes you, Luke, trusts you, too. That's something ain't never happened to her before."

But obviously plenty else had—more than Luke would ever have guessed. Feeling awkward, humbled even, he kicked the edge of the rug up and shuffled his boot against the floor. "Why are you telling me all of this, Calam? It's none of my business."

"Maybe it is and maybe it isn't," she said, approaching him. "I'm just looking out for her as best I can. You got to be patient with her, careful, too, especially about them babes." She looked him in the eye. "I wouldn't bring the subject of them little ones up if I were you."

Luke's mouth fell into a solemn frown. "I sure as hell wasn't planning on it."

"Good, then." Calamity linked her arm through his. "Got a couple other things to tell you about, but first there's a favor or two I got to ask. While I'm gone. . . ."

8

Over the next few days, Stormy barely had a moment to herself. Her days were spent working in the store, the nights, making taffy and chocolate dainties. Smiling Will Hawkes showed up on Thursday night as was his wont, and Stormy finally met the man who mined during the week and looked after his family and the store at the end of the week.

He looked a good deal like Justin, especially around the eyes with his upswept, windblown features, but his mouth was the most fascinating thing about him, and no doubt, the origin of his nickname, Smiling Will. A thick, clean scar ran from just below his chin through both his lower and upper lips, ending on his right cheek. A series of white dots indicating the path the doctor had taken with his stitches stopped under the ledge of that cheek where the catgut had been tied into a knot—a tight little knot that pulled the right side of Will's mouth into a perpetual grin.

Stormy liked him immediately, especially after he informed her that Deadwood's population would swell from a few hundred to several thousand men between Friday night and Sunday, when all the miners came to town for supplies, visits to the assay office, and just plain rabble-rousing.

With this encouragement, Stormy spent the entire afternoon and evening of Friday in her cabin, creating her specialties to meet what Will was certain would be a huge demand. By noon Saturday his prediction had come true. Better than half of her extra-large supply had been sold. And more miners were on their way to town.

As her workday drew to a close, Stormy dumped the contents of her last sack of candy into a bowl near the cash register, and then began to collect her things.

Eudell Hawkes, who rarely agreed with her husband, had conceded that Stormy simply didn't have the time to try out her pies just yet, and that she ought to get busy on a new supply of chocolate taffy as soon as possible. She called to Stormy as she removed her apron. "One other thing before you go."

"Yes, ma'am?"

Eudell excused herself to the pair of miners she'd been waiting on, and moved up close so only Stormy could hear. "Justin's out front loading wagons with his pa. I expect that boy's going to want to stop you, and I know the reason why. He's wanting to ask if he can escort you to the show at Langrishe's theater tomorrow."

"Don't worry, Eudell," Stormy assured her. "I'll turn him down gently but firmly."

"I don't think you should this one time."

If Eudell had said that she'd triple her wages, Stormy couldn't have been more surprised. In fact, nothing, except for Luke's odd, almost cavalier behavior, could have surprised her more.

He'd been fussing over her like a mother hen, waiting outside the store each day to make sure she returned to her cabin safely, occasionally coming to near blows with Justin over the honor, and generally acting more guardian than beau. She supposed that this might be his way of courting her, and even dared to hope that it might be the reason for his sweet and thoughtful gestures.

But this comment, from a woman who'd threatened her in no uncertain terms if she were to flirt with her son, was unfathomable.

To make certain she'd understood, Stormy said, "Excuse me, ma'am? I'm not sure I heard you correctly."

"I said that it's all right with me if you let Justin escort you to the performance tomorrow."

"But I thought you were worried that Justin might get ideas about courting me. This seems—"

"I never said that Justin has permission to court you, for heaven's sake!" She narrowed her gaze. "He knows better than that even if you don't! I thought you might want to attend the performance, and if you do, you simply cannot go unescorted—not with all these men in town. I have a reputation to think of, and I don't want the precious few ladies around here to get the idea I got a loose woman working for me."

"Oh, I see. I didn't think of that."

"You *were* planning to attend, weren't you?"

With Luke McCanles and Wild Bill Hickok as the major draws, nothing could have kept Stormy away. "Of course. I've been looking forward to the show."

"And your sister? If she's planning to go too, I'm just sure that Justin wouldn't mind escorting the both of you."

"Oh, ah—no, my sister can't make it. She had to leave town for a few days."

"Leave town?" The loose skin on Eudell's forehead wrinkled up as she raised her eyebrows. "How'd she manage that? We haven't had a thing but a few oxcarts pulling out of Deadwood lately. Surely she didn't—"

"Ma?" Justin called, interrupting her as he burst through the front door. "Who are we supposed to load up next? I got Pancake Bill out there cussing up a blue storm about Cheating Sheely taking his place in line. Sheely swears—and I do mean *swears*—that he was there first. Pa and I don't know which one of 'em's lying, or who to load up next."

Eudell squared her shoulders. "I'll go see to them. Why don't you take a break—a *short* one—and walk Miss Cannary on home. You can ask her about tomorrow if you like while you're at it."

His cheeks puffed up and his eyes glazed over with joy, but Justin managed to keep his excitement in check. Only his high voice with its tendency to creak when he was nervous betrayed him. "Yes, ma'am. Right away." He took the empty sacks from Stormy's arms and extended his elbow. "If you're ready, Miss Cannary, so am I."

"I'm ready, Justin, and thank you."

They stepped out into the street, more correctly into the muck, just beyond the store's small boardwalk, but Stormy was well prepared. On her first day of employment, she'd purchased a sturdy pair of miner's boots to wear through mud, animal droppings, and even ankle-deep puddles—which today seemed to be everywhere.

It had rained yesterday afternoon, and now the sky was clouding up again, the rumble of distant thunder warning of yet another drenching. Above nature's din, the endless crack of hammers and screeching saws could be heard, and when one particularly sharp clap of thunder exploded through the gulch, Stormy practically jumped into Justin's arms.

"Scare you a little, did it?" he asked as he gripped her elbow tighter, enormously pleased to be of service to such a delicate female.

"Just a bit," she had to admit, "but it really shouldn't have. I heard much worse when I lived in Colorado."

"Don't you worry, ma'am. I'll get you home before it comes down on us." He patted her arm possessively as they passed by the Langrishe Theater, a haphazard building made of canvas and wood. "Ah," he began awkwardly, "I was a-wondering if you'd like to go to the theater show with me tomorrow." He pointed at the building. "Mr. Langrishe has promised to have a couple of singers, a poetry reading, and the best of all, some storytelling by Wild Bill Hickok and Lucky Luke McCanles, after which they will do a shooting exhibition in the street. What do you say, Miss Cannary? Will you go with me?"

She smiled primly, as if mulling over the idea. "Why, thank you, Justin. I guess I should have an escort."

He beamed, his smile as brilliant as a noonday sun, but it took five full minutes—the time it took to reach the cabin—before Justin could find his tongue. As Stormy went inside, he said, "Thank you for doing me the honor of going to the show tomorrow. If there's anything, *anything* a-tall I can do for you, you just say the word, Miss Cannary."

"Thanks, but no, Justin. I have to get busy making candy, and I'm afraid it's something I must do by myself. Thank you again for walking me home and for the invitation. I'm sure it will be a great show."

After he'd gone, Stormy secured the door, rolled up her sleeves, and got to work. Her only interruption came not two hours later when a very solicitous Luke stopped by to make certain she'd gotten home safely. The gesture warmed her all the way to her toes, even if she still didn't understand exactly what he was after, or what kind of impression he was trying to make on her. The only thing that mattered was the attention he'd been heaping on her. Daring to dream of a future with a man such as this, an exhausted Stormy stumbled off to bed just before midnight.

Sometime later, she awoke with a start. For the last three nights, she'd been disturbed by strange, frightening noises. Had she heard them again? Or was her mind playing tricks on her? She sat up in bed. Scratching sounded at the back window. Something bumped against the log walls—a man's boots?

Whatever the source, she now knew without a doubt that the noises were not in her mind, but real.

Then suddenly, voices filtered through the walls of the cabin. Men arguing, she thought. Drunken miners? Or some of her new self-proclaimed "suitors," lonely men who'd stopped by the grocery store for something other than supplies over the last two days. Desperate men who'd heard about the new woman in town.

When the noises had come last night and the night before, Stormy had stayed in bed frozen, her heartbeat a furious cudgel against her ribcage. Tonight, things would be different. No longer could she lie there, terrified and trembling, her eyes wide open until dawn. She was exhausted, the neck of her nightgown sticky with perspiration, but she threw back the bedsheet and reached for her heavy cotton robe. As she slipped into it, she searched the wall behind her in the darkness until her gaze rested on Hickok's double-barrelled shotgun. Carefully lifting the weapon from its corner cradle, she split it open, checked to see that it was loaded, and then quietly slammed it shut.

Armed now, she cocked the twin hammers as she made her way to the center of the room, and then stood rock-still to listen for further disturbances. More noises, this time toward the front of the cabin. More voices too, louder, insistent, sounding angry. Then a bump against the door.

Stormy whirled toward the sound and lifted the shotgun upward in an effort to get it into position. On the upswing, her finger pressed lightly against the lead trigger. Old Martha responded in an instant. She hurled the load from the first barrel at the door—and lifted Stormy completely off her feet.

Eerie silence followed the explosion. Then a man yowled, and another cried out in surprise. Stormy lay flat on her back in almost the same position she'd found herself on her first day in Deadwood.

A figure stumbled through the now open door, calling, "Miss Cannary? Miss Cannary, where are you? Are you all right?"

"Get out of the way, you idiot," said another gruff voice in the darkness.

Boots scuffled across the floor, and then one connected with Stormy's outstretched hand. She let out a yelp.

"Oh, my Lord!" Justin hunkered down beside her. "Did I hurt you, ma'am?"

Before she could answer, or even make certain she was decently covered, someone lit the lamp on the table, setting the room aglow.

"Get on out of here, Justin!" Luke ordered, sickened to think how close he'd come to shooting the young man as he prowled in the darkness. Turning the wick on the lamp up another notch, he saw Stormy frantically trying to cover her exposed legs with her robe. *"Now!"*

But Justin set his jaw and remained at Stormy's side, patting her injured hand as she tried to wrestle it away from him.

Luke muttered an oath under his breath and drew his pistol. "Damn your skinny hide—you'd best have your ass up and out of here in one second, or I'll be forced to blow it off for you!"

Justin hesitated long enough to take another glance at Stormy. She was breathing raggedly, sitting sideways now, her robe carefully arranged so that nothing showed but yards of white cotton, and looking completely stunned. Not sure exactly what he ought to do at this point, he scrambled to his feet and faced the gunman. "I got just as much right to see to Miss Cannary's safety as you do, and I—"

Luke fired three quick rounds between the young man's legs, effectively cutting off his conversation. Without another word, Justin spun around and fled through the open doorway.

As he crossed the room to secure what was left of the split-log door, Luke reached down, took Stormy by the hand, and pulled her to her feet. "Are you all right?"

His words and the sudden movement jolted her into action. She jerked out of his grip. "No thanks to you! What in the world was going on outside? Why are you here? And what was *Justin* doing out there with you?"

Luke frowned. "I don't know why in hell he was prowling around your cabin, but I was just . . . well, hell, I just thought I'd look in on you now and then, what with Calamity gone and all. I'd have expected a little thanks instead of a faceful of birdshot!"

He continued on to the door, still muttering, "What in hell is it with you Cannary women and guns? Bill told me how Calamity damn near took his legs off at the knees a few days ago, but I never thought I had a worry coming from you!"

"You wouldn't have if you'd have stayed in your

room where you belong! Have you been here every night since my sister left?"

Luke tugged at the door, whose hinges were bent, and finally got it to close. Wedging a small piece of the shattered pole between the door and the jamb, he secured it for the time being. Then he turned and answered her. "I've stopped by a time or two, I suppose, but I sure as hell wouldn't have bothered if I'd known you had old Martha lined up with my head!"

Wobbling on her feet, Stormy smoothed the folds of her robe and retied the sash around her waist. Her head was spinning, and she wasn't exactly sure what had happened, or even how, but Luke's words kept the fighting side of her at the forefront. "That was an accident. I never even pulled the trigger on the gun. Why, I barely even touched it."

More shaken by the turn of events than he let on, Luke snatched the weapon up off the floor, released the hammer for the second barrel, and then propped it against the door. Keeping his back to Stormy, he admitted, "I guess maybe I did forget to mention that ol' Martha is Bill's 'persuader,' the kind of gun he expects quick action from. To make sure he gets that action, he filed the firing pin down so it would have a hair trigger."

Luke rubbed his left arm where a flying piece of lumber had smacked him hard enough to knock him off his feet. "At least Bill had the decency to load the shells with birdshot instead of buckshot! I suppose I should consider myself lucky—*again*."

Even in the dim light, Stormy could see that Luke's hand came away from his shirt with smears of blood on it. Her anger and fears forgotten, she rushed to his side, "You've been shot!"

Luke glanced down his shoulder to the spot where his shirt was torn, and then shrugged. "I thought I just got hit by a chunk of that door, but maybe I did pick up a pellet or two."

"Come over here and sit at the table." Stormy led him back toward the light. "And take off your shirt."

Turning her back to him as he peeled off his damaged clothing, Stormy filled the teakettle with fresh water, stirred up the embers in the stove, and then started a fresh fire.

After Luke removed his vest and shirt and tossed them on the table, he eased down on the chair nearest the stove and noticed that Stormy had done a little housecleaning. Even in the near darkness, the place looked brighter somehow, fresher.

The floor, though still uncovered, was not only swept, but oiled as well, and on his old bed she'd draped a bright yellow quilt patterned with purple and lavender lilacs. Completing the new look, crisp white curtains trimmed with ruffles hung at both the front and back windows. No wonder he hadn't been able to see into the cabin to make certain she was all right!

"There," Stormy said, sure that the fire had taken hold. She turned away from the stove and glanced down at Luke to study his injuries. "Now let's see if this is something I can take care of, or if we'll have to wake the doctor."

"No doctors."

"I'll be the judge of that." She circled him, taking a

careful look at the damage. Luke lounged in the chair
with his wounded arm stretched out across the table.
But she couldn't seem to concentrate on his injuries.

Stormy had glimpsed other men in various stages
of undress—her father in his undershirts, even the
Parker men completely bare-chested on several occasions—but seeing Luke nude from the waist up was a
sight she was totally unprepared for.

His shoulders were even broader and more muscular than she'd imagined, his skin tan and smooth,
but something else completely captured her attention, a sight that set her heart tripping and her belly
aching down low. Luke's burly chest was richly matted with lush dark curls that tantalizingly narrowed
and then disappeared beneath his belt.

Struggling to keep her fascinated gaze off the
buckle near his waist, her imagination away from
what might lie below it, Stormy gripped the edge of
the table, forcing her attention on his wounds. "I—"
She cleared her throat. "It doesn't look as bad as I
thought." She leaned in close. "In fact, I don't think
you were shot at all."

"Not shot?" Luke peered down the length of his
arm. "Then why in hell do you suppose I'm bleeding?"

She chuckled lightly as she made her way to her
trunk to gather some supplies. "It looks like you only
scraped off a little skin and picked up a few splinters.
One of them seems to be kind of deep, but I think I
can dig it out."

Splinters. Luke fought a shudder at the word, the
bitter memories hanging just out of reach. In a state
one step this side of panic, he looked up as Stormy

came back to the table carrying a sewing basket and a few pieces of toweling. She set the basket on the table and withdrew a large needle and a long-legged instrument made of silver. *Tweezers.* His stomach convulsed.

"Hell," Luke said in his gruffest voice, suddenly desperate to leave the cabin. "If that's all that's wrong with my arm, I'm not even going to worry about it. After a couple of days, those slivers will just fester up and fall out on their own." *Fester up and fall out.* The words echoed in his mind, but he heard his mother's voice, not his own. No doubt about it.

"You're not going anywhere." Stormy jerked the shirt out of Luke's hand. "I'll do my best not to hurt you, but those pieces of wood have to come out. The sooner, the better."

She took the bottle of whisky from the windowsill, poured a few ounces into a clean glass, and then dropped the needle and tweezers into the liquid to disinfect them. When she returned to the stove, Luke peered into the glass of alcohol. The needle didn't look too deadly, but the sight of those tweezers—an instrument somehow more vicious and deadly than any weapon ever turned on him—raised goosebumps all the way down to his liver. What in hell was wrong with him? It was just a few silly splinters. Hell, he'd had three bullets dug from his body on two separate occasions, not to mention the patching job required after he'd taken a knife in the back. How could he think of bolting like a bawling calf over a few bits of wood?

As Stormy came back to the table with a bowl of

hot water and some clean rags, she couldn't help but notice Luke's worried expression. "Why not concentrate on something besides what I'm doing? I'll be finished before you know it." She took the tweezers out of the whisky and laid them across a clean rag.

Luke glanced at his fingers, saw the tremors in them, and clenched his jaw. God, what a baby! Determined to get hold of himself, he searched the room for an object, anything that might capture his attention as Stormy had suggested. His gaze settled on her quilt, the damaged door, every corner of the room, but kept returning to her. So he left it there, taking his really first good look at her that night.

She was a little disheveled, with her strawberry blond hair hanging in lengths across her shoulders and over her brow as if caressing her face—that angel face. He considered leaning over to test the softness of her smooth skin with his free hand, hoping to prompt the appearance of her dimples, when a jolt of pain shot up his arm, making him cry out instead.

"I'm sorry," Stormy quickly said as she splashed a little of the whisky on his wounds. She glanced up at him, noticing how pale and drawn he'd become. "I didn't mean to be so rough, but that big sliver is a little deeper than I thought."

"Then leave it be," he said hoarsely, panic ricocheting up his throat.

Something in his voice, the barely masked desperation, made her look up again. Luke's expression was almost comical—that of a little boy trying to be brave—but the pale white of his skin and the beads of perspiration along his hairline told another story. He looked almost . . . terrified. Because of this minor surgery? Sure that she'd misread him, she shook her head. "I'm the one who shot at you—I can't just leave your arm this way. Either let me get the doctor, or hold still and let me finish."

He nodded briskly, stone-faced. "Go ahead."

As she picked up her tools again, Stormy tried a different approach. She decided to get him talking about himself. "How did you get the nickname Lucky?"

Pretty sure what she was up to, but willing to try anything if it could help him ignore her deft fingers and the cruel instruments they held, he said, "When I was about fourteen years old, I went gunning for Wild Bill Hickok and lived to tell about it."

The tweezers clattered to the table. *"What?"*

Luke chuckled uneasily. "It wasn't because I was faster on the draw than him, that's for sure. If his gun hadn't jammed, he'd a blown me all the way to hell and back before I even knew what hit me. As it was, I accidentally winged him, then I turned tail and tried to run away. That's how I got the name Lucky."

Astounded by this information, Stormy had a hard time concentrating on her work. She slowly began to dig out the largest piece of pine as she asked, "What in heaven's name ever possessed you to even go after a man like Mr. Hickok?"

Luke flinched as the needle burrowed under his skin. "Revenge, I guess."

"How could a boy of such tender years possibly be after that kind of revenge?"

Luke uttered a strange little groan, a kind of cross between a moan and a chuckle. He caught his breath and then went on. "Have you ever heard of the McCanles Massacre?"

"Of course, but—" Stormy cut her inquiry off as a horrifying thought crossed her mind. "Surely you're not a true McCanles . . . are you?"

"A *true* McCanles?" Luke snatched his arm out of her grasp. "What in hell is that supposed to mean?"

"I—I didn't mean anything except to say that since you were in all those wild west shows with Mr. Hickok, I assumed you'd taken the name to play the part. Surely a real McCanles would never—"

"Never do what? Throw in with the man who killed his father? Well, he would." He lowered his head, wondering at the sudden connection he felt between splinters and his last memories of his father.

Stormy sucked in the corner of her lip and chewed on it. If what he said was true, how could Luke have been Marshal Hickok's deputy, or even performed right alongside him as part of Buffalo Bill's Dramatic Company? It simply couldn't be true. Sorry that she'd ever begun the conversation or heard his distorted answer, she abruptly dropped the subject and devoted her energy to that last big sliver.

Stormy took hold of Luke's arm, dipped her instruments into the wound one more time, and finally pulled the section of wood out of his flesh. "There." She held the tweezers up for him to see the size of the splinter. "That's the last one."

Luke sank back against his chair, relieved, yet disturbed once again by the sight of those tweezers.

Stormy chided him. "I never would have guessed that a famous pistoleer like you could get so upset over a few little splinters. Are you always so squeamish?"

Luke chuckled nervously. "Not as a rule. In fact, I can only think of one other time. "On one of my not very smart days, I decided to ride our family bull, Old George, who didn't want to be ridden. That beast took off at a dead run, then skidded to a stop, tossing me not over, but *through* the slats of the corral." He smiled slightly at the memory. "After I regained consciousness, I discovered that I was covered from head to toe in pieces of that fence, and looked more like an overgrown porcupine than a kid."

Still trying to forget the earlier conversation, Stormy laughed along with him. "I would imagine it took your mother a little longer to clean you up then than it took me now."

"Yeah . . ." Pain lanced his heart, deeper, more cutting than any physical discomfort he'd endured as he thought back to the day. "I guess it did at that." And then he remembered.

His mother—and her tweezers. She'd begun plucking him clean, wiping his tears, patching him with loving hands until their neighbor Mrs. Warren had burst into the kitchen. His memory was patchy after that, with bits and pieces of the conversation jabbing at his mind the way those splinters had pierced his body, but Luke remembered one thing for certain. That was the day his father had stolen the county funds and run off with Sarah Shull.

Yes, that was the day all right. Luke could hardly

believe that he'd forgotten for even one moment the
way his mother had tried to finish doctoring him that
day. Her eyes were red, her bottom lip blanched and
trembling, and worst of all for him, she'd lost her
gentle touch. Her tweezers poked and prodded, hurt-
ing him beyond the limits he could endure until he
finally had to beg her to stop. He remembered the
torment in her eyes and the anguish in her voice as
she said, "I guess it's all right to leave the rest of
them where they are. They'll fester up and fall out
sooner or later." It was then that he discovered the
cruel difference between emotional pain and physical
pain.

Luke closed his eyes, understanding finally that
neither his mother nor Old George was to blame for
what lay festering in his body that day. Credit for that
belonged to his father, David McCanles. He tight-
ened his fists until his fingernails cut into his palms,
wishing all the while that he could squeeze away the
years of humiliation for both himself and his mother.
He never saw her smile after that day. No matter
what he did or how hard he tried, a flicker of amusement never lifted the corners of her mouth again. He
had failed her then as surely as he'd failed her the day
he went after Hickok.

Luke's long silence, coupled with the torment she
could see clearly etched into his handsome features,
left Stormy feeling as if she'd walked in on a very private conversation. She pushed her chair back and
stood up. As she reached for the supplies on the
table, Luke caught her by the wrist.

"Leave them."

She glanced at him, saw the pain and something she didn't understand shining in his dark eyes. Not knowing what to do or say, Stormy tried to back away from the table.

Luke's reaction was swift and impulsive. He pulled her down onto his lap before she could speak, much less object. Her robe fell open, revealing not the woman beneath but a crisp cotton nightgown buttoned up to the throat. They were the bedclothes of a spinster, but in spite of that, Luke could see a jiggle here, a suggestion of curves there, and could imagine the soft rewards lying so close he could touch them. Needing her, needing something to make him feel good again, he slipped his hands between her robe and the nightie to stroke her through the thin cotton gown.

"Luke," she choked out, feeling a conflicting need and apprehension. "Luke, please."

"You don't have to beg me, sweetheart," he murmured, forgetting about Calamity's warnings. "I'm yours. All yours."

Before she could protest, before she could even *think*, he began kissing her, using his mouth most wickedly, teasing her lips, her throat, and God, yes, even her breasts through her gown. Luke lavished her with hot, fiery kisses until she was trembling all over. Just when she thought she might faint, he pulled back, allowing her to catch her breath.

"Luke, please . . . stop," she managed to say, wondering how she would ever find the strength to repeat the request if he should persist.

"Stop what?" He winked to feign innocence, but

the suggestive gleam in his eye told another story. "I haven't asked you to do anything—yet."

"I know, but this . . ." She considered her position on his lap, her practically naked bottom pressing so intimately against his rigid body. "This just isn't right. It doesn't look right either."

Luke glanced around the cabin. "No one here but us, and I can assure you that your curtains will keep out the prying neighbors. I've been trying to catch a peek of you for three nights running." He wrapped her tighter in his embrace. "What are you really afraid of? Me?"

She shook her head resolutely.

"Then unless you're planning to hang on to that stupid rule about marrying, there's really nothing to stop us, is there?"

Stormy hesitated, wanting him, cherishing the moment, but needing to remain true to herself above all. "That *is* the one thing," she whispered, her voice resigned. "I'm not ready to change my mind about that rule."

Luke stared hard into her eyes, looking for another answer, but he knew that he'd already heard the only one he would be getting that night. It was curious how those words affected him. He'd known that a tempest was brewing inside him all night long, growing in intensity as surely as the one nature was planning for the gulch tomorrow, but it was odd that such a burst of insight should catch him now, when he least expected it.

Even though he knew the reasons for most of his inner turbulence, his reaction to Stormy's words had him stymied. Her refusal, if that's what it was—in fact, *any* woman's refusal—should make him feel anger, frustration, or irritation at the least. But he felt none of those things. Instead, Luke McCanles felt like crying.

In an attempt to ward off that sudden, mercifully foreign sensation, Luke pulled Stormy close, pressing his face against her fragrant hair. What a night this was turning out to be! Afraid of splinters and crushed by a female's refusal! What in hell was happening to him? He had to get a grip on these sudden emotions, *had* to find the strength to control himself, to somehow feel like a man again.

But God help him, all he wanted to do was cry.

9

Sunlight filtered in through Stormy's new white curtains, teasing Luke's eyelashes apart. Not knowing where he was or what burden had crushed his lungs so that he could barely draw a breath, he opened his eyes. He was still sitting in a chair at the cabin—and holding an angel in his arms. Stormy's head was nestled against his neck just below his ear, and one of her hands rested on his chest, her slender fingers buried in the thick curls there. She was still sleeping, her breathing rhythmic, exhaling in little sighs far too adorable to be called snoring. Luke smiled.

He moistened his mouth, tasting salt, then quickly brought his free hand to his cheek. It felt dry, but chalky, briny. Had he given in and cried after all? Had he been awake or asleep? Luke couldn't remember—could she? He glanced down at her, so peaceful in slumber, and convinced himself that, no, he would have remembered breaking down in front of her, if indeed that's what he'd done. Whatever had happened to him as he slept, he felt curiously refreshed and relieved. And numb.

Luke wriggled his toes, or tried to, but nothing happened. Both of his legs were asleep. He would have to wake her or risk permanent paralysis! As he settled on a way to rouse her, he smiled again. Then he lowered his head and began helping himself to several stolen kisses.

When he touched her, she moaned softly and stretched her limbs, her bottom grinding against his groin. At the sudden sensations, Luke sucked in a sharp breath and then let it out in a slow hiss. Stormy's lashes fluttered, revealing a glimpse of her languid dove-gray eyes as she sleepily whispered, "Hi."

"Good morning, beautiful," he whispered back, his voice anything but drowsy.

Stormy's eyes popped open. "Oh!" She glanced around the cabin, and then down at herself. Her robe was open, and her thin nightgown clung to her body as if it were damp. "Oh, my Lord!" She hopped off Luke's lap and quickly turned her back to him. As she adjusted her robe, she stammered, "I—I must have fallen asleep. I haven't had much rest these past few nights."

Luke glanced down at the telltale shape of his groin and dropped his arms into his lap. Assuming that she knew what he was referring to, he said, "Thanks to you, I haven't gotten much sleep myself. I hope you weren't as cruel to your husband as you are to me."

The minute those last words left his tongue, Luke wanted to reach out and snatch them back. God, how the thought of her with another man sickened him, even if that man *was* her husband.

Her clothing adjusted, Stormy spun back around. Eyes wide with surprise, she repeated, "My husband? What are you talking about?"

Luke paused, thinking back to what Calamity had said about the three little ones. She hadn't exactly mentioned that Stormy had been another man's wife, but hell, whatever else she might be, she never struck him as the kind of woman who'd start a family without a legal husband. He shrugged as he said, "I assumed you'd been married . . . or something."

After brushing her hair back out of her face, Stormy headed for the stove. "I don't know why you'd think a thing like that, but you assumed wrong."

If not a formerly married woman, then what? Trying to make sense of it all, Luke studied her as she ground the beans for the morning coffee. Nothing seemed to fit. Not the children without benefit of a husband. And not the dire warnings Calamity had given him about messing with her sister.

"You watch yourself with her," she'd cautioned, "cause that kid keeps a mighty sharp razor stowed in the waistband of her bloomers. I can't begin to tell you the kind of grief she's visited on any man dumb enough to mess with her if she didn't want to be messed with, or fool enough to cross her. She's crazy that gal is. Crazier than me by a long ways." She'd rambled on, extracting Luke's promise to look after

Stormy day and night, to keep watch and see that no harm came to her.

Luke shook his head. The more he knew Stormy, the less any of Calamity's revelations or warnings fit. The only thing he did know was that one of the Cannary sisters was lying. Was it Calamity Jane, a friend he'd known and trusted for several years? Or was it Stormy Ann, a wildcat of a woman he didn't know half as well as he wanted to?

When the coffee was ready Stormy turned to find Luke staring at her. Clutching the edges of her robe to hold it closed at her throat and waist, she said, "Thank you for, ah . . . looking after me or whatever it was you were doing last night, but I think you should leave now."

He sighed. "I suppose I should. I'll just see what I can do about fixing that door before I go." Luke pushed himself halfway out of the chair, testing his tingling feet and sluggish muscles before he finally stood and lumbered across the room.

Stormy glanced toward the front window curtain, judging the time of day. Bright sunlight filtered through. Thinking of the neighbors, she hurried past Luke, and blocked his way to the door.

"What have you got in mind, sweetheart?" he murmured, "A fond farewell?"

"I just want to make sure no one is outside." Stormy pulled the curtain aside and peered out into the alley to make certain that her night visitor could depart unobserved. From behind her, she heard Luke snicker. She turned back to him and said, "It doesn't matter to me who sees you leave, but people like Mrs.

Hawkes might get the wrong idea. I just don't want to get fired before I'm ready to open my own sweet shop. You understand, don't you?"

Thinking of the new life she was trying to build, he nodded, "I sure do, darlin'." Luke smoothed his hair with his fingers and donned his hat. Then he removed the chunk of wood he'd used to secure the door, handed it to Stormy, and took a good hard look at the damage. "I think a couple of new braces and another pole ought to get this door through at least one more attack by the sisters Cannary. I'd be happy to stop by before the show and take care of it for you if you like."

"Thank you," she said quietly. "And if possible, I'd really appreciate it if you could fix it well enough so my sister won't guess what happened."

Luke glanced up at the two neat bullet holes in the loft, then down at the mess Calamity had made of the floor when she shot up Stormy's book. "Looks to me like she's got more to explain than you do around here." He stepped across the threshold, adding, "I just hope Johnny the Oyster gets back to Deadwood to reclaim his cabin soon. If he doesn't, there isn't going to be anything left of it." Then he disappeared up the alley.

An hour later, after donning her best Sunday dress—a two-piece calico polonaise affair in dark plum with black lace trim and buttons—Stormy glanced at the prune-colored bonnet hanging from a peg near the door. She smiled, recalling Luke's reaction every time she wore it, and then impulsively reached into her trunk to lift the dustcover off a hat she'd purchased in Colorado but never before worn.

It was a love of a bonnet, fashioned in black velvet and satin, made to sit squarely on the top of her head. She'd been down at the mouth the day she bought it, depressed over her lack of success in locating even one member of her missing family. Then she'd seen the hat in the window of the Denver Millinery Shop and it had brightened her entire day. Of course, she'd never donned it except in the privacy of her own room. Should she wear it even now? Reveal that much of her hair—and of herself?

Stormy thought of Luke's response to the new hat, imagined the way his dark eyes would sparkle with admiration, and grew warm all over. She fit it to her head without another minute's hesitation. Feeling slightly wicked, as much by her saucy headgear as by the unintentional indiscretion with Luke in her cabin, she hurried off to join the Hawkes family for church services, which were being held in the street near their store. The morning skies were overcast, warm, and sultry, but the storm had stalled somewhere to the south. With a little luck, the rain would hold off until nightfall.

Methodist preacher Henry Weston Smith, who worked at odd jobs during the week, stood atop a large packing crate before his congregation. He addressed a respectful audience of eight women and forty men, speaking about the evil lurking throughout the gulch and offering ways to recall the wandering sinners home, until his flock became bored and began to thin. Most, Stormy noticed, headed up the street to where a crowd had formed at Langrishe's theater—but not the Hawkeses.

At Eudell's insistence, the family, including Stormy, remained behind as rapt observers until Preacher Smith had said his final amen. By the time Stormy and Justin arrived at the theater, the only seats remaining were at the back of the hall. She carefully eased down on her makeshift chair—a stake driven into the ground with a section of tree trunk tacked to the top—and waited for the show to begin.

The aroma of pine was all around her, due, she supposed, to the fresh-sawn lumber on which she was sitting—a clean scent that she found invigorating. The wind whistled against the building, picking up speed, and the distant rumble of thunder announced that the storm was on the move again.

Jack Langrishe strode up to the elevated floor at the far end of the hall and shouted above the murmurs of the excited audience. "Welcome to the first performance of our little theater! Sorry we can't offer better furnishings just yet"—he pointed up to the framework that supported the canvas roof and then down to the sawdust floor—"but with your continued patronage, we hope to soon have a finished theater complete with velvet armchairs!"

The crowd roared its approval.

"And now, without further ado, I present Miss Donna Leigh!"

Stormy leaned forward on her stool, straining to hear the vocalist above the rapidly increasing thunder.

Accompanied by her husband's fiddle, Donna

began her program with a mournful version of "Rose of Killarney." To that she added a few Yankee tunes that had come out of the War between the States, and by the time she finished with "I'll Take You Home Again, Kathleen," the audience was cheering and stomping.

Next came Ed Brown, a placer miner who strummed the guitar while reciting poetry, some of it just this side of decent. It was during his performance that a stranger stepped into the theater with his young son and daughter in tow.

"Excuse me," he whispered to Justin, who was sitting on the aisle. "Looks like all the seats is taken. Mind if we just hunker down on the floor beside you?"

Justin glanced at the man, then beyond him to his daughter. "Ah, no . . ." His Adam's apple bobbed, but it took a full minute for the words he'd formed to tumble off his tongue. "Your girl's welcome to my seat if she wants it." He rose, turning awkwardly toward Stormy. "I'm gonna stand if'n it's all right with you."

Seeing the newcomers, she nodded. "Of course."

Justin stepped aside to allow the young woman to take his chair, and then he slipped around behind her.

Stormy smiled as the newcomer sat down, admiring her abundance of rich chestnut curls and delicate, sparrowlike features. She looked to be around sixteen, and certainly a young woman who wouldn't have gone unnoticed in a place like Deadwood. Her curiosity piqued, she said, "I don't believe I've seen you in town before."

The girl offered a shy smile. "That's because we don't live here. We're from down the road a mile or so just outside of Lead. I'm Savannah Ross, named after the town my kinfolk are from. Well, me too, of course." She giggled.

"A pleasure to meet you, Savannah. My name is Stormy." She considered asking if the girl had seen Calamity during her trip to Lead, then thought better of it as Jack Langrishe took center stage again.

Spreading his arms wide, he announced, "And now for the highlight of our performance! A conversation with two of the most famous citizens to ever walk the streets of Deadwood . . ."

As the man went on about the stars' lives as Indian slayers, gunmen, and scouts of the plains, the door behind Stormy blew open again, this time to admit Jack McCall and his friends along with a particularly strong gust of wind. She glanced over her shoulder at them and watched as they made their way along the north wall of the building. Finding no vacant seats, they stood in place just six feet from the stage, observing as Langrishe arranged two chairs and set a small table in between them. On that table sat a bottle of whiskey and two glasses.

After stepping down from the platform, the showman waved his arm toward a canvas flap that served as a curtain, and continued the introduction. "Ladies and gentlemen! We at Langrishe's theater are proud to present . . ."

"Hickok," the man himself said as he strolled into view. He stroked his luxuriant stallion-tail mustache. "Wild Bill Hickok."

The audience burst into applause, and Hickok, who was dressed in his rawhide show costume complete with his favorite fur hat, took the chair on his right. Then he signaled for silence. "With me this afternoon is my good friend ..."

"McCanles," Luke said as he strutted onstage to the accompaniment of a particularly loud rumble of thunder. Before the crowd had a chance to react, Luke drew his guns, twirled them around his index fingers several times, and then sheathed them all in the space of a heartbeat. "Lucky Luke McCanles." He grinned a bad-boy grin, then took a seat next to Hickok.

The crowd went wild. Men whistled. Women squealed with delight. Justin hooted and hollered. And young Savannah Ross gripped her throat, leaned in close to Stormy, and said in a breathless drawl, "Lawd! Have you evah seen anything quite like *him* before?"

As affected by Luke's entrance as anyone else—maybe more—Stormy felt her heartbeat flutter in her throat, making it difficult to draw a breath, much less speak, but she managed to smile and say, "Not that I can remember."

But she did. Oh, how she remembered. Luke had been dressed in the same black-and-charcoal suit he wore now on the day he had come to collect his kiss—right down to the silver conchos, fancy black hat, crimson tie, and pearl-handled guns. He'd not only collected that kiss and more since then, but spent the night with her wrapped in his arms.

Worst of all, instead of being ashamed at the idea,

no matter how innocent it had been, she had a sudden urge to *brag* to this young stranger next to her, just how well she did know Luke. Stormy blushed as she thought of how debased she'd become during her short time in Deadwood.

She took a quick peek at the young woman, afraid that her shameful thoughts had been observed, but Savannah had long since returned her attention to the stage—and to Luke, who looked confident, rakish, and impossibly handsome. Caught in his spell herself, Stormy watched as he poured a good measure of whisky into the glasses. Hickok accepted his drink, brought it to his lips, and tossed it down. He sputtered loudly, then spit most of it across the stage.

"Damn it, Jack!" Hickok complained. "What in hell is this crap?"

Langrishe, who was kneeling just at the edge of the platform, leaned forward and whispered, "Tea, sir. I thought you just wanted the whisky bottle for atmosphere."

"Atmosphere!" He glanced at Luke. "What's say we blow that bottle of painted water so far into the atmosphere it never comes down again?"

A sudden clap of thunder seemed to split the sky, adding even more menace to Hickok's threat. Langrishe flinched. "Please, fellows, no gunfire in here. Obviously I didn't quite understand what you wanted."

"What I wanted," Hickok explained, "was a glass or two of whisky. You get us a little bourbon, or you don't get any stories. Got it?"

The showman nodded and then disappeared behind the curtain.

From her seat way in the back, Stormy couldn't hear the conversation, but she realized something was amiss. Before she could figure out what, the bright flash of a nearby lightning bolt illuminated the canvas roof for a split second, and then another series of ear-splitting thunder strikes rolled through the gulch.

"Lawd!" Savannah cried. "I just don't think I can evah get used to this part of the country."

More than willing to help the lovely young lady recover from her fears, Justin stooped down between the women, careful to keep his conversation out of the reach of Mr. Ross's ears. "Are you scared, Miss Savannah? You don't have to be with me around."

She batted her lashes, averting her gaze. "And why is that, kind suh?"

"Suh?" He chuckled to himself and glanced at Stormy. "Did you hear what she called me, Miss Cannary? *Suh*. Don't that just beat all?"

"Yes, Justin," she answered, trying to keep her expression impassive. "It most certainly does."

Grinning broadly, he turned his back on Stormy. "Where are you from, Miss Savannah?"

"Georgia . . . *suh*." She giggled and hid her mouth with her fingertips. "Savannah, Georgia, of course."

"Oh, of course!" Justin slapped his forehead with a dramatic flare, nearly knocking Stormy off of her perch.

"Would you like to take my seat, Justin?" she asked.

Completely missing the hint of sarcasm in her tone, he said, "Really? You sure you wouldn't mind?"

Hiding her surprise, for Stormy hadn't really expected him to accept the offer, she said, "No, of course not."

"But Ma says a real gentleman ain't supposed to sit down in mixed company unless all the ladies is seated."

"Really, Justin," she said as she rose, "it's fine with me. This stool is a little uncomfortable anyway."

From up on the platform, Luke tried to keep his cocky show grin in place as he scanned the audience. He'd been looking for Stormy since he'd walked out on stage and finally spotted her at the back of the theater. He smiled, hoping she'd realize the gesture was meant for her, and then took another glance to his left to check on McCall and his companions. They were still leaning against the support beams, grinning as if they knew something the audience didn't. The malevolence radiating from that small group of men was so ripe, Luke could almost smell it. A chill rolled down his spine.

As if to add to his sudden sense of foreboding, the wind howled overhead, lifting sections of canvas and then dashing them against the pine ribs supporting the entire structure. Heavy splatters began to drum against the cloth roof, intermittent drops that quickly grew more frequent and torrential. The storm had finally arrived at the gulch.

Luke returned his increasingly uneasy gaze to Stormy. Even from that distance, he noticed something else about her, a different, more feminine look. Was it a new dress, or—the hat!

Luke craned his neck and waved, trying to catch

her attention, but before he could succeed, a vicious gust of wind grabbed a corner of the theater's roof, tearing the canvas from its moorings and flinging it to the muddy streets below. Rain poured down on the crowd, drenching even the most prepared from head to toe, and in that maelstrom, Luke lost sight of Stormy. Amid the squeals of fright, delight, and just plain surprise from the audience, he leapt down off the stage and plowed through the crowd.

When he found her at the back of the building, Stormy was in the midst of removing her lovely new, and completely saturated, bonnet. He took her into his arms, half-blinded by the steady torrent of the rain pouring in through the opened roof. "Hey? Are you all right?"

"Fine," she hollered back, "if wet to the bones can be considered all right."

"Then let's get out of here. I'll see you get home all right."

She paused to glance at Justin, a young man whose hormonals were clearly in the throes of the uproar his mother had fretted about, and then laughed. "That sounds like an excellent idea. Besides, I think I've just lost my escort—permanently."

Guiding her to the door, Luke pulled Stormy across the two-by-four that served as a threshold and led her right into an ankle-deep puddle. "Oh, dammit it all the way to hell and back!" he said. "I forgot that Langrishe hadn't built his boardwalk yet." He tugged his hat low on his brow, warding off the rain, and checked the road. Main Street was a veritable river of slime, an open sewer with every manner of muck, mud, and water flowing in search of the lowest point. Without even bothering to ask, he scooped Stormy into his arms and made a dash for the cabin.

Once they were inside, Luke gently set her on her feet, pulled off his hat, and shook the water out of it before hanging it on the usual bedpost. Then he glanced at Stormy, who was shaking out her bonnet, and all at once his heart seemed to melt. Her hair, golden in color now that it was wet, had come loose and hung in dripping sections that were plastered to her face and the bodice of her dress. She looked vibrant and young, impossibly young.

That thought prompted the image of her three children—and a knot the size of the Homestake Claim formed in Luke's stomach.

Stormy felt his eyes on her, caught his gaze, and said, "What's wrong?"

He considered shrugging her inquiry off but found himself blurting out the truth instead. "I promised Calamity that I wouldn't mention this, and I don't want to get you upset, but I was just thinking about those three little ones of yours."

"Why would that get me upset?" She tossed her bonnet onto the bed and pushed her wet tresses back off her brow. "I don't mind that Calamity told you about our youngest sister and little brothers."

"Bro—" Luke rubbed his knuckles across his chin, wiping off yet another rivulet of rain. "You mean those little ones aren't, you know . . . yours?"

Her mouth fell open. "You mean, as in my *babies?*" At his nod, she began to laugh. "I don't know how you've managed to get everything so messed up, but let me clear the air once and for all. I have never been married, nor do I have any children."

Luke studied her as she spoke, sure now that she must be telling the truth. Damn Calamity's black heart! She'd tricked him—for what reason, he couldn't imagine—but she had. He grumbled to himself, wondering how many other lies Calamity had told about her sister.

"Are there any more questions?" Stormy asked, seeing the confusion in his expression.

"Several for your sister, but just one for you." Luke reached out, caught Stormy's hands in his, and dragged her into his arms. "Exactly what is it you want from me?"

She stiffened with surprise, and then shivered as Luke's expression transformed from confusion to hunger. His eyes were darker than the skies during a new moon, his passion as obvious as stars on such a night, but she hedged and said, "I—I don't know what you mean."

"I think you do." He tugged her even tighter against his hips, surprised at the amount of heat they generated together—so much, in fact, he could almost imagine steam rising up from their damp clothing and bodies. "You've been teasing me since the day we met, acting a lady one minute, a wildcat the next. Which are you?"

Stormy moistened her lips, buying a little time. She wanted to be the wildcat, oh, how she wished she could be the wildcat each time Luke took her into his arms, but she was a lady. In her heart and soul, she knew she could never be anything *but* a lady.

"Silence, huh?" He slid his fingers into her damp hair, gripping her head between his hands as if it were a crystal ball. "I'm trying to get some answers here. Can't you help me a little? You're running me around in circles, and dammit all, woman, I can't figure out in which direction you're trying to steer me. If it's this—" he gave her a hard, searing kiss, "tell me now, and I'll be happy to lead the way from here on out."

Stormy's mouth was still open, waiting, she supposed, for another kiss, and she couldn't seem to close it. She couldn't think, couldn't move. How could she with Luke holding her so tightly, so very, very intimately? *Yes,* she wanted to scream—yes, she wanted him, *needed* him in the worst way imaginable, but how could she possibly admit such a thing when she'd only just begun to acknowledge that she even *had* such feelings? And where would such an admission lead, if not to trouble? She had to tell Luke no, explain to him somehow that she simply wasn't ready for this kind of relationship, but the best Stormy could manage was to shake her head in very weak denial.

"Then, near as I can figure," he said, sighing with disappointment, "you're leaving me with just one other path." He fit his knuckles under her chin, forcing her to look him in the eye. "If you weren't kidding about that last rule, I hope, for your sake, that you haven't got your heart too set on marrying me."

If Luke had kissed her again, whispered how much he wanted and needed her, or even simply carried her off to bed, her resistance was so low, Stormy guessed she might have succumbed to his charms right then and there. But this suggestion—even if it were true—was too much for her to take.

Her strength restored and then some in the face of such arrogance, she laughed as she said, "Marry . . . *you?* Who said anything about marrying you?"

Uncharacteristically tongue-tied, Luke sputtered, "B-but what about that rule, the part where—"

"I said something about the day I wed, *not* the day I wed you. What gall!"

She exploded out of his embrace, accidentally slapping him across the face with her long wet tresses as she whirled out of his reach, and then marched across the room.

Luke held out his hands, palms upward, as if the gesture would somehow make everything all right again. It didn't, but he found a humbleness in the posture, a sort of absolution for letting his mouth run away with his brain. Stormy's forgiveness for his lack of humility, he suspected, would be a lot longer in coming.

The following Saturday, Stormy leaned against the counter at Smiling Will's Grocery and thought back over the last week. She almost laughed as she considered how solicitous Luke had become. He appeared at her door every morning, walked her to the grocery, then returned each evening to see that she got home all right. On every one of those nights except for the last, he had even taken her to supper at the hotel.

To say that he acted the gentleman was too mild a term. Luke McCanles, the man who'd tried every which way to get her out of her bloomers, had never once tried to kiss her good night or even hinted that she drop that last "rule" again. His good behavior should have pleased her, but it didn't. It almost made her angry.

Worse yet, she knew why. Shameless hussy that she'd become, Stormy missed Luke's intimate caresses and passionate kisses. Missed them more than she ever would have dreamed possible. Just *thinking* about them now set her blood to boil.

When had she turned into such a wanton? And why had Luke suddenly decided to evolve into such a perfect gentleman? Could she dare to hope that he'd decided to court her in earnest, and this was the way he went about such things? Or had he completely lost interest in her as anything but the sister of a good friend? And how, just how was she ever to know the difference without coming right out and asking him?

"Ahem!" Eudell Hawkes drummed her knuckles against the counter where Stormy's elbows rested. "You've spent half the morning wandering around in a daze and the best part of noon daydreaming. Are you planning to get any work done today? Saturday *is* our busiest day, you know."

Stormy straightened and smoothed her apron, surprised to discover how easily thoughts of Luke could block out the constant chatter of so many miners catching up with one another. "I'm sorry, Eudell. I guess I am a little distracted today." Then she walked to the end of the counter, picked up the grocery list of the next man in line, and began taking supplies from the shelves.

She'd filled about half the order for a miner named Mysterious Jimmy when a commotion from the street caught her attention, distracting her yet again from her duties. She thought she heard chickens—a lot of chickens squawking in terror. Then Eudell thundered past the counter.

"My hens!" she cried as she ran out the door. "Something's after my layers!"

Stormy had been hearing wild tales about raucous bullwhackers who liked to drive their oxcarts past Eudell's pen and make a game of lassoing her chickens. She set Jimmy's order down on the counter and hurried out to investigate. As she'd suspected, the driver of a passing freight wagon had found the hens too tempting to ignore. What Stormy didn't expect was to find her sister driving the rig.

"Eeee—ya—*haaa!*" Calamity bellowed as she cracked her whip yet again, this time actually managing to lasso one of the chickens. After hauling it up to the bench where she sat, she belted out a horse laugh and said, "There'll be a hot time in my old frying pan tonight, or my name ain't Calamity Jane! Eeee—ya-—haaa!"

"Thief! Thief!" Eudell screamed at the top of her lungs.

Horror-struck and a little sick to her stomach, Stormy ducked into the doorway and hid herself from both Eudell's and Calamity's view. How could Martha have done such a thing? Why here, at her place of employment? And why now, as her life was finally coming together?

Miners filed past her, eager to join or at least observe the growing ruckus. Above their retreating footsteps, Stormy clearly heard Eudell say, "I'll have you shot for this, you disgusting pig! Gimme back my chicken!"

Not knowing exactly what to do but compelled to do something—and *now,* before her sister got to rambling on and mentioning her family ties—Stormy stepped out onto the boardwalk.

Calamity leaned backward, nearly falling off the seat as the oxcart lurched over a mudhole, and then turned her glassy-eyed gaze on Stormy. "Hey, kid— how're doing? I'm back!"

Wanting only to shut Martha up and send her on home before any more damage was done, Stormy hiked her skirts and ran alongside the wagon. "Stop a minute, won't you?"

"Just what I was a-planning to do, kid! Got a saddle of venison and a big ol' cow elk to deliver to the meat store. Now get out of my way so's I can get this dumb old ox up a little closer to the shop."

Stormy hurried on ahead of the wagon, hoping Calamity wasn't so drunk as to slip and reveal their true relationship, and then turned to watch the "docking" procedure. The chicken, who'd either died or passed out, lay in her sister's lap. Her movements less than gentle, Calamity removed her bullwhip from around the hen's neck and then popped the length of rawhide high over the ox's head. "Get your overfed hide next to that building you-good-for-nothing, low-down, stinking fly barge!" Again she cracked her whip, this time with a string of curses as accompaniment. When she was satisfied the rig couldn't get any closer to Shurdy's Meat Shop, Calamity set the brake, grabbed the hen by its throat, and hopped down off the rig.

Eudell set upon her the minute her feet touched the ground. "Give me my chicken, you filthy piece of garbage!" She held out her hand.

Calamity grabbed that offered hand and shook it, practically jerking the older, and considerably larger, woman off her feet. She smiled, her mouth crooked and more than just little wobbly. "I missed you, too, Miz Hawk-Nose. How ya been?"

Eudell grimaced as she pulled her fingers out of Calamity's grimy hand. "Don't you ever touch me again! Now give me back my chicken."

Calamity hung her head, feigning sadness. "I'm afraid he's a goner, but don't you fret none about that. I intend to give him a right decent burial." She patted her belly, and then staggered backward a few steps, chuckling to herself between hiccups.

Taking the opportunity to get between the two women, Stormy approached her employer. "I think she's drunk, Mrs. Hawkes. Why don't you let me see what I can do with her? You go on back inside the store."

"Humph!" Eudell pointed an accusing finger toward Calamity. "That woman is *always* drunk. She's a vile, disgusting creature of the lowest sort. I just wish Marshal Hickok would agree to become sheriff of this town! He'd lock her up and throw away the key! In fact, I really think she ought to be . . . shot!"

A strange and awful sense of quiet settled over

Stormy at Eudell's tirade, a feeling of hot rage. By now all the miners—Smiling Will and Justin included—had filed out of the grocery store, and several others approached from across the street. They were laughing, pointing at Martha Jane as if she were some kind of freak, giving the pious Mrs. Hawkes a wide berth to do as she pleased.

Stormy's jaw trembled with humiliation, but she managed to keep herself in check enough to say to her employer, "We're causing quite a scene. Why don't I get Calamity out of here? I'll just walk her on home."

Eudell's breasts—enormous by anyone's standards—seemed to swell even more as she set her chin and said, "That woman isn't going anywhere until she pays for my chicken. This isn't your business anyway. Get on back to the store and get to work, missy."

When Eudell moved as if to barrel past her, Stormy blocked the way. "I said I'd walk her home. Take the price of the chicken out of my wages if you like. I'll be right back." She turned as if to do just that while she still had a civil tongue in her head. Then something clamped over her collarbone, nearly breaking it.

"I simply will not put up with the help sassing me," Eudell declared as she twisted Stormy's shoulders around until she faced her. "Either apologize and go back to work, or . . ."

Stormy shook the meaty hand off her shoulder and gathered every bit of her self control before she trusted herself to speak again. "Or what, Mrs. Hawkes?"

The older woman didn't say a word. She just raised her chin and pursed her lips.

Spinning on her heel, Stormy once again offered her back to her employer. Head held high, she started down the street, pausing just long enough to grab Calamity's hand before resuming her journey. From behind her, she heard Eudell's voice ring out.

"Go ahead then, but I hope you realize what you're doing!"

Willing herself to remain quiet while she still had a job, Stormy's back went rigid, but she continued on her way.

"You're ruining your life, missy! And over what? A smelly old sot who isn't fit to clean the bull dung off your shoes, that's what, a rheumy-eyed drunk! Have you gone completely crazy?"

Stormy dug in the heels of her new boots, jerking herself and her sister to a stop. She'd heard enough. Way too much, in fact. She propped Calamity—who was giggling and fondling her ill-gotten chicken—against the corner of Shurdy's Meat Shop, and then turned back toward the woman.

Sisterly pride mingling with a healthy dose of guilt, Stormy slammed her hands against her hips as she said, "I guess I have been a little crazy, idiot enough anyway to let a bully like you intimidate me into pretending I'm someone I'm not. This"—she pointed at Calamity—"fine young woman happens to be my sister. Now, if you don't mind, I'm going to take her home."

"Your *sister!*" Eudell clutched her bosom. "God in heaven! You mean I've been harboring the kin of a filthy whore who'd give herself to the devil himself for a bottle full of whisky? How can you even *admit* that that daughter of satan is your sister?"

Beyond rational thought now, Stormy nearly tripped over her own skirt as she marched back up to where Eudell Hawkes stood. She meant to give her one more chance, to reason with her and try to extract an apology, but as soon as Eudell's self-righteous features were in range, she lost what little control she had left. Stormy drew back her arm and slapped her as hard as she could.

Trembling from head to toe, her voice quivering with both horror and rage, Stormy issued a warning. "If I *ever* hear that you've spoken of my sister in such vile terms again, I swear to God, I'll run you down and knock you all the way to hell and back!"

10

After her impulsive diatribe, Stormy somehow managed to alert Mr. Shurdy that his shipment
had arrived, to arrange for his assistant to care for
the wagon and the exhausted animal attached to it,
and then to maneuver her sister back to their cabin.
Now, two hours and ten cups of coffee later, Calamity sat at the table looking as if she might finally be
sober enough for a coherent conversation.

Over at the stove, Stormy wiped her brow with the
back of her hand and then lifted the final piece of
chicken from the frying pan with a pair of twisted
metal tongs and dropped it on the platter. After
removing the empty skillet from the heat, she
admired the results of her labor as she said, "I suppose I should be grateful you managed to lasso a nice
fat hen for our supper. At least we won't go hungry
tonight."

Calamity clamped her head between her hands

JOIN THE
TIMELESS ROMANCE READER SERVICE AND GET FOUR OF TODAY'S MOST EXCITING HISTORICAL ROMANCES FREE, WITHOUT OBLIGATION!

Imagine getting today's very best historical romances sent directly to your home – at a total savings of at least $2.00 a month. Now you can be among the first to be swept away by the latest from Candace Camp, Constance O'Banyon, Patricia Hagan, Parris Afton Bonds or Susan Wiggs. You get all that – and that's just the beginning.

PREVIEW AT HOME WITHOUT OBLIGATION AND SAVE.

Each month, you'll receive four new romances to preview without obligation for 10 days. You'll pay the low subscriber price of just $4.00 per title – a total savings of at least $2.00 a month!

Postage and handling is absolutely free and there is no minimum number of books you must buy. You may cancel your subscription at any time with no obligation.

GET YOUR FOUR FREE BOOKS TODAY ($20.49 VALUE)

FILL IN THE ORDER FORM BELOW NOW!

YES! *I want to join the Timeless Romance Reader Service. Please send me my 4 FREE HarperMonogram historical romances. Then each month send me 4 new historical romances to preview without obligation for 10 days. I'll pay the low subscription price of $4.00 for every book I choose to keep — a total savings of at least $2.00 each month — and home delivery is free! I understand that I may return any title within 10 days without obligation and I may cancel this subscription at any time without obligation. There is no minimum number of books to purchase.*

NAME_____

ADDRESS _____

CITY_____STATE_____ZIP_____

TELEPHONE_____

SIGNATURE _____

(If under 18 parent or guardian must sign. Program, price, terms, and conditions subject to cancellation and change. Orders subject to acceptance by HarperMonogram.)

and propped her elbows on the table. "Gawd, kid. I'm really sorry about you losing your job, and all. I hadn't figured on lollygagging at the Shoofly Saloon for so long, but them fellas just wouldn't let me out of Central City till I'd stayed a day or two. None a this'd happened if I'd a been thinking straight. Maybe old hawk-nose is right about me—"

"I'm *not* in the mood for that kind of talk tonight." Stormy brought the platter to the table and took a seat across from her sister. "Besides, there isn't a job in the world worth that woman's evil opinion. Let's try to forget about her and eat before our supper gets cold."

Keeping her gaze pinned on her sister, Calamity tugged her chair up close to the table. She chuckled as she reached for a golden brown drumstick. "You've managed to collect quite a little pile of grit in your craw since you come to Deadwood, kid. Gawd, even drunk as I was, I still remember the expression on that old biddy's face when you popped her one! She looked like someone'd rammed a hot poker straight up her—"

"Calamity, please!" Stormy covered her face with her hands, pressing her eyes to keep the tears from falling, tears that she knew were prompted as much by her own denial of her sister as by remorse. "I've never slapped anyone in my life, and I'm none too proud to lay claim to such a violent deed now. Can't we just forget about it and hope that the others in this town will too?"

Calamity rolled her eyes as she dug through the platter of meat searching for the other drumstick. News of any kind traveled fast in an isolated community like Deadwood. Ten minutes after Stormy had nailed Eudell Hawkes, Calamity would have bet her last shot of whisky that everyone in town knew about it. But she wasn't going to be the one to tell her sister she was living on false hope. No, siree. And maybe, if they knew what was good for them no one else would either.

Licking the grease off her dirty, chapped fingers, Calamity grinned and said, "It's a closed subject as far as I'm concerned. I just want to make sure you understand how I feel about all this. I'm real sorry for causing you to lose your job, but I tried to warn you about this town and what they thought of me the day you came here."

"I remember." The words were barely audible, a whispered prelude to what Stormy knew she had to say next. "I knew from the moment I arrived in Deadwood what kind of person you were, and how some of the townsfolk might look down on you, but instead of standing beside you, of having the good sense to be proud to call you sister, I denied you. I pretended my sister was someone else. Someone who wore dresses and never ventured out of our home because of her sickly nature, not because of her reputation." She lowered her head. "Can you ever forgive me?"

Calamity groaned. "Gawd, kid—you ain't done nothing to forgive. You stood up for me today like no one ever has."

"Today, yes. But I should have done so from the very moment I arrived here."

"Aw, that's a bunch of crap. I ain't exactly what the ladies call acceptable, but it don't bother me none. Really, it don't. I like what I am and what I do—hell, no I don't! I *love* it!" She pounded the tabletop. "There ain't no man who can drive an ox team better than me, or shoot or ride better for that matter, and it's cause that's what I like to do! Some people have a problem with that, ladies in particular. 'Course, you know as well as I do that a lady just can't do all them manly things and be a lady too, so I had to make a choice. I made that choice a long time ago, and near as I can figure, I ain't got no reason a'tall to apologize for what I am. I do see why you might have to, though."

Stormy's eyes misted. "Well, I don't, and I'll never apologize for you, or disclaim you again."

Calamity bit off a big piece of chicken and swallowed it, hoping somehow the meat would push the sudden lump in her throat back down to wherever it came from. She licked her lips clean. "I appreciate you saying so, but all I want is for you to know that I'm about as happy as I can be—except, of course, when me being me hurts you." She sighed heavily. "Gawd, kid, I still think you'd a been better off not telling anyone that you even know'd me."

Stormy had to wipe away her tears before she could speak. "I'm proud to claim you because I love you, Martha—"

"What'd I tell you about that name?"

Stormy's hand went to her bosom. "Sometimes I just *have* to call you Martha. In here you'll always be Martha to me, no matter how many other names you have. I just want you to know that I'll always love you—whoever and whatever you are."

Calamity drew in a deep breath, but it couldn't stop the burning behind her eyelids or keep her vision from growing watery. "Gawd, kid," she muttered, her voice a bare whisper. "How can you say that after all I done to you today?"

"You didn't do anything to me but help me be myself again. As far as that job goes, maybe you actually did me a favor. My taffy has been going over really well with the miners. I know I can sell it myself, even if I have to peddle it up in the badlands!"

Calamity laughed raucously, glad to purge herself of the incessant ache in her chest. When she calmed down, she shook her head and wagged a finger across the table. "You won't do any such thing. You're a lady and I know you *like* being a lady as much as I like being a bullwhacker. If anyone moseys up to the badlands to sell your taffy, it'll be me. Say, kid! That ain't a half-bad idea. That's it!" She slapped her forehead. "We'll make us up a batch tonight, and tomorrow I'll run it up to the badlands! I bet we'll sell a ton!"

"That sounds like a great idea—and it just might work!"

"Damn right it'll work!" The sisters linked fingers, squeezing each other's hands in a kind of victory salute when a knocking sounded at the door. "Thank God for that," Calamity said, her voice choked. "I was about to turn into a maudlin ninnyhammer!" She released Stormy's hand and bellowed, "Yeah? Who's there?"

The door inched open a crack. "You gals decent?" To see for himself, Luke stuck his head inside the cabin. "Oh, dammit, you are." He checked to make sure ol' Martha was in the corner where she belonged before he came inside. "Afternoon ladies," he greeted as he sent his hat spinning toward the bedpost.

"Well, why don't you just come on in without an invite, you old polecat," Calamity suggested. "What's on your mind?"

He grinned as he sauntered across the room. "I just stopped by to congratulate the newest contender to Joe Goss's throne."

Stormy frowned. "Who's that?"

Trying to hide her chuckles, Calamity said, "He's a heavyweight champion boxer."

"Oh." Stormy's eyes popped open wide as she whipped her head around toward Luke. *"Oh!"*

With a wide grin on his face, he grabbed the last empty chair at the table, spun it around, and straddled it. "I hear Smiling Will's poor little wife is still hearing bells and seeing stars. What'd you get her with? A right cross or a left hook?"

Stormy groaned and buried her face in her hands.

"Surely you didn't drop her with an uppercut! That doesn't sound very sporting to me."

"Ease up on her, Luke," Calamity said. "I don't think she wants to talk about it—now, or ever."

Shrugging, he eyed the platter full of chicken. Without asking, he helped himself to the last breast, took a large bite of it, and then began to moan dramatically as the spicy flavor filled his mouth. "Damn, that's good." He glanced at Calamity. "There's no way in hell you made this." Then he glared at Stormy. "So you must have fixed it. And to think I've spent my hard-earned money buying restaurant suppers all week long, while here sits the best cook in town. It's robbery, is what it is."

Stormy let her hands fall to her lap. "No one forced you to ask me to supper."

"You've been taking her to supper?" Calamity's eyes lit up. She rapped Luke across the biceps. "Hey! You been a-sparking my li'l sis whilst I was gone?"

"No, I haven't been *sparking* anyone, Calam." Luke grumbled as he finished the piece of chicken. "I just did exactly what you told me to do—nothing more, nothing less."

"What she—" Her heart in her throat, Stormy fixed an accusing gaze on Calamity. "Just what did you ask him to do?"

"Nothing much. Just to kinda watch after you at night and such."

"And such." Stormy leaned back in her chair, not sure who she was angrier with—her sister for treating her as if she were still a baby, or Luke for pretending to court her, for making her feel as if he truly cared. She folded her arms across her breasts and set her jaw.

Luke, assuming Stormy's anger was directed at her sister, turned on Calamity and demanded, "Speaking of which, why don't you tell me all about Stormy's husband and children one more time since we're all together? What in hell was that all about?"

Calamity moved out of his range and offered a lop-sided grin. "I don't recall mentioning that she had a husband."

"Yeah, well, maybe not in those words, but you

sure as hell said something about her worrying over her 'babies.' Three of them to be exact."

"Gawd, Luke. I never said they was hers."

Luke sighed. "What about the razor? Did I misunderstand that, too?" He turned to Stormy. "Do you keep a razor in your bloomers, or not? The truth."

"A raz—" Her gaze darted to Calamity, who rolled her eyes, and then back to Luke. He looked so smug, so sure of himself. Too sure of himself. She lifted her chin and snapped, "I *wish* she hadn't mentioned the razor. There are *some* things a girl ought to be able to keep private."

Again came a knock at the door, muffling Calamity's snicker. "Well, ain't we the popular ones tonight!"

"I'll see who's there." Grumbling to himself, still wondering about the existence of that razor, Luke hopped off his chair and crossed the room. He opened the door to see the entire Hawkes family standing before him.

"Evening," said Will. "Hope we ain't disturbing you, but the Mrs. has a couple of things she'd like to say to the Cannary gals. They here?" he asked, even though he could see past Luke and knew that they were.

Luke inquired over his shoulder, "Are you ladies in for—"

"I heard him," Calamity cut in. "Tell 'em to come on in."

"Martha!" Stormy whispered. "I don't want to talk to her—to any of them."

Calamity smiled and then leaned across the table

to whisper back, "What happened to all that grit you had stuck in your craw? Swallow it, did ya?"

Stormy groaned but looked over to the group in the doorway and said, "It's all right, Luke."

At the invitation, Will gave his wife a little shove.

Eudell stumbled into the room, and then, with her husband and son directly behind her, lumbered over to the tables. Keeping her gaze away from the sisters, she stared directly ahead—at the platter of fried chicken. "I came by to . . . apologize for my earlier conduct. I didn't mean all those nasty things I said. I was upset about my chickens."

"I reckon you had every reason to be upset about that, Miz Hawkes," Calamity said. "In fact, I'd like to pay you for that bird." She dipped into her pocket and pulled out her poke. Dangling the leather pouch before the woman, she said, "Take whatever you think you got coming."

Eudell eyed the small sack of gold dust, hesitating a long moment before another jab in the ribs from her husband prompted her to say, "No, thank you. Consider the chicken a peace offering for the dreadful names I called you."

"That's right neighborly of you." She looked to her sister. "Ain't that real friendly of her?"

Struggling to produce even the shadow of a smile, Stormy offered a brief nod but still couldn't find it in her heart to accept the woman's obviously forced apology.

Prodded again by Will, Eudell went on to say, "There's one other issue I'd like to discuss." She turned her gaze on Stormy. "I hope I didn't leave you with the impression that you are fired. I'd like to see you back to work tomorrow morning."

From behind her, Will added, "We *all* would."

At Stormy's frown and the refusal it suggested, Calamity kicked at her leg under the table. "I'm afraid you're a-gonna have to talk to me about that, Miz Hawkes. I'm, ah, my sister's business partner." Stormy gasped, and Calamity kicked her again. "From here on out, Stormy will keep doing all the cooking, but I'll decide where to do the selling."

Eudell bristled. "What are your terms?"

Calamity scratched her head. "Well, I'll tell ya . . . after the commotion at your store and all, I had to go out and get us some new customers. Got us booked pretty solid now for at least the next—"

"I think I can manage to work a few days for the store and still fill all my candy orders," Stormy piped up.

Calamity glanced up at Eudell and gave her a tight smile. "She's a regular go-getter, that one, but I don't see how she can manage but one day a week. How about she comes in on Wednesday. We ought to be caught up on orders by then if we don't get no more new ones."

Eudell seemed to swallow her disappointment. "Wednesday it is, then."

"And Saturday, too," Stormy added, dodging the toe of her sister's boot. "I know how busy you are then, and I'm *sure* I can manage both days."

"Thank you. I'll see you Wednesday, then." Eudell turned as if to leave when Calamity jumped out of her chair and offered her hand.

"It's been a real pleasure doing business with you, Miz Hawkes."

Eudell hesitated as long as she dared but finally touched Calamity's fingers for a brief moment. Then she shuddered, sending a ripple of quivering flesh from her jowls to her belly.

Calamity grinned. "Allow me to see you and yourn to the door."

The Hawkes family had no more than stepped out into the alley before Calamity turned to Luke, and added, "That goes for you, too. My sister and I got work to do. You'll just be in the way."

"You?" He laughed. *"Making candy?"*

Glancing back to the table at Stormy, she said, "You could use an extry taffy-stretcher or something like that, couldn't you?"

Pride bursting in her chest, Stormy nodded, and said, "She's right, Luke, and besides, she's my business partner now, the one who gets all the customers. What Calamity says, goes—and I guess that means you."

Grumbling to himself, he grabbed his hat and slammed it down on his head. "Customers," he muttered. "You don't have any other customers . . . do you?"

The sisters grinned in unison, and then Calamity said, "You'll see soon enough."

As Luke took his leave, Stormy watched his profile disappear around the corner, and then threatened, "He'd better *not!*"

*   *   *

Wednesday, August 2, 1876, fell right smack in the middle of the dog days of summer, when the elements separated the hearty from the frail. While Luke would never entertain the idea that he was anything less than sturdy, he had to admit that today he was somewhat "under the weather." The storm system had completely left the area, clearing the way for the relentless summer sun, but it had left behind just enough moisture to create a walking steam bath out of any soul brave enough to toil in the daylight hours. Luke McCanles was not one of those men.

He wiped the sweat from his brow again and then donned his hat. He should have joined Bill over at the Number Ten Saloon at least an hour ago, where Missouri riverboat Captain Massie was holding court at the poker table—another from an endless list of gamblers who couldn't wait to lose all his worldly possessions to famous men like Lucky Luke and Wild Bill Hickok. Luke hadn't been up to joining in when the game began, and he wasn't up to it now, except that the heat in his room was no longer oppressive but suffocating.

As he stepped out onto the boardwalk in front of his hotel, he glanced first to his left, toward the Number Ten and the badlands beyond, and then to his right. Three doors, one alley, and two boardwalks in that direction, Stormy would be selling taffy, laughing, he supposed, and socializing with the customers. Offering little bits and pieces of herself the way she hadn't found the time to do for him over the last three days.

The poker game would probably go on for hours,

Luke figured, maybe for days. Even if Bill had cleaned Massie out by now, the game would continue. Hell, he could join the group later and relieve Bill of his winnings. He chuckled to himself at the thought. Then, indulging his sweet tooth—for the woman, not the taffy—Luke headed to the right.

When he stepped into the store he spotted Stormy at the back counter. She handed the editor of the *Black Hills Pioneer* a large sack of candy, and then turned as if to go into the storeroom. Luke caught her gaze, and she froze in place. His grin smug and self-assured, he approached her. "Afternoon. How's business?"

"It simply couldn't be better. Can I help you?"

Luke sighed, dropped the act, and got right to it. "You most certainly can, sweetheart, but will you? That's the question."

Stormy heard the innuendo in his voice and knew he was hinting at something other than groceries, but he didn't seem at all amused, or flippant. "What would you like?" she asked, knowing full well that she'd opened the door to any number of ribald remarks but to honesty as well.

Luke didn't disappoint her with nonsense. "I'm not exactly sure *what* I'd like from you, Stormy. That's why I want to talk to you. In relative privacy. Can you take a walk over to the hotel with me? I'll buy you a nice cool sarsaparilla."

Excitement poured over her, warming her system as Stormy grinned and said, "That sounds lovely." Then she glanced down the end of the counter to where Eudell Hawkes stood. She was fanning herself with a copy of the newspaper, her fleshy upper arm swinging up and down. Stormy called to her, "I need to leave for a few minutes, Eudell. I'll be back within the hour."

If the woman had any reservations about the help skipping out for personal business, she didn't let them show. She nodded and said, "Try not to be gone too long, will you? I'm feeling mighty poorly this afternoon. I think I ought to lie down for a while."

"I'll be back as fast as I can." Stormy reached around behind her waist to untie her apron. Then a single shot rang out from somewhere down the street. Her gaze darted up to Luke. "What was that?"

"I don't know, but I think I'd better find out."

Luke turned on his heel and ran toward the front door but hung back out of sight when he reached the jamb. From behind this shield, he scanned the buildings on each side of the street from one end of the gulch to the other. As he narrowed his gaze toward the badlands, Luke saw Crooked Nose Jack McCall dash out of the Number Ten and start to mount his horse. McCall fell to the ground but quickly regained his footing. Then he began running up the street, toward the grocery store. Luke slipped his gun out of the holster, preparing to step in front of the man and detain him long enough to investigate, when Stormy rushed up beside him.

"What's happened?" she asked, horrified to see that Luke's weapon was drawn.

He grabbed her by the arm and flung her back inside the store. "Get down and stay down!" As he turned toward the street again, he saw McCall disappear into the meat shop next door. Both guns drawn, Luke decided to go in after him.

Stormy, who was shaken but still on her feet, cautiously made her way back to the doorway. She peered out into the street, surprised to see several men running in her direction, shouting words too garbled for her to understand. Just before they reached the grocery store, they each filed into Shurdy's. And then the most surprising sight of all: Calamity Jane stumbled out of the saloon, and she, too, started toward the meat shop.

No longer concerned about her own safety, Stormy rushed out to stop her. "What's happened?" she cried, her hems dragging in the muck.

Calamity didn't answer. She just kept on fighting her way through the mud and slime toward Shurdy's.

As she drew near, Stormy could see tears streaming down Martha's face, and blood on her shirt. "My God!" she cried, sprinting to her side. "What's happened to you? Have you been shot?"

Through her sobs, Calamity managed to say, "I ain't shot! It ain't me he ambushed!" She pushed Stormy aside and headed for the entrance of the meat store.

"Who's been shot?" Stormy called after her. "Please tell me—is someone hurt?"

At Shurdy's doorway, Calamity paused long enough to knuckle the tears off her cheeks. Then she looked over her shoulder and cried out, "That crooked-nosed bastard gunned down my Bill, that's who. Shot him *dead!*"

11

Later that same evening, Luke entered the Bella Union Theater, the structure Jack Langrishe had leased while repairs were being made on his own damaged building. Tonight there would be no singing or dancing, no laughter or applause. Tonight the outraged citizens of Deadwood had decided to hold a miners' court in order to try Jack McCall for the murder of James Butler Hickok.

Luke chose to sit on a bench at the back of the hall. If he were close enough to look McCall in the eye, he knew he would never be able to listen to the interrogation, much less allow the man to live long enough to hang. No, he would have to wait until after the trial to extract some small measure of revenge for the best friend a man could have had—whether through the hangman's noose or his very own Colt. Luke slid his hands down along his hips, feeling decidedly naked without his guns, and cursed the committee that had voted to confiscate all weapons at the door.

A group of miners filed by him, their holsters empty, and the theater began to fill. Luke noted sourly that the crowd was comprised more of morbidly curious people than actual friends of the man he'd come to regard as a father figure. And then in through the door came Stormy, accompanied by her very agitated sister. He quickly looked away, trying to blend in with the wall, but Calamity spotted him.

She leaned in close to Stormy and whispered, "Go sit with him, and make sure he don't do nothing stupid when they bring McCall in. Luke's what they call a good friend but a bad enemy. No telling what he's a planning for Crooked Nose. I got to go sit in front so's they don't forget I'm witnessing."

As Calamity continued down the aisle, Stormy seated herself on the bench beside Luke. His gaze flickered over to her, and then he looked away. Trying to reach out to him in any way she could, she quietly said, "I—I'm sorry about what happened. I know how much Mr. Hickok must have meant to you."

In spite of the wall of steel he'd erected around himself, the intentional numbing of his very core, Luke flinched at her words. She didn't know a thing. She couldn't have. How could she possibly know what Bill had meant to him when he hadn't realized it himself until this afternoon? Hell, he hadn't felt this much grief the day they'd buried his father. And for a very good reason. David McCanles had never earned the kind of respect Luke held for Bill Hickok.

He glanced at Stormy, noting the concern in her

soft gray eyes. No, she didn't understand, and probably never would accept the fact that a man could turn from his natural father and then throw in with the man who killed him. But he needed to say *something* to her, to acknowledge her attempts to console him.

Hell, it wasn't her fault he could still hear the voices of the townsfolk echoing in his ear, repeating over and over, "Wild Bill has been shot! Wild Bill is dead!" He was the one who would have to live with the agonizing uncertainty, the possibility that somehow he could have prevented Bill's murder. Had he gone straight to the Number Ten instead of the grocery store, surely he could have stopped McCall—maybe before the bastard even drew his weapon.

Luke canted his head toward her and said, "Thanks for coming and . . . sitting with me. You wouldn't happen to know what they've done with Bill, would you?"

Although she trembled at the look in his eyes, a chill so viable she could almost reach out and touch it, Stormy softly repeated what Calamity had told her. "Colorado Charlie and a few others took him to the tent by the river. Doc Pierce laid him out, and Preacher Smith is going to hold services first thing in the morning."

Luke nodded abruptly and then leaned back against the wall. He supposed that was the way he'd have arranged things, but suppose was all he'd had time to do. From the moment he'd cornered McCall in the meat shop, and then been joined by the angry mob from the saloon, he'd never let the bastard out of his sight—that is, until the self-appointed committee decided Luke might not be the wisest choice as a guard for the man who'd killed Wild Bill Hickok.

If only he'd known the nature of McCall's deed before the crowd had gathered in Shurdy's! Hell, he'd have shot the bastard then and there and in just the same way McCall had shot Bill, showing every bit as much mercy. Luke clenched his jaw and gritted his teeth.

"They're about to start," Stormy whispered as she slipped her hand in his. Luke stiffened as if to pull away, but then relaxed and allowed the gesture.

"Quiet please," said W. L. Kuykendall, one of nine lawyers who lived in Deadwood. Stepping up on the stage, he held his hands high over head. "I've been chosen by the people's committee to serve as judge over this trial. Before we proceed, I have to remind you that while I am legally empowered to perform such duties as the recording of claims and the vows of matrimony, what we are about to undertake here should not be viewed as anything more than a kangaroo court."

The crowd came alive at that, a few indignant citizens suggesting that they skip the illegal trial and hang McCall right away and get it over with.

Again Kuykendall gestured for silence. Then he took his place behind a desk brought in for just that purpose. "Gentlemen?" He waved to two other lawyers, one representing the defense, the other, the town. "Shall we proceed?"

From the back of the room, Luke and Stormy watched as twelve miners were chosen from the crowd to serve as jurors. Then acting sheriff Isaac

Brown brought Jack McCall in through the front door and led him down the aisle, his hands tied behind his back. Luke clenched his fists, including the one that held Stormy's hand, but then quickly relaxed again when she gasped in pain.

The gavel sounded, and "Judge" Kuykendall called the first witnesses. All three men who had been sitting at the poker table with Hickok—Charlie Rich, Carl Mann, and Captain William Massie, who now had the bullet which passed through Hickok embedded in his right wrist—gave the same account.

They had been playing five-card draw when McCall came in the saloon looking a little drunk, "histed" another drink or two, and then proceeded to have a quiet talk with a stranger at the bar. After that, McCall circled the poker table, checking each player's cards, until he came to a stop behind Hickok. McCall screamed an oath and muttered a few words, but no one could make sense of them— the blast of his pistol obliterated his statement forever along with the man known as Wild Bill Hickok.

And finally Calamity was called. She leapt up on the stage, swore to tell the truth, and then just plain swore a little for good measure before Kuykendall invited her to sit down in the chair beside his desk.

Colonel May, representing the people, said, "Please tell us in your own words, Miss Cannary—"

"Calamity Jane's my name, and I'll thank you to use it!"

He sniffed in disdain, and then said, "I stand corrected, Miss *Jane*. Please tell us what you saw in Nuttall and Mann's Number Ten Saloon this afternoon."

"I seen *him,*" she said, pointing her finger at McCall, "stagger in some time between three and four."

"Would you say that Mr. McCall was drunk?"

She shrugged. "I'd say he was just this side of tanglefooted, but not so bad off as to be D and D."

"D and D?" May raised his eyebrows. "Please explain to the court what that means."

"It means drunk and disorderly—just like you was night before last."

The colonel exchanged an indignant glance with Judge Kuykendall and then proceeded. "Please describe what happened next."

"I would if you'd quit interruptin' me. As I was saying, McCall come in, got a beer—I wasn't drinking, mind you. I just stopped in the saloon to say hi to the fellas."

"You're not on trial here. Please go on."

"Sure. So after he gets his beer, McCall sneaks over in a corner with John Brody where they commenced to whispering."

"You used the term "sneak." Please explain to the jury the rationale behind your choice of words."

Calamity had to think about that for a minute, translating what he had said from lawyer talk to plain English. "If you mean why did I say they was sneaking around, it's 'cause they was! They talked real quiet like, you know, like they had some big damn secret, and I guess it looks like they did!" She leaned over and glared at McCall. "Ya dirty bastard!"

Judge Kuykendall banged his gavel. "Please refrain from badgering the accused. Go on with your testimony."

Her lip curled into a cross between a frown and a sneer, but she continued. "After the bastard over there finished his visit with Brody, he did just like Charlie said—strolled around the table as casual as you please and looked at everyone's cards. Hell, Crooked Nose played poker at that same table the night before and lost big to Bill, but Bill being the nice fella he is, loaned him some money to buy a nice big breakfast this morning—*this very morning*, gawd-dammit all to hell!"

"Please," Kuykendall said, "get on with it."

Straightening her rawhide jacket, Calamity said, "After he made it all around the table, McCall come up behind Bill hollering something like 'Take that!' and shot him right through the back of the head!" Again she leaned forward, this time shaking her fist. "You miserable low-down good-for-nothing coward! You never even gave him a chance!"

Kuykendall's gavel fell three times before Calamity, red-faced and out of breath, finally sat back in her chair. "That'll be all, Miss Cannary," he said. "You can return to your seat."

"But I got one other thing to say!"

The judge sighed wearily. "It is pertinent to the case?"

"I don't know, but it could be important." At his nod, she continued. "I was walking from the Number Ten over to Custer's saloon shortly after the accused over there first come to town, and I overheard Brody, a fella named Tim, and McCall discussing killing someone. Never did hear a name, whether this poor soul was dead already or if they was just planning for him to be dead, but it coulda been Bill they was talk-ing about. It sure as hell coulda been."

"Thank you for your testimony. Now will you please take your seat?"

After Calamity finished, only a handful of miners were called, their stories more of the hearsay variety than anything. The defense eschewed the opportunity to cross-examine the witnesses and instead called the defendant to the stand.

After the preliminary testimony in which he did not deny shooting Hickok, McCall said, "I come here with just one thing on my mind. Getting revenge for my little brother, Tom."

Judge Miller, defender for the accused, asked, "And why did you feel you needed to take that revenge with Mr. Hickok?"

"Because back in Hays City, Kansas, where I'm from, Marshal Hickok went after my little brother for stealing chickens, and shot him in the back!"

Luke leapt to his feet. "That's a goddamn lie!"

Kuykendall banged his gavel. "I will have order!"

"But I was with Bill in Hays City," Luke persisted. "He never shot anyone in the back, much less a kid! McCall's lying!"

"You will sit down this minute, Mr. McCanles, or I'll have acting Sheriff Brown remove you from this courtroom!"

Not simply grumbling, but growling to himself, Luke sank back down on the bench beside Stormy. "That son of a bitch is going to get away with it. I just know he is."

Although she had the feeling that Luke wasn't

really talking to her, Stormy took possession of his hand again and said, "They'll find him guilty. They have to—everyone saw him shoot Mr. Hickok."

By then, the defendant had been excused, and Judge Kuykendall rose to address the jury. "I'm going to ask that you men go backstage for your deliberations, but before I do, I must in all good conscience remind you again that this court is for all purposes, illegal. The Black Hills still belong to the Sioux, and because of that, our nearest legal federal government is nearly two weeks away in Yankton. While I will not instruct you to render a not-guilty verdict, may I remind you of the consequences should you find Mr. McCall guilty. We cannot legally impose the punishment prescribed by law for a verdict rendered during an unlawful trial. Have I made myself clear?"

Several of the jurors scratched their heads and a few whispered among themselves, but without issuing further explanations or instructions, Kuykendall ordered them to begin deliberations.

Stormy, who understood only too well what the judge was asking of the panel, stole a surreptitious glimpse at Luke. His profile was rigid, his dark eyes unblinking and so full of outrage and pain it nearly broke her heart. Oh, how she wished she could reach out to him, to soothe him somehow and bring the sparkle back to those obsidian eyes. But she sensed that nothing and no one would reach him this night. Not her—and not the love she felt for him.

Sucking in her breath, Stormy glanced again at Luke. *Love?* Was that what this was all about? Had she really and truly fallen in love for the first time in her life? There was so very much about him to love, she thought, studying Luke's strong profile, recognizing the sensitivity lying just beneath the rage.

It was certainly more than his outward flash, the persona he affected as a showman. Although she couldn't deny her attraction to Luke the celebrity, she suspected these deeper feelings and this love—if that's truly what it was—were directed at the man beneath.

Feeling closer to him at that moment than she'd believed possible, Stormy gently squeezed Luke's hand as the jury began to file back on stage. Warming her, fulfilling a need he could not possibly have imagined, he squeezed her back.

Kuykendall read the slip of paper jury foreman Whitehead gave him and then handed it to the court clerk and instructed him to announce the verdict.

"The jury has voted for acquittal."

At the crowd's instant uproar, Kuykendall banged his gavel again and again, and then shouted over the din. "Mr. McCall, you are free to go on one condition. You've got exactly 60 seconds to get out of Deadwood as long as you promise never to return again."

McCall stood, waiting as the bailiff cut his bonds, and said, "I'm gone the minute my hands are free!"

"Over my dead body, you are!" Luke shouted as he jumped into the aisle, ready to strangle the man with his bare hands.

"Sheriff Brown!" Kuykendall called. "Arrest that man, McCanles. Take him out of here and lock him up until time for the funeral in the morning."

"No!" Stormy cried, rising. "He hasn't done anything wrong!"

Brown and two of his "deputies" rushed Luke, scuffling with him briefly, but in spite of his resistance and Stormy's heated protests, they managed to drag him out of the theater and into the night.

Relieved to see that Jack McCall had already made his escape through the rear of the building, Judge Kuykendall banged the gavel one last time, and then said, "This court is adjourned."

Back in their cabin for the night, Calamity poured a glass of whisky and shoved it across the table to Stormy. "Here. Drink this up. It'll help a little."

Stormy was sorely tempted but shook her head. "Thanks, but I'm really not up to it. I can't quit thinking about poor Luke locked up in that cabin for the night. How in God's name could they have put him in the very same place they kept that evil man, McCall? It's not only unfair, I think it's downright cruel."

With a shrug, Calamity reclaimed the drink she'd offered her sister. "They couldn't just let him go chasing after McCall, and since we ain't got a jail, and Cold Deck Johnny's cabin is the only vacant one in town, there weren't any where's else to put him. 'Sides, kid—they only arrested Luke so's they wouldn't have to put *him* on trial for murder, too. It's for the best."

Stormy pictured Luke, angry and alone with his grief, and then softly sighed. "He'll be safer, I suppose, but I don't see how he'll be better for this." She looked up in time to see her sister take a big swig of her drink. Even though she had yet to see Martha cry, her eyes were red and swollen, forlorn. Humbled with sudden guilt, she said, "What's done is done. I shouldn't be rattling on about Luke anyway. He may not be too comfortable, but at least he's alive, when the man you love is—is, well, gone."

"Love?" Calamity blinked, shuddering as her first swallow of liquor in three days coursed through her system. "Who said anything about love?"

"I assumed, that is, I thought that since you and Mr. Hickok shared so much, that you, well, loved him."

"Oh, kid, I dunno." She sighed and stared down at the bottom of her glass. Her voice pensive, even a little wistful, she admitted, "I supposed maybe I did love Bill a little—he'll always have a right special place in my heart, that's for sure. That man never gave me a moment's grief. Well," she amended, "maybe that one time when he run off and married Agnes Lake, but other than that, never. I guess folks could say that I loved Wild Bill Hickok and not be too wrong. But I don't think it's the same kind of love you're a talking about though, is it?"

Stormy's gaze fell to her lap. "I don't know, Martha," she whispered. "I don't know what to think about love or anything anymore."

"You're thinking one thing from where I'm sitting, kid—you got it in your head that you're in love with Luke, ain't ya?"

Keeping her chin low, Stormy hid a grin as she eyed her sister. "That would be a little outrageous . . . wouldn't it? I mean, is it even decent, much less possible to fall in love with a man you've only known a few days or weeks?"

Calamity let out a whoop of laughter. "How the hell should I know? I ain't never fallen in love with anyone. Stumbled a few times, I suppose, but that's it."

Looking back down at her hands, Stormy began to pick at her flower-patterned skirt.

Calamity observed her sister. " 'Course just 'cause it never happened to me, don't mean it can't happen. I just wish you'd a picked someone else to get all mooney-eyed over."

Stormy pushed her coyness aside. "What's wrong with Luke? He's the most fascinating man I've ever met, not to mention handsome and famous, too! What more could I ask for—could anyone ask for? Why, I should think it'd be more difficult for a woman *not* to fall in love with Luke."

"Simmer down, kid, that ain't what I meant. I got eyes in my head enough to see that Luke is one fine chunk of a man. But I already told you why I didn't want you taking up with Luke McCanles. He ain't the marrying kind." She pointed across the table. "You are. And that, li'l sis, is a problem—a mighty big one from where I sit."

Stormy leaned back in her chair and let out a long sigh. She hadn't thought that far ahead, or even considered that somewhere down the road she might expect Luke to marry her. And she certainly hadn't entertained the notion that when that day came, he'd turn and run the other way. And then she thought of something else.

Turning an accusing eye on her sister, she asked, "Is that why you told Luke all those crazy stories about me having a husband and babies? To run him off?"

Calamity howled. "Hell, no, kid! I was trying to do something nice for you. You made out like you wanted him, you know—And I thought Luke was looking a little nervous around you, you being a lady, and all, so I just roughed you up around the edges a little."

"By giving me a family and a razor in my undergarments?"

"Nice touch, huh?" At Stormy's frown, she said, "Gawd, if I'd a said to him, 'Luke, old friend, I got to leave town for a few days. My li'l sis is a right fine lady and a virgin to boot. I want you to look after her real good whilst I'm gone—but you keep your hands to yourself.'" She snorted. "Why, that boy'd a left a trail of dust clean down to Texas."

"Oh, Martha. I can't believe Luke is so afraid of respectability."

"No? My little plan worked, didn't it?"   .

Again her eyebrows drew together, this time with more worry than puzzlement. "I—I'm not sure what you mean."

Calamity stretched over the table, getting as close to her sister as she could. "He tried to get in your bloomers a time or two, didn't he?"

Stormy colored, and her lashes fluttered against her cheeks.

"Ah, hah!" Calamity banged a fist against the table. "Just as I thought he might. Did you let him jump you?"

"Martha!" Hardly able to believe she was having another of these sordid conversations, Stormy choked on the words as she said, "Of course I didn't."

"Humm, I was afraid of that." She drummed the tabletop with her blunt-nailed fingertips. "I'll just bet it's that damnable Dr. Tuttlebutt and his load of crap that got you too scared to give it a chance. I should have—"

"I'm not afraid," Stormy cut in. "I want Luke in that way, more every time I see him, but—"

"But what, kid? Why not jump him and take what you can get?"

Although she found the idea of doing just that, or even *thinking* about following up on her desires, scandalous, Stormy thought about Calamity's suggestion. Really thought about it, and not for the first time, but the answer was the same as always. She sighed heavily as she said, "I can't. Not yet anyway, because that's not the way I want it to happen for me. Can you understand what I mean at all? It's important to me—I don't even know why—but it's important to me to be wed first."

"Uh, huh." Calamity sat back in her chair and linked her fingers across her belt buckle. "In that case, I'm gonna say this just one more time—jerk that line of yours out of Luke's pond *now,* and go dangle it somewhere's else."

"But Martha, what if I—"

"That's the end of it, kid." She pushed out of her chair and stretched her arms high overhead. "It's been one hellacious day and tomorrow ain't looking

any kinder what with Bill's funeral and all. I'm gonna
turn in early for a change and get some rest." As she
headed for her bedroom, she glanced over her shoulder to add, "Hell—I might even surprise old Bill by
stopping at the bathhouse first thing in the morning
before I pay him my last respects."

12

The following morning, Stormy and Calamity trudged up the steep incline behind the mule-drawn cart which carried the body of Wild Bill Hickok. His coffin, a hastily constructed crate made of raw pine, rattled against the wagon bed, creating a series of eerie, almost ghostlike thumps as the iron wheels bumped their way up the mountain slopes to Boot Hill. A crowd of black-draped mourners trailed the main procession, following the path to the cemetery like a column of ants.

Glancing down the hillside for her first really good look at the settlement below, Stormy could see the clear outline of the town. The principal streets of Deadwood—Main and Sherman—joined together in a V shape and then slithered out of view between the folds of the mountain range. The day was warm and bright, yet even under a full complement of sunshine, the thick pines were so deeply verdant, they seemed to fade into a dark shadowy purple along the horizon.

Stormy glanced toward Calamity, thinking of remarking on her observation, when something in her sister's expression stopped her cold. While she wasn't stone-faced or somber, Calamity seemed curiously detached, insulated against her pain as well as the whispered comments of the crowd following behind.

Today the murmurs were not filled with innuendo, as was the norm when conversation centered on Deadwood's most notorious woman, but with surprise. In fact, Martha "Calamity Jane" Cannary hadn't merely surprised but shocked them all—Stormy included—by turning up for Wild Bill's funeral in full female regalia.

She had draped herself in a black mourning gown complete with bustles, buttons that went all the way to her chin, and a simple gold brooch fastened at the throat. To that utterly proper beginning, she'd added her faded Cavalry scouting jacket. The contrast between the feminine dress and army coat would have been jarring enough, but she'd compounded the error by donning a wide-brimmed hat mounted high with ostrich feathers. The frothy profusion of plumes dyed in shades of pink, purple, and white made her look as if she were wearing a berry meringue pie on her head.

Trying not to appear too preoccupied by her sister's eccentric appearance, Stormy glanced down at her own dark green dress. It was stylish, if a few years out of date, finished with a matching black-and-green jacket, and topped with her saucy, slightly damaged velvet hat. Yet instead of feeling proper and ladylike beside her more garish sister, she felt drab, almost spinsterish. More than spinsterish—alone.

It was not because of Calamity's apathy this morning, Stormy realized, but because of Luke. She hadn't seen him anywhere. Not at the cabin where he'd been detained for the evening, and not in front of Smiling Will's Grocery, where the mourners had met for the procession up the hill. What if he'd broken out of the cabin and gone after McCall? she thought with horror. Or maybe he'd only attempted to escape, and in the ensuing melee been wounded or . . . worse.

At the crest of the knoll where Boot Hill began, the procession came to a halt. Stormy glanced at the scattered headstones, some sticking straight out of the ground, others listing at impossible angles, and then looked beyond them to the perimeters of the cemetery. There, almost hidden by a small stand of young pines, stood Luke and a pair of "deputies."

"He's here!" she blurted out.

"That he is," Calamity agreed solemnly, staring straight ahead as several men removed the casket from the cart. "Did you happen to take a look at my Bill 'fore they nailed the coffin shut?"

Berating herself for being so insensitive—so selfish as to be thinking of Luke instead of Hickok— Stormy's gaze fell to the ground as she murmured, "No, I'm afraid I didn't."

"You should have," her sister said, shaking her head slowly. "Bill's was about the prettiest corpse I ever did see."

Stormy swallowed a groan, but couldn't quite hide her grimace as an image of the dead man came to mind.

Calamity, whose attention had been diverted

toward the stand of trees, never saw or heard her response. She reached out blindly, slapping Stormy's shoulder, and hollered, "Hey, kid! Lookie over yonder— Luke went and made it to Bill's funeral after all! See him hiding in the pines?"

Stormy nodded weakly. "Yes, I do. Maybe I ought to go over and ask him to join us."

"Nah. He ain't gonna come over here with them two fellahs a-guarding him." Calamity frowned but just as quickly brightened as she suggested, "I don't see the harm if you go join him. Hell, this is a funeral, not a social, and 'sides, I bet ol' Luke could use a friendly face about now."

"B-but I was going to stay with you during the services. I thought you wanted me to—"

"Luke needs a friend right now a hell of a lot more than me and Bill do. I'm fine, kid. Now get on out of here."

"If you're sure you don't need me." At Calamity's nod of assurance, Stormy kissed her cheek. "My thoughts will be with you."

She weaved her way through the headstones, careful not to stumble over the jagged stumps of pines that had been chopped down to clear the area, and approached the tree line.

One of the guards called out to her. "Morning, ma'am. Something we can do for you?"

"There certainly is," she said, surprising herself with her own temerity. "You can leave me and Mr. McCanles alone to express our sympathies. Do you mind?"

One deputy glanced at the other, and then both

men shrugged. "Guess not." They walked away but repositioned themselves in the center of the grave-yard in order to have a view of both the services and their charge.

When she was sure the men were out of earshot, Stormy moved closer to Luke. His face was shadowed with heavy stubbles of a day-old beard, and dark smudges of exhaustion dulled the usual sparkle in his eyes. "I was worried about you last night. Are you all right?"

He nodded abruptly. "No need to worry. Nothing wrong with me that a little sleep won't cure." He removed his hat, glancing at hers as he smoothed his hair with his fingers. "I meant to tell you before; I like that bonnet a lot better than the other one."

She smiled and touched the velvet. "Rain splatters and all?"

"You could dip it in mud, and I'd still like it better." He inclined his head toward the crowd gathering around the gravesite. "Speaking of hats, I couldn't help but notice you and another gal following behind the wagon when you got to the top of the hill. Who in the hell was that walking with you?"

A little chuckle sneaked out before Stormy could stop it. "*That* was my sister, Miss Martha Jane Cannary."

Luke whipped his dark head around. "*Calamity?*" He looked back at the crowd, narrowing his focus on the woman in question. Whistling softly, he said, "I'll be go to hell. Calamity in a *dress*. How in God's name did you get her into it?"

"I didn't have a thing to do with it. She took off early this morning for the bathhouse, and then met me at Will's like everyone else. I was as surprised to see her like this as you are."

Again he whistled. "How's she doing otherwise? You know. About Bill."

"Fine," she said automatically, frowning as she added, "At least, I think she is."

"Why do you say that?"

Stormy shrugged. "I don't know exactly, but it seems that she's a little too accepting of Bill's death. Too *calm* about the whole thing. Do you know what I mean?"

Luke knew precisely. Calm, he understood from recent experience, could mask a lot of things—sorrow, grief, anger. In his case, white-hot rage. But he hinted at none of them. He just shrugged and said, "She's tough. She'll be just fine."

From across the way, Preacher Smith announced the beginning of the services. A hush fell over the crowd. Smith spoke highly of Hickok, dwelling on his days as a peace officer in particular, and then went on to lament his senseless death. With a fully supportive crowd egging him on, the preacher ended his sermon with a plea for justice.

"... and although I have no doubt whatsoever that Mr. McCall did indeed murder James Butler Hickok, I shudder to think what the result might have been had the jury returned a verdict of guilty in this case. Private parties must not and cannot take the law into their own hands!" His frock coat blew open as he raised his hands high. "If, heaven forbid, our community suffers another homicide—and this seems likely when you consider nearly half a dozen men have been killed each day in these parts over the past few weeks—let us proceed in a manner befitting an intelligent people. It is time we appointed a U.S. deputy marshal, a man sworn to take offenders to Yankton where they will have justice meted out in proportion to the crime."

He clasped his hands at his waist and lowered his head. "Let us pray now for an end to the killings and a new beginning for Deadwood. Let us pray for all these things as we pray for the soul of our brother, James Butler Hickok."

Their heads still bowed, each consumed by their own thoughts, Luke and Stormy remained silent as the crowd began to file away from the grave site. Shortly after that, acting Sheriff Brown approached the stand of pines holding a pair of pearl-handled guns.

"McCanles, Miss Cannary," he said, nodding as he greeted them. "As far as I'm concerned, my sheriffing days are over." He handed the pistols to Luke. "I hope you'll be smart enough to stick around town. Ain't nothing you can do about McCall now, and besides—we need you here."

Luke took the guns and slammed them into their holsters. "I don't know what in hell for."

Brown's response was a tight smile. "Talk has it that you'd fill those U.S. deputy sheriff boots just fine. We need someone with your reputation, a man who can handle a pair of Colts the way you do."

"The *last* thing you need is someone like me cleaning up this town."

Brown sighed. "Just promise you'll at least think about it. We're counting on you, McCanles."

Luke pressed his lips together and gave Brown a short, noncommittal nod.

"Thanks. And one other thing." He canted his head toward Hickok's final resting place. Two young men were shoveling dirt into the grave, the hollow *thump* each shovelful made as it hit the coffin echoing along the mountaintops. "Try not to think about that too much. Hickok was a fine man, but this ain't worth getting yourself killed over. He just caught a lousy break."

"About as lousy a break as a fellah can catch, wouldn't you say?"

"Yeah. I guess it was at that." Brown's gaze darted from Luke to Stormy. He touched the brim of his hat. "Good day, ma'am." And then, turning back to Luke, he added, "Sorry about the inconvenience last night. You understand we was just doing our duty." He turned on his heel then, joined his "deputies," and started for town.

"Son of a bitch," Luke muttered, forgetting that he wasn't alone.

"He's right, you know. Preacher Smith, too. You can't expect this town to survive if people keep taking the law into their own hands . . . unless, of course, you *are* the law."

Luke snorted. "Are you suggesting what I think you are?"

"That you'd make a fine sheriff? Yes."

He laughed bitterly. "You don't have any idea what you're talking about, lady."

"I don't?" Her mood lifting a little, she said, "Then why don't you tell me what I don't know."

Luke knew but two things for certain as he stood at the edge of the graveyard. He didn't want to become the sheriff of Deadwood, and he didn't want to talk. Not to Stormy. Not to anybody. He sighed heavily and glanced around the cemetery. The mourners had gone back to town and their own lives, leaving just the boys, who were still working on Hickok's grave, and Calamity, a sad figure who stood nearby watching them. Without returning his gaze to Stormy, he said, "Maybe we can talk about this some other time. I think now you ought to join your sister."

Stormy had a pretty good idea that Luke was trying to evade her, but she didn't push the issue. She turned and called across the cemetery, "Are you ready to go yet?"

As if she hadn't heard the question, Calamity hollered back, "Wasn't that a great sermon? Could ya hear over there?"

"We heard just fine," Luke called back. "I'm sending your sister back to you now."

"Don't bother!" She turned and started down the hill. "I got other plans. You keep her."

Chuckling to herself, Stormy said, "I get the feeling she doesn't want to be seen in that dress any longer than necessary. What do you think?"

Again Luke sighed, this time with a weariness that went all the way to the bone. "I gave up thinking sometime around dawn."

If she'd seen pain in his expression, or even heard it in his tone, Stormy might have gone on and left him alone. But pain wasn't what she saw in Luke's lusterless eyes. He looked despondent, lost somehow. Unable to leave him in such a state, she took hold of his hands. "Come on. Let's get out of here. Is it safe to walk in these woods?"

He resisted. "Thanks, Stormy, but I'm really not in the mood for a walk. Why don't you go on back to town."

"Oh, come on!" she persisted, this time pulling him forward. "Show me around—I haven't been out of that smelly gulch since the day I arrived."

Curiously enough, as he considered her proposal, the burden which had weighed so heavily on Luke's heart and mind seemed to lift a little. Why not take a little walk? Hell, it might even do him some good. "All right, but I have to warn you—if you're expecting a tour of the Black Hills from me, I might just get you lost. My internal compass has failed me every day of my life since I was born. Spin me around in a circle, and I couldn't even find Lead from here."

Stormy looked up in surprise. "But how can that be? In one of the romances I read about you—I think it was called *Lucky Luke, the Indian Slayer*—you were a *guide!*"

Luke rolled his eyes. Those damn novels again, tall tales written to set the readers' hearts a flutter with nary a kernel of truth to them. He ought to set her straight about his fictional life once and for all, he thought with a twinge of guilt.

He really should, but he didn't. As they began walking, Luke found himself bluffing instead as he explained, "That was different. Knowing north from south is less important than reading tracks."

"Oh." Stormy was apparently satisfied by his answer.

Pleased with the deception, if not proud, Luke cleared a path through a thick tangle of deadwood and brambles, and followed the edge of the slope until it narrowed into a small ravine. Steering her toward the little valley, their steps cushioned by a thick matting of pine needles and the damp earth beneath it, Luke was pleasantly surprised to discover they'd reached a pretty little stream.

"Want to rest here a spell?" he suggested, enticed by the lush green meadow, the thickets of aspen and willow lining the creek, and the tall pines overhead.

"Yes. Oh, yes!" If ever she'd seen heaven, this was it. Stormy sank down onto the thick blanket of grass, carefully tucking her legs beneath her skirt. "It's so beautiful here, it's hard to believe there's a town just below us." She breathed deeply, sucking in the clean pine-scented air, and was at once struck by the contrast between the fresh forest and the horrid odors wafting throughout the roadways below. "Just imagine how wonderful this entire area will be once Deadwood is cleaned up—and I mean the streets as well as the rowdy citizens."

Luke sat down beside her, stretched his legs out, and leaned back on his elbows. "Whether this town gets respectable or not is none of my concern. I don't plan to be around long enough to see it happen."

"You're thinking of leaving Deadwood?" At his nod, she gasped. "But surely you're not still planning to go after Jack McCall!"

"I can't just let the bastard get away with this!"

"But *Luke*—"

"I *know* McCall's lying about the murder of his brother, I know it! Bill didn't do it, that's for sure, and if it's the last thing I ever do, I'll prove it!"

"But what possible good will it do for you to hunt

the man down? He's been acquitted. You'll be the one in trouble with the law, not him."

Luke had thought of little else during the night: How to find McCall, what to do when they met again, how to justify killing the man without finding himself at the end of a hangman's rope. And he had come up short of ideas. He sighed. "I'm not thinking of running blindly after him. Hell, I wouldn't know where to look by now anyway." Or *how*, he amended silently.

He picked a blade of grass and slipped it between his teeth. "A man like that is bound to have a lot of enemies. If I don't get him, someone else will. Hell— maybe I should just leave it to Colorado Charlie. I've never been much good at getting revenge anyway."

As she thought back to the night she'd removed the slivers from Luke's arm, there was no question in Stormy's mind that he was referring as much to his own father's death as he was to Hickok's murder. Had he opened that topic for discussion? Hesitantly, she said, "You know, you never did explain why you stayed on with Mr. Hickok after you tried to shoot him. I realize that you became very good friends, but how did you get over your hatred for him after what he'd done to your family?"

Luke gave her a sideways glance. He'd been sure he didn't want to talk—especially about a subject as sensitive as this—but as he pulled the blade of grass from his mouth, he found himself saying, "Simple. Bill was right. My father was wrong."

"That doesn't make any sense to me, Luke. How could you even have *spoken* to the man who killed your father, much less become his friend? How could you just forget your loss so easily?"

"Forget?" Luke uttered a short, harsh grunt. "I've never forgotten a day of it." He began picking pebbles out of the grass, surprised at how easily he was discussing what had long been a closed subject. "My father wasn't what you'd call a very nice man. Some even suggested that he was the leader of a gang. I don't know about that, and I guess I never will. I just know that he stole some money from the county we were living in and ran off leaving us behind."

"You mean he abandoned his family? Your mother, too?"

"He sure as hell did," he replied, thinking of Sarah Shull. "He didn't have much use for any of us until almost a year later. That's when he sent for us—my mother, my younger brother, and me. We joined him at Rock Creek, a little settlement in Nebraska Territory."

"I remember reading about Rock Creek," she said, recalling an article she'd seen in *Harper's New Monthly* magazine. "That's where the McCanles Massacre took place, right?"

He laughed. "There was no massacre, Stormy. Just three men were killed that day. My father, who was pretty much the local bully by then, hired a couple of thugs and then got into an argument with the man who ran the Pony Express station set up on our property. My brother was with him that day, and Bill had just stopped by the station. The argument got out of hand, shots were fired, and that was the end of David McCanles and the men he'd hired."

"And your brother saw it all?"

Luke draped his arms across his knees. "I don't know if he actually saw what happened or not. By the time he got home, he had one story for me and one for my mother." He shook his head. "That boy must have changed the facts about a dozen times, but the story my mother believed, the one that made her beg me to go after Hickok and settle the score, was the one charging *Bill* as the leader of a massacre." He glanced at Stormy. "That, by the way, is also the story the newspapers picked up, and probably the one you read."

Shrugging because she couldn't remember any of the details of the massacre, she said, "If your brother actually reported that Mr. Hickok had murdered your father, why didn't your mother call in the law?"

"Oh, but we did!" Again he shook his head. "The whole damn family marched into Beatrice, our territorial government, and swore out warrants for Hickok's arrest. He was released at the preliminary hearing after pleading self-defense in the protection of company property."

"But if Mr. Hickok was found innocent, why did you go after him?"

"McCall was acquitted too . . . remember?"

Stormy lowered her gaze and whispered a faint, "Oh."

Luke hated to see her so distressed, especially since he hadn't been completely honest with her. He climbed to his feet and said, "There's a little more to it than that. When we got home from the hearing, my mother begged me as the oldest son to go after Bill and see justice done."

Stormy raised her hand, and Luke tugged her up from the grass. As she dusted the back of her dress, he went on, "I guess you could say my mother was desperate for justice, willing to sacrifice her firstborn to get it on the chance it might help wipe away her pain."

"And you thought by killing Bill you could gain favor in her eyes, or at least ease the hurt of your father's death?"

"I suppose that's what I thought at first." He laughed bitterly and tossed a pebble into the stream. "Later it came to me that what she really needed was some kind of justice for the hurt she'd suffered while David McCanles was *alive*." At her shocked gasp, Luke placed a finger over Stormy's lips so he could finish. "When my father left us behind in North Carolina, he didn't leave town alone. He took another woman with him."

"Oh, Luke." She slipped her hand between his arm and rib cage and gave him a gentle squeeze. "How awful that must have been for your mother— for all of you."

"Yeah," he said so softly she almost couldn't hear it. "Trouble was," he added, flinching as he recalled the sting of splinters all over his body, "shortly after we arrived in Nebraska, my mother discovered that he was still keeping that woman in a house just outside of town."

"How perfectly horrid!"

"It was certainly that, and, I suppose, part of the reason she sent me after Bill. My father had robbed her of her pride, and there wasn't a thing she could do about it. Instead, I think maybe she hoped to find her revenge with the death of the man who robbed her of her husband."

"And so you, hardly more than a boy, tried to kill Mr. Hickok."

Luke couldn't help but laugh at the picture he must have made by stalking Wild Bill Hickok. Still chuckling, he said, "I'll never know exactly what Bill thought when he saw this snot-nosed kid calling him out, but after the smoke cleared, he sat me down and told me exactly what happened at the station. His version matched one of the stories my brother told, and I knew then for sure that he was telling the truth."

"And so you decided to stay with him? What about your family?"

Luke averted his gaze, his jaw clenched. She'd finally touched on the subject he'd hoped to avoid, but how could he now? And what difference did it make any longer? "I couldn't give my mother the peace of mind she needed," he admitted with a candor that surprised him. "I failed her, and I guess I just couldn't face her."

"But Luke, I'm sure she would have—"

"It doesn't matter now," he said cutting her off. "Bill understood at the time. I was just a kid of fourteen when I went after him. The ten-year difference in our ages at that time was considerably wider than it is—was—now. He taught me to shoot, ride, and just plain be a man. In a real sense, I suppose you could say he became my family. He sure as hell filled in as father, the difference being that Bill Hickok was a hell of a lot better man than David McCanles ever was."

At that admission, Stormy uttered a low murmur of understanding, but Luke didn't look at her. He couldn't. A sense of shame washed over him, a feeling of regret as he thought of his lost family. At once, and for the first time ever, his failure to ease his mother's troubled mind seemed small beside such a loss. Luke hurled the rest of the pebbles into the stream, blasting vicious darts of water up along the bank where a small flock of sparrows pecked at the earth. They fluttered up into the trees, squawking their complaints at the disturbance, and then drifted back down to their feeding grounds one at a time.

Stormy circled him until they were standing face-to-face. Smiling up at him, she lightly touched his chest with her fingertips as she said, "Thank you for being so honest with me. I know how difficult it can be to discuss family matters—even within your own family."

In control of his emotions again, Luke returned her smile and tapped the tip of her nose. "My family history isn't a pretty one. Yours has to be better."

Stormy laughed. "You already know my sister Martha. I'm afraid the rest of us are pretty boring by comparison."

Not so, Luke thought, once again admiring her dimples, the silver sparkles in her eyes. He wondered if the others were like Stormy or her rough-and-tumble sister. "Do you really have three little ones somewhere?"

"Oh, yes! I hope to receive a wire from Brigham Young any day now telling me where they might have been taken by their adoptive families, but even if he doesn't answer me, I intend to start looking for them by next spring. By myself if I have to."

Luke felt humbled by her resolve, small even, in the face of such devotion. He didn't know how to respond, so he just said, "That's, ah, nice. Really nice."

Stormy playfully slapped at him. "I told you the Cannary family is boring. I'd rather hear more about your fascinating life. Tell me about your 'scout of the plains' adventures. Did you really spend a whole year doing nothing but hunting buffalo and trapping beaver in hostile Indian territory? And what about your years with Buffalo Bill and his theatrical troupe? That must have been *so* exciting!"

Humbled once again by a sensation he'd never experienced before meeting her—guilt over a female's adoration of his fictional persona—Luke rolled his eyes. "It's nothing, Stormy, really. I don't want to talk about it."

She winked and flashed a grin. "Aren't you the modest one! Why if even *half* of your exploits in the novel *Lucky Luke's First Trail,* are true, you're nothing less than a national hero!"

Luke had grown so uncomfortable with the conversation, he simply couldn't chance another barrage of compliments. He took Stormy's hands between his and said, "Thanks for all the kind words, but I think we ought to head back now. I need to get some sleep."

"Of course, Luke. I'd forgotten how tired you must be." She started to pull her hands from his when a sudden, undeniable impulse struck her—she had to kiss him. When they'd begun their walk, Luke had been sullen and grief-stricken, and unwilling participant. But now he was smiling at her, actually smiling.

As if somehow in the throes of all his sadness, he'd found some solace in talking to her. Gripped with a happiness she couldn't deny, Stormy's heart seemed to blossom in her breast as she leaned in close to him and said, "There's just one other thing before we go. I'd like to kiss you. May I?"

Caught off guard, Luke stumbled backward, feeling awkward, confused. "I, ah, guess you didn't notice, but I wasn't given much chance to shave this morning."

Stormy moved close again. "I don't mind. Really I don't." At his look of indecision, she added, "It's not as if I'm planning to kiss you all the way to hell and back. I simply want to kiss you. Is that all right?"

Her dimples flashed, and suddenly Luke couldn't imagine what had held him back in the first place. He grabbed his hat by the crown, removed it, and then waited. "Be my guest, sweetheart."

He didn't have to wait long. Stormy leaned toward him again, almost, but not quite touching his body. Then she slowly slid her hands up to either side of his face, caressing him for a long moment before she finally touched her lips to his cheek, stubbles and all. Her kiss was so gentle, so very tender, at first Luke wasn't sure if he'd imagined the sensations. But then those satiny lips fluttered to his other cheek, and finally moved over to his mouth where they landed so softly and delicately he was stunned by the intimacy it suggested.

She stepped away from him and smiled, those dimples dipping to new depths, and Luke couldn't help but return her grin. What in *hell* was going on here?

he wondered. With her or him? He recalled the way she had clung to him during the trial last evening, sharing his pain and anger no matter how uncommunicative he was, and then he thought of how she'd sought him out at the funeral. Now this, a gesture of affection beyond anything he'd ever experienced.

Although he had no idea what was going on, Luke gave up on thinking and let instinct guide him. He tossed his hat to the ground and wrapped his arms around her. In a voice thick with emotion, he said, "You're something, woman, you know that? You make me, I don't know . . . *feel* something, too."

With just a hint of hope in her tone, Stormy asked, "And what do you think that might be?"

"I told you, I don't know. Maybe there isn't a word for it." Luke tucked her head beneath his chin and continued holding her close, swinging her gently in his arms. Then it occurred to him that what he felt might have a name after all. Releasing her with an abruptness, Luke bent down to retrieve his hat. "Let's go back now."

"Oh . . . of course." Stormy did her best to hide her disappointment as she fell in step with Luke, but inside, she felt as if her heart would break in two. They'd been so close for those few moments, she'd felt almost like a part of him, especially as he held her in his arms. What had gone wrong? She knew that the things they'd discussed had been difficult for him and that he'd probably never really talked about his family with anyone else before, but she was just as sure that he'd been the better for it when they finished.

How could he have grown so cold, and so quickly? And why? The Luke she'd glimpsed—the real man, she suspected—had simply faded away, blending into the lavender horizon along with the thick forests.

As she walked alongside him toward Deadwood's muck-strewn avenues, Stormy couldn't help but wonder, Would he ever let her get this close again?

Over the next few days, Stormy felt as if she were walking on eggs around both Calamity and Luke. If one was ornery, the other was sulky, and vice versa, until she wasn't sure she wanted to open the door to either of them ever again. It wasn't that she didn't understand their suffering or the various and unexpected ways grief had of manifesting itself. She'd dealt with that kind of anguish after her mother's and father's funerals, and to a lesser extent had grieved for her lost brothers and sisters every day since the family had broken apart. What she didn't understand was how to help these two in their time of need.

Calamity was slipping back into her old habits, even to the point of either forgetting to get orders for taffy during her excursions to the badlands or just plain neglecting to deliver the orders she already had. Even worse, her bout of temperance had come to an end, and she'd started drinking again, a little more heavily as each day passed. Stormy had tried to suggest that she slow down, but Martha had let her know in no uncertain terms that she was "Calamity Jane and I can say and do what I want to!"

Luke, she suspected, had also been hitting the

bottle more than usual. She'd only seen him during daylight hours of late, and when they did meet their conversation always drifted to his vacillation about remaining in Deadwood. While he hadn't actually made up his mind to go, he'd never hinted that she might be worth staying for. And right or wrong, grieving or not, his ambivalence hurt her.

Dwelling once again on Luke's suddenly indecisive nature, Stormy gave the rope of molasses taffy she was pulling a vicious twist. Then somebody beat on the cabin door.

"Eee—ya—haaa!" Calamity roared through the new pine slats. "Open up, li'l sis!"

Grumbling, Stormy removed the length of taffy from the bedpost she used as a stretcher. She dropped the candy on the marble slab, wiped her hands on her apron, and then went to the door to let her sister in.

Without so much as a hello, Calamity stumbled into the cabin, nearly tripping over the part of the floor she'd shot up, and then propped herself against the wall. Grinning crookedly, she hiccuped and said, "Morning, kid."

Although she knew exactly what time it was, Stormy glanced out at the sky as she closed the door. "It's evening, not morning. After seven, I'd say."

"No matter, kid." Calamity pulled a small flask from inside her jacket, unscrewed the top, and took a swallow from it.

"Why don't you go on to bed? You look tired, and I have a lot of work to do."

Calamity shook her head vigorously and little bits

of dust sprinkled down her rawhide jacket. "Shut up, kid. Just shut up and listen." She wiped her nose. "I got to tell you something, and you got to listen straight out 'cause I don't think I can say it but once't."

"I'm listening."

"I just stopped by to tell you I'll be gone a few days. Don't want you to worry none about me."

"You have another delivery for No-Teeth?"

She hiccuped and took another swig of whisky. "No. I just got to leave. I got some problems—" She beat on her chest. "Hurts like hell in here. I just got to go, you know, forget about it for a few days."

"Go? But where? Why leave?"

Calamity staggered over to where Stormy stood. "I'm riding up to Lead or maybe Central City for a few days. Got to meet up with the fellahs and have a drink or two to get rid of this—" Again she beat her chest. "Can't stand the way this feels! Now let me by."

"Oh, but—do you have to go? Why don't you just stay here in Deadwood?" At Calamity's incredulous look Stormy added, "I promise I won't say a word about your drinking ever again. If that's what you have to do to get Mr. Hickok's death out of your system, I swear I won't say a word or try to stop you."

"Hickok? He ain't got nothing to do with this." She pounded her chest this time. "He ain't got nothing to do with nothing." She wiped her nose again, dragging a few tears off her cheeks in the process. "I got to leave 'cause I don't want you to see me like this."

"Calamity, please listen to me!" Stormy implored. "I don't care if you get so drunk you can't crawl. Do you hear me? It doesn't matter."

Calamity swayed. "It matters to me, kid." She dragged the sleeve of her jacket across her face. "For the first time in my life it matters—and I'm gonna make damn sure you don't never see me like this again. Now get out of my way."

She barreled her way to the door, leaving Stormy with no choice but to follow along behind her. "All right!" she cried to her back. "Go if you must, but please wait until morning when you're . . . feeling better. Please?"

Calamity jerked the door opened. "Gotta go *now*." She stumbled over the threshold and grabbed hold of the jamb to steady herself. "You get that pole over this door and leave it there, you hear?"

"Please don't go tonight," Stormy begged in a last effort. "Wait until tomorrow."

But Calamity went on as if she hadn't heard her. "Don't let no one in here while I'm gone, especially not Luke."

"Luke? But why wouldn't—"

"I don't like the way he's been carrying on tonight." She wiped her nose again. "If he comes by, you be sure and don't let him in. That crazy bastard's on some kind a rampage."

13

After her sister left, the only disturbance in Stormy's small part of town came when one of the neighbors discovered that his mule was missing. Calamity, it seemed, had "borrowed" her transportation to Lead. Other than that, all was painfully quiet. No howling coyotes, no whistling winds, and most noticeable of all, no Luke banging on the door.

Stormy fixed herself a small supper of bacon and beans when her candymaking chores were finished, and then took the family Bible from her trunk and carried it to the table. With no clear understanding of why she'd chosen to peruse it on this particular night, she turned up the lampwick and opened it to her father's wide, slashing scrawl on the overleaf: "Property of Robert and Charlotte Cannary, given by Grandfather Cannary on the occasion of the birth of our first child, Martha Jane Cannary. May 1, 1852, Princeton, Missouri."

Stormy sighed as she brushed her fingers across her father's handwriting, and closed her eyes. She thought of her days in Princeton, especially of the thick pine forests behind her grandfather's cornfields and the yellow-green foliage of nearby sycamore trees. She recalled lazy summer days spent racing around the muddy shores of their favorite swimming hole with Martha and neighboring youngsters, and nights watching her father read this very same Bible.

She couldn't remember her grandfather's name. Grandfather Cannary was all she'd ever known, and all she ever would know, it seemed. He and her grandmother were long since dead, as were her parents. Who would remember *her,* she suddenly wondered? Would anyone ever care enough to write her name in a family Bible?

Disturbed by her wandering thoughts, Stormy opened her eyes and slowly thumbed through the book. What was it she expected to find in these pages, she wondered. Answers? To what? Surely biblical passages couldn't help her to make up her mind about Luke. She would have to decide on her own whether to keep her love for Luke hidden or to go seek him out and let him know how she felt. The latter didn't sound plausible for someone as reserved as Stormy, and yet, what else was she to do? Sit there night after night and hope that he'd figure it out on his own? And what if he just rode out of her life without so much as a good-bye?

Sighing with frustration, Stormy thought of the many nights her father had sat by the fire reading this Bible. What had he found in its gilded pages? Solace and comfort, she supposed, and maybe the strength to go on living with his flamboyant wife. Or had he needed that? As she considered it, Stormy realized she couldn't honestly remember a day when her father wasn't happy, or any instance in which he'd seemed the least bit regretful that he'd married Charlotte—wild, wicked woman that she may have been. Maybe that's what reading the Bible had given him: a way to accept the ones he loved for what they were, sinners and saints alike.

Stormy finally decided to close the Bible when she realized she was reading the same passage again and again, yet not quite getting its message. She yawned, unaware until then of how late the hour had gotten, and rose from her chair. She'd just taken her nightgown from the nail on the back of the bedroom door when a knock sounded at the front of the cabin.

She froze for a moment, gown still in hand, and then tiptoed across the room.

"Stormy?" Luke called through the split logs. "You awake?"

She remembered Calamity's warnings. *He's on a rampage.* Luke didn't sound like his usual mirthful self, but his tone was hardly that of a crazy man. Why not let him inside?

The door rattled as Luke pounded on it again. "Stormy? Open up!"

"Ah, just a minute," she finally answered as she tossed her nightgown on the bed. After quickly untying her soiled apron, she hurled it to the loft above, straightened her skirt, and smoothed the sides of her hair back. Then she opened the door.

Luke stood just back from the threshold, feet apart, arms at his sides. He was rumpled, his white dress shirt opened at the throat, and he wasn't wearing a tie, a vest, or the jacket that matched his charcoal trousers. He looked weary but edgy as he peered in through the doorway, staring at her in a way he'd never done before. His gaze was intense and so full of implication Stormy felt as if she could reach out and pull his darkest thoughts inside the room. Maybe opening the door hadn't been such a good idea after all.

"Aren't you going to invite me in?" he asked, his voice deep, husky.

"Oh . . . of course." Throwing her reservations aside, she allowed him to enter.

After pulling the door shut behind him, Luke removed his hat. He didn't spin it toward the usual bedpost but dropped it onto the bed. Square in the middle of her nightgown.

Stormy swallowed hard and then took a breath. She picked up the aroma of whisky. "Can I make some coffee for you?"

"I didn't come here for refreshments."

Luke pinned her with his gaze, stinging her with its intensity. Stormy backed away from him, both frightened and thrilled at once. She felt a nervous twitter quivering in her throat, but she couldn't seem to quell it as she swallowed again and sputtered, "C-Calamity warned me you were in a bit of a mood tonight." She laughed, the sound high-pitched, girlish. "She even suggested that I keep the door locked if you should stop by."

Luke advanced on her. "Maybe," he murmured, "you should have listened to your sister."

He was close—too close. Stormy braced her arms, holding him off as she said, "Luke, please stop it. You're scaring me. What's wrong with you?"

Holding back for a moment, he admitted, "I don't know for sure. I just know that I'm tired—tired of pretending, of lying, of playing games. I've decided it's time to make a few decisions."

"A-about . . . leaving Deadwood?"

"Among other things." Luke brushed her hands aside, his movements rough, jerky, and tugged her into his arms. "Is there any reason for me to stay?"

He fit her body to his, adjusting each of her curves to complement his angles, and then leaned forward just enough to bend her spine. Stormy's head fell back, exposing her throat, and Luke's mouth immediately went to that most vulnerable of areas. He kissed her wildly, moving as far down her neck as her blouse would allow, and then maneuvered his lips back up to her cheek where he paused, breathing heavily.

"I'd have left town three days ago if not for you," he whispered against her skin, his voice dark and thick. "You're the reason I'm still here. Because of you."

In spite of the heavy aroma of whisky and the glaze in his dark eyes, Stormy tried to reason with him. "Then you're mad, is that it? Mad at me for keeping you here?"

"I'm mad all right." He lifted Stormy off her feet, spreading kisses across her cheeks and mouth, muttering between those kisses, "Crazy, in fact. Crazy to have you."

Before she could react to either his suggestion or the fact that he'd carried her across the room, Luke propped her against the cabin wall near the bedroom door. Then slowly he let her slide down through the circle of his arms while he positioned his hard thigh between her legs. His hands slid to her bottom where he lifted, then settled her, even more intimately. He began kissing her again—this time, all the way to hell and back.

Stormy's mind, her body, everything, seemed to be spinning completely out of control. Luke was kissing her in a way he'd never kissed her before, with so much heat and passion, she feared they might catch fire. His hands were on her, stroking her everywhere, *feeling* her through her clothing. She couldn't breathe, couldn't think, could only feel.

Hoping that if she got her feet back down on the floor, she might be able to regain at least a bit of her reasoning powers, Stormy tried to slide down off his thigh. The friction that the movement created between her and Luke sent a current of electricity through her entire body, scattering sparks of desire to all of her nerve endings. She gasped for breath and sought to regain her balance.

Luke released Stormy's lips and leaned back just enough to focus on her expression. Liking what he saw there, he locked her in his equally heated gaze. "It seems to me that you're done playing games, too. I want you, Stormy, and tonight by God, I mean to have you." He nudged her with his thigh, slowly moving it up, and then down. "I think it's time we went to my hotel room."

Stormy tried to catch her breath. Luke's scent was all around her, in her, that same earthy blend of smoke, whisky, and sheer masculinity that had been invading her body night after night as she slept on his pillow. He was a part of her already, she realized, inside her in all but the most basic and animalistic of ways. Why *not* allow this final penetration? she wondered through a fog of passion. What had she been saving herself for if not this man she loved?

Luke sensed that she was wavering. Keeping his voice low, he reminded her, "You already broke the one rule by kissing me with a faceful of whiskers—and I didn't even ask you for the favor. It's time to break that last rule, Stormy. Come back to my room with me now."

She wanted Luke badly, no question about that. If she were honest, she would have to admit she lusted for him. But incredibly, she heard herself say in a strangled whisper, "I . . . *can't.*"

Luke's spine stiffened as if he'd been shot, and then he released her so quickly she nearly turned her ankle when her feet hit the floor.

"That's it? You're sure that's your final answer?"

Afraid of what she might see if she were to look at him, afraid of herself, too, she hung her head and slowly nodded.

"You're tough, lady," Luke said, his black eyes aglow. "So tough you make your sister look like a preacher's wife."

Then, without another word, he turned on his heel and stomped out of the cabin.

Thirty minutes later, Stormy was still sitting on the bed, holding Luke's hat in her hand, stroking it. This was not his show hat but a plain black gambler whose low crown and curled brim were worn at the edges, ragged. That was how she felt. Her tears had dried some time ago, but the ache deep inside would take a lot longer to ease. After all, it wasn't every night she could boast of driving away both her newly found sister *and* the man she loved.

Stormy couldn't count the times she'd gotten up and thought of going after Luke, of boldly striding into every bar in Deadwood to find him and offer herself to him. The way she should have done earlier.

But each time her feet hit the floor, some vicious, hateful part of herself forced her back down on the bed as if it were determined to keep her from finding true happiness. And so she sat, still stroking Luke's hat, wishing it were him.

This time when a knock sounded at the door, Stormy was so entrenched in her reverie that she screamed as she cried, "Who's there?"

"It's Luke, Stormy," he said quietly, almost apologetically. "Let me in."

This time she didn't freeze or hesitate. Her heart in her throat, Stormy jumped off the bed and opened the door. As before, Luke stood just back of the threshold. He'd changed into a fresh white shirt, this one buttoned to his Adam's apple, and added a vest and jacket, but still no tie. He'd donned his show hat, the one made of black felt and silver conchos. She noticed too that he was freshly shaved and that he still smelled of whisky.

As he'd done earlier, he stared at her with an intensity that couldn't be denied, but this new look was as fresh as his clothing. Now Luke was cocky, confident, and maybe even a little drunk. For the second time that night, Stormy wondered if opening the door had been a mistake.

"Well?" he said. "Aren't you going to invite us in?"

"Us?" Stormy peered around Luke's shoulder and noticed that someone stood behind him. When she recognized the face of Judge Kuykendall, she gasped. "Oh, excuse me. Please—come in."

"Sorry to disturb you at this time of night, Miss Cannary," Kuykendall said as he strode into the cabin behind Luke. "But our friend Mr. McCanles insisted that you wanted to be married tonight."

Stormy's mouth fell open, but Kuykendall, who was looking at his pocket watch, didn't notice. He said, "Since it's nearly midnight, I think we'll have to get started if we're going to meet those requirements."

Her mouth still agape, Stormy glanced at Luke. *"Married?"*

"You win," he said, calling her bluff. "The judge brought his Bible and everything. Shall we let him get started?"

Finally able to close her mouth, Stormy glanced from Luke to the judge. The latter looked solemn and embarrassed, and the former mirthful, as if he couldn't quite keep from snickering. What exactly was going on? Was Luke playing a little joke on her, or was he actually asking for her hand? Thinking back on their earlier encounter, and more on her reaction after he'd left, Stormy decided she wouldn't be taking any more chances with her heart. She would call his bluff.

She brushed her hair back with her palms, straightened her plain brown skirt, and then turned to the judge and said, "I would imagine you're used to marrying folks who are a little more prepared than this."

Kuykendall chuckled quietly. "Against my better judgment, Miss Cannary, I have recently wed not one, but two couples of dubious reputation in the Bella Union Theater under far less appropriate conditions than these." He walked over to the table and opened the ledger he carried in addition to his Bible. "Your full name please?"

Stormy could feel Luke's eyes on her, but she didn't dare catch his gaze. Even if this turned out to be a joke of some kind, she had to play it out. With her chin high she said, "Ann Marie Cannary. Stormy is my nickname."

He nodded as he wrote, and then asked, "And your full name, Mr. McCanles?"

Luke cleared his throat, hoping to elicit some kind of response from Stormy, but she stared dead ahead at the judge. "Ah, it's Lucas David McCanles."

Silence hung over the trio as Judge Kuykendall finished his paperwork. When he finally straightened, and turned to them with Bible in hand, Stormy stepped forward and said, "Wait a minute, please."

Luke's breath whistled out in a relieved sigh.

Missing the significance of his reaction, Stormy walked over to the table and reached down to pick up her family Bible. "I'd appreciate it if you'd use this one instead of yours. It belonged to my father."

Luke's Adam's apple bulged against the inside of his collar, and suddenly he could hardly draw a breath. He stuck his finger between the shirt and his throat and tugged, loosening the material.

"Now, Mr. McCanles," Kuykendall said. "If you'll stand here." He pointed to a spot on the floor directly in front of him, and then at another alongside it, "and Miss Cannary, you can stand there."

Each cast a furtive glance toward the other, but both Luke and Stormy obeyed the judge's instructions.

When Kuykendall began the actual ceremony, the words he spoke were lost on Luke. He was too busy trying to figure out Stormy's next move, whether she would toss in her cards now or stay with the game a little longer. His gaze darted over to her time and time again, but not once did she turn to meet it. What did she intend to do? Run her bluff until the last possible moment? And just exactly what part of this ceremony *did* constitute the last moment?

Kuykendall droned on, delivering the shortest possible discourse on what they should each expect from the holy state of matrimony, and finally said, "Do you, Ann Marie Cannary, take Lucas David McCanles as your lawfully wedded husband to love, honor, and obey as long as you both shall live?"

Luke heard those words as clearly as if he'd spoken them, and this time when he glanced at Stormy, she met his gaze. *At last,* he thought, encouraged, *she's finally coming to her senses.* But after chewing her bottom lip for just a moment, she surprised him by quietly murmuring, "I do."

I do? He was alarmed and impressed by her spunk under fire. She looked calm, almost serene, her silvery eyes smiling on the judge. *Damn,* he thought with an ill-timed burst of admiration, *now here stands a woman who'd make one hellacious poker player.*

". . . and do you, Lucas David McCanles, take Ann Marie Cannary as your lawfully wedded wife to love and support as long as you both shall live?"

Dumbfounded, not sure when or where the ceremony would come to an end, or even more important, at what point it became *legal,* he tugged at his collar again.

"Mr. McCanles?" the judge asked, his brows raised. "Do you wish to take Miss Cannary as your bride?"

Stormy glanced over at Luke, smiled as if she knew something he didn't, and then looked away. He turned to the judge and said, "Hell, yes."

Judge Kuykendall solemnly shook his head, but closed the Bible and said, "That rather irreverent remark makes you husband and wife. You may kiss your bride, Mr. McCanles."

"What did you say?"

"Which part didn't you understand, Mr. McCanles?" Kuykendall asked with just a hint of weariness in his tone.

Luke pulled at his collar again, this time tearing the button free of the material. He gulped. "That's all there is to it?"

"You were the one in a big hurry. I simply try to please."

"B-but—I mean, is this, you know . . . *legal?*"

"I assure you," Kuykendall replied as he strode back to the table, "this wedding is as legal as any performed in the States." He wrote something in his ledger and then beckoned them over. "If you'll both sign at the bottom where I've put the X's, I'll be on my way home."

Painfully aware that Luke had yet to kiss his bride, Stormy joined the judge at the table and quickly wrote her maiden name for the last time.

Directly behind her, Luke stared at the ink as it dried on the page. When Stormy finished, she turned, handed him the pen, and stepped back out of his way. Still in shock as he leaned over the table, he turned toward the judge, and whispered, "Are you sure this is *really* legal, you know—legitimate?"

"Absolutely, Mr. McCanles. I can be both witness and preacher when necessary. Please sign your name so I can be on my way."

Without further hesitation, Luke bent down and scrawled the signature he'd affixed to thousands of theater programs throughout the years. The ceremony concluded, Kuykendall retrieved his pen, the ledger, and his Bible. Then Stormy saw him to the door.

After the judge had gone, she turned back to face her new husband. He was leaning against the table as if it were holding him up. Looking dazed now, not cocky, Luke repeatedly rubbed his hand back and forth across his mouth and chin.

Not sure what to make of this new expression, she said, "Do you still think we ought to go to the hotel, or would you rather stay here tonight?"

"Hotel?" Was this a dream, or had he just . . .

"It's probably a little nicer than this cabin, isn't it?"

He nodded, incapable of speech.

"I need to pack a few things, but I won't be a minute."

Luke watched as she took a small valise from her trunk and stuffed her nightgown, robe, and a few toiletries into it, but he felt as if he weren't in the same room with her—rather as if he were viewing some distant panorama through the glass eye of a telescope.

After slipping into her plain black jacket, Stormy walked over and stood by the door, valise in hand. "I'm ready."

Feeling numb from head to toe, Luke slowly crossed the room. *Jesus!* he thought, rapidly sobering as he led Stormy out of the cabin and into the alley. *It's true!* He'd gone and played a reckless hand of showdown, winner take all, and now he was a married man—*married!*

His thoughts jumbled, clouded by alcohol and panic, Luke somehow managed to guide Stormy across Main Street and then escort her into the Grand Central Hotel. Once inside the gaily decorated lobby, he quickly pulled her over to the landing at the stairs. Then, glancing around to make certain they were unobserved, he slipped the key to his room in the palm of her hand.

"You go on ahead," he whispered, wiping his brow. "It's room 302. I'll, ah . . . be along in a little while."

Pleased that he'd extended the courtesy of allowing her to prepare for their wedding night in privacy, Stormy brushed his cheek with her fingertips and lightly kissed his lips. "I promise I won't be too long." Then she spun around and started up the narrow staircase.

Luke remained on the landing, watching Stormy gracefully make her way up the steep flight of stairs and disappear around the bend at second floor. When she was out of view, he dragged his palm across his mouth again, and then backhanded the sweat from his brow.

From the reception desk, the clerk called out, startling him, "Evening, Mr. McCanles. I've never seen her in here before. Is the lady with you?"

Luke groaned, his face ashen, and turned toward the man. "The, uh, lady . . . well, you see, she isn't just *any* lady." The game was over, time to toss in his hand. He took a deep breath and finished the sentence. "That was my . . . wife."

The sound of those words coming from his very own mouth was a little too much, even for a seasoned gambler like Luke. He twisted his body, nearly falling over the rug he'd wound around his boot heel, and then bolted out the door.

14

Stormy lay alone in her marriage bed for what seemed like hours. She supposed her new husband was simply extending her a extra little time for privacy, but she couldn't help but wonder if some of the things she'd seen in his expression during the wedding ceremony had been genuine—shock, surprise, and even a little panic among them. Maybe, she thought in annoyance, if she'd bothered to read the entire text of Dr. Tuttle's guidebook, she wouldn't have to wonder why Luke hadn't yet joined her for their wedding night.

Stormy punched her pillow and rolled to the left side of the bed. If she hadn't been so preoccupied by the "forbidden" sections of that book, she might have learned a little more about what to expect after the "I do's." But instead, she'd rushed right ahead to what she'd thought were the titillating parts, filling her head with "crap," as her sister would put it, and now she didn't know whether to be pleased by Luke's overly thoughtful gesture, angry at his indifference, or worried about his safety. She only knew that earlier that evening, back in her cabin, Luke had given her a taste of the pleasure Martha had hinted at. And now she wanted more.

Restless, Stormy rolled over to her right and tried once again to fall asleep. Just as she began to drift off, she thought she heard a few muffled thumps coming from down the hall. Then the door to her room burst open. Jerking herself upright, her first impulse was to scream, but when her visitor's identity became clear in the glow of the hallway lamp she relaxed. It was Luke. And he appeared to be inebriated. He wavered in the doorway for a moment, and then stumbled across the threshold, kicking the door shut behind him.

With the room cloaked in darkness again, Stormy could no longer see anything of Luke except his vague shadow, but she could hear him quite well. He bumped into the dresser, knocking something to the floor with a crash—the lamp, she assumed—and then muttered an unintelligible oath under his breath as he worked his way toward the bed. His boots scuffled across the floor, moving ever closer, and she finally felt his weight as he sank onto the edge of the mattress.

Feeling awkward and more than just a little nervous, Stormy pulled the sheet up under her chin and quietly remarked, "I was beginning to think that I'd have to spend my wedding night alone."

Luke lurched forward, nearly falling to the floor,

but somehow managed to right himself as he whipped his head around and glanced at her.

"Well, I guess I'm here now, aren't I?"

He turned away from her, a thin beam of moonlight illuminating his profile and upper body, and began to strip off his clothing. Stormy watched, as alarmed by this coarse-sounding Luke as she was nervous, but managed in spite of her doubts to fill her gaze with the sight of her new husband as he disrobed. His back muscles worked to a satiny sheen, showing her his incredible strength, and Stormy trembled with as much fear as desire. When Luke unbuckled his belt and pushed his trousers down over his hips, she gave in to a sudden attack of nerves and slid down under the covers, her body going rigid.

Luke fell onto the bed and the mattress pitched, rolling her toward him. The aroma of whisky was strong, more pungent than ever, as he reached out for her in the darkness and warned, "Brace yourself, Mrs. McCanles. . . ."

"I know," she whispered, speculating on the rest of the sentence. "All the way to hell and back."

With a husky chuckle, Luke pulled her close. "You catch on fast. I like that in a woman." He tugged at her nightgown, pulling it up past her knees. "I like skin, too—what's all this you're wearing?"

Blushing from her toes to her forehead, Stormy tried to acquiesce to his demands. She reached for the satin ribbons at the throat of her nightie, carefully releasing the bow, and then paused, wondering how much of herself to reveal.

An impatient Luke made the decision for her. He

yanked the nightgown above her hips and slipped it over her head all in one quick movement. Chuckling again, this time more hoarsely, he tossed the gown across the room, and then fell on her, running his hands across her naked torso.

Luke's touch was raw, a little rougher than she would have liked, but Stormy moaned at the sensations, stiffening too, as her concern about the state of his mind grew. Luke gathered her in his arms and began to kiss her, his sensual mouth moving down from her lips to her throat, and then lower still to the small mounds of her breasts.

She gasped as he nuzzled there and drove her to near madness when he teased each nipple with his flickering tongue. Even though she still had misgivings about Luke's drunkenness, Stormy felt herself responding to him, swelling and blooming under his touch. Then he slid his hand down to her thighs, skimming the golden blond curls at the apex, and she sucked in her breath with both shock and surprise.

"You like that, huh," he said through a thick chuckle. Again he brushed his fingers across those silken curls, and then with a heavy sigh, Luke rolled to her side and nestled his head in the valley between her right arm and breast. "Umm, soft," he murmured, his voice faint, dreamlike. "You're so very . . . very . . . soft."

Stormy waited in the darkness, wondering what came next and when or if she ought to begin kissing him back. And waited a little longer. "Luke? What do you want me to do?"

He inhaled noisily, and his reply came out in the form of a snore.

The following morning, Stormy awoke with the dawn. Luke was lying next to her, one hand clasping her breast, the other tangled in her hair. His lashes, she noticed, were sooty, fanning the upper shelf of his cheekbones in far longer sweeps than any man had a right to. The waves of his hair had separated during the night, especially along his neckline and at the top of his brow where they veered away into thick curls. His dishevelment made him look adorable, innocent even—the exact opposite of the man who'd stumbled into her bed last evening.

How often was he like this? she wondered. Had she unwittingly married a drunk? The only time she'd ever seen Luke even slightly tipsy was on the day they'd met. She glanced at him again, still so appealing in sleep, and another thought tickled the back of Stormy's mind. Although she couldn't seriously believe that Luke might have been as nervous as she on their wedding night, maybe he'd needed a few drops of courage before coming to her as a husband. She could have used a couple of drinks herself.

Even now, she could hardly believe that she'd lain beside him stripped naked for the entire night! Stormy considered her circumstances, the sinfully delicious way she felt knowing that not only was she nude, but the six feet of muscular man beside her was naked as well.

She let her gaze drift from his handsome face

down past his chest. The sheet was draped across him there, barely hanging on his angular hipbone. If she were to catch a bit of material between her toes and pull, the cover might just slip completely off his body, exposing him. If that happened, Stormy thought with a wickedness that surprised her, she would finally get a look at this mysterious thing which . . .

Luke raised his arms high overhead and then flopped over on his back. Something bothered him, but before he could identify what it was, he became aware of an intense throbbing against his forehead. A mother lode of horrors was waiting just inside his brain, eager to remind him of exactly how much whisky he'd poured down his throat last night.

Desperate to avoid the confrontation, Luke tried to burrow his way back down into sleep. It didn't happen. Too much of last night had already floated to the surface of his thoughts, and way too many of those memories contained flashes of Stormy. His heartbeat picked up at the thought of her, beating a tattoo against his sensitive temples, yet oddly enough, the pain seemed to ease as her image grew clearer. Luke drew in a deep breath, recalling her scent so vividly he could almost taste the hint of vanilla and lemon that always seemed to surround her.

Again seeking comfort from his thoughts, a way to allow his throbbing head to drift into dreams of Stormy and things that could never be, Luke rolled back over on his side—and collided with something soft. He reached out blindly, groping what he instantly recognized as the body of a woman. With a heavy groan of surprise, he flipped over onto his back. *Jesus, McCanles!* he cursed to himself. *What in hell did you do last night?*

He feverishly tried to remember, but it was like looking down the shaft of a bottomless mine, a great black hole of nothing. He hadn't visited the badlands in weeks, and he sure as hell would never have dreamed of sneaking a "soiled dove" into his hotel room. How could he have gotten so damned drunk?

The woman beside him inched closer, and then tentatively began walking her fingers along the center of his chest. Knowing he had to face her, to let her down as quickly as possible, Luke muttered, "Move over a little, would you, sweet darlin'? I'm not feeling too good this morning."

Stormy stroked his brow, brushing a few of those damp curls off his forehead. "Small wonder," she whispered, not quite as sympathetic as she supposed she ought to be. "You smell like you must have drunk up half the town last night."

Stormy's voice? *Stormy!* How had she gotten into his room? His headache forgotten, Luke quickly tried to retrace his steps. He remembered going to her cabin, desperate to have her, pressing her against the wall, and wanting her so damn badly that he nearly lost all control and embarrassed himself in a way he never had before. She'd turned him down. He remembered that little rejection clearly. Stormy had sent Lucky Luke McCanles away, even though he knew she'd been every bit as eager as he to find a little satisfaction in their relationship.

But then how the hell did she wind up in his *bed?* Luke covered his face with his hands, squeezing the truth from his memory, until the events of last evening collided in a mélange of echoed voices. A mob of informants suddenly filled his mind, demanding to be heard. One by one they called out, uttering bits and pieces of fragmented conversations. He clearly heard Judge Kuykendall say, "What part don't you understand, Mr. McCanles? Kiss your bride." Raising her voice above the crowd, Stormy declared, "I *do!*" And then, strangest of all, Luke heard his own voice shouting in the night, "It's true! It's *true!*"

He sat bolt upright, the forgotten headache cracking against the inside of his skull like a bullwhacker's whip. Groaning in agony, he clasped his head between his hands and turned to see Stormy lying beside him.

"Are you all right?" she asked, concerned by his facial contortions and obvious pain.

"Yes—no. Hell, I don't know." He collapsed against his pillow but left one eye open, pinned on Stormy. It *was* true. All true. He'd married her. Just like he had good sense, he'd up and married the sister of Calamity Jane, and now he was trapped. *Jesus, McCanles!* He hadn't wanted a wife—he'd just wanted . . . *her.* And here she was, streaks of golden-red hair streaming down over one shoulder and spread over his pillow as if it had every right to be there.

"Can I get something for you, Luke?" she asked, not sure what to make of his odd expression. "When my mother felt like you do, she used to mix day-old coffee grounds with raw turkey eggs, and then add boiled turnip juice and a pinch of—"

"Oh, Jesus—no!" His stomach rolled and then seemed to flip over backwards. "I—I'll be just fine the way I am."

She laughed, the sound infectious, and when he glanced at her again, Luke noticed that the sheet had slipped low on her left breast, nearly exposing it. He moistened his lips, staring at the outline of her pink nipple, and then drew in a ragged breath. In spite of the fact that she'd tricked him, turned his own bluff around until he had no decent way out, they must have been good together last night—he just *knew* they had to have been good. Damn good.

He tried to remember what had happened after the wedding, but no informative voices called to him this time. Just the voice of Cold Deck Johnny bartending at the Texas Star Saloon, asking him why didn't he just buy the whole damn bottle and get it over with.

Jesus, but he'd wanted Stormy last night. And he wanted her now. Why in hell couldn't he remember even one little moment of what had gone on between them? Luke glanced into her silvery eyes, aware suddenly that she was still watching him, even though she looked uncomfortable, maybe a little embarrassed. After last night? Confused by her modesty, testing her, he reached over and tugged the sheet lower, exposing her down to her navel. Stormy immediately drew her arms up to her breasts but then slowly let them fall away.

Confusion replaced by instant desire, Luke sucked in his breath. *Oh, yes,* he thought, they must have been *more* than good last night. Eager for a return match, he rasped, "Come here."

Stormy slid across the sheet. "What do you want me to do?"

"I think you know damn good and well what I want by now." He pulled her into his arms, crushing his mouth to hers in a fevered, almost angry kiss, unaware until that moment that he even felt a certain resentment. It was there, whether it sprang from disgust at himself or disappointment in her, the anger was definitely there. But as Luke rolled over with Stormy still in his arms, he brushed those thoughts aside and concentrated on another kind of feeling.

He hovered over her, staring down at her startled expression, caught for a moment by the sight of her silken hair spread along her creamy white shoulders and around the pillow. He lowered himself to her waiting body, his hands and mouth eager to touch her everywhere at once. Stormy trembled at first, almost resisting his advances, but then she began to ripple where he touched her, to writhe and shift her hips, the movements innocent and awkward, yet impatient, too.

What a match they were! he thought again, stung by the intensity of his desire. Had he really ever believed that one stolen interlude with Stormy would be enough to get her off of his mind? Last night and the forgotten encounter seeming less important somehow, Luke coaxed her legs apart with his knee. She moaned softly at first when he slid his fingers between her thighs, mewing almost like a startled kitten, and then groaned from deep in her throat as he began to stroke her there, preparing her for him.

When she was damp and swollen, as ready as he'd take the time to make her, Luke took her quivering mouth with his own, kissing her deeply, and raised her hips to meet his. Then he thrust into her. Stormy cried out and arched her spine, but Luke drove ahead, taking her response as encouragement. He recognized some difficulties as he penetrated her, even cursed himself for being so clumsy, and finally recognized that all was not as it seemed.

What in hell? he wondered groggily. But he couldn't seem to reason it out, couldn't really grasp the situation for what it was. He was only aware of the exquisite feel of her body, so hot and tight around him, he feared the slightest movement might end their lovemaking before it really began. It *couldn't* have been this good last night, he thought, his passion reaching new levels, it just couldn't have been or he would have remembered it.

Then, from somewhere deep in his impassioned haze, Luke finally understood that there had been no last night, that this, in far more significant ways than he could ponder now, was a time of many firsts—and that he had to forgo his own pleasure long enough for Stormy to reach his level of excitement. Following his instincts, Luke forced himself to slow down, to curb his runaway urges and give her a chance. *Don't think about what you're doing,* his mind whispered, *don't stop to consider how very good she makes you feel: Think of splinters, of anything but here and now, and slow down. Slow down . . .*

Stormy's pain had been sharp but mercifully fleeting as well. She tried to relax in the moments after Luke first penetrated her, to think of what had transpired in terms of pleasure, but everything was happening too fast, too frantically. When she thought she could bear no more of his invasion, as she brought her hands to his chest in order to try and fight him off, Luke suddenly slowed his rhythm and shortened his strokes. As she caught her breath, he slipped his hand between their hips, sliding his fingers down through her mound of golden strands, and began to caress her there, slowly, wickedly. Stormy's breath caught at the sudden explosion of sensations, and then she spread herself beneath him, ready now to learn all she could about this thing called pleasure.

They were better than good together, so hot and so very in tune that in no time, Luke was racing out of control again. He was gripped by an intensity he'd never experienced before, a primal need to possess her in this, the most rudimentary of ways. The time for slowing down had passed for them both, Luke realized as Stormy matched him stroke for stroke, moan for moan, for the urge to lay claim to this woman as his own was far more powerful than any he'd ever experienced before, more forceful even than the most basic instinct for survival.

She shuddered at last, her entire body arcing, and then cried out in ecstasy moments before the first vigorous jolt of Luke's release. He was lost to her then, lost to himself even as he spurted what seemed like his very soul into the depths of her womb.

After Luke's movements slowed and then stopped

altogether, he rolled over onto his back and covered his brow with his forearm. Stormy lay beside him, stunned, adrift on a still-trickling current of pleasure—deluged with the very sensations, she supposed, that Calamity had promised she would find in the marital embrace. *Pleasure.* The word rolled off her tongue in a whisper, and then rippled through her body. *Pleasure.* Pure and natural pleasure. Such a lovely word for such intensely erotic sensations. She sighed, blushing inwardly as she thought of her earthy responses to Luke's touch, at the surprises he'd unleashed in her body. Had any woman before her ever felt quite this good, she wondered dreamily, or this completely and utterly alive?

When his breathing had returned to normal, his mind muddled but functioning again, Luke kept his arm over his brow as he said, "I didn't touch you last night, did I."

It was a statement, not a question, and Stormy wasn't quite sure what he wanted to hear. "No," she admitted, "but that's because you were—"

"I know what *I* was. What I didn't know, what I'm wondering about—" Luke cut his words off just short of mentioning her virginity. Instead, he said, "Remember your rule about not kissing men with beards?"

At his tone and his odd question, Stormy finally glanced his way. His face was hidden beneath his forearm. "Y-yes. Why?"

"Just exactly how many clean-shaven men have you kissed, Mrs. McCanles? Precisely."

Alarmed by his tone, Stormy looked away from

him. She paused, remembering Calamity's warning about how Luke preferred his women a little rough around the edges, and then softly said, "You mean since I've been in Deadwood?"

"Since ever!"

She hesitated again, still not sure how to handle this interrogation. "Including you?"

"Jesus—fine. Yes, including me."

She couldn't stall him any longer, Stormy knew. And she couldn't out and out lie. She sighed as she admitted, "I'd have to say . . . just the one."

"*Me?*"

"You."

Exhaling heavily, Luke closed his eyes. *Why me?* he wondered, incredulous. And why in hell had a woman like Stormy, a lady in every way he could think of, agreed to marry him? Could she really have gotten so moony-eyed over the "star" of those fictional romance novels that she'd cheerfully turned her virtue over to *him,* a man who hardly deserved the honor? Hell, to Luke's knowledge, he'd never even been within kissing distance of a virgin before, much less deflowered one, but here he was with Stormy, sated to his toenails from their lovemaking. It was an honor he hadn't expected or asked for, and a heavy responsibility weighing him down like a huge stack of those novels.

Then another thought occurred to him. What did he know of virgins? Had he hurt her? She had seemed tense when he'd first come to her, and afraid, now that he thought about it, and no damn wonder! He had driven into her with no thought but to sate his own lust. With a low groan, Luke lowered his arm and took a quick glance in her direction.

Stormy's eyes were closed, and her face so still and white, she almost looked lifeless. Was it a look of contentment or agony? And how was he to know the difference with a woman like Stormy? He'd never known a woman even remotely like her.

Luke rolled over to her, reaching tentatively at first, and then took her into his arms. Stormy was trembling all over, nervously chewing on her bottom lip, but giving herself up to him as if he actually deserved all her sweetness. He didn't, he knew without question, but he also knew that he lacked the strength to push her away.

"Open your eyes," he whispered. "Look at me."

When she blinked up at him with those languid gray eyes, Luke's heart began to thump against his ribcage. She didn't look like a woman in pain, and certainly not a woman with regrets, so he indulged himself with her softness, pulling her close until their bodies met from head to toe. Stormy was shuddering now, not merely trembling, but Luke had no idea if her responses were prompted by desire or fear. He made no move to reclaim her.

Instead, he kept her folded in his arms, content somehow just to hold her close. He hadn't envisioned a moment like this before, when he'd want nothing more than to crush Stormy, or any woman for that matter, against his body with no purpose but to embrace her. And never had he imagined how *good* it could feel, how utterly gratifying.

Shaken to his core by the depth of these sudden

and surprising emotions, Luke took another peek at her. Her eyes were closed again, her mouth turned up at the corners in supreme bliss. Luke groaned under his breath. None of this made sense. Not his reactions, or hers. He only knew that he'd deflowered the only virgin he'd ever met and tricked her into marrying him to boot! If he didn't know another thing, he knew that much to be true. But why had she gone along with him?

Releasing her, Luke eased Stormy back down on his pillow and said, "Answer me something, sweetheart. Why did you agree to marry me last night?"

Taken off guard by the question, she stumbled around in her mind looking for the answer until she was hit with a sudden realization. She'd known all along that something had been missing in the marriage ceremony, something that loomed large, but until that moment, she hadn't understood what it was: words of love.

There was no doubt in her mind that she loved Luke, loved him even more by morning's light, but what of him? Had it all been a gamble to him, a drunken mistake? Unwilling to hand over the only thing she had left of herself—her heart—to a man who might not even want it, Stormy lowered her lashes and looked away from him.

That was answer enough for Luke. If it hadn't been painfully obvious before, it was now. She'd married her fantasy man, the star of the show, and now she hadn't the words to explain it to him. Maybe, he thought wryly, he hadn't done the tricking after all. Disgusted with himself for not coming clean sooner about who and what he really was, and disgusted with her for being so shallow, Luke rolled over to the edge of the mattress and began to tug on his clothing.

When he was dressed, he strode to the foot of the bed and faced her, clinging to the brass railing for support. In a hoarse whisper, he said, "I'm sorry, Stormy. Sorrier than you'll ever know."

"Sorry?" She sat up in bed, pressing the sheet against her bosom. "What for?"

"About last night," he said, with difficulty. "And especially for . . . everything since." He reached down, took his hat off the floor, and fit it to his head. As he walked to the door, he added, "I'll just go on downstairs now and give you some privacy."

Privacy? Why on earth would she need privacy now after all that had transpired between them? Stormy opened her mouth to speak, to call him back and tell him the only thing she wanted right now was him, but she was too late. The door closed quietly, and then Luke was gone.

15

Two days later, Stormy leaned her elbows across the counter at the grocery store and began to tap her foot. She was nervous, she realized, more fidgety than she could ever recall being. Not that she had any good reason to be. For the most part, things were going her way for a change. Her candy was selling well, even better than before, and the ladies in town—the same ones who'd look down their noses at her when they found out that Calamity Jane was her sister—had finally decided to accept her as one of their own, now that she was Mrs. Luke McCanles. Even Eudell, who'd taken her into the store grudgingly, seemed positively thrilled to have the wife of such a famous man as her employee. In fact, everyone seemed mighty impressed with her new status. Everyone except her husband.

She'd barely seen Luke since the morning after their marriage. Oh, he'd shared supper with her the past two nights, that and several colorful stories of his exploits at the gambling tables, but meals were all they seemed to have time for. She went to bed alone and woke up alone. And Luke, a man whose passion for her had been zealous at the start, didn't seem to mind the separation a bit.

It wasn't as if he didn't explain his lengthy absences. Luke had illustrated how his work schedule demanded that he be at the poker tables when most of the miners were in town and itching to lose all their hard-earned gold dust. He'd also pointed out that a good game usually lasted all night and into the following day, the hours during which she made candy or worked at the store. It *seemed* reasonable enough, yet she still couldn't help but feel abandoned, orphaned all over again for the third time in her life.

As she thought of Luke, daydreamed about the night he would come to her and make her feel so special again, one of Luke's defensive statements rang in Stormy's ears, reminding her not only of the words, but of the way he'd said them. *You knew what you were getting into when you married me, didn't you? I'm nothing but a gambler and a show-off these days. Surely you didn't expect a picket fence and a vegetable garden from Lucky Luke McCanles.* The words were bad enough, but the way he'd said them were even worse; he'd sounded almost angry. Who was he so upset with, and why?

"Excuse me, Mrs. McCanles."

Justin cut into Stormy's thought, startling her. She jumped.

"Sorry, ma'am, but kin I just get a handful of taffy? Miss Savannah's here again and she wants to give that licorice flavor a try if you got any left."

Glancing up to see that Savannah and her father were perusing the canned goods on the shelf near the stove, Stormy decided to take the opportunity to ease another concern from her mind—her sister's well-being. "I'll see to them, Justin," she said as she took the entire bowl of candy off the counter, stepped out from behind the cash register, and made her way down the aisle.

With Justin right on her heels, Stormy approached the Rosses and greeted them. "Hello again, Mr. Ross, Savannah. Your visits to Deadwood are getting to be pretty regular, aren't they?"

Ross shot a knowing glance between his daughter and Justin as he said, "It seems my girl can't get enough of your candy, ma'am. Has to try each new batch while it's fresh, isn't that so, Savannah?"

The girl blushed and nodded, but when Stormy offered the bowl of candy, she picked out only a few pieces. Smiling to herself as Justin crept closer to Savannah, Stormy turned back to her father. "Didn't you mention that you live down the road near Lead?"

"Yes, ma'am, we do."

"I wonder . . . have you seen a lady named Calamity Jane in your town over the last day or so?"

Ross worked the brim of his hat between his hands as he muttered, "That ain't much of a lady for someone like you to be discussing, ma'am. I just seen her riding a mule up the gulch, a foot in each stirrup like the lowest common—"

"Calamity Jane is my sister, sir," Stormy said, "and as Calamity Jane, I guess she can ride a mule any darn way she wants to. Now, were you saying that you saw her in Deadwood today?"

His tired brow furrowed for a moment, but then he just shrugged and said, "Yes, ma'am. She just rode up Main Street and then took off up the side of the hill."

Boot Hill, Stormy thought, knowing exactly where her sister would be heading. "Thank you for the information, Mr. Ross. I appreciate it." As she turned to Justin, Stormy handed him the bowl of taffy and then her apron, too. "I have to leave for a while. I don't know if I'll be returning today, so you'll have to take over for me."

On foot, it took Stormy just under thirty minutes to reach the crest of the hill where the cemetery began. Pausing to catch her breath, she spotted her sister sitting cross-legged near Hickok's grave. Calamity looked sad but not tormented, almost resigned to his death, as if she'd managed to find the peace and solace she'd been seeking. Hoping that she would not be intruding on Martha's privacy, Stormy quietly approached her.

Calamity heard footfalls and turned around. "Hey, kid! How ya doing?"

"Good," Stormy said as she sat down beside her on a small patch of grass. "How about you?"

"I'm all right, kid, really." She reached over, patted Stormy's hand, and then removed her hat. A thin band of clean skin ran around her forehead between her hairline and the spot where her hat fit down on her head. Streaks of sweat cut jagged paths through the dirt on her cheeks and throat, and her hair, matted and dirty, stuck to her neck even after she shook her head. Calamity laughed as she said, "I 'spect I look like I been drug beneath a skinner's wagon through Splittail Gulch, but believe you me, I feel one hell of a lot better than I look."

Watching as Calamity struggled to finger-comb her hair, Stormy said, "I've definitely seen you looking better, but I'm glad you're back home safely. I've been a little worried about you."

Giving up her attempts to groom herself, Calamity flipped the clumps of her hair over her shoulder and then went back to what she had been doing when Stormy approached. Carefully arranging the cards, she fanned a pair each of black aces and eights, and then drove a tenpenny nail into the cards, pinning them to the earth. "Bill was holding a hand like this when he got shot," she explained, her voice unusually soft. "Up to Lead, they're a calling this a 'dead man's hand.'"

"Maybe I should go and leave you alone for now. I didn't mean to disturb you."

"You didn't. I told you—I'm fine. What about you, kid?"

Stormy dropped her gaze to the dried pine needles littering the edges of Hickok's grave. She'd figured on telling Martha about her surprise marriage, but this didn't seem to be the time or place. "I'm fine, too."

Calamity nudged her with her elbow. "Come on—there's something you're not telling me. What is it kid? Is that Luke still giving you some trouble?"

"Trouble?" She looked up at her sister, blushed, and lowered her lashes.

"Out with it kid! If that Luke's been pestering you, or up to no good, I swear—"

"Luke hasn't done anything he shouldn't have—at least, nothing that a husband shouldn't do."

"Well, that's good to know." She brushed a clump of mud off the sleeve of her buckskin jacket. "I have to tell you, when I left here the other night, I wasn't exactly—" Calamity's lips froze while still formed in the shape of that final word, and her bloodshot eyes bugged out as her sister's message finally sank in. "Did you say something about a *husband*?"

Grinning like a shy schoolgirl, Stormy said, "Yes. Luke and I got married after you left."

"*Married?* You married Lucky Luke McCanles?"

Stormy's grin widened as she nodded.

Her mouth agape, Calamity mimicked her sister by bobbing her chin along with her. Then she narrowed her gaze and said, "Are you *sure* we're talking about the same fellah?" She raised her hand high above her head. "Tall, maybe a little over six feet, dark hair, black eyes, better looking than a man ought to be with a smile that could charm the bloomers off a nun—*that* Luke McCanles?"

Stormy giggled. "The very same one.

Calamity stared at her, mouth still agape, for several minutes. "*Gawd*, kid!" She stared at her another minute. "How'd you do it? How'd you trick him into marriage?"

Pausing only a moment to think about it, she said, "I didn't. In fact, if anyone got tricked, it was me."

Calamity whistled her astonishment. "I cain't hardly believe it! Luke McCanles up and marrying you just like that! When did all this happen, and hey—are you sure it's legal?"

"The night you left town, and yes, it's quite legal. Judge Kuykendall married us right there in our cabin."

Again Calamity stared at her sister, her shock apparent in yet another long pause. *"Gawd."*

Laughing softly, Stormy offered a few details. "The judge used the Bible Grandfather Cannary gave us the day you were born. I thought you might like that."

Nodding, a silent Calamity considered her sister's revelations a little longer before she winked, nudged her ribs with her elbow again, and said, "Well? What'd you think of your wedding night? Wasn't it everything I told you it'd be?"

Again Stormy blushed, and this time, she turned her face away from Martha's view. "Nothing much happened the night we were married. Luke got a little drunk and he fell asleep as soon as he got into bed."

"Do tell." Calamity snickered, and then persisted. "That'll happen to the best of 'em, but you musta tangled with him sometime or another—them roses on your cheeks didn't bloom without a little help from someone."

Beyond embarrassed, Stormy got to her feet and wandered a few steps away from her sister. "Luke and I have consummated our marriage, if that's what you're so interested in. Does that satisfy your curiosity?"

"Ain't me what should be having the satisfaction

around here." Struggling to regain her footing, Calamity stumbled over to where Stormy stood and gripped her by the shoulders of her crisp white blouse. "Why aren't you more excited than this? What is it, kid? You kin tell me. Wasn't that Luke as kind and good to you as he shoulda been?"

Tears she hadn't known were there erupted, spilling down Stormy's cheeks.

"Gawddamn that miserable polecat!" She doubled up her fist and shook it. "I'll take my whip to his ass, I swear I will!"

"N-no," Stormy said between sobs. "Luke didn't do anything wrong, in fact he was wonderful the one time we did spend together. I—I don't know what's wrong with me, but I feel alone all the time, unwanted too."

"Unwanted?" Calamity scratched the top of her scalp. "What are you saying? That you and Luke been married three days now, but just had the one roll under the sheets?"

Stormy blushed and her tears fell even harder, but she did manage to nod.

"I'll be go to hell," she whispered with awe. "That's just stranger than strange. Luke always struck me as the, you know, *vigorous* type, if you get what I mean."

"Well, I *don't* know what you mean because I hardly ever see him!" The tears continued to fall.

Calamity leaned right into her sister's face, taking her shoulders between her hands and shaking her a little as she said, "There's got to be a reason for this. What'd you do that one time—keep your bloomers buttoned up to your chin, or did you just lay there like a slug?"

"I don't have any idea *what* I did wrong, and I don't want to talk about it anymore!" Stormy tore out of her sister's grip, whirled around, and headed for the trail to town.

Calamity caught up with her, blocking her path as she said, "Come on, kid—it's me! I ain't trying to poke fun at you. I just want to know why you look so unhappy. Gawd, it ain't every gal who's been able to slap a harness on Luke—and don't think a few haven't tried. I want to know how you managed the job, and why you aren't happier about it."

Stormy dried her tears with the sleeve of her blouse, absently wiping at the smudges her sister had left at the shoulders with her dirty hands. She sighed heavily. "I'm sorry if I snapped at you. I guess I'm a little touchy about the subject of me and Luke right now."

"It's all right to be touchy—just as long as you keep talking to me."

Shaking her head slowly, Stormy whispered through a sigh, "There's really no point in talking about this. Luke doesn't want me anymore, and that's all there is to it."

"Talk to me anyways, kid. Tell me why you think you and that husband of yours ain't getting together more often."

Leaning back against a pine tree, Stormy closed her eyes and then finally relayed Luke's many excuses for staying away. She concluded, "When he's explaining all his late hours and the reasons we can't be together, I suppose it makes sense at the time, but after he's gone, I just feel more lonely and unwanted than ever. It's almost like we're not really married. Is it wrong for me to feel this way?"

"Hell, kid, I don't know ox shit—'scuse me—I don't know beans about marriage, but it does seem to me that you got every reason to be upset." Calamity caught the sleeve of Stormy's blouse between her fingers. "Come on. Let's walk while I think on this a spell."

The sisters weaved their way through the cemetery then, Calamity deep in thought, Stormy following aimlessly beside her, trying not to step on any unmarked graves. They'd gotten halfway down the side of the hill in the direction of the stream she and Luke had discovered after the funeral, when Calamity came to a sudden halt, turned, and snapped her fingers.

Looking Stormy square in the eye, she said, "Got to ask you something personal, but I don't know how without coming right out with it."

Although she had a feeling Calamity's idea of *personal* could get downright vulgar, she agreed. "Go on."

"Did Luke know what kind a woman he was getting when he married you?" Stormy wrinkled her nose in confusion, so she added, "Did he know you was a virgin?"

"I—I don't know for sure, but if I had to guess about his assumptions, I'd say . . . no."

"Ah, hah!" Calamity scratched her scalp again. "And that one time you was together—did Luke figure out you was ninety-nine percent pure then?"

Color crept up her throat, but Stormy kept an unruffled demeanor as she said, "Again, I can't say for sure, but if I were to make a guess, I'd say . . . yes."

"Well, there you have it, kid!"

"I *do?*"

"Sure! Remember what I told you about Luke liking his women a little rough around the edges?" At Stormy's nod, she went on, "Well, gawd, kid—don't you get it? You plum scared hell outta that boy!"

"What? How could someone like me scare a man like Luke McCanles? Why, the very idea is just preposterous."

Calamity considered it a moment longer, then nodded resolutely. "Believe me, li'l sis—you're the *only* person alive who could scare the Luke I know. I'd bet my bloomers—yours actually—that you and your fine moral character is what's got him spooked."

Stormy's head spun with the thought. "Even if that were true, and I'm not saying that I believe it, I can't help what I am, or what I was. How am I ever going to make a marriage with Luke if he keeps running away from me?"

"That might not be too tough, li'l sis." She leaned in close, whispering conspiratorially. "I could have me a talk with ol' Luke, if you like, and then—"

"No!" Stormy cut in, horrified by the idea. "Please don't even mention to him that we've had this conversation. I'll die if you do!"

"Okay, okay. Got enough dead people in this town as it is." Calamity rumpled her brow as she tried to think of another way to reach Luke. "All right," she said at last. "How about this? There could be one other idea that might just work, but you're gonna have to make a few changes"—she winked—"loosen your stays a little if you know what I mean, for it to have a chance."

"I love Luke," Stormy said, sure only of that fact at the moment. "And I'll do anything I have to in order to make our marriage work. Anything at all. What do you have in mind?"

Calamity wrapped her arm around Stormy's shoulder and began walking her back toward town. "Mighty glad you asked, kid. Now here's what I think you should do. . . ."

Later that night at the Texas Star Saloon, Luke sat at a poker table with Colorado Charlie, California Jack, and one of the proprietors of the now infamous Number Ten Saloon, Carl Mann. Luck as well as his ability to concentrate had eluded him all night long, and as the evening stretched into early morning, he tossed in yet another losing hand, pushed his chair away from the table, and said, "Deal me out, Carl. I'm not worth a shit tonight."

Mann glanced around the unusually quiet saloon. "You can't drop out now, Luke—hell, we can't play with just three men."

"That's really all you've been playing with for half the night," he muttered, getting to his feet. Ignoring the men's complaints, he worked his way to the bar, and then pounded his fist against the scarred top to capture the bartender's attention. "Give me a beer, would you, Johnny?"

Johnny the Deuce, who'd been half-asleep, grabbed a bottle of the local product brewed in lower Deadwood at the Spring Creek Brewery and presented it to the town's last remaining celebrity. "This one's on the house." He watched, eyes shining with admiration, as Luke took a long refreshing pull from the bottle, and then asked, "What about it, McCanles? You gonna run for deputy marshal?"

"'Course he is," a feminine voice chimed in, "ain't you, honey?"

As he took another swallow of beer, Luke's gaze flickered over to Blonde May, a blowsy saloon "entertainer" and waitress who'd taken a shine to him the moment he arrived in Deadwood. Tonight she was a vision in pink, a frothy confection of organdy and ostrich feathers set off by piles of stark white hair, brightly painted lips, and burgeoning breasts straining the boundaries of her low-cut gown.

Luke gave her a tired smile as he said, "I don't know what I'm going to do yet, May. I have to think about it some more."

"But we need you, honey," she murmured with a pout. Wrapping one of the dark curls at his neck around her finger, she added breathlessly, "You're the only fellah in this town man enough to do the job. Say yes, sugar." She moved closer to him, suggestively rubbing her breasts against his satin vest. "I'd just feel so safe at night if I knew you were watching out for me."

After taking another swig of beer, Luke grasped

May by the shoulders, intending to remove her from his person. At the same moment his fingers curled around the exposed flesh of her arms, the loud crack of a bullwhip sent him ducking for cover.

"Eee—ya—haaa!" Calamity bellowed as she rolled up her whip and strode across the room. "I been looking for you all over town, *brother* dear." She stepped up beside Luke, elbowing Blonde May aside. "This fellah's taken. Get lost, sugar face."

No stranger to the rougher side of life, May returned Calamity's greeting with a vigorous swing of her ample hips, bumping her back out of the way. "I was here first, you smelly old sot," she said with a sneer. "Why don't you go up to the bathhouse and soak your head?"

With no warning whatsoever, Calamity drew back her fist and drove it into Blonde May's chin. The woman fell back against Luke, nearly knocking him to the floor, but he managed to set her back on her feet and regain his balance.

"You stinking *bitch!*" May screamed as she lunged forward and grabbed clumps of Calamity's hair. "I ought to kill you for that!"

"You and what army, you ten-cent whore!"

Although he was sorely tempted to let the two fight it out, Luke drove his arms between them, shouting, "That's enough, *ladies.*" He pried them apart, each coming away with several strands of the other's hair, and said, "Unless you're planning to put on a jiggling match and strip down to your suspenders, I doubt anyone wants to watch any more of this. May, why don't you go entertain someone else for a while, sweet darlin'."

"Yeah," Calamity tossed in. "Go drop your fanny on Mysterious Jimmy's lap. Maybe he can rise to the occasion for you. Luke and I got family business to discuss, ain't we Luke?"

"Family?" May stepped up between Calamity and Luke. "What is that supposed to mean?"

"Just that my ol' friend here up and married my li'l sis not three days past. Ain't that right, Luke?"

"Your sister?" May gasped and clutched her bosom. "Is that right, Luke?"

The muscles of one eye twitching at the corner, Luke glared at Calamity as he said, "This is none of your business, May. Now leave us be."

She laughed, pointing first at Calamity and then at Luke. "I heard you picked yourself up a little bride, handsome, but I had no idea she came from a family of such high breeding."

This time when Calamity let her fist fly, Luke was ready for it. He caught her hand in his palm, turned to May, and said, "If you don't get out of here now, I'm going to turn her loose and then *help* her snatch you bald-headed!"

Still laughing, May flounced out of harm's way and began looking for another prospect for the evening. When she settled in at a table with five poker players, propping her left forearm and breast on John Brody's shoulder, Calamity narrowed her gaze and said, "Now that's a man more suited to the likes of her. If I ever saw a meaner, rougher ol' cob than that Brody fellah, I don't know where. Him and that bunch of ruffians he runs with would shoot a prospector in the back and then roll him over just to watch him die."

Luke's gaze flashed to the man, but just as quickly returned to Calamity. "You didn't stop at this particular bar just to grumble about the criminal element in town. From the few things you've already said, I suppose you've spoken with Stormy since you got back."

She gave him as bright a smile as she ever managed. "Guess I have, at that. So are you gonna buy your new sister a drink, or not?"

Luke gestured to the bartender. "Whisky for the lady, and I'll have another beer."

"Give us the whole damn bottle," Calamity said, amending the order. "We might be *discussing* for a while."

Luke sighed heavily but followed Calamity to a table near the front door where few patrons were around. After she settled into her chair, Calamity poured herself a drink and said, "I got to tell you—I cain't hardly believe you just up and married my sister like that. Why'd you do it?"

"That's none of your damn business."

Calamity took her bullwhip off her lap and waved it under his nose. "That little lady is my sister, and that damn well makes it my business! Now why'd you do it?"

Showing an exterior calm he didn't feel inside, Luke turned his beer bottle in slow circles. How the hell could he respond to a question like that when he wasn't sure of the answer himself? He finally shrugged and said, "I got drunk and then I ran a little bluff on her."

"You tried to bluff my *sister*?"

At her tone, Luke glanced over at Calamity. She

looked as if she knew something he didn't—the exact same way Stormy had looked at him on the night they wed. He furrowed his brow and hesitated as he said, "I've been known to run a pretty good bluff in my day."

Calamity slapped her palms against her filthy buckskin trousers and howled. Through her raucous laughter, she finally said, "Hell, that gal and I been playing one-on-one poker since we was both knee-high to a rattlesnake. You sure picked the wrong girl to try your card-playing talents on! Gawd, she can outbluff me with one arm in a sling and blindfolded to boot!"

Luke took a long swallow of beer and then stared dead ahead through the saloon's only window. The hour had grown late. Stormy, he supposed, would be at the hotel by now, in his bed sleeping. A wave of desire slowly drifted through him. Luke clenched his teeth and began to roll the pads of his fingers across the top of the table, strumming the pits and burns along the scarred surface as if they were the strings of a guitar.

Laying her elbows on the table, Calamity leaned in close and said quietly, "I don't know heads nor tails about what's going through that mind of yours now, or how you got so muddled as to get caught in your own trap, but I would like to know this much—when Stormy called that bluff of yours, why'd you go through with it, Luke? Why didn't you just toss in your hand and call it a night?"

He took a long pull of his beer, evading the question. "I told you—I was drunk. Why ask me, anyway?

Talk to your sister, and ask her why in God's name *she* went through with it."

But Calamity already had the answer to that little puzzle, and a whale of an answer it was—Stormy was in love. Was Luke? She cocked her head, studying him, but his expression was guarded, cautious. She thought of coming right out and asking him the way she'd have done had he married anyone but her sister, but then she thought of Stormy and remembered her pleas.

Knowing she'd already overstepped her boundaries by simply having this conversation, Calamity tossed down her drink. "Hell, Luke—I don't know any more about Stormy's mind than I know about yours. Maybe she up and married you just cause you're so damned good-looking."

With a bitter, explosive laugh, Luke offered his own explanation. "There's only one reason a woman like that would marry a man like me—because I'm the famous 'Lucky Luke McCanles.'" He finished his beer in one swallow, and then banged the empty bottle down on the table as he pushed out of his chair. "You ought to do her a favor and tell her that she's gone and tied herself to a person who only exists on the pages of a book." He slammed his hat down on his head. "Don't take this personal, Calam, but I'm not in much of a mood for talking, and I've already done more than I wanted to. I'm going to another saloon now. Don't let me turn around and see you in it— understand?"

Calamity's expression softened, as did her voice. "Sure, Luke. Sure."

Over at the table where Blonde May had fled, John Brody lounged in his chair, his pockmarked features puckered in contemplation. Fingering the handle of his pistol as he watched Luke leave the saloon, he turned to May and said, "Did I hear you right earlier? Is McCanles thinking of running for deputy marshal?"

May shrugged. "He went and got himself married, you know, so my guess is that he will. Can't imagine why he'd want to settle down here unless he knew this town was gonna get cleaned up good and proper." Her fingers dipped into the valley between her breasts as she added, "Since he's the only fellah man enough in this town to do the job, I expect he'll be our first official marshal."

But Brody hadn't heard a thing she said past Luke settling down in Deadwood with his wife. He was on his feet and out of the door before her crimson lips could even form the word *marshal.*

Later that morning, when Luke was sure that Stormy had had enough time to groom herself and leave for the day, he fit the key in the lock and let himself into his hotel room. Rubbing his weary eyes with the palm of his hand, he walked toward the bed and flung his hat in the direction of the brass ball atop the post. It missed, as it had almost every day since he'd moved to the hotel.

Heaving a sigh, he slipped out of his jacket and hung it on the post. As he added his shirt and vest to the makeshift hanger, Luke paused, noticing that Stormy had tossed her own bright yellow quilt over the plain white bed covering. A sharp pang of longing pierced his chest, and then grabbed hold with a vengeance.

Jesus. How had he—a man whose already healthy appetites had more than doubled since bedding Stormy—found the strength to stay away from her night after night? Why hadn't he simply come to her a time or two and been done with it? The answers stirred in the back of his mind, lolling there as if hiding just out of reach, but Luke made no attempt to prod them loose. He already had enough troubles. And he was tired.

Reaching for his belt buckle, he turned toward the chiffonier against the wall behind him, but froze when instinct warned him that he was not alone. Dropping into a crouch, Luke went for his guns, almost drawing them before the figure in the corner came into focus. When he identified her, Luke straightened his spine and dropped his hands to his thighs. "Stormy!"

"Good morning," she murmured, her voice soft and low.

Draped in one of his dress shirts, the edges clutched between her hands at the throat and midsection, she was bare clear up to her shirttails, which ended at midthigh. Luke's incredulous gaze clung to the vision of her long slender legs—legs he'd never had a good look at before now.

"S-stormy . . . Jesus." He backed away. "I'm sorry. I thought you'd be gone by now. I'll just get dressed and leave you to—"

"You don't have to go, Luke."

She took a step in his direction, forcing herself to release the material she clutched, and the shirt fell open to reveal one breast and a long expanse of hip and thigh.

"Stormy," he said again, his heartbeat erratic. "I really ought to—"

"I don't have to be at Will's until noon," she cut in, prepared for his excuses. "And I'm all caught up on my candymaking. I thought maybe you'd like to . . . visit awhile."

She took three more steps toward him, the motion widening the gap between the edges of the shirt until Luke had far more than a mere glimpse of the golden blond thatch at the juncture of her legs.

"Jesus, Stormy," he said, catching a sharp breath. "Sweet Jesus, what in hell . . . ?"

She was upon him then, boldly linking her arms around his neck just before she pressed her breasts and their hard nipples against his bare chest. Then with graceful, swanlike movements, she arched her neck, looked up into his eyes, and whispered, "I realize I have a lot to learn, so I'd appreciate any suggestions you might have. Is there anything in particular you'd like for me to do?"

Luke's erratic heartbeat skidded to an abrupt halt. He sucked in his breath and moistened his lips, but when he thought to speak, to say something, *anything,* all he could manage was a hoarse groan.

She smiled. "Nothing yet, huh? Maybe I'll just go ahead and try a few of the things I thought of while I was waiting for you. Be sure and let me know if I do something you like."

Stormy unbuckled his belt, and Luke's guns and holsters fell to the floor with a heavy thud. Then she slipped her fingers inside the waistband of his trousers and set to freeing the buttons.

16

Luke was silent as her hands dipped below the fabric of his trousers, so very rigid in his manner that Stormy caught her first breath of panic. What if after all this he didn't want her? She'd brushed her hair again and again until it shone like fresh-spun gold, and to add to her allure, she'd spent some of her hard-earned pay on a small bottle of rosewater, which she'd splashed along her throat and breasts. What if none of it helped and he sent her away? She would simply crumble and die on the spot if that were to happen!

But as the last button on Luke's trousers slid loose from its confines, his fly gaped open to reveal a tremendous swelling beneath his drawers, and Stormy decided that she didn't have much to worry about.

Opening the edges of Luke's shirt to expose her body was the most reckless thing she'd ever done, but as Stormy faced what she must do next, the feat paled by comparison. Trying to appear unruffled, poised even, she slid the garments down from his hips. Although she knew pretty well what to expect after their first encounter, she wasn't quite prepared for her first look at Luke in all his male glory.

She gasped, and her gaze darted up to his eyes.

"I like what you're doing so far," he muttered, his hands going to her shoulders. "What else did you have in mind?"

He looked amused, but something more, almost as if he were straining against himself, holding back. Little dots of sweat sprang out on his upper lip, and his complexion took on a gentle glow, a thin sheen of perspiration. His nostrils flared, and then his jaw went as rigid as the rest of his body.

Smiling as she recognized the signs of intense arousal, feeling her own body spring to life with a fiery surge that amazed her, Stormy shook off the remainders of her shyness, and let her fingers drift down to the dark curls at Luke's groin. The moment she touched him, he lurched toward her, heating her with his warm breath, melting her uncertainty. She took him into her hand and instinctively began to stroke him.

Luke's fingers dug into Stormy's shoulders, and with a harsh intake of breath, his eyes rolled to a close. Buoyed by his response, surprised by her own boldness, Stormy smiled. She hadn't expected the velvet soft skin or the enormous sense of heat throbbing against the palm of her hand, but as she quickened her movements, what she saw in Luke's expression far exceeded her hopes. He was burning up with desire, his dark eyes opened, glazed with lust, and soon he would—with a feeling akin to panic, Stormy realized she didn't know what to do next.

Luke burst through his passionate haze and tore her hand away from his body. "That's enough of that. Let's try something different . . . something we'll both like a hell of a lot better."

Moving quickly, he kicked off his clothes, tugged off his boots, and then stripped his shirt from Stormy's shoulders. Lifting her into his arms, he carried her a few steps past the chiffonier and pinned her against the wall. Desperate to be inside of her, to feel the moist glove of her warmth around him, Luke pleaded in a husky whisper, "Open up to me, Stormy. I have to be inside of you right now."

Nudging her hips against his thigh as she'd done at the cabin, she moaned softly as she gave her consent. "Yes, Luke—oh, yes."

Balancing her body with one hand clasped firmly against her nude bottom, he moistened the fingers of the other and slipped them between her legs. The gesture was unnecessary. Stormy was hot and slick, more than ready for him. His desire so intense he could bear it no longer, Luke lifted her above his hips, and then slowly eased her down over his body. Her eyes were wide with surprise as he drove into her, and Luke's breath shuddered out in staccato gasps. Then he went still, satisfied for now to be a part of her.

His lips sought hers, his tongue, the recesses of her mouth, and their union was complete. They remained as one, fused, embedded in each other for a long, fulfilling moment. Then Luke buried his face in her silken hair and began to move inside of her, keeping his thrusts short and gentle as he whispered, "What other things did you think of while you were waiting for me, sweetheart?"

Stormy gave a throaty chuckle. "Nothing as scandalous as all this."

"If not this, then what?" He spread wet kisses across her mouth and throat.

Still struggling with her innate shyness, distracted by Luke's body thrusting inside of her and his very busy mouth, she said, "I—if you didn't want to stay when you found me here, if you tried to leave me alone again, I was going to . . ." The sentence trailed off and bright spots of color lit Stormy's cheeks.

"What, sweetheart?" Luke went still again and caught her chin with his free hand. "You were going to do what?"

"I—" she lowered her lashes and bit the corner of her lip, "I was going to push you down on the bed, leap on top of you, and, uh . . . force you to be a husband to me."

"Were you now?" Luke lifted Stormy off his body and set her on her feet. He gazed deeply into her eyes. "That sounds like one *hell* of a fine idea, Mrs. McCanles." Then he swept her into his arms, carried her over to the bed, and threw the both of them on top of her quilt.

He rolled onto his back, his arms spread in submission. "What are you waiting for? I'm all yours."

Again fighting timidness, Stormy slid over to Luke's side and tentatively draped her leg across his. He was staring at her with that bad-boy grin, his eyes dark with both passion and mirth, his mouth curved crookedly to one side, but he made no move to instruct her, to guide her in a way the little marriage manual hadn't.

Dr. Tuttle would condemn her to hell for just considering such wantonness, she thought with a fleeting sense of shame as she rolled to her knees, and then straddled her husband. She would most *surely* burn in hell for this, she decided, but as Stormy lowered herself over Luke's eager body, hell suddenly seemed like a very attractive place to be. Some baser instinct took over then, tossing the remains of her shyness aside, and Stormy began to ride Luke like a woman possessed.

She ground her pelvis against his, burying him inside her and crying out in rapture as each new burst of pleasure spiraled up to touch her very soul. Luke clamped his fingers to her hips, trying to help her adjust the rhythm of her movements, but Stormy relinquished none of her control. Instead, she relished the sudden and very real sense of power and freedom.

Her head fell back and then forward as an orgasm finally claimed her and she began to shudder all over, calling out Luke's name. He took control then, flipping her over on her back while she was still in the throes of passion, and drove deep within her, triggering his own release.

When it was over, and they were both quiet and still, Luke rolled to his side and gathered Stormy into his arms. She was damp from head to toe, her breathing still irregular. He reached over to brush the hair from her cheeks, and then touched his mouth to hers, softly, more a caress than a kiss. When she opened her eyes and looked up at him, an enchanting blend of wonder and sensuality sparkling up from their silvery depths, Luke knew that he and Stormy were far from finished with each other—at least for this day.

And why not? he thought to himself as he rolled over onto his back. He hadn't meant for this to happen again, and he sure as hell hadn't planned it. He'd honestly expected her to have come to her senses by now, to realize exactly what kind of man she'd married, and set out to obtain an annulment or a divorce before he could sully her any more than he already had.

Obviously she hadn't done much by way of clear thinking since the night they wed or she wouldn't be here in his arms. And he apparently wasn't gentleman enough to set her straight—not yet, anyway. And didn't he just know why. Hell, his entire life was nothing more than one big fantasy. Why not allow her a part in the performance for a few more hours? Just how much more ruined could she get in only one day?

Stormy sighed, stretching her arms and legs luxuriously, and then sat up and tossed the long damp strands of her hair over her shoulder. Feeling a residual twinge of modesty, she crossed her arms over her breasts as she moved forward to slide down off the bed. Luke reached out and caught her by the waist, pulling her back down beside him.

"Luke," she murmured, her voice a feeble, breathless protest. "I have to get dressed."

He dragged a fingertip down her throat to her breast where he lazily circled the nipple. "Not yet you don't. I was hoping you'd want to try a few of the things I thought of while you were, ah, *forcing* me to be a good husband." His mouth replaced his finger.

Surprised by a renewed spurt of desire, Stormy gasped as Luke's tongue worked its magic. "B-but you need to get some sleep, and I told Mrs. Hawkes I'd be at the grocery store around noon today."

Luke flashed her a wicked grin as he moved his hand lower to caress her smooth flat tummy. "I think you're going to be a little late today, sweetheart. In fact," he added, sliding his fingers through the golden curls down at her groin, his moist lips to her navel, "there's a very good chance that you might not make it to Will's at all today."

When Luke awakened much later, the room was heavily shadowed, threatened by the approaching night. He glanced at Stormy, her slender body curled up next to his, her delicate face and glorious hair snuggled into the crook of his arm, and knew that he couldn't ignore their predicament any longer. She'd caught him with his guard down today, but now he had a chance to make things right. Now he had to face not just the situation he'd created but himself as well. And this, he figured, was as good a time as any to do it.

In fact, the only time he ever dropped his Lucky Luke McCanles persona was during the moments after he first awakened. For that reason, Luke never liked to spend the whole night with a woman, and he *sure* as hell hadn't ever wound up in the spot he was in today—sleeping with a *real* lady, not to mention one who also happened to be his wife. Luke didn't count that first morning he'd found Stormy in his bed, because he hadn't known she was there, much less remembered that he'd married her. But here and now, this time, he was caught by the balls, and he knew he wasn't going to get away until he reasoned his way out of his troubles.

Luke's gaze flickered over to Stormy again. Her sweet bow-shaped lips were slightly parted and swollen, he supposed from their long hours of love-making. He wanted to kiss her, to feel that satin smooth mouth against his skin one more time, but he resisted the urge. It was a surprisingly easy denial, for as with most of his awakenings, he didn't much care for the Luke McCanles he woke up with, and this particular afternoon, his dislike was even more intense than usual.

Wake up and look at me, he wanted to shout to Stormy. *Take a good look at the man you married. See, he is not some fabulous, heroic gunman destined to save the West from all evil!*

But he didn't do that, of course. Instead, he carefully eased down off the mattress, covered Stormy with the corner of her quilt, and quietly slipped into his clothes. And out of her life.

As she slept Stormy's languid mind convinced her she was stretched out in sweet clover near the banks of the little stream she and Luke had discovered. Warm sunshine poured down over them, heating their bodies between bursts of passion, and lime-colored leaves from the quaking aspens fluttered nearby. Up higher, hidden deep in the branches of a black spruce, a woodpecker drove his beak into the bark in an ongoing search for nourishment. Tickled at first by the steady *rat-a-tat-tat* from the bird's efforts, Stormy quickly became annoyed by the racket until she finally awakened.

She sat bolt upright on the mattress and shook her head to clear it. Still the hammering continued, and she realized there was no woodpecker at all but someone knocking on the door of her hotel room. She glanced around the nearly darkened room. Luke was gone. Shivering against her nakedness and just a sliver of fear, she wrapped the quilt around her body and called out, "Who's there?"

"It's just me, kid!" came the voice of her sister. "Open up!"

After Stormy let her in, Calamity marched into the room and settled her gaze on her disheveled sister. "I seen Luke riding through town a little while ago, so I figured it'd be okay to come looking for you. You been in this room with him *all* damn day?"

Blushing to her roots, Stormy walked back to the bed, sank back down on the edge of the mattress, and nodded.

Calamity traced her sister's steps, stuck her finger under her chin, and forced her to look up. "I guess I don't have to ask if you managed to loosen up enough to go after your man. Hell, I got eyes enough to see that you did. Looks to me like that Luke's gone and planted a whole damn garden of roses in them there cheeks of yours." She snickered and pinched one of those cheeks between her fingers. "How ya feeling, kid?"

"Embarrassed." Stormy removed her sister's hand from her face and smiled. "I also seem to be having an attack of shyness. If you don't mind, I'd like a little privacy so I can get cleaned up and dressed."

Again Calamity snickered. "Might's well put on your nightgown as anything. Take a look at the hour."

Although she could hardly believe she'd slept the afternoon away—at least part of it—she said, "I know how late it is—I'm starving! When you saw Luke, did he mention anything about meeting me downstairs for supper?"

"I said I *seen* him in town, kid, but I didn't get a chance to talk to him. In fact," she added with a chuckle, "when I called out to him, he galloped off through the badlands and headed towards Charlie's camp like his ass was on fire. You *sure* we don't need to talk?"

Stormy bit back a satisfied grin. "I'm sure. Now I'd appreciate it if you let me get dressed in privacy. And tell you what, why don't you wait in the lobby for me. You and I can have supper together, and we'll put it on my husband's tab!"

Calamity, who'd agree to damn near anything as long as she didn't have to pay for it, accepted the invitation, let herself out of the room, and headed down the stairs.

Feeling more feminine than usual, Stormy washed and carefully dressed in her favorite gown, a gauzy princess-style frock in violet and purple lawn. As she tied her hair back with a matching satin ribbon of royal purple, she thought of her ugly prune-colored bonnet and began to laugh. What a difference Luke and the love she felt for him had made in her life!

For the first time ever, Stormy actually felt pretty, as if it were all right to show off her strawberry-blond hair and bat her eyelashes. Here she was, actually trying to look a little more attractive, and didn't it feel good! Not just good but *great* to feel so happy about being a woman—finally to feel free enough and proud enough to allow herself a small modicum of vanity.

She dashed over to the freestanding mirror and fit her black velvet bonnet to her head. She stood preening for a moment, delighted to see a rosy-cheeked woman with a bright smile staring back at her. Then, humming to herself, she went in search of her sister.

The lobby was deserted. Calamity was nowhere to be found, and neither was the desk clerk or the regulars who sat around the glass-topped walnut table and groused about claim jumpers and confidence men. Deciding to carry her investigation outside before checking the restaurant, Stormy stepped through the glass-paned front doors and discovered a noisy group of townsfolk gathered in the street. The crowd, Calamity included, were huddled around a man on horseback, grabbing at something he carried.

"Damn ya all anyways," the rider complained. "I ain't got time for this nonsense. I got to deliver some mail up to Spearfish yet tonight! Fight it out amongst yourselves!"

The man heaved a large sack toward the board-walk where Stormy stood, but it missed the mark and landed in a nearby mud puddle instead, splashing her new dress.

She didn't even have a chance to look down to assess the damage. As the man rode off, the group sprang toward the sack, a man called Pink Bedford leading the charge. Just as he bent over to retrieve it, Calamity dove down between his legs, landing with a gluey splat, and then bounced up from the puddle with the mail sack clamped to her breast.

"Get back!" she warned, mud dripping off her elbows and chin, boots sliding against the boardwalk as she tried to regain her footing.

"Come on, Calam," shouted a man in the crowd. "Give me first crack at it! I ain't heard from my wife for nigh on to six months."

"Then you probably ain't got a wife no more, you danged idiot! Now back away. Ladies first!"

Before anyone could stop her, Calamity ducked inside the hotel, dragging Stormy with her, and slammed the doors behind them. She leaned against the door handles and then tore open the sack. "Come on, kid. Grab a handful and look through it for anything with our name on it. While you're at it, keep anything you find for Luke, Bill, or even the Hawkes if you've a mind to."

Stormy kept her eye on the men, several of whom were pounding on the glass inserts of the door. "But what about the people outside? This doesn't seem fair to me."

"Ain't no such thing as fair on mail day. In case you haven't noticed, we don't get no regular postal service here in Deadwood. Hell, if we left sorting the mail to them yahoos outside, they'd scatter what don't belong to them in the street and leave it to mix with all the . . . fertilizer. Now quit feeling sorry for them and help me!"

Trying to avoid the mud splattered not just on but inside the sack, Stormy dipped her fingers into the bag and withdrew several envelopes. After they'd sorted through each letter and gathered all the pieces addressed to them or those they cared to protect, Calamity handed all the envelopes she'd collected to Stormy—with the exception of one. Then she ordered her to stand back.

Spinning around to the door, she hollered, "Get out of the way, fellahs! Here it comes!" After the men had retreated and stepped off the boardwalk, she tossed the sack out into the street. Chuckling as the crowd fell on it, she muttered, "See what I mean, kid? Mail day in Deadwood is a lot like slopping the hogs."

Stormy, who was only half-listening to her sister, slowly nodded as she dropped the letters on the table generally reserved for the regulars. She sat down on a matching walnut chair with a soft velvet cushion, her gaze and attention riveted to the surprisingly large number of envelopes addressed to Lucky Luke McCanles. Most of them were from Cheyenne, Wyoming, and all of them were scripted in flowing, delicate letters. Feminine writing as far as Stormy could tell.

"What do we got here, kid?" Calamity said as she sat down beside her and began sorting the letters by name. "Gawd! Would you look at all the mail for Bill? Too bad he couldn't a got this 'fore he died. He always loved hearing from folks who thought kindly of him." She sighed wistfully.

"Luke has quite a few pieces of mail, too," Stormy said holding up a stack of letters. "I think his are all from women, and look at this one." As she read the name inscribed on the back near the seal, she lifted the pale pink envelope and sniffed. "It smells like Miss Daisy Summers dumped an entire bottle of perfume on her note. Who do you suppose she is?"

Calamity snatched the letter out of Stormy's hand. "It don't matter who she is no more, kid. When Luke met her, he weren't no married man. I 'spect he'll set her"— she grabbed the other letters Stormy had sorted— "and all them other females straight once he has a look at these. It might be best if I take 'em to him."

Fighting the urge to reach out and yank the envelopes back, Stormy swallowed her curiosity. "Maybe you're right." She sighed, and then studied the rest of the mail. "That's it? Everything is for Luke or Bill?"

Calamity nodded, and then reached into her shirt pocket. "'Cept for this un, a course." She pulled out a crumpled envelope whose yellow edges were torn. "It's addressed to Ann Marie Cannary. Know her?"

"A telegram! For me?"

Laughing to herself, Calamity flipped it across the table. "For you, kid."

Stormy ripped it open, read the first few lines, and then shot a wide-eyed look across the table. "It's from Reverend Young in Utah!" Her gaze dropped back down to the telegram, her mouth silently forming each word as she read and then reread them. "Oh, Martha!" she cried when she was certain her eyes hadn't deceived her. "He's found the boys!"

"Found 'em? Where—in Salt Lake City?"

"He didn't exactly find them," Stormy said, amending her statement. "But Reverend Young sent the name of the family that took them in and says that when they left Utah they were headed for Idaho Springs in *Colorado!* Do you know what that means? I was practically in shouting distance of the little ones the whole time I lived in Denver, and I didn't even know it!"

"Hey, kid," Calamity said softly, hating to spoil Stormy's excitement. "That sounds real spooky and all, but that was a long time ago. Maybe they was headed for Idaho Springs, but there ain't no way of knowing if they actually made it, or if they're still there today."

Stormy was undaunted. In fact, nothing could dim her excitement. "It doesn't matter in either case. I have more than I ever thought possible—the name of the family and a place to start looking. We'll find them. I know we will."

Although she'd heard her sister's references to *we,* Calamity ignored them. "What's the name of the family you're a looking for?"

Stormy's gaze dropped back down to the piece of paper. "The O'Malley's. Charles and Gloria O'Malley."

"Anything there about our little sister?"

She shook her head, still reading. "Only that the reverend intends to continue asking about her."

"Well, hell, two outta three ain't too bad. I suppose now you're gonna set to making plans to go look them up."

"Right away!" Stormy dropped the letter on the table. "I can't wait to see them, can you?"

Calamity shrugged. "It'd be nice. I got to admit that."

"And Luke!" Caught up in her own excitement, Stormy began making plans. "There's really nothing to keep him here. I know for a fact that he's not interested in the deputy marshal position. There isn't a reason in the world that all three of us can't head to Colorado! Do you think we can make the arrangements soon? We have to arrive in Idaho Springs before the first snow hits the Rockies, you know."

Although she was far less enthusiastic about the plan than her sister, Calamity smiled and patted her hand. "Sure, kid. I'll bet we can make it before the leaves begin to turn."

Stormy jumped up from her chair. "Let's go find Luke and tell him."

Calamity clamped her hand over Stormy's shoulder and pulled her back down. "Like I told you, as far as I know, he's out past the badlands at Whitewood Creek. Ain't no place for a lady."

"Oh," she said with a sigh. "I guess not." Then she brightened. "Will you—"

"I'm on my way, kid."

"Oh, and after you find Luke? Why don't both of you come to the cabin. I'll fix us some supper there and then make up a batch of chocolate dainties to earn a little extra money for the trip."

From over her shoulder, Calamity muttered as she opened the door. "I just hope ol' Luke's gonna be as worked up about all this as you are."

"He will be!" Stormy declared, sure of herself. "I just know he will."

17

"*She* . . . what?" *Luke whipped* his head around toward Calamity, nicking his chin with the straight-edge razor. "Ow—shit!"

Giving him a wide berth as droplets of blood oozed through the surface of Luke's shaving foam, Calamity stepped around him. "You know, now that I think of it, this little matter we got to discuss might just get a bit on the lively side. It probably ain't the sort of thing the others should hear." She glanced around the area, noting the half-dozen men gathering around the cook fire, and then started walking in the opposite direction. "Why don't you mosey on down yonder near the creek when you're done chopping yourself to bits. We'll talk there."

Although he could see no good use in discussing Stormy with her sister, or even in considering the wild proposal for dragging him off to Colorado, Luke said, "I'll join you in a minute—that is, if I don't bleed to death first, thanks to you."

Chuckling to herself even though her heart was heavy, Calamity picked her way through the thick tangle of deadwood littering the ground and wandered down to the banks of the creek. There, among the white-barked aspens, she sat down on a fallen log near the drooping umbrellalike branches of a willow tree and propped her feet on a large boulder protruding from the earth.

"Gawd," she muttered to herself as she pulled a flask from her hip pocket. How had everything gotten into such a helluva mess? Calamity unscrewed the cap and took a healthy swig of whisky. Until Stormy had come along, her life had finally gotten some order to it and almost, even a purpose. Then in rapid succession she'd become the big sister again, feeling a responsibility she'd long since shrugged off. After that, she'd lost the best friend a man or woman ever had, and then had to sit quiet while his murderer was released.

Now she had to deal with this obsessive quest of Stormy's. Who'd a thought that Reverend Young would ever locate the family that took in the little ones? And where in hell did it say that that quest had to be as important to her as it was to good little Annie? "Gawd," she muttered again, equal parts of guilt and frustration eating away at her. She took another drink.

The truth was, she finally admitted to herself, she didn't *want* to search for or find her missing family. It was sad, perhaps, selfish even, but all too true. Taking another, longer swallow of whisky, she reminded herself that she shouldn't be sitting there drinking. Shouldn't be swilling whisky when she still had to face her sister and tell her she had no intention of accompanying her to Colorado. Hadn't she promised herself and Stormy after that fiasco with Miz Hawkes that she'd never get swizzled around her again? But Calamity couldn't bear the idea of confronting Stormy without a little fortification any more than she could bear the idea of leaving Deadwood.

Maybe that was part of the problem. Leaving this town, a place so very much like her. Like Deadwood, she was ruffled and dirty around the edges, raucous and lusty, and every bit as lawless and untamed.

She smiled at the thought, at the rare sense of belonging. For the first time since the family had pulled out of Princeton, Calamity felt as if she'd found a true home, a place where more folks than not accepted her. Nothing, she knew then, not Stormy, and not a healthy dose of guilt about the little ones, would ever make her leave this town until she was damn good and ready to go.

Calamity reached for the cap again but paused when she heard the crackling of twigs and leaves snapping under the weight of Luke's boots. A moment later, he was standing before her, a dab of newsprint stuck to the cut on his chin. He was dressed in his card-player's costume complete with satin vest and black hat surrounded by conchos. In addition to the clothing, he also wore the arrogant, cocky attitude he usually took to the poker table. Calamity sighed. Convincing him to nursemaid Stormy on her journey wasn't going to be easy.

Giving him a bright smile, she piled on the flum-diddle. "Ain't you the handsome one tonight. I'll bet

the fancy women over to the Texas Star ain't hardly
gonna be able to keep their hands off'n you or their
skirts below their knees!"

"I am *not* going to Colorado, and all the flattery in
the world isn't going to get me there." He straightened his crimson bow tie. "If that's the only reason
you stopped by to pester me, I'll just be on my way. I
have business in town."

"No—there's more." She patted the log beside her,
and then reached into her jacket pocket. "Sit a spell.
The mail come today. I brung a few interesting-
looking letters for you."

Grumbling to himself at the delay, Luke nudged
Calamity's feet off the boulder with the toe of his
boot and sat down across from her. Then he stuck out
his hand. She gave him the mail along with several
minutes of silence in which to thumb through it. He
flipped each envelope aside, unopened, including the
aromatic note from Miss Daisy Summers, and tore
into the one sealed with the stamp of William F.
Cody.

After Luke read the letter, he glanced at Calamity
and said, "It's from Buffalo Bill."

She nodded. "My Bill got one, too, but I ain't had a
chance to have a look to see what it said. What's he
want?"

"He wants us to join him as part of the show he
now calls The Buffalo Bill Combination and start
touring again." He laughed bitterly. "He even thinks
maybe we ought to look up General Custer and see if
we can't talk him into performing with the troupe
when we reach Bismarck. I guess word of what hap-

pened at the Little Bighorn hadn't reached him when he posted this."

Calamity's expression softened, and then fell. "He probably don't know about Bill getting shot yet either."

"He'll find out soon enough, I expect." Luke tore the letter in half and tossed it into the stream.

"Hey! Why'd you go do that? Ain't you gonna answer him or even think about joining up with him again?"

Cocking a jaundiced eye her way, Luke muttered an oath to himself. He didn't know much these days, but he knew damn good and well that Buffalo Bill would not be interested in hiring Lucky Luke McCanles if Wild Bill Hickok weren't standing alongside of him. Knew it as sure as he knew his days of fame and celebrity were over. Finis. Gone with a puff of smoke from Jack McCall's pistol. And like that puff of smoke, the persona of a showman known as Lucky Luke McCanles had vanished into thin air.

"Luke?" Calamity persisted. "What are you gonna do?"

He shook himself out of his dark thoughts, away from the realization that he'd spent better than half of his life as little more than decoration on Hickok's shirttails, and said, "I'm going to stop wasting my valuable time, that's what. Haven't you heard? The Christman brothers washed up over a thousand dollars in gold nuggets this morning—*each.* If he's running true to form, the oldest ought to be about half-shot by now. There's money to be made off those boys tonight, and I plan to get my fair share."

When he started to rise up off the boulder, Calamity

clamped her fingers against his knee and gave him a
rare smile. "Just a minute more of your time. Enough
anyways for you to give me your promise that you'll
see Stormy reaches Colorady safely."

Luke took a deep breath. *Stormy.* Hell, what was
he supposed to do about her? Be a pretend husband
until the real thing came along and she didn't need
him anymore? Hah! If he was nothing else, Luke was
done pretending. "Your sister doesn't need me.
Besides—you're her family. I believe that *you* are
quite capable of seeing her to Colorado safely."

"Oh, but Stormy does need you." Calamity took
the cap off the flask, tossed down another swallow,
and then offered it to Luke.

He shook his head. "No, thanks. Drinking's what
got me into this mess in the first place."

"What mess you talking about now?"

He measured her, wondering how she'd react to
the truth. "This ridiculous excuse for a marriage is
the mess I'm talking about." Calamity froze, not even
reaching for her bullwhip. He went on. "I already told
you—it never should have happened in the first place.
It's not like your sister and I have a real marriage, you
know. What we have is one big accident."

Although she was startled by the unexpected turn
in the conversation, Calamity brushed his remarks off
and clung to her original topic. "Don't matter what
you call it—you are my sister's husband, and as such
you *got* to take her to Colorady. It's real important to
her, Luke. *Real* important."

"Then you take her if it's so goddamn important."

"I cain't! Don't you see that?" She took another

drink and wiped her mouth with her shirt sleeve. "I just cain't face up to them babies. I don't know what to say to them! I couldn't stand it if they asked me why I run off and left 'em the way I done, couldn't stand it at all. Don't you see, Luke? I cain't do it and I ain't gonna. That just leaves you."

With a weary sigh, Luke propped his elbows on his knees and buried his face in his hands. Calamity had a couple of valid points. After all, mistake or not, he *had* been fool enough to say, "I do." He probably had a moral obligation to consider escorting Stormy on the trip, but in that same moment, he realized something else as well. His motives for doing so would be purely selfish. He was really only thinking of the hours, the days, the *weeks* he would spend with Stormy if he should agree to guide her to Colorado—*guide* her, for Christ's sake, as if he even knew in which direction to start!

Luke's stomach rolled into a tight ball. He couldn't do it. Not just couldn't, but *wouldn't* accompany his "wife" to Colorado or even across the streets of Deadwood again. And didn't he just have the ghost of an idea as to why not. Luke figured that his decision might have something to do with an elusive thing called love—the little "splinter" festering at the back of his mind, wriggling there each time he awakened, trying to work its way up to his consciousness.

If that was indeed the name for what nagged at him, he suspected that one morning soon he'd wake up to find that sliver free, forcing him to discover that yes, that's exactly what he'd felt for Miss Stormy Ann Cannary while she'd been a part of his life.

Love. If not that exactly, he did care enough to step out of her life.

But he shook off those thoughts almost as quickly as they came. Luke McCanles wasn't the kind of man who sat around thinking about things like love. Love was meant for others, for sensitive, caring folks like Stormy, not for men like himself and Wild Bill Hickok, men who took what they could get where they could get it and left a beautiful memory behind. He smiled at the thought, hoping to lift the sudden burden in his chest as easily as he lifted the corners of his mouth.

"You'll do it then?" Calamity asked, seeing some cause for hope in his expression.

"No, Calam," he said. "I absolutely will not, and don't ask me why not because I won't tell you."

She threw her flask against the boulder he was using as a chair. "Gawddamn your black eyes anyways, Luke! I was a-counting on you!"

"Sorry to disappoint you."

"B-but . . . but hell! What am I gonna do now?"

"Why don't you just do what you usually do—count on yourself."

"I already told you!" She jumped up from the log. "I cain't go see them little ones. *You're* the one should go. You swore to protect my sister when you married her, accident or not, and now you got to do your duty!"

Luke rose up off the rock slowly, giving himself time to calm down before he said, "What in hell is the matter with you, woman? I thought you cared about your sister."

Taken aback, she said, "I do. 'Course I do."

"Then I should think you'd be happy to have me out of her life. What the hell kind of a husband can someone like me be to a lady like her?"

Calamity scratched her scalp. "Well, I dunno. I never thought about it much."

"Obviously, neither did your sister."

Squinting up at Luke in the waning light of dusk, she considered telling him how much Stormy loved him, of suggesting that maybe, just maybe, that's all Stormy wanted back from him as a husband, but when she tried to arrange those thoughts, to make them seem reasonable and logical even to herself, they got more jumbled than before. Laughing nervously, she said, "Gawd, Luke, this business between you and my sister just ain't something I ought to poke around in, and it sure ain't the sort a thing I can understand."

"Which part don't you understand, Miss Cannary? That your sister let her head get turned by a paper hero? That I was fool enough and just drunk enough to play a little game with her? That because of that game, we *both* lost a bet—one, I might add, that cost both of us our freedom?"

Calamity tried hard to digest this information.

"The thing is, Calam, the marriage was a mistake— a *huge* mistake—and one that I have no intention of paying for with the rest of my life. I can't imagine why you'd want your sister to pay so dearly either."

She jutted out her chin, and then took another swallow of whisky. "Maybe you *are* what Stormy wants—have you thought of that? Maybe she don't think being your wife *is* such a danged mistake."

"Then Stormy is a fool," he said in a deceptively quiet voice. "A fool who has no idea who I really am." He paused, weighing the rest of his thoughts, and then offered them anyway. "Apparently, neither do you. Maybe if you'd bothered to look past the bottom of a whisky bottle before now, you'd have noticed that I'm not even close to good enough for your sister, this town isn't good enough for her, and hell, for that matter . . ." He stopped just short of saying something he knew he'd regret.

Calamity finished Luke's sentence in a wisp of a voice. "I ain't good enough for her either."

"Oh, hell, Calam. I didn't say that."

"No, you didn't, but don't think I don't know it's what you wanted to say." She hung her head. "And you had every right to say it. I know it's the truth."

Luke wanted to reach out to her, to tell her that she was wrong and offer some sort of comfort, but he couldn't seem to manage the lie. "All I'm saying is that none of us are fit to mingle with her kind, and no matter how hard we try, we never will be either. I say let her go now while she's still relatively pure of both body and heart."

"Let her go?" Calamity's grim brown eyes became as luminous as they ever did. "You mean send her away—alone?"

"That's how she got here, isn't it?"

"Well, yeah, but . . ." She shrugged.

"What other choice is there? If she stays here, we'll just wind up dragging her down with us and this town."

A tear found its way to the corner of Calamity's

eye. She blinked it down along with another swallow of whisky.

Hating her look of defeat, and himself even more for being the cause of it, he said, "Aw, hell. Maybe I'm wrong. Maybe if we try to talk some sense in her, or—"

"You ain't wrong, Luke," she said, pushing herself to her feet. "You ain't wrong a'tall. I know what I got to do." Tugging up her buckskin trousers, Calamity turned away from him and started back toward town.

Luke stood rigid for a moment, his heart aching as he watched her shuffling away, and then impulsively called out, "Calam?"

She paused and then answered him over her shoulder. "What?"

"When you see Stormy?"

She sighed. "Yeah?"

"Tell her I won't stand in the way of whatever she decides to do about me. You know, if she gets an annulment, or even talks Judge Kuykendall into forgetting the wedding ever happened. Whatever she decides is fine with me."

Calamity nodded and resumed her journey.

"Oh!" he shouted, halting her again. "And be sure to tell her . . . to mention that I said good-bye."

"Anything else?"

Luke hunched his shoulders and drove his hands into his pockets as if warding off a sudden chill. "Just one other thing, Calam. Try not to . . . hurt her too much."

Calamity hesitated for several moments, then continued her trek to town. "Yeah, sure Luke. Hell, yeah."

∗ ∗ ∗

Much later, close to midnight in fact, Stormy wrapped the final chocolate delicacy in a bit of waxed paper and carefully arranged it with the others in her basket. She had just cleaned her copper pot when at long last she heard several sharp raps on the door accompanied by her sister's familiar, "Eee—ya—haaa!"

When the door opened, Calamity practically fell across the threshold. "Hi ya, kid!" She sniffed the air. "What ya up to in here? Smells like you set fire to a sugar barrel!"

Ignoring Calamity's remarks, Stormy stuck her head through the opening and glanced up and down the alley. "Where's Luke? And what took you so long to get back?"

"Luke ain't gonna be joining us."

Alarmed by the tone of her sister's voice, Stormy quickly pulled the door shut and secured it with the pole. She turned toward the table and watched her sister stagger and then tumble into a chair. "What happened tonight?" she asked as she crossed the room. "Why isn't Luke with you, and how come you're so. . . . Where have you been? Supper's been ready for hours."

Calamity eyed the whisky on the shelf above the stove. "I ain't hungry. Fetch that bottle down here 'fore you sit down kid. We got us a couple a things to straighten out."

Although she knew her sister had already had far too much to drink, Stormy also knew better than to deny her. She grabbed the bottle and took a seat at the table. "Where's Luke?"

"Where he is about every night." She hiccuped, and then poured herself a cupful of whisky, spilling as much on the tablecloth as in the glass. "Mining the miners at the poker tables."

Stormy sighed. "What took you so long to come tell me that? I've been worried."

After a quick drink and a loud belch, Calamity snickered. "Hell, kid. Don't ever go worrying your head about me."

"It's not you I was worried about!" Nerves that had been tight as bow strings over the past few hours suddenly snapped. Stormy banged her fist against the table. "It's me I'm worried about for a change—understand? I worked like a madwoman around here while I was waiting for you! I was terribly excited about finding the little ones and making plans for the trip to Colorado and all, but then when you didn't come back, all that excitement flew right out the window. How could you have forgotten about me and gone out drinking in a saloon instead?"

Calamity pushed the bottle and her glass of whisky aside. Then she leaned across the table and said, "'Cause I'm no damn good, that's how."

Stormy's first impulse was to leap across the table, latch on to her sister's ears, and box them but good. She took several deep breaths, reminding herself that Calamity was somewhat in her cups, and searched for the reason behind her sister's insensitive behavior instead. It wasn't particularly hard to find.

Showing a great deal more compassion and understanding toward Calamity than she'd received from her, Stormy took her sister's hands in her own and said, "The little ones are going to be as happy to see you as I was. Not a one of us would ever even think of blaming you for what happened to the family after Ma and Pa died. That's what's got you so nervous about going to Colorado, isn't it?"

Calamity snatched her hands away and brought them to her eyes in an attempt to rub away the sudden stinging there. "That ain't it a'tall! I ain't got time to go lollygagging around the countryside with you. I got work to do right here in Deadwood. In fact, not two hours ago I signed up for a mail run to Custer in the morning. And don't forget—I got my oxcart business to tend, too. You want them little ones so bad, you go find them. Just leave me the hell out of it."

At those words, the tension slid right out of Stormy's shoulders. She smiled, knowing she'd guessed right about the guilt. Now she knew for sure that her sister's sense of shame had a big part in her reluctance to make the journey to Colorado. There was something else, too, something Stormy sensed, but it wasn't as clear. And it really didn't matter. Calamity didn't want to go search for the rest of the family, and there would be no point in trying to persuade her.

Careful to keep her tone nonjudgmental, she said quietly, "I guess I did forget about your business ventures, and I'm sorry if I sounded as if they didn't matter. We can easily make it to Colorado without you, and I'll be sure to tell the little ones how much you miss and love them when we get there. You can count on it."

"We?" Calamity said even though she knew exactly who her sister was referring to. "You got a weevil tucked inside your corset?"

"I'm talking about Luke, and you know it. If he's willing, I don't see why we can't leave with the next oxtrain that rolls through town."

"Well," Calamity grumbled, eyeing the glass of whisky, "He ain't."

"Ain't?" Stormy's breath froze, and then whistled out. "Surely you're not suggesting that he doesn't want to go to Colorado either . . . are you?"

At the panic in her sister's expression, Calamity lost the last thread of her resolve. She reached for the glass and downed the shot of whisky. Through a terrific shudder she said, "Sorry, kid. But, yes, I am. He don't want to go to no Colorady. Asked me to tell you that."

Stormy bit down on her lip, forcing her frozen lungs to contract again, to breathe. This couldn't be happening—my God, not after all she and Luke had been to each other in their room today! She'd seen how much he cared then, and not just in the way he touched her or made love to her. She'd seen it in his ebony eyes. If not quite love, she'd seen at least a deep affection. Luke cared about her. Stormy knew it in her heart, doubted that fact not for one minute. The question was, did he care enough to help her fulfill her dream?

With a pleading gaze, she whispered, "What did Luke say to you? Please tell me his exact words."

This, Calamity figured, was where she was supposed to mention Judge Kuykendall, the huge mistake, and the annulment, but how could she? Stormy looked so frightened and vulnerable, it was almost like seeing her as a child again. Calamity blinked, trying to rid herself of the sight, but when she opened her eyes, there sat Muffin, the little sister she'd sworn to protect from harm. She looked a lot like she had the day their mother died, that horrible afternoon they'd laid not just Charlotte but their stillborn baby sister to rest. Stormy had been inconsolable then, and nothing Calamity said or did had helped. There was no way she'd be able to console her if she mentioned what Luke had in mind, no way in *hell* to help heal her broken heart.

Deciding to let Luke do his own dirty work, Calamity struggled up from her chair. "I cain't remember his exact words, kid, but I do remember Luke's thoughts on the matter. He ain't going to no Colorady with you and that's that. Why don't you just figure on making the trip yourself?"

Stormy leapt out of her chair, following Calamity as she tottered into the bedroom. "But *why* doesn't he want to go? Surely he must have given some reason."

"I—I don't remember, kid. I just cain't remember." As she shrugged out of her jacket, Calamity came up with a way to keep from having to answer any more questions or tell any more lies. She fell heavily onto the bed and rolled face first onto the pillow.

Stormy leaned over the foot of the bed. "Calamity? Please don't ignore me. There's something you're not telling me—I know there is." A loud snore rattled up from the heavy woolen blanket. "Oh," she snapped.

"Good night, then. I'll see you when you get back from Custer."

She slipped out of the bedroom, banging the door shut behind her, and began to unbutton her blouse. In her heart of hearts, Stormy had known that Luke might not take to the idea of Colorado right away, but she'd counted on Calamity and their long friendship to help convince him to make the trip. Now that her sister's help was out of the question, she would have to broach the subject on her own. How difficult a task would it be to change her husband's mind?

Maybe things weren't as gloomy as they seemed. Near as Stormy could figure, all she really had to do was seek Luke out, clear up any misunderstandings Calamity may have caused during the evening, and make sure he realized how very much it meant to her to find the rest of her family. Surely he would change his mind about Colorado then. If Luke didn't exactly love her, he most certainly cared enough to want to ensure her happiness—didn't he?

Daring to fill herself with hope, Stormy slipped her nightgown down over her head and finalized her plans. She would stay the night here with her sister, and then in the morning, go to the hotel and wait for her husband. When he arrived, they would talk, he would see her point, and the future would look very bright indeed.

As she climbed between the sheets of Luke's old bed and closed her eyes, Stormy could almost see the snow-capped Rocky Mountains.

18

Waiting for her husband turned out to be the most ominous phrase imaginable. Stormy had done little else for the last two days. She'd even gone so far as to return to the hotel several times throughout the day just to see if she could catch Luke napping in their room, but she had yet to lay eyes on him. He was gambling, she supposed, or resting up at Charlie Utter's camp, but there was no way for her to find out for sure. If her sister were still in town, there would be no problem. Stormy would simply have sent her after him by now, but true to her word, Calamity had left the cabin the morning after they'd talked about Colorado and headed to Custer before dawn.

Her frustration rising, Stormy smoothed another square of waxed paper against the grocery counter, tearing a corner in the process. How was she to make plans for the future when she didn't even know when she'd see Luke again? Bit by bit, he seemed to be disappearing from her life. This morning had been the worst. When she'd gone to the Grand Central Hotel, she discovered that the few articles of clothing Luke usually left in the chiffonier were missing. As was his shaving gear. And his spare hat. Room 302 had never seemed so empty.

Maybe she was expecting too much as the bride of a Deadwood gambler. Perhaps catching bits and pieces of each other was the best any couple could manage in this ramshackle excuse for a town. Even ladies like Eudell Hawkes had to settle for "occasional" husbands, men who worked the mines at the edge of town, returning to town on Saturday for supplies and brief visits with their families only to head back to the hills the following night. In fact, that way of life seemed to be more the norm.

Normal or not, as the afternoon sun dropped behind the high mountains to the west, Stormy knew only one thing for certain. A time of reckoning was at hand for her. She couldn't get Colorado and the little ones out of her mind any more than she could forget the fact that neither Calamity nor Luke had shown an interest in making the journey with her.

Worse, the more she thought about it, the more her memory drifted back to the aromatic letter scripted on pale pink stationery. Suppose Miss Daisy Summers had something to do with Luke's sudden disappearance? What if he'd already left town! For all Stormy knew, he could have saddled up and ridden off the same morning as Calamity.

Stormy doubled up her fist in frustration, accidentally crumpling the used squares of waxed paper she'd smoothed out for reuse. "Damn," she muttered under her breath, surprising herself with a seldom-used oath.

"Excuse me, Stormy?" came the voice of her employer. "I'm busy tallying the day's receipts and didn't quite hear you."

Stormy whipped her head toward the other end of the counter where Eudell Hawkes was busy weighing gold dust on what was touted to be the most sensitive scale in town. "I, ah, said nothing, ma'am. Just cleared my throat."

"Oh." Eudell sacked up the last scoop of gold and cinched the bag tight. "Got any more of those chocolate dainties of yours? Lord if they aren't a little bit of heaven, I can't imagine what is."

Eudell's upper lip was shadowed with remnants of the many chocolates she'd already eaten during the day. Stormy glanced into the bottom of the basket and said, "I just have two left."

Working her way around the cash register to the front of the counter, Eudell reached into the basket and snatched them out. "Might's well take them for myself, in that case. Wouldn't want to disappoint someone who wanted a dozen or so, now would we?"

"No, ma'am."

Eudell unwrapped one of the candies and popped it into her mouth. "I have to run over to the bank for a while. Will you please mind the store until I get back?"

Although Stormy hadn't quite decided what to do

next, she said, "I really ought to get back to the cabin and make a batch of taffy. We're out of that, too."

"Don't worry, dear. I won't be long, and if Justin should return from his deliveries before I come back, he can take over for you." With a loud slurp, she started for the door. "If you get time tonight, we'd just *love* it if you'd make another batch of these chocolates. They're simply *wonderful.*"

Stormy thought of telling Eudell that she didn't have the time or the heart or the inclination to mess with chocolate dainties tonight. In fact, it suddenly occurred to her that if she didn't locate her husband soon and find out exactly what was going on with him, she wouldn't have time for anything. She'd be too busy packing up to leave this disgusting town—too busy planning a solitary journey to Colorado. But she didn't say a word. She smiled and waved as Eudell disappeared out into the streets of Deadwood, streets that Luke prowled night after night. Streets that she, a lady, was not allowed to navigate once the sun went down.

Or could she? Stormy wondered as thoughts of the evening she had gone after Calamity in the Number Ten Saloon surfaced. *If the mountain will not come to Mahomet, then Mahomet must go to the mountain.* Dressing up in miner's garb to seek out her loved one had certainly worked well enough before. How would Luke react if she were to stroll into his place of business and demand an audience? Outraged or flattered? As Stormy mulled over the idea, the very real dangers to both her heart and physical safety, Justin bustled in through the door.

"Hey there, Miz McCanles! How are you this fine day?"

"Not as fine as you, I would say from the look of it." Stormy gave him an indulgent smile. "What has you in such fine mettle today?"

He shrugged and spoke through a watery grin. "It's coming up on Friday, ma'am. That's when I get to run the regular supplies up to Lead . . . and thereabouts."

Thereabouts could only mean the home of Miss Savannah Ross, Stormy surmised, and she found herself envying Justin his joy, coveting the blush of new love lighting his youthful features, a love that had yet to go astray. The way her own might if she were forced to choose between Deadwood and Colorado. "Have you seen Mr. McCanles today?" she asked him.

"No, ma'am." He poked around in the empty candy basket. "Last I heard of Luke, he was busy consoling poor Ned Parker over at the Custer Saloon."

"Consoling Mr. Parker? Whatever for? My Lord, has something happened to Adelaide?"

"Not yet." He snickered. "I guess you ain't heard that last night poor old Ned was a-sitting at a poker table with Luke and at least three other gamblers when in marched Mrs. Parker."

"*Mrs. Parker?*" Save for Justin's mother, Adelaide Parker was the most respected woman in Deadwood, an assistant to Preacher Smith, no less! Why, how could she have found the gall to do such a thing? "Are you quite certain it was Adelaide Parker?"

"Oh, yes ma'am. It was her all right."

"But why on earth would she willingly go into a *saloon?*"

Again Justin snickered. "I don't know none of this firsthand, of course, but I was told that even though old Ned ain't never been what you'd call lucky at the tables, he just can't seem to stay away from them. Got the gambling sickness, I suppose. Anyway, last night, there was a huge pot of gold piled up in one of them games that'd been going on forever. That's about the time Miz Parker blew in through the door wearing an expression like a meat ax."

"You mean she risked her reputation just to collect her husband from a poker game?" Which suddenly didn't sound like such a bad idea.

"Yes, ma'am, she did that and then some. She didn't say nary a word. Just stomped up to the card players as pretty as you please, swept her arm across the table to scoop the entire pot into her big ol' apron, and then she marched back out of the saloon."

Stormy practically laughed out loud at the image. "Didn't Mr. Parker even try to stop her?"

"No one did, Miz McCanles. When she walked out that door, the saloon was quiet as a graveyard. Hell— oh, excuse me, heck—from what I heard, half them men are still sitting there in a complete state of consternation."

"And that half," Stormy guessed with a chuckle, "no longer includes Mr. Parker. Correct?"

"That'd be key-rect. No point in him staying, or even coming back to the Custer or any other saloon in this town either from what I hear. No one wants to play poker with a man got a wife as crazy as that. They're all scared she might do it again!"

And didn't it sound like a wonderfully clever bit of

insanity to Stormy at that moment. If *she* were to follow in Adelaide Parker's steps as early as this evening, the timing would be perfect. The incident with the Parkers should certainly be fresh enough in Luke's mind so that he would at least hear her out. And she wouldn't have to dress up like a grubby old miner after all.

"Got something else on my mind too, Miz McCanles," Justin said with his usual timidness. "I wonder if I might ask you to do me a favor?"

Although her mind was elsewhere—wondering how she could locate Luke without having to check in every saloon—she gave Justin a bright smile. "I suppose I would consider it as long as it's within reason."

"I was wondering if you could spare me one or two of them chocolate dainties. You know, free-like."

"Free-like? I'm not sure I understand what you mean. I sell my candy to your mother and she resells it, so actually, by the time I bring them here, the store owns my goods. You'll have to ask your mother about free candy."

Justin glanced over his shoulder as if just hearing the word *mother* might actually make her appear. They were still the only two people in the store. "You see, Miz McCanles, it's like this. I can't ask my ma cause I don't exactly want her to *know* I got the candy." He rubbed the boils on his neck. "She won't let me eat such things, and if I was to try to talk her out of a couple of pieces, she'd want to know what I want 'em for and such."

"Oh, I think I see." She glanced at the eruptions on his skin. "Next time I make a batch, I'll set a piece or two aside for you. I don't see how that little bit of chocolate could hurt your complexion anyway."

"Oh, golly, ma'am. They ain't for me. I wanted to give the candy as a kind of gift."

Wondering why she hadn't realized it on her own, she said, "You want them for Miss Ross, is that it?"

Justin's gaze fell to the floor and he nodded vigorously.

"Does it have to be chocolate dainties? Won't some taffy do as well?"

"Oh, no, ma'am. Miss Savannah dearly loves your chocolates, she does, and I so wanted to get her heart's desire for her, you know, if I could, that is. Before Friday, if possible."

Stormy sighed heavily at the thought, but her spirits lifted immediately as something else occurred to her. Smiling as the idea took shape in her mind, she said, "You know, Justin, making even a small half-sized batch of chocolate dainties is a lot of trouble for me."

He hung his head. "Sorry. I didn't know that, ma'am. Just forget I mentioned it."

"Oh, I don't think we have to do that. There might be a way, but I'd have to ask an awfully big favor of you in return."

"Anything, Miz McCanles! Anything a'tall!"

"All I really need from you is a little time and a lot of discretion. Do you know what that is?"

He squinted as if squeezing the information from his brain. "Keeping my mouth shut, ma'am?"

"Precisely, Justin. Can you manage that?"

"Yes, ma'am! What do I got to do?"

Even though no customers had passed through the door, Stormy motioned him to move closer. Then she leaned across the counter and whispered, "Just about the time it gets dark, I want you to go on a little manhunt for me. It means you'll have to poke your head in every saloon in Deadwood until you find the man I'm looking for, but once you find him your job is essentially finished. I don't want you to talk to him or anyone else about it. All you'll have to do after you find him is report back to me. What do you say?"

"Don't sound too hard, ma'am. Who are we looking for?"

Stormy flashed her dimples for the first time that day. "Another gambler whose luck is about to run out on him."

Later that night at least a full hour after dark, Stormy tied a ribbon of emerald satin around the cigar box she'd filled with chocolate dainties and set it aside for Justin. Then she slipped into a plain skirt and jacket of charcoal serge set off by dull pewter buttons, and finished her look in Sunday-go-to-meeting fashion. After twisting her hair into a tight little bun at the top of her head, Stormy reached for her favorite black velvet hat but at last second changed her mind, and donned the prune-colored bonnet instead.

Luke wouldn't care for her choice of headgear, she knew that of course, but she hadn't selected the over-sized bonnet out of spite or even stubbornness. She'd decided on the hat for personal reasons. The only man Stormy wanted gazing into her eyes or searching her expression tonight was Luke McCanles. As she studied herself in the mirror, she decided the ugly bonnet would assure her of that. Going over the things she planned to say once she confronted her husband, Stormy tugged on her heavy boots and began pacing the floor.

Justin arrived ten minutes later, his face flushed, his breathing rapid as she opened the door. "I found him," he said, panting as he caught his breath. "I was about ready to give up the search when I had a look in the Texas Star Saloon. Why is it always the last place you go looking for something that you find what you're after?"

In no mood for idle chatter, Stormy practically buried the cigar box in Justin's gut as she said, "I think it has something to do with providence. Here's your candy."

"Why, thank you, Miz McCanles." He tested the weight of the box, beaming. "Thanks a heap!"

"You're welcome. Now tell me—what was Luke doing?"

"Playing poker with some other fellahs."

"You didn't speak to him or mention that I'm looking for him, did you?"

"No, ma'am. I just seen him, and then I come right here like you said."

"Good." She pushed the door shut behind her and stepped out into the alley. "There's just one other thing I'd like you to do for me. Will you please escort me to the Texas Star Saloon?"

Justin's upswept eyes bugged out. "You ain't

thinking of going in there, are you? You ain't—
Lordy! You ain't planning on doing what Miz Parker
done, are you?"

Her resolve wavering, Stormy inhaled deeply as she
said, "I'm not exactly sure what I intend on doing. I
just know that I have to do it there. Now please,
Justin. Let's go now before I lose my courage."

And she was most definitely in danger of losing
more than her courage, Stormy realized as she took
the young man's arm and started down the alley. Her
stomach was doing slow, nauseating rolls, making her
feel as if she'd eaten an entire batch of her own
chocolate dainties, and her heart was beating so fast
she could hardly draw a full breath. How in God's
name, she wondered again, had Adelaide Parker
found the pluck to do what she'd done?

Keeping that woman's courage foremost in her
mind as she and Justin reached the wide double doors
of the saloon, Stormy made a solemn vow to herself:
No matter what happened next, up to and including
the worst scenario possible—that Luke would carry
her bodily from the bar and toss her into a mud puddle on Main Street—she *would not* cry. There would
be plenty of time for weeping later if the outcome
didn't go as planned. A lifetime to shed her tears, in
fact.

"Here we are, ma'am," Justin announced. "Are you
still so sure you want to go in there? Luke ain't gonna
like it much if you do, you know."

Stormy straightened her shoulders and drew in a
deep breath. "I'm aware of that, Justin, but thanks for
reminding me and for all your help tonight. I'd appre-

ciate it if you'd go on home now. I think I'll have enough of an audience as it is."

"Whatever you say, Miz McCanles." He tipped his hat and snapped his suspenders as he backed away. "And good luck to you in there."

"Thank you." Stormy waited in the shadows by the doors until Justin had gotten completely out of sight before she risked a peek inside the saloon. The room, she noted with relief, was blessedly cursed with poor lighting, the glow from an inadequate number of lamps murky at best. Still, she could see that there were some twenty or thirty men inside, most of them sitting at the tables where female faro dealers flipped cards at customers from out of long wooden boxes. Other women, the "entertainers" or dancing girls she surmised by their gaudy and scandalously skimpy costumes, wandered through the crowd serving drinks and flirting. At one of the few tables that didn't feature a female faro dealer, she finally recognized the features of her husband. He was sitting with five other men.

Steeling herself against the wave of protest her presence was sure to bring, Stormy parted the doors and marched into the saloon. Luke and the gamblers with him didn't notice her or even look up from their cards until she reached their table and said over the noisy crowd, "Excuse me, gentlemen. I'd like to have a private word with my husband. Would you mind leaving us alone for a few moments?"

If the funny little jesters decorating the pair of aces Luke held had jumped down off the pasteboards and started dancing a jig, he couldn't have been more surprised than he was when he looked up to see Stormy standing across the table from him. "W-what in *hell?*"

None of the other gamblers spoke or moved. They sat in stunned silence, their mouths opened like baby birds. Moving ahead with her plan, Stormy gazed down at the pot of gold, narrowed her silver eyes, and warned, "I can scoop up a lot more of those winnings with the skirt I'm wearing than Adelaide Parker could have if she'd donned *three* aprons. Perhaps you gentlemen didn't hear what I said?"

The five gamblers answered as one. Their chairs screeching in protest, the men pushed away from the table, leapt up, and took off for the bar. The saloon grew quiet after that, the only conversations hushed and too muted for Stormy's ears, but she could feel the curiosity and astonishment of a thousand eyes boring into her back. Concentrating on the only pair that concerned her—the cold black orbs cutting into her from across the table—she sat down and let her gaze linger on the pot of gold.

"I don't know what in *hell* you're up to," Luke muttered hoarsely. "But if you even *think* about touching that pot, I swear to God I'll blow your fingers all the way to hell and back."

Stormy thought of defying him, of impulsively scooping up a handful of gold dust just to call his bluff, but wisely folded her hands into her lap instead. "I didn't come here to pick up where Adelaide Parker left off, but if you force me to, I will."

Luke's gaze darted around the room. He lowered his head and his voice as he said, "The only thing I intend to force you to do is leave this bar! Now what in hell do you think you're doing in here? I don't happen to think that this little stunt of yours is particularly smart or amusing."

Stormy met Luke's nervous gaze. He was as angry as she'd ever seen him, and embarrassed too. Feeling as if the latter expression gave her the upper hand, she forged ahead. "I didn't come here to be smart or funny. I just wanted to get your attention."

"Then I'd have to say you succeeded handsomely." He glanced around the room again, this time shooting barbed glances at any man fool enough to be caught staring at him. Then he leveled his gaze on Stormy. "You also managed to get the attention of every other man in this room. Is that what you have in mind?"

"All I'm after is a conversation with my husband. I've been trying to find you for three days now, but you've been extremely difficult to locate. I thought you might even have . . . left town, or something." Stormy reached into her pocket, withdrew the telegram, and dropped it on the table. "This came for me with the mail you got the other day. It's from Reverend Brigham Young in Utah. He says that my little brothers were taken in by a family heading to Colorado, and that—"

"I know all about your plans to go to Colorado," he said, cutting her off. "Didn't Calamity tell you she spoke to me about it?"

Her gaze fell to the table. "Yes. She said you didn't think you wanted to go with me, but she'd been drinking and I hoped that she was wrong."

"She wasn't. I don't want to go Colorado now or ever." He glanced around the saloon again. Even though most of the patrons had gone back to what they'd been doing before Stormy burst in the room, far too many eyes were still upon them. Forcing a stern tone, he said, "Why don't you skedaddle on out of here before what's left of your reputation is ruined?"

"There are several things more important to me than my reputation, Luke." Stormy's gaze, more determined than ever, met his and held it. "One of those things is my family. Another is the fact that I'm your wife. Do you really expect me to pack up and leave for Colorado without you?"

At the determination and challenge in her words, the whispered comments and prying eyes of the other gamblers seemed to fade into meaningless chatter. All Luke could see or hear was Stormy. God but she was beautiful, ugly bonnet and all. Beautiful, courageous, and ridiculously naive to think she could march in here and convince him to do her bidding.

So bold was she, in fact, that it almost gave him second thoughts. It'd be so easy to scoop Stormy into his arms and sweep her away with him. Easy and self-serving like every other thing he'd ever done in the past. This time, he swore to himself, he would put his own needs aside. Luke couldn't be certain exactly what drove him to such chivalrous heights, but for the first time in his life, he felt the magnificent anguish of sacrifice.

Struggling with that anguish, he said to Stormy, "You managed to find Deadwood from Colorado alone. I don't see why you need me to find your way back."

His tone set off some ominous alarms of panic in Stormy. "Of course I need you, Luke," she said with near desperation, "and I want you with me wherever I go! You're my husband."

"Calamity told you how to get yourself out of that little inconvenience, didn't she?"

"Inconvenience?" She faltered, taken off guard by the remark. "I—I don't know what you mean."

"Didn't your sister say anything about us?"

"Us? I have no idea what you're talking about."

His fists dropped to the table. "Calamity was supposed to tell you how to go about getting yourself out of this marriage. You mean she didn't?"

"*Out?*" Stormy's heart turned a somersault. "What's that supposed to mean?"

Luke sighed heavily and glanced around the room again. There were sacrifices, but then there were *sacrifices.* Knowing he couldn't handle much more of this conversation under these circumstances, he said, "It seems your sister forgot to mention a couple of things she promised me she would. I guess you and I do need to talk, but we'll have to do it some other time and at some other place. Go back to your cabin now, and I'll look you up when I get a chance tomorrow."

"No." The word was spoken in a tone as flat and dead as the sudden demise of Stormy's heartbeat. If she'd been carved from all the gold in Deadwood, she couldn't have felt more leaden. In a voice as heavy as her heart, she said, "We'll finish what we have to say to each other here and now. I'm not leaving this table until I know exactly where I stand with you."

Again came the urge to sweep her into his arms and carry her away forever. Fighting that impulse, Luke pushed both hands through the hair at each of his temples, and said, "Dammit all, Stormy. This isn't the way I wanted things to end between us."

Her heart lurched, but remembering her vow, she blinked back a tear and kept her voice low and steady. "Exactly how *did* you think it would end?"

Luke hesitated, studying her expression thoroughly for cracks in her suddenly tough demeanor before he would answer her. She looked cool and determined on the outside, ready for anything he had to say, but he also thought he noticed a little flicker in the steel gray of her eyes, maybe even the hint of a tear. He hadn't wanted to hurt her before, and didn't want to now, but had she left him any other choice?

Choosing his words carefully, Luke finally admitted, "I think it'd be best for us both if you were to go see Judge Kuykendall and ask him about giving you an annulment or something like that."

"An—" But Stormy couldn't form the syllables to repeat the word. In all her suppositions as she prepared for this little showdown, never, *ever,* had she considered that Luke might have tired of her, or that he didn't want her in his life anymore. How could she hope to hang on to a man who wanted nothing but to be free of her?

Feeling defeated, too miserable even for tears, Stormy spoke so softly that her voice almost couldn't be heard. "I won't fight you if getting rid of me is what you want, Luke. I had no idea you were so unhappy with me."

Again Luke's hands fell to the table. "Aw, Jesus, Stormy. This doesn't have a damned thing to do with happiness. Surely you haven't really considered that impulsive little wedding of ours as a real marriage, have you? We both made a stupid mistake—why compound it by tangling in each other's lives?"

Her gaze fell to the table and she sniffed back a tear. "It doesn't feel like a mistake to me. Except for these last few moments, I've rather enjoyed being Mrs. Luke McCanles."

Until then, Luke had been ready to take back his words, maybe even to give their marriage a try for a little longer—long enough anyway for her to discover that she'd tied herself to a man who didn't exist in her own time. But Stormy had just made sending her away easy for him. She was beginning to remind him of Agnes Lake, the woman who'd married Wild Bill Hickok not for the love she professed but for the privilege of using his name to help advertise her circus show.

Smiling grimly, he said, "You may keep the title of Mrs. Luke McCanles, if you wish. I don't think you have to worry about running across another one in the near future."

Startled by his sudden arrogance, Stormy glanced up into his eyes. His gaze was intense, those black eyes as full of purpose as they'd been the night he'd come to her with Judge Kuykendall. The intent this time, of course, was quite the complete opposite. She swallowed, steeling herself against further rejection, and served up not just a dash of truth but her heart as well. "I don't care about the title, Luke. I care about you. In fact . . . I love you."

The only visible sign Luke gave that he even heard the words was a subtle tightening of his fingers. His gut was churning and his heartbeat was out of control. He took in the shape of her mouth as Stormy formed the words, the subtle dipping of her dimples, and the way her cinnamon lashes shyly brushed the upper reaches of her cheekbones as she'd said them. God, what he wouldn't give to watch her form those words again, to have her say them when they were meant for the man inside and not some fictional hero. What he wouldn't give!

"Luke?" Stormy whispered across the table. "Did you hear what I said?"

"Yes," he snapped, fighting his own emotions and a sudden surge of anger. "It's just that having young women fall in love with him is a hazard Lucky Luke McCanles has contended with throughout his career. I am sorry that you've become afflicted with the malady, but let me assure you of this—you will get over it. Now I'd really appreciate it if you'd leave so I can finish my poker game."

Luke's declarations didn't make complete sense to her, especially when he'd referred to himself in the third person, but Stormy did understand one certainty above all: He didn't want her anymore. It was done. The anger and hatred glittering in his ebony eyes gave testament to the futility of arguing with him further. A wave of nausea swept through her. Stormy gripped the edge of the table for balance, her heart in her throat, her stomach roiling like a kettle of hot taffy, and struggled to get control of herself. Then she opened her eyes again, daring to hope she'd been wrong, maybe even to discover Luke smiling at her, *loving* her. What she saw instead was that a buxom dancing girl had cozied up behind him.

"Need some help, sugar?" Blonde May asked, giggling as she gawked at Stormy's bonnet. "You two are looking a little agitated."

Without glancing up at her, Luke said, "I can take care of this myself, May. It's a private matter."

May looked around the room, rolling her voluptuous hips from one side to the other as she adjusted her stance, but she made no move to leave. "I wouldn't say this conversation is as private as all that. After what happened over at the Custer Saloon last night, we can't afford to have this sort of thing happening all over town. It's bad for business, not to mention a real blot on your record if you want to be the first sheriff of Deadwood."

Stormy gasped. "You mean you're planning to take the position after all?"

Although he had no intention of seeking or accepting the job of U.S. deputy marshal, Luke saw it as a quick way to end the increasingly uncomfortable conversation. Not pausing long enough to think what the entertainer's reaction might be, he gave Stormy a slow, careful nod.

Blonde May immediately whirled around toward the crowd, her scarlet petticoats flying up above her knees. "Listen up everyone," she shouted above the din. "He's gonna do it, folks! Lucky Luke McCanles has just agreed to become the first sheriff of Deadwood!"

This news was greeted with cheers and whistles,

and above the roar of approval, the voice of an excited miner declared that he was buying drinks for the house. Thinking he would have to repay the man anyway once he reversed his position, Luke pushed up from his chair to claim the tab for himself. Just then a man in a blue flannel shirt ran past him, smashing against Luke's shoulder and knocking him back into his chair.

"Hey!" Luke hollered, but the man had already fled the saloon. Stormy, he noticed, looked shaken and startled. The rude gambler forgotten, suddenly all Luke could think of was getting her out of the saloon before the "happy" crowd got even happier.

Toughening his voice and his expression, Luke leaned across the table and said, "Get out of here before this crowd really gets to partying. Go to Colorado, gather up the rest of your family, and have a happy life."

Encouraged by Luke's declarations, Blonde May slid her arm across his shoulder. "You heard him, sugar," she purred. "This ain't no place for the likes of you."

Luke shrank from May's touch, but instead of flinging her arm off his shoulder, he fought the impulse and decided to use her brazenness to help drive home his point with Stormy. Forcing himself to relax, looking as if he were enjoying the attentions of the other woman immensely, he stared woodenly across the table and said, "I suggest that you look up your lawyer tomorrow and explain that you made a little mistake. Tell him you accidentally married a bastard who abandoned you and that you'd like to take steps to correct the situation. I'll be sure to back up anything you say if he should ask."

Feeling even bolder, May stroked Luke's broad shoulder with intimate caresses, and then slid her fingers into the thick sable curls at the back of his neck. "I'll just bet she's got plenty to say about the kind of trouble you've been giving her, too, hasn't she, Luke honey?"

"That's about the truth of it, sweet darlin'."

Stormy had seen and heard all she could bear. Her heart felt as if it were splitting in two, and her pulse pounded against her throat and ears in a terribly erratic rush. Hands and knees trembling violently, her gaze still locked in Luke's, she slowly rose up from her chair. With a quick glance at May, who was smiling triumphantly, Stormy took a last look at the man who was still her husband. He smiled back at her. Not the bad-boy grin, and not even a smug told-you-so kind of expression. Rather, he looked grim. As if he were smiling to acknowledge the mourners at his own mother's funeral.

Collecting the shreds of her dignity, not daring to chance the betrayal of what her own voice might reveal, Stormy offered Luke a curt nod and then, on legs stiff and wooden, with her chin held high, she turned and slowly walked out of the saloon.

19

The cool night air smacked against Stormy's face as she stepped out of the saloon. She swallowed several times in succession in a feeble attempt to keep her tears inside, hoping to maintain control of herself just long enough to reach the cabin safely, but it didn't work. She burst into sobs despite her efforts.

With tears of anguish streaming down her cheeks, Stormy stumbled around the corner of the Texas Star Saloon and ducked into the shadows of the narrow, littered alleyway. With her legs trembling, she flattened her back against the wall of Sally Mae's Bathhouse and slid down to her haunches. There she gave up the battle and dropped her head against her knees, allowing the tempest to run its course.

When she'd left for the saloon tonight, she'd been excited, if a little anxious, but filled with more hope than trepidation. How could all her well-laid plans, her very *life,* have gone so terribly awry? She'd figured on Luke being a little stubborn about changing his mind over the trip to Colorado. She'd even suspected that he'd put up some resistance about leaving Deadwood in the near future. But to shut her completely out of his life? To ask her to forget that she was ever his wife? Never had she considered that possibility.

Stormy knew but one thing in all her confusion: She'd lost the only man she'd ever loved, and she didn't even know why. Her thoughts returned to the aromatic letter he'd received. Suppose she *had* been right about Miss Daisy Summers's connection to Luke's sudden lack of interest in their marriage? Or perhaps the blond woman in the bar was more to his liking.

Stormy shuddered with both anger and disgust as she thought back to the intimate way the painted entertainer had moved her hands across his shoulders, rubbing her hips against his body like a shameless alley cat. She also recalled the words her sister had used when she tried to warn her off Luke: "He likes 'em a little rough around the edges." Maybe that was the problem in a nutshell. She was just too damn priggish to keep her man.

Inside the bar, Luke sat as rigid as the wooden stallion gracing the roof of the Kentucky Stud Saloon across the street. He watched as Stormy slipped through the double doors, disappearing from view. Unaware until then that May's fingers were still in his hair, still touching him and stroking him down to the very nerve endings, he clenched his fists and said, "Take your hands off of me. I want to be left alone."

"Golly, honey pie." She pouted, removing herself from his person. "There's no need to get so nasty."

"I haven't even begun to get nasty, May," he warned. "Why don't you run along before I get that way, and while you're at it, have someone bring over a bottle of whisky."

"Sure thing, you big grump!" With a toss of her blond curls, she flounced away, leaving Luke to his thoughts.

And dark thoughts they were. If he didn't know another thing, he knew then that he'd never get the memory of Stormy's crushed expression out of his mind—or the fact that he could have kept her with him for a short time longer, living the lie perhaps, but living it in her arms. It seemed a fair enough exchange for the use of his name, now that he thought about it. Especially as he recalled the boundless rewards of lying in those soft arms.

But then indulging in those rewards wouldn't be fair to Stormy. The very fact that he'd chosen not to do so again had been a damned generous gesture on his part, and a responsible one, too. So why didn't he feel better about sending her away? Why did the idea of life without Stormy twist his insides like colick did in the gut of an old mule?

The odds of understanding that little mystery weren't good. Luke knew that as well as he knew anything. Hell, he'd never been able to figure out what attracted him to Stormy in the first place, much less understood what insanity had driven him to marry her. It sure as hell wasn't the spinsterish way she made herself up in that disgustingly ugly bonnet!

In spite of his mood, Luke almost laughed as he remembered how hard she'd worked to hide those incredible silver eyes, that innocent, eager mouth, and her seductively guileless body from him in the beginning. Since then, he'd come to know the true beauty beneath the prudish garb, and as an added bonus, glimpsed deeper to discover an inherent decency deep in her soul. Stormy Ann Cannary, the woman who'd become his wife for a brief period, possessed the kind of purity that even the corrupt streets of Deadwood or a has-been like Lucky Luke McCanles couldn't contaminate. And thank God for that. Women like Blonde May were more his style. Hell if they weren't—but hadn't he just sent her away, too?

Shaken when he realized the reason why—that the memory of Stormy would haunt him forever, ruining him for all other women—Luke craned his neck toward the bar and shouted, "Where in the hell is that whisky I ordered?"

"Coming up, sugar," May called back.

As Luke waited for the drink and the relief he hoped it might offer, the men he'd been playing poker with returned to the table. Keeping their wary eyes on Luke, each gambler sank down on his chair, picked up his discarded hand, and perused the cards as if they'd never been interrupted.

Luke glanced over at Al Harvey, a placer miner known simply as "the Poet," and said, "Deal me out."

"But Luke, old friend," said Al, "the pot ain't been touched, and yur woman's on the mend. So forget about Ned—this weren't near the same. Pick up yur cards and let's get on with the game."

Luke shot a vicious gaze in the Poet's direction.

Al kept his next rhyme to himself and resumed shuffling the cards.

Luke closed his eyes, his thoughts drifting back to Stormy. He could almost see her sitting across from him in that goddamned bonnet. Her chin was set defiantly, her smoky eyes flashing as she made her case for going to Colorado. Had she ever looked more adorable than she had tonight, bonnet and all? How had he ever managed the lies he'd told her, the cruel remarks? He'd been rough on her. Too rough, he decided.

Maybe he should have taken the time to explain things better, to humble himself before her, and to let her know exactly what kind of man she'd married. She'd have been disappointed to discover who the real Luke McCanles was—no doubt about that—but at least she might have understood better his reasons for turning her away. Hell, she'd probably be grateful for his honesty and the end to her illusions. Luke sighed. He'd go to her and explain everything. Maybe then he wouldn't have to worry about the memory of Stormy's stricken features burning into his mind for the rest of his life.

"Here's your whisky, sugar," May said as she set the bottle on the table.

"Why don't you drink it, sweet darlin'?" Luke pushed out of his chair. "I'll join you a little later." Then he headed for the doors.

* * *

In the alley, Stormy's sobs had finally eased to intermittent sniffles. Collecting herself, she dabbed at her cheeks and eyes and then slowly rose and leaned against the wall. Before she could turn and start for the street, she heard the rumble of several pairs of boots thumping against the boardwalk connected to the bathhouse. Realizing the jeopardy she might be in if the owners of those boots were to spot her, Stormy flattened herself against the rough-hewn logs and waited for the men to pass by.

The footfalls stopped just short of the final plank on the boardwalk. Shortly after, fat curls of cigar smoke drifted into the alley and under Stormy's nose, tickling the inside of her nostrils. She pressed a finger against her upper lip to stifle a sneeze and prayed that the men would continue on by her.

Raucous piano music from inside the bar reverberated against the wall, pounding out a rhythm that matched the frantic beat of her heart. In the distance a lone wolf howled, drawing her attention to the full moon overhead. A violent shudder racked Stormy from head to toe, pushing her against the wall, driving tiny spears of splintered pine through the material of her jacket to scratch her delicate back.

When one of the men began speaking in hushed tones, she nearly cried out with terror but bit it back and kept her silence.

"Are you sure Buck isn't too damn drunk to handle this, Tim? Look at him! He's asleep on his feet."

"He's no drunker than Crooked Nose was," said

another voice. "McCall's aim was straight enough to get the job done."

A pause, and then, "I guess you're right." Boots scuffling, and then the same voice. "Straighten up, Buck. Tell us one more time exactly what you're gonna do when you get inside the saloon."

A hiccup. "Find Luke McCanles and . . ." He made a sound with his mouth that mimicked gunfire.

"And after that?"

"Go to Shh-sherman Street where you'll be—" he belched loudly, "waiting with the horses."

"Christ, you're a mess. Stay away from the whisky when you go inside, and don't come out until you're sure McCanles is dead."

Unable to stop herself, Stormy gasped in horror.

A second later, a man wearing a blue flannel shirt rounded the corner and grabbed the collar of her jacket.

When Luke stepped through the double doors of the Texas Star Saloon, the first shock to his system was the realization that night had fallen. How had he managed to lose track of the time so completely? Jesus, he'd sent Stormy out into the streets of Deadwood after dark! Before the full impact of that glaring error had time to sink in, the second shock struck. From his left came the blood-curdling screams of a woman in distress.

Stormy! With no thought to his own safety, Luke bound down off the boardwalk and dashed into the alley. Spotting a group of shadowy figures moving toward a moonlit path some fifty yards away, he drew his pistol and called out, "Stop right there in the name of the law!"

Stormy clawed at the rough, dirty hand clamped against her mouth, dislodging it long enough to cry out, "Go back, Luke! They—" The hand found her lips again, squeezing them and her nose so flat she could barely breathe, much less finish her warning. The owner of that hand, a big brutish man the others called Brody, began to drag her backward, issuing a fast order to his friends as he slipped around the corner to Sherman Street. "What are you waiting for, Buck? There stands your target—unload your gun into the bastard!"

Luke shouted another warning as he rushed farther into the alley. "Stop or I'll shoot! Identify yourself!"

The hulking shadows of two, maybe three people, disappeared around the corner, leaving one figure silhouetted in a cloak of moonlight. Luke had to make a decision. Fire on the man blindly with no clue to his identity, or take a chance on getting shot himself. What would Hickok do under these circumstances? Too late, Luke realized that taking the time to make that decision cost him a split second he couldn't afford.

As he brought his gun up level and took aim, a flash of gunpowder caught his eye. In the next moment, the Colt was ripped from Luke's hand and a lancing pain seared the heel of his palm. He fell to his knees, blindly groping for the pistol with his bloodied hand, and he heard another shot ring out in the darkness. Less than an inch from his right knee, a clump of earth kicked up, spraying him with particles of dirt. Luke dove for the ground, gripping the Colt with both hands, and began firing at the figure as he rolled toward the wall and the cover of its shadow.

The man in the alleyway swayed drunkenly for a moment, then crumpled and fell. Luke belly-crawled to where the body lay, his gun and gaze pinned on the man's bulk, ready for even the slightest movement. The gunman was dead. A stranger at that. Puzzled, Luke quickly rounded the corner and scanned Sherman Street. There he found what he assumed was the dead man's horse, but no sign of his accomplices. Or Stormy. Turning his attention to the road, he picked up the sound of two or more horses galloping away toward Lead.

Frantic to catch up to the riders before any harm could come to Stormy, Luke ripped off his tie and used it to wrap his injured hand. Then he glanced around in the shadows with thoughts of amassing a posse, the way Bill would have done. A few curious citizens hid in doorways and around corners, but none ventured forth to offer assistance. If he took the time to go from saloon to saloon in order to seek help, Stormy's abductors would gain an even bigger head start. It was going to be tough enough to track them in the dark.

Seeing no other choice, Luke named himself temporary sheriff of Deadwood and launched his body onto the dead man's horse. He spurred the animal into a gallop down the main road and then veered up a narrow trail to the east where he spotted a strip of white petticoat sparkling out from the dark earth.

The new path led him deep into the forested hills surrounding Deadwood, but Luke followed the course set by the outlaws with surprising ease, especially for a man with a deficient sense of direction. If he didn't know better, he would have sworn the kidnappers purposefully laid out an easy trail for him to follow. As he neared the crest of the hill where the ground was thick with deadwood from a tornado, he spotted Stormy's bonnet lying atop a large tangle of deadfall. Luke pulled the horse to a halt and listened.

At first all he could hear was the heavy panting of his tired mount, but then he picked up the rustling of leaves and a few grunts and groans—noises from a scuffle. When a feminine yelp accompanied those sounds, Luke climbed down off the horse and proceeded on foot. Save for the whisper of pine needles and leaves under his own boots, all was quiet as he reached the crest of the hill. There a huge boulder rose up from the earth, its center cracked, dividing it nearly in two. Butt Rock, as the locals liked to call it. Directly below, a few tall pines stood watch over their fallen cousins, but other than that, the landscape here was bleak, almost barren.

The moon shone directly down on the huge boulder making the surface seem slick and wet, although the night was as dry as Luke's suddenly parched throat. Instinct warning him that the men he sought stood directly behind Butt Rock, he used one of the surviving pines as cover and drew both of his weapons.

Even though he doubted his throbbing right hand

would be of much use, he raised the pair of Colts and shouted into the calm of the night. "Give it up, fellahs! You're surrounded. Let the woman go!"

On the other side of the boulder, Stormy grappled with her abductor. He held her tight against his body, her back lashed against his chest with a strong right arm, her mouth buried beneath the coarse crust of his left hand. She fought him anyway, twisting and kicking, seeking an unguarded moment, an area of vulnerability. When she found it, accidentally spearing his solar plexus with her elbow, she was almost too surprised by his howl of pain to react.

But she managed to tear out of the man's grip as he sought to catch his breath, and then she screamed as loud as she could, "Run, Luke! They don't want me—it's you they're after, *you* they want to kill! Run, Luke. *Run!*"

Following her own advice, she broke to the left, bolting blindly down the incline, away from danger. Her loose hair streaming behind her like a river of gold, she ran headlong into the man in the blue flannel shirt. Catching the bulk of those unfettered locks in his fist, he hauled her up short.

Luke saw the figures darting in and out of the pines, and heard Stormy's cries of pain, but he couldn't chance a shot. Moving higher on the mountain in hopes of gaining a better viewpoint, he shouted a warning at the kidnappers. "Let her go now, or I swear—I'll see you hang for this!"

The outlaw chuckled hoarsely as he wound Stormy's hair tighter around his fist, balling it up so snug against her scalp that she heard several strands popping like corn against the inside of her skull. A guttural cry escaped her lips, but rendered helpless by the paralyzing pain, she was unable to speak or move.

Pleased by the whimpering pleas of his captive, John Brody called out to Luke, "I don't want to hurt the woman. My gripe is with you. Show yourself and I'll let her go."

Did he have any other choice? From higher on the mountain, on the north side of Butt Rock, he could hear someone creeping through the mat of pine needles and twigs. The man who'd spoken was dead ahead, concealing himself and Stormy behind a thick pine tree that listed dangerously downhill. The other man was getting closer. Soon, Luke guessed, he would be surrounded and of no use whatsoever to Stormy.

Offering himself as a target, he stepped into the clearing and under a beam of moonlight. "Turn her loose," Luke demanded, onstage again, but this time for real. "Once the woman is safe, we'll talk."

The outlaw holding Stormy brayed his laughter. "There's nothing to talk about, McCanles. We like Deadwood just the way it is. We don't need you or Wild Bill Hickok cleaning it up for us either! Ready, T.J.?"

From fewer than twenty yards to his left, Luke heard the other man declare, "Ready!"

And then everything happened in a blur. From the south, a man dragged Stormy out from behind the dead pine. He laughed, and then threw her down the side of the mountain. Enraged, Luke raised the barrel of the gun in his injured hand and leveled it on the man. Before he could pull the trigger, he heard the retort of gunfire. Then something slammed into him, lifting him off his feet and smashing him down to the ground with such force that his head spun.

After a long moment of stunned silence, Luke heard men's voices. And then Stormy's cries reached him from off in the distance. With the sudden, agonizing return of his senses came an unbearable explosion of pain. He'd been shot, gut shot if he had to make a guess. Truth was, Luke couldn't pinpoint exactly where he'd been hit. He just knew that everything south of his chest and north of his kneecaps had caught fire, and the flames were growing in intensity, spreading throughout his entire body.

The voices came clear again, confident, full of arrogance. Stormy's cries were louder, too, closer to danger than before. Why hadn't she run away when she had the chance? *Fine, then,* he muttered to himself, recognizing a slight insanity to his thoughts. *If that's what she wants, then let her be the sheriff for a while.* Being a showman wasn't nearly as much fun as it used to be anyway.

Luke relaxed then, snuggling his head against the carpet of pine needles as if preparing to nod off to sleep. Just before he drifted away, a spurt of lucid thought alerted him to the danger of the situation—and the fact that the outlaws were so close, he could smell the days'-old sweat and cigar smoke on their clothing.

"Get the girl," said one. "I'll make sure McCanles is dead."

Figuring he was already about as dead as he could get, Luke failed to entertain any thoughts for ensuring his survival. But there was still a chance to save Stormy. Drawing on all his strength, Luke rolled over onto his back, his pistols raised, and began firing blindly at the two shadows coming toward him.

As Stormy clawed her way back up the side of the hill, she saw the outlaws working their way down to Luke. Then the firing began, and one on top of the other, the kidnappers fell. When she reached Luke, he was still lying on his back, still clicking the hammers of his empty Colts.

Overcome with residual terror, ecstatic to find him still alive, Stormy threw herself to the ground at his side. "Luke!" she cried, ducking between his flailing arms. "Oh, Luke!"

"I told that idiot not to give the Indians guns!" The pistols fell from his hands and his arms flopped down beside his head. "The Rough Riders have to win . . . that's what the public wants!" He lifted his head. "It's that goddamn Buffalo Bill and his giant ego! What in hell does he know about Indians anyway?" Luke groaned, and his head fell back against the ground. "That's it for me," he declared in an agonized whisper. "No more shows. I quit. I . . . quit." And then he passed out.

Two hours later, although after what Stormy had been through it seemed much longer, she paced in the parlor Doc Pierce used as his waiting room. Her serge suit was mottled with Luke's blood, her loose hair tangled, hanging down over her shoulders and back. She was exhausted, and her tears continued to fall. But she couldn't sit or rest.

Luke was gravely injured. She knew that much when she'd discovered his wound. He'd been bleeding profusely, even after she bandaged him with not one but two of her petticoats. By the time she roused him enough to help her slide him up on a horse, he'd soaked through the yards of cotton. After that, the slow, tedious trip down the side of the mountain became a blur, a nightmare of terror.

"Mrs. McCanles?"

With a startled intake of breath, Stormy whirled to see Doc Pierce standing near the doorway of his office. "Is Luke going to be all right?" she asked, sweeping across the room.

The doctor's features, sad-eyed and droopy by nature, seemed to darken as he slowly shook his head. "I'm sorry to have to tell you this, but—"

"He's not dead!" She grabbed the sleeves of his shirt. "Tell me he's not *dead!*"

Doc Pierce took her by the shoulders, his expression unchanged. "No, Mrs. McCanles. The bullet went clean through your husband and didn't seem to do a lot of organ damage, but he's lost an awful lot of blood. I don't think he's going to make it."

20

He's not going to make it. Over the next two nights and days, Stormy fought the echo of those words, but each time she stopped tending Luke long enough to nap, she woke up to the memory of them, like it or not. As she slowly awakened on the third morning, Stormy thought she heard a different phrase echoing in her ear, one spoken in a voice a little more familiar to her than Doc Pierce's.

"Eee—ya—*haaaa!*"

Stormy sat bolt upright on the worn emerald-and-gold damask couch in the doctor's parlor and rubbed her eyes. She heard the crack of a bullwhip followed by yet another "Eee—ya—haaa!"

"*Martha's back!*" she whispered under her breath.

Stormy rose up from her makeshift bed, went straight to the window, and tore back the lace curtains. Calamity was riding a horse with a foot in each stirrup, as the proper ladies in town would describe her, and popping her whip high overhead as she trotted down Main Street. When she passed by Smiling Will's Grocery, she cracked the whip one more time and then lassoed one of Eudell's prime layers.

Laughter bubbled up Stormy's throat even as her tears began falling again. Martha was home. Everything would be all right now. Wiping her cheeks with the back of her hand, Stormy went to the door and opened it. As she walked out onto the porch, Eudell Hawkes came barreling out of the grocery store.

"Stop! Thief!" She marched out into the street, animal urine and droppings be damned. "Give me back my chicken, you vile excuse for womanhood! Give it back, I say. Halt thief!"

Smiling for the first time in three days, Stormy lifted the teal blue skirts of the gingham wrapper she'd donned the morning after Luke was shot and started down the stairs to attract her sister's attention. Before she could take a step, Doc Pierce called to her from his office.

"I think you'd best come back inside, Mrs. McCanles."

Her heart in her throat, Stormy whirled around. "Luke—is he . . . ?"

The doctor's hangdog expression was as melancholy as it ever got, but he surprised her by saying, "The fever broke and I think he's coming around. It looks like he might just make it after all."

A fresh batch of tears spilled down her cheeks as Stormy hurried across the room to embrace the doctor. "Oh, thank you, thank you," she cried, dampening his rumpled smock.

"You don't need to thank me," he said, coloring as he pushed her away. "Your hard work saved Luke as much as mine did. To pull through, he's gonna need a lot more of that specialized nursing you've been giving him." He pushed open the door to his office and gestured for her to enter. "Try to keep him as calm as possible and don't let him get out of bed yet. I'll check on him again this afternoon. Right now, I'm going upstairs to get some sleep."

Stormy started to say thank you again, but Doc Pierce shook her off and disappeared down the hallway. Blinking back tears that finally sprang from joy, not anguish, she walked into the room, sat down on the chair at his bedside, and began wiping the sweat from her husband's brow.

Aware that someone was touching him, still too far removed from reality to know who or why, Luke struggled for consciousness. A blast of heat flared in his innards, the flames licking at his bowels, and his head felt as if it might explode.

When at last his heavy eyelids parted a fraction of an inch, the first thing he saw was what he thought might be a bright ball of sunlight. His lids slammed to a close, and then slowly opened again. As his eyes focused, he discovered the sunburst filling his vision was nothing more than Stormy's yellow quilt. And that he was nestled deep inside of it.

"Good morning," came her voice so softly, so ethereally, at first Luke thought he'd imagined it—or that he'd died and there was an angel that sounded just like her. Then she spoke again. "Are you thirsty?"

He turned his head to the right, and there she was. Stormy wearing a delicate blue dress with white lace fluttering up from the round collar. "Is it morning?" he rasped, surprised at how scratchy his throat felt. She nodded, blinking back what looked like tears. Luke groaned.

It was time for the truth, for his usual moments of insight, but strangely enough, on this morning, nothing nagged him from the back of his mind. The sliver was free. *I love her,* he thought, surprised at how good it felt to admit it, if only to himself. Luke started to turn to her, to take her hands, or to simply touch her, when a blinding pain lanced through his gut, singeing him down to his toenails. He cried out in agony.

"Don't move," she said, placing her arm across his chest. "You'll break the wound open and start bleeding again."

"The wound?" he said through a groan. And then he remembered. The men, the night, and the silvery patina of the moon shining down on Butt Rock. Again he groaned. "I've been shot."

"Yes," she whispered softly. "You've been shot."

"And those men? What happened to them?"

"You shot them back. They're about six feet under, probably polishing Mr. Hickok's boots at the cemetery."

As another thought occurred to him, Luke tried to sit up. Again the pain, and again Stormy's firm hand pushing him back down on the bed. "What about you?" he said between clenched teeth. "Did they . . . hurt you?"

She shook her head. "I'm fine. They just scared me a little—as you have for the last three days."

"Three—" Luke's eyes rolled to a close as Stormy began mopping fresh droplets of sweat from his brow. When he felt up to speaking again, he quietly asked, "Why are you still here? I thought by now you'd be on your way to Colorado."

"You know why I'm here. I love you and I'm *not* going to leave your side."

He opened one eye, then the other, and all his defenses fell by the wayside. With a surprising amount of ease, he admitted, "What you love is a figment of your imagination."

Since she couldn't make sense of those words, Stormy shrugged them off. "You've been through a terrible trauma, Luke. Don't try to think or talk about anything but getting well."

Her soft fingers stroked his brow, and for a moment, Luke coasted along with her in her fantasy world. Then he reached up and caught her wrist, forcing her to look him in the eye. "I'm not crazy, sweetheart. Maybe I'm just being ethical for a change. I should have told you what an imposter I am a long time ago, but I guess I just didn't have the decency."

"An imposter?" She laughed. "Try to get some sleep, darling. You're a little confused."

"I've never been more clear headed than I am at this moment. Please, sweetheart. Hear me out."

Stormy was pretty sure that she *didn't* want to hear what Luke had to say, and even more certain that her frazzled emotions would give out if she were subjected to any more heartache, but she gave him a lame smile and a nod of encouragement anyway.

Luke took her hand in his. "Everything you've read about me is nothing but a pack of lies. I've never been a scout, an Indian fighter, a buffalo hunter, *or* a guide. Hell, I've never been much of anything, not even when I followed Bill around pretending to be his deputy. That's what I've been trying to tell you. You married a man who doesn't exist."

She chuckled lightly, her relief palpable. "If that's all that troubles you, don't give it another thought. It doesn't matter, Luke. None of it matters now. All I care about is you getting well again."

"You may think it doesn't matter now, but it will later. Someday it will finally occur to you that the Luke McCanles you married is a fraud, not a dime novel hero, but a common man. A nobody. It'll matter one *hell* of a lot then."

"A *nobody?* Who came riding after me the night I was kidnapped? Who saved me from those men and almost died in the trying? I don't remember reading any stories where this fictional 'Lucky Luke' McCanles did anything so heroic as all that."

"Oh, hell, Stormy. That was nothing. Those bastards would have killed you. I just did what I had to in order to keep you from harm."

She smiled. "You've finally said something that makes sense. *That's* what a real hero is, Luke. A man who just does what he has to without thinking about himself or the consequences. You put my safety ahead of everything, including your own life. If that's not a hero, I don't know what is."

A hero? A *real* hero and not part of a show or an act meant to impress the crowd? Luke closed his eyes again. The idea was unfathomable, at least it had been until Stormy came into his life. What if she'd spoken the truth—about any of it? Luke had lived in a pretend world for so long, he didn't know truth from fiction anymore, how to react or what to say. What would a *real* hero do now? he wondered.

Stormy continued to stroke his brow, whispering softly, "There's another reason I'm still here, Luke. You love me."

His eyes blinked open. "Is that so?"

Stormy's grin was secretive, self-assured. "Yes. You called my name a lot during the fever of the last few days, and if you said that you loved me once, you said it a hundred times. I believe *that* Luke McCanles, and I want to be his wife for as long as I live. What do you think of that?"

Emotions washed over him, soothing an ache that went much deeper than his wounds. Allowing himself to envision a future with Stormy, liking what he saw, he said, "That depends on what you think about making the trip to Colorado with a guide who doesn't know east from west."

"Luke . . ." Tears welled up in her eyes. "You'll go to Idaho Springs? You'd do that for me?"

"I'd do anything for you, sweetheart. Anything." His own eyes misting over as he saw the love in her expression, again Luke let them roll to a close.

"Anything . . . at all?"

Too choked up to speak, Luke nodded.

"Then there's one other thing we ought to discuss before you go back to sleep. While you were out of your head, you called another woman's name almost as often as you called mine."

Luke's eyelids flashed open at that. "I swear that no one and nothing has ever mattered to me the way you do. If you're talking about the mail—"

"No," she laughed, "I'm not, but one day, I'd like to know a little more about this Daisy Summers."

"Daisy Summers?" He frowned. "I don't know who the hell she is—or anyone else I may have mentioned."

"Yes, you do, and this one is a woman I think you love very much."

"I said—"

"Hear me out," she insisted, pushing him back down on the pillow. "I thought once you're well, you might want to see her again. I thought maybe we could make a stop on the way to Colorado. Wouldn't you like to drop by Rock Creek, Nebraska?"

Luke's breath caught, and then whistled out in a long sigh. "My mother."

"Yes, your mother."

Turning his head away from Stormy, he sighed heavily. "I thank you for the suggestion, but that could be a tough reunion for us all, sweetheart. Real tough."

"But you have to do it, Luke. You know you'll never be truly happy until you do, don't you?"

He paused, thinking for a long moment before he finally admitted in a whisper, "Yes. I don't suppose I will."

"Then it's settled." Stormy tucked the blanket up around his chin. "When you're well enough to travel, our first stop will be in Nebraska."

Turning back to her, Luke reached out and caught her hands in his. "Agreed." He pulled her down toward him, gently kissed her lips, and then pulled back and said, "Hey—are you sure Rock Creek is on the way to Colorado?"

Stormy laughed and cried at the same time. "Not according to most maps, but I have a feeling with you as our guide, it will be."

"Ah, Stormy," he said, chuckling along with her. "Maybe you'd better think twice about following an incompetent guide like me out of Deadwood."

"There's nothing to think about, Mr. McCanles." She blew him a kiss. "If I have to, I'd follow you all the way to hell and back."

Author's Note

Although *Wildcat* is a work of fiction, I have tried to present as many historical facts as possible. The murder of Wild Bill Hickok and the arrest and subsequent trial of his killer, Jack McCall, are as accurate as historical research can provide. Once he was acquitted, McCall fled to Cheyenne, Wyoming, where he boasted of his deed. He was arrested there by a U.S. marshal, taken to Yankton, territorial capital of the Dakotas, and then tried. McCall was convicted when a real jury learned that he had never had any brothers, and that he could not have shot Hickok as an act of revenge. His true motive was never known, but many believe it was simply to keep Deadwood as lawless as possible. McCall was hanged for murder.

Historians have for the most part dismissed Calamity Jane as a drunk and a prostitute. I believe that she was simply ahead of her time with regard to career matters and men, but her battles with the bottle were legendary. There is no question that she and Wild Bill Hickok were at the least friends, and probably for a brief period lovers. She finally decided to give marriage a try, and in 1885 married a man named Clinton Burke. Two years later she gave birth to her only child, a daughter, but marriage and motherhood proved to be too confining for Calamity Jane. She left her husband and child and went back to her wild, wicked ways in Deadwood.

As it slowly gained a small amount of respectability, Deadwood opened a new cemetery, Mount Moriah, three years after the death of Wild Bill Hickok. The townsfolk moved several of its more colorful citizens, Preacher Smith and Wild Bill among them, to the new location. At her request, Calamity Jane Cannary Burke was laid to rest beside Hickok after her death in 1903.

Throughout the pages of *Wildcat,* I have made several references to Calamity Jane's six siblings. Sister Lena, brother Elija, and the three "little ones" were actual people. The heroine of this book, Ann Marie Cannary, is fictional. Lucas ("Lucky Luke") McCanles is also a fictional character, but his family and the McCanles Massacre are not.

Others such as Johnny the Oyster, Blonde May, Colorado Charlie, Old Frenchy the Bottle Fiend, Cold Deck Johnny, California Jack, Cheating Sheely, Pancake Bill, Mysterious Jimmy, Pink Bedford, and Swill Barrel Jimmy were actual characters who helped make Deadwood's history so colorful.

AVAILABLE NOW

LORD OF THE NIGHT by Susan Wiggs
Much loved historical romance author Susan Wiggs turns to the rich, sensual atmosphere of sixteenth-century Venice for another enthralling, unforgettable romance. "Susan Wiggs is truly magical."—Laura Kinsale, bestselling author of *Flowers from the Storm*.

CHOICES by Marie Ferrarella
The compelling story of a woman from a powerful political family who courageously gives up a loveless marriage and pursues her own dreams finding romance, heartbreak, and difficult choices along the way.

THE SECRET by Penelope Thomas
A long-buried secret overshadowed the love of an innocent governess and her master. Left with no family, Jessamy Lane agreed to move into Lord Wolfeburne's house and care for his young daughter. But when Jessamy suspected something sinister in his past, whom could she trust?

WILDCAT by Sharon Ihle
A fiery romance that brings the Old West back to life. When prim and proper Ann Marie Cannary went in search of her sister, Martha Jane, what she found instead was a hellion known as "Calamity Jane." Annie was powerless to change her sister's rough ways, but the small Dakota town of Deadwood changed Annie as she adapted to life in the Wild West and fell in love with a man who was full of surprises.

MURPHY'S RAINBOW by Carolyn Lampman
While traveling on the Oregon Trail, newly widowed Kate Murphy found herself stranded in a tiny town in Wyoming Territory. Handsome, enigmatic Jonathan Cantrell needed a housekeeper and nanny for his two sons. But living together in a small cabin on an isolated ranch soon became too close for comfort . . . and falling in love grew difficult to resist. Book I of the Cheyenne Trilogy.

TAME THE WIND by Katherine Kilgore
A sizzling story of forbidden love between a young Cherokee man and a Southern belle in antebellum Georgia. "Katherine Kilgore's passionate lovers and the struggles of the Cherokee nation are spellbinding. Pure enjoyment!"—Katherine Deauxville, bestselling author of *Daggers of Gold*.

COMING NEXT MONTH

ORCHIDS IN MOONLIGHT by Patricia Hagan
Bestselling author Patricia Hagan weaves a mesmerizing tale set in the untamed West. Determined to leave Kansas and join her father in San Francisco, vivacious Jamie Chandler stowed away on the wagon train led by handsome Cord Austin—a man who didn't want any company. Cord was furious when he discovered her, but by then it was too late to turn back. It was also too late to turn back the passion between them.

TEARS OF JADE by Leigh Riker
Twenty years after Jay Barron was classified as MIA in Vietnam, Quinn Tyler is still haunted by the feeling that he is still alive. When a twist of fate brings her face-to-face with businessman Welles Blackburn, a man who looks like Jay, Quinn is consumed by her need for answers that could put her life back together again, or tear it apart forever.

FIREBRAND by Kathy Lynn Emerson
Her power to see into the past could have cost Ellen Allyn her life if she had not fled London and its superstitious inhabitants in 1632. Only handsome Jamie Mainwaring accepted Ellen's strange ability and appreciated her for herself. But was his love true, or did he simply intend to use her powers to help him find fortune in the New World?

CHARADE by Christina Hamlett
Obsessed with her father's mysterious death, Maggie Price investigates her father's last employer, Derek Channing. From the first day she arrives at Derek's private island fortress in the Puget Sound, Maggie can't deny her powerful attraction to the handsome millionaire. But she is troubled by questions he won't answer, and fears that he has buried something more sinister than she can imagine.

THE TRYSTING MOON by Deborah Satinwood
She was an Irish patriot whose heart beat for justice during the reign of George III. Never did Lark Ballinter dream that it would beat even faster for an enemy to her cause—the golden-haired aristocratic Lord Christopher Cavanaugh. A powerfully moving tale of love and loyalty.

CONQUERED BY HIS KISS by Donna Valentino
Norman Lady Maria de Courson had to strike a bargain with Saxon warrior Rothgar of Langwald in order to save her brother's newly granted manor from the rebellious villagers. But when their agreement was sweetened by their firelit passion in the frozen forest, they faced a love that held danger for them both.

Harper **The Mark of Distinctive**
Monogram **Women's Fiction**